**Praise for *New York Times* bestselling author
LORI FOSTER**

"Foster's writing satisfies all appetites with plenty of searing sexual tension
and page-turning action in this steamy, edgy, and surprisingly tender novel."
—*Publishers Weekly* on *Getting Rowdy*

"Foster's third Love Undercover novel is a steamy delight
with characters so beautifully and painfully real that every wrenching,
joyful and steamy scene is worth savoring."
—*RT Book Reviews* on *Getting Rowdy*

"Foster hits every note (or power chord) of the true alpha male hero...
a compelling read from start to finish."
—*Publishers Weekly* on *Bare It All*

"A sexy, believable roller coaster of action and romance."
—*Kirkus Reviews* on *Run the Risk*

"Bestseller Foster...has an amazing ability to capture a man's emotions and
lust with sizzling sex scenes and meld it with a strong woman's point of view."
—*Publishers Weekly* on *A Perfect Storm*

"Foster rounds out her searing trilogy with a story
that tilts toward the sizzling and sexy side of the genre."
—*RT Book Reviews* on *Savor the Danger*

"The fast-paced thriller keeps these well-developed characters moving....
Foster's series will continue to garner fans with this exciting installment."
—*Publishers Weekly* on *Trace of Fever*

"Steamy, edgy and taut."
—*Library Journal* on *When You Dare*

LORI FOSTER

up in flames

Recycling programs
for this product may
not exist in your area.

ISBN-13: 978-0-373-77879-9

UP IN FLAMES

Copyright © 2014 by Harlequin Books S.A.

The publisher acknowledges the copyright holder of the individual works as follows:

BODY HEAT
Copyright © 1999 by LORI FOSTER

CAUGHT IN THE ACT
Copyright © 2001 by LORI FOSTER

Printed in U.S.A.

CONTENTS

BODY HEAT

CHAPTER ONE

She was the only female fully clothed.

On an enormous party boat filled with people, a dozen half-naked women vying for masculine attention, her subtlety made her stand out. And he wasn't the only man noticing, a fact that was starting to get to him.

He should thank her. After all, he needed all the distractions he could get right now. Trying to keep his mind off the importance of the deal he'd finalize once they reached Marco Island was making him crazy. He'd worked long and hard for this day, and now it was almost at hand.

She walked to the railing, leaning out over the clear blue Gulf waters, watching the sky and the endless seas; she seemed aloof. A damp, salty breeze picked up and plastered her loose, colorful skirts to her body, emphasizing a sweet little bottom and long legs.

Adam Stone shifted his carry-on bag from one hand to the other, then flexed his fingers. The expensive leather bag, bought for him by his younger brother, Kyle, was a celebratory gift specifically for this trip. The bag was attached to his belt by a long leather strap, securing it to his person. It held important papers as well as a sizable check. Beyond that, the bag held significant sentimental value. This bag was a sign of his future, his family's future. There was little chance of being robbed on the yacht, but his innate sense of caution was hard to shake off when so much was at stake.

He considered approaching the woman, but held back, mostly because he knew he didn't have time to get involved beyond small talk. Not only that, she appeared to be ignoring all the males on the boat, himself included. So far, she'd kept her back to him, almost as if she knew of his interest and rejected it out of hand.

The Florida sun was hazy today, the sky overcast, but that didn't deter the bikini-clad boaters who approached him. They'd been coming on to him since he'd climbed aboard, determinedly seductive, despite his disinterest. All his attention remained centered on that elusive woman as she walked away, separating herself from the crowd once again.

Without his usual charm, Adam excused himself to follow her. It was her glossy black hair he spotted first. Even without the glare of sunshine, that dark hair shone silky soft. The wind ruffled the short, fine curls and sent her colorful skirts billowing like a flag.

Adam swallowed.

Ridiculous that seeing the shape of a slim thigh through a filmy skirt should have such an effect when he'd just walked away from a topless woman, but there was no denying his interest. He felt it clear to the bottom of his stomach, and somehow, the feeling was damn familiar.

Her elbows were braced on the handrail, so he could easily trace the feminine line of her nape, her spine, down to a narrow waist. Her halter top, modest in comparison to the tiny bikinis, still afforded him a teasing view of honey-colored skin and tempting curves. Enthralled, he stepped a little closer, again shifting the bag in his hand.

She hadn't yet noticed his approach. With a sigh that he detected even over the loud music and the rush of the water against the hull, she lifted her face to the breeze. Adam stepped slightly to the side, curious to see her profile, to decide if her looks warranted all the interest she'd generated in him.

His shock almost knocked him over.

"Mel? Mel Tucker?"

Rather than turning to him with equal surprise, she abruptly stiffened. Her hands gripped the rail a little harder, and she slowly swiveled her head in his direction. Eyes narrow, mouth set, she said, "Old habits die hard, I see. But the name is Melanie. Ms. Tucker to you."

Adam laughed, his entire mood suddenly lighter. The cursed fate that had put him on this boat no longer seemed so cursed. "You haven't changed a bit, Mel." His gaze coasted over her as she turned to face him fully, hands on her slim hips. His voice dropped the tiniest bit, and without his mind's permission, he muttered, "You're still sexy as hell."

Her mouth tightened, and the pale blue eyes that still haunted his dreams looked more ominous than the approaching storm. Lifting her nose slightly in a gesture she'd perfected as far back as grade school, she said, "You obviously haven't changed, either."

Her words hit him like a blow—just as she'd no doubt intended. His muscles knotted. The *hell* he hadn't changed. He had—in too many ways to count.

Adam held onto the burst of anger by a thread. Always, for as long as he could remember, Mel had been able to rile him with very little effort. The last time he'd seen her back in Brockton, Ohio, his family had been incredibly poor, while *her* family owned the entire town. She lived on a hill with a view while he lived down by the river in a trailer nearly rusted through. Though he'd gotten a job at a young age, what he made went into helping out his folks—and his father had died anyway. Mel had gone off to an elite college, and he'd dealt with some of the worst grief of his life.

And she dared to suggest he'd survived it all without changing?

Because he was older and wiser and had long since outgrown taunting any lady, he forced a smile. "Seven years have gone by. I think it's safe to say we've both changed."

She blinked hard and her jaw worked. "What do you want, Adam?"

Incredulous, he stared at her, his mouth open, his brows up. "You're still angry," he accused. "After seven years, you're holding a grudge!" He finished with a short, rough laugh that sent her back straight and her chin up.

Several tense seconds passed, then she abruptly turned away and marched the last few feet to the very back of the boat. She ducked under a slide that sloped from the upper deck to just above the water, opened a double gate and sat on the dive platform. Gathering up her skirts to her knees, she plunked her small feet into the blue water, dismissing him.

Adam fumed. The hell she would dismiss him! He, too, ducked under the slide, sitting cross-legged beside her and propping his bag in his lap. She remained silent and stiff. Too silent. He didn't like it.

Mel had always had an undeniable effect on him. From the first time he'd seen her, when they'd both been no more than kids, there'd been a chemistry of sorts, something she'd denied and he'd continually struggled with. He felt it still, but he wouldn't let her know. He wouldn't let her and her wealth and social position intimidate him after all this time. He'd done all right for himself, though it hadn't been easy. He had no reason to feel like the poor trash her family had once looked down on.

The boat moved lazily, barely slicing through the Gulf waters, yet the surface was choppy. He glanced at the sky, then frowned at Melanie. Searching for innocuous conversation to show his nonchalance, he murmured, "It looks like a damn storm. I'm going to be late."

He wanted her to ask him, Late for what? But she didn't, of course. Nothing with Mel had ever been easy. Instead she said, "You shouldn't be on this boat, Adam."

She hadn't looked at him, and that bothered him even more. All his life he'd thought of her as the one that got away, the one out of reach. There were still nights when he couldn't sleep for thinking of her, imagining....

When they were younger, he'd teased her unmercifully. Though he was two years older, he'd been held back in first grade after missing too much school due to illnesses that didn't get treated by a doctor. Real doctors were often too expensive, and trips to the clinic took his parents away from work.

He and Mel saw each other often back then, and her lifestyle, her obvious wealth, had been like a pounding toothache; it prodded at him always, reminding him of what he didn't have, while she had way too much. As a kid, he'd almost hated her, at least on some level.

By junior high school, though, he'd learned to hide his feelings...and he'd gradually become aware of her as a female. She represented all the things in life he wanted to obtain; security, comfort, importance. After a while, he'd wanted to obtain *her*. But that was like wanting the moon in the palm of his hand. Ridiculous.

He'd watched her constantly, dwelling on their differences, feeling equal parts obsessive and possessive. When her innocent eyes began looking more sad, more lonely, he was the first, maybe the only, to notice. In a small, moderate town, her outstanding wealth had isolated her.

He'd wanted to chase that sadness away. It gave them some-thing in common, something he gravitated to.

But that was so long ago. She'd hated him then.

Evidently she hated him still.

"I should have taken a charter," he growled, ignoring the pang of old regrets and the bite of her scorn that could still bother him regardless of his denials. The wind whistled around them, and a colorful float went flying off the deck to bob wildly in the churning water. "But the damn captain of the charter came down ill. I would have missed an important meeting, but then your buddy, the captain of this boat, saw me and offered a ride. I accepted."

"He's not my buddy. I barely know him."

"Then what are you doing here?"

She stared out at sea, constantly pushing her wind-tossed curls out of her face. Her hair was shorter now, but he liked it. The casual style suited her small features. The hem of her skirt was getting damp, but she either didn't notice or didn't care. He noticed. He'd always been painfully aware of every little detail that concerned her.

Ignoring his question, she said, "I saw you earlier." She glanced at him, then away again, her expression still set. "You've had at least two women hanging onto you ever since you stepped on board. Some things, I guess, never change."

Stunned, he stared at her profile. "You saw me right away but didn't say hello?"

"Why would I?" She looked right at him, and her eyes blazed. "We didn't exactly part as friends. You were a mean, petty jerk who enjoyed making my life miserable."

He searched her face, his frustration extreme. "For God's sake, Mel, that was seven years ago. We were kids, and when we got older I didn't..."

"Melanie. My name is Melanie, damn it."

He couldn't recall ever seeing her temper before. Mostly she'd been nervous with him, shying away if he got too close, never defending herself, no matter how hard he'd tried to get her to do just that. He lifted one brow, more frustrated by the second. "Well, excuse me all to hell and back." Then he asked, "You have changed, haven't you?"

There went that chin again. "If you mean you no longer intimidate me, yes."

"I intimidated you?" He knew it was true, that he'd played on her vulnerability, but it wasn't something he wanted to own up to now. Jealousy, need, a very basic emotional hunger, had driven him then. He wasn't proud of that time in his life. "Honey, you were the one with all the clout. If you'd wanted, you could have had my whole family tossed out of town."

She blinked, as if surprised by what she'd said, what she'd admitted. A few raindrops fell, lightly at first, but quickly picking up ferocity. Behind them, the partyers began scurrying about, laughing and squealing. Women grabbed for their tops or towels, couples jumped out of the upper deck hot tub. Within minutes, everyone was under cover in the cabin. Everyone except them.

Finally Melanie looked away and Adam drew a deep, starving breath, still watching her. For a minute there, with her gaze locked on his, he'd felt caught, and the feeling wasn't altogether uncomfortable. She stirred something in him that had been missing for quite some time.

The rain came a little harder, wetting his hair, but Adam ignored it.

He should take her arm and help her into the cabin. But he didn't want to. He wanted to talk to her, alone, away from the damn drunken crowd. Once they reached the island, he likely wouldn't see her again. Somehow, he wanted to apologize to her for his behavior of the past. Somehow, he wanted her to know all he'd accomplished since then, exactly how much he'd changed.

He didn't want her thinking of him as the poor kid down by the river.

The boat was suddenly put in full throttle, and they both lurched, grabbing a section of handrail—and a part of each other. Mel's fingers clutched his pant leg while he held her elbow. Gently, his heart pounding, he slid his hand down her arm to her slender fingers. Her hold loosened, and when she would have let go, he captured her hand, steadying her. Mel's eyes widened and she looked behind her, as if only then aware of the storm and the deserted deck. The bouncing boat kept her from shaking him off. Over the roar of the engine, she said, "We should go inside."

An abandoned beach towel hit him in the back, plastered to him by the rain and wind. He held her just a little tighter while struggling to untangle himself from it. Thank God he had dry clothes in his bag or his meeting would be ruined. He couldn't exactly make the deal of his life looking like a drowned rat. Another float whipped by, disappearing into the churning waters.

Growing alarmed by the strength of the wind, Adam carefully stood, then helped her to do the same. From the sound of the revelers inside the cabin, the laughing and loud music, no one even knew they were still on deck. And just as Mel got to her feet, the boat veered sharply to port and she lost her balance. With wide eyes and a horrified scream, she crashed overboard. Adam cursed viciously and made a wild grab for her but missed. His bag fell from his grasp, and the strap to his waist jerked him off balance. He, too, went over with a gigantic splash, but more awkwardly than she, his head hitting the slide as he flew past.

Just before he went under, he heard the roar of the receding boat motor, the louder roar of the storm, and worse, Mel's nearly hysterical screams. Her fear galvanized him. Ignoring his aching head, he pushed himself to the surface and frantically searched for her while wind, rain and waves lashed his face. The side of his head hurt like hell, but he didn't have time to complain yet. Mel was already several yards away from him, thrashing about wildly as if drowning. Adam felt a crushing fear when he twisted to see the boat going out of sight. Fighting the dragging weight of his heavy bag, he began stroking through the water toward her. Just as she let out another garbled scream, he reached her...and they both went under.

Melanie felt a slick, sliding movement against her lower body and opened her mouth to scream again. She managed to gulp a mouthful of salt water. Visions of sharks made her panic real and unmanageable.

But then Adam's blond head broke the surface, and he dragged her upward against his solid body. "Mel!" She felt his legs brush her, tangling with her long skirts, his hard arms around her. Nothing in her life had ever felt so reassuring.

"Oh, God." She gripped him fiercely, trying her best to ignore the reality of her situation. She loved boats, the sunshine and fresh air, but she had never quite envisioned herself thrown overboard, at the mercy of the Gulf and all its aquatic denizens. "Oh, God, oh, God..."

"Mel, you're drowning me! It's okay."

He tried to ease her away, but she got one hand knotted in his hair and held on for dear life. His familiar scent, one she'd never forget no matter how long she lived, surrounded her, and she crowded even closer. His hair was the same, still too long, too sexy, damn him, and she used it like an anchor, holding him tight. She didn't want to be shark bait.

Her voice shook uncontrollably when she spoke. "Where's the damn boat? Where is it!?"

"Sh. It's all right," he said. "We need to swim, honey."

"Swim? *Swim!*" A vicious wave slapped her in the face, water going up her nose, making her choke and sputter. The furious storm continued, almost pushing them under. Would the turbulent water draw the sharks or chase them away?

Shouting to be heard, Adam said, "The boat is gone. Mel, loosen up, you're ripping my hair out."

She tried, she really did. She'd so badly wanted to make a good impression on him, and this surely wasn't it. But she couldn't get her fingers to unknot. "This isn't happening… this isn't happening…."

"Mel, calm down. The idiots on board are either too drunk or too stupid to realize they lost us. We're on our own until they dock and count heads."

If they counted heads. He was right about them all being tipsy, and she'd so deliberately separated herself from them, wanting to be alone, needing the solitude. Would they even notice she was gone? She moaned long and loud. "We'll drown!"

"No, we won't." His voice was calm, sure, just as she remembered it. "We're not far from shore. Can you swim?"

"What about sharks?" She looked around wildly, terrified, not certain if what she saw were shadows in the water or merely waves.

"There's no sharks here."

Her head whipped back around, and she tightened her hand in his hair, making him wince. "How do you know?" she demanded, shaking his head, wanting confirmation. It would be just like Adam to pull her leg, to play on her fear.

"Mel, damn it, turn me loose!"

Through her panic, she read the pain on his face and struggled to relax her grip. Adam circled her waist with his strong arms and held her closer. The contact with his body startled her, despite her predicament. Always, when she'd imagined such a scenario, they'd been on dry land, he'd been filled with abject apologies, and she'd been benevolent in her forgiveness.

Instead, she managed to make a total fool of herself. Not that it mattered if they were going to die, anyway.

Speaking close to her ear, he said, "I've got a Florida guide-book, *The Key to the Keys.* No sharks in these waters, I promise. Now can you swim?"

"Don't let me go!"

"Honey, I'm right here. But we need—"

Something bumped into them. It was huge and...red. She gasped, again choking.

"A float, surely heaven sent." Adam smiled at her, his eyes narrowed against the impact of the waves, his lashes spiked with the rain and sea, his blond hair plastered to his skull. But he smiled, and she felt ridiculously reassured as she treaded water. "Mel? Can you climb on?"

She remembered the float blowing off the deck, and he had offered it to her. Lord love him. She gratefully grabbed the rubber edge and with more panic than grace heaved her body mostly upon it. She gripped it so tightly, there was no way she'd lose her hold until she felt solid land beneath her feet. Her wet, clinging skirts were everywhere, and whether or not they covered her backside, she couldn't say. She felt too numb to know, too frightened to care.

She felt Adam rearrange the skirt, felt his hands on her flesh and merely said a prayer that they'd survive.

"Now just hang on." Moving to the back, Adam levered himself up over her until his head was even with her derriere. She felt his heavy, sodden leather case placed on the small of her back but didn't begrudge him that. As long as she was out, she was happy to accommodate him. He began paddling and kicking, propelling them forward.

She felt like an ineffectual idiot, like a hysterical dolt, but she couldn't seem to help herself. She continued to look around, watching for signs of creatures of any kind. If she spotted so much as a goldfish eye to eye, she'd lose her fragile grasp on control.

A thought occurred to her, and she yelled over the storm, "How do you know which way to go?"

"I'm guessing."

"What!" He mumbled something she couldn't hear and his chin bumped her bottom, then he shouted, "The guidebook, remember? I figure we're still somewhere between the Keys and Marco Island. Trust me, I know what I'm doing."

She thought to question him further but decided against it. Talking was too difficult at the moment, and her teeth were chattering too badly to make good sense anyway. It was easier to trust him and let him take over.

But when it seemed like an hour had gone by and her lips were numb from the cold rain, she began to panic again. He could well be swimming them farther out into the Gulf, rather than inland. There could be whales as well as sharks, maybe even giant eels— She jumped when he reached up and touched her cheek.

"Almost there, Mel. How're you holding up?"

For a moment she couldn't believe what he'd said, then, incredulous, she asked, "Almost *where?*"

"Shore. Look ahead."

He had better eyes than she if he could penetrate the sheet of rain, but when she looked as hard as she could, she thought she could see the outline of land. Her breath left her in a whoosh, and her heart began racing. "Where are we?"

"Damned if I know. But if it'll be solid beneath my feet, then it's good enough for me."

Absolutely. She wanted out of the water and she didn't care where. With a deep breath to fortify her, she released her death grip on the raft. Her knuckles hurt, her fingers felt stiff, but she extended her arms and began paddling.

"Good girl. We'll get there, Mel. You'll see."

She kept paddling, but she closed her eyes, too, saying a silent prayer. *Please, please, please let me live long enough to put my feet on land again.*

Almost ten minutes later, her prayers were answered.

CHAPTER TWO

When she realized Adam was standing, she almost cried with relief. She wanted to slide off the raft to make it easier for him, but the rain had let up and she could see more clearly. The land they approached looked ominous with an abundance of skinny, mangled palm trees, some practically hanging in the water, and spreading, spidery mangrove trees, making the island look more like a scraggly forest. The ocean floor was visible, and what she saw scared her to death. Shells, small fish, water weeds. She curled a little more tightly on the raft.

"Do you think there's…*anything* in the water?"

At first Adam didn't answer, just kept trudging forward, dragging her along. Finally, with weariness evident in every word, he said, "Nothing's bit me yet."

Just the thought made her squeamish. A few more feet, and Adam walked past her, going the rest of the way to shore and collapsing onto his back.

Alarmed, Mel realized the raft couldn't very well be dragged in with her on it, and if she didn't move, she'd float right back out to sea. Not that he seemed to care.

Mustering her courage, she jumped off the raft—and sank as

deep as mid-shins. The water was so shallow, Adam couldn't have pulled her any farther along.

Disregarding her blatant cowardice even as she carefully surveyed the shallow water, she attempted to act blasé, to hide her fear. She grabbed the raft and pulled it behind her as she waded out of the water.

Her strappy little sandals were long gone, and her toes sank into the white sand. Her skirts, made to wrap twice around her waist, were sadly tangled, sticking wetly to her thighs, hindering her every movement. She stopped to shake them loose, to squeeze out some of the water, but it was useless. They clung to her like a second skin. She plopped down on the fine sand beside Adam. He didn't move.

His eyes were closed against the now gentle rain, his clothes every bit as ruined as hers, his mouth tight. And still he looked incredibly gorgeous.

All the old feelings of inadequacy swamped her. For as long as she could remember, Adam had been vital, outgoing, easily the center of attention whenever he entered a room. And she'd been a fading wallflower, crippled by her vulnerability and shyness. When she'd seen him on the boat, she'd begun reviving plans to show him how she'd changed, to prove she wasn't the little girl he probably remembered with pity. She'd thought to wait until they'd docked, change into something more sophisticated and then approach him.

Instead, he'd approached her, taking her totally off guard, and she'd behaved like an idiot. "Adam?"

"Hmm?" He looked a little pale, his mouth pinched.

"Are you all right?"

"Just dandy. I always take an hour-long swim to get the old blood pumping."

Her eyes narrowed. Just like him to be so sarcastic at a moment like this.

But then she realized he had to be worn out. To her shame, she hadn't helped him a bit. She looked at him again and considered apologizing, but couldn't decide how. He was still her high-school nemesis, yet now he was her hero, as well. The circumstances had her grinding her teeth.

She looked around, up and down the shoreline, and saw nothing but bent and twisted trees, sand, a few pelicans. The island wasn't large by any stretch, and she wondered how it would fare if the storm returned. "Adam…"

He groaned and reached up to rub at his head. "Talk softly, okay? I've got a ringing headache."

She lowered her voice appropriately. "Do you have any idea where we are?"

"Not a clue."

She looked around again. It was a safe bet they weren't on Marco Island, so it had to be one of the smaller islands. She started to stand, her intent to locate people, houses, anything that looked even remotely domestic or civilized. But Adam caught at her arm.

"No, don't wander off. I don't want to take the chance we'll get separated. Just give me a few minutes and we'll start exploring together." He said it all with his eyes closed, and her concern for him doubled despite her resentment of the situation.

Sinking into the sand, she looked him over. He lay on the shore like a starfish, arms and legs spread, his posture one of complete exhaustion. His tie remained tight around his throat, his bag still attached to his belt. Melanie figured the least she could do was try to make him comfortable, to prove he no longer cowed her. And he had jumped in after her, had kept her safe. If it hadn't been for him, the sharks—she gulped—probably would have had her for lunch. Though she hadn't actually seen any sharks, she was still certain they were there.

And if nothing else, his presence had given her immeasurable comfort.

She reached for the strap on his bag, but before she could get a good grip on it, his fingers bit into her wrist.

His eyes opened and they pinned her, hot and intense. "What do you think you're doing?"

Uh-oh. Melanie remembered those eyes from high school, so compelling, so sexy. Adam Stone had always had the ability to turn females into mush. Though he'd been poor and oftentimes dangerous, women had gravitated to him in hordes. But she'd resisted. She'd had little choice. His only interest in her had been spite.

"I was going to move your bag and undo your tie."

"Why?" The visible signs of exhaustion momentarily left his body, and he looked ready to attack.

She made a sound of disgust. "You look miserable, that's why."

"Like you care?" He snorted. "Aren't you the same woman who just a while ago was ready to bite off my face?"

She blushed, annoyed that he'd point that out. Damn him, how did he constantly do this to her? They'd only been reunited a very short time, and already she was on the defensive! Since she'd first met him, it had been that way. Right before she'd left for college, he tried to pretend an interest in her, but she'd been wise to him by then. She knew he was only setting her up so he could humiliate her. She'd refused him as quietly and with as little confrontation as possible.

But she'd come home from college a changed woman. Away from her parents' smothering influence, she'd grown into her own, able to stand up to anyone when the situation warranted. She'd anxiously looked forward to her next meeting with Adam Stone, anxiously practiced all the things she'd say to him, how she'd put him in his place.

How she'd make him see her as more than a pawn.

Only he was gone by then, moved away after his father's death. And she'd forever felt cheated of her big moment.

She'd never forgotten him; she doubted she ever would. Other than her parents, he'd had more influence in her life than any other person.

Damn him, she would not let him do this to her again! She was a mature businesswoman, and she'd behave as such, no matter his provocation.

With her hands fisted in her ruined skirts, she forced a calm tone and said, "I was trying to be cordial, Adam, considering you played the gallant and rescued me."

He scowled. "What the hell are you talking about?"

"You dove in after me," she reminded him. "You didn't have to do that, all things considered. The least I can do now is try to be nice."

He stared, his expression stunned. "Nice?" Then he laughed and dropped his head onto the sand with a groan. He was silent a moment before muttering, "Well, what do you know. You owe me."

"I didn't say that."

"Didn't you? It's appropriate, don't you think? My clothes are ruined, and it's for certain I've missed my damned meeting." He cocked an eye open to look at her. "All because I jumped in to save you."

"Don't curse."

Coming up on one elbow, he growled, "I'll damn well curse if I want to! You have no idea what missing that meeting means."

She leaned back, away from the force of his anger. Subdued just a bit, she said, "So tell me."

He glared at her, then turned his head away. After a second, he plopped back on the sand. "Forget it."

She shrugged, but since he wasn't watching her, he didn't see it. Guilt gnawed at her. "I suppose I do owe you. A little."

"A *lot.*"

She sighed. "Very well. I owe you a lot. How much money will you be out because of our…misfortune?"

His gaze turned lethal, and the words were little more than a whisper. "You're not going to offer me money, are you, sweetheart?"

"But you said I owed you."

"You owe me gratitude, that's all. I don't want your damn money."

"Oh." The money would have been so much easier.

He shifted, putting one arm behind his head, watching her, a half smile on his sensuous mouth. "Okay, Mel, since we're agreed, have at it."

"Excuse me?"

"Go ahead and make me comfortable. That was your original intent, right? I await your efforts."

He said it like a dare, and her temper pricked. She would not let him, or any other man, intimidate her ever again. So what that he was more muscled now, that maturity made him even more masculine, more sexy? His blond hair was streaked from hours in the sun; his eyes were dark gold. He looked incredible, while she knew she looked a wreck.

It was bad enough that he'd spotted her in the casual outfit she'd chosen for the boat. Her halter and loose, lingerie-style shorts were made of the same silky material, and covered by the long, thin skirts, but she'd still felt too physically exposed to face him. The cabin had been too crowded to hide in, and then she'd realized she didn't want to hide from him. Not ever again. But she thought he'd be too involved with the women swarming him to notice her.

She'd obviously been wrong.

Now, after her ordeal, she looked wretched. She could feel her eye makeup smeared on her cheeks, knew her short hair stuck out at all angles. She'd lost even more weight over the years; while he was thick with muscle, she was lacking the lush curves men seemed to admire, and in her outfit, there was no way to disguise her figure.

But she couldn't change any of that, so she'd simply have to make the best of an awkward, unimaginable situation.

Mustering her courage, she again reached for his bag. Unfortunately, it couldn't be unlatched at the handle; it had to be undone at his belt. The front of his belt. Without looking, she could sense Adam's smirk. He didn't think she'd do it; she intended to prove him wrong.

To distract herself from his body, she said, "It's finally stopped raining." She slid her fingers under his belt and tried to work the latch.

"It's going to get hot as hell, you know."

She felt the heat already. Adam's stomach was solid rock against the backs of her fingers. And warm. Very warm in comparison to his clammy clothes.

"Humid, too," he added more softly, his voice a rough growl. "Downright steamy."

"Will you stop that!"

He gave her an innocent, surprised look. "Stop what?"

"Stop…talking like that. All sexy and low."

He quirked a brow.

"Oh, forget it. You probably don't even know when you do it." The latch came free, and she pulled the strap away, then immediately started on his tie, giving it a good jerk first, making his head bounce in the sand. Before he could reprimand her, she said, "Ever since I've known you, you've done that. You're nothing more than walking testosterone, and while *some* women might like it, I do not."

She gave the tie another vicious jerk, loosening the knot, and he grabbed her hands. "Will you stop before you strangle me! Damn, woman, I was discussing the weather, and somehow you got on the topic of my hormones!"

Melanie jerked away and came awkwardly to her feet. She shoved her tangled hair out of her face and tried again to untwist her long, wet skirts. After a moment of futile effort, she gave up. Propping her hands on her hips, she said, "I brought it up because that's all you are! Male hormones waiting to burst." She threw her arms wide in apt description.

Adam slowly sat up and had his elbows resting on his bent knees, his head cocked to stare directly at her. "Is that right? Well, I'd say that puts you in something of a predicament then, doesn't it."

Warily, she asked, "What do you mean?"

"I hate to break it to you. No, actually I'm glad to break it to you. This little island appears to be deserted. We're all alone—just you, me, and my bursting hormones." He grinned wickedly. "For who knows how long?"

Frozen for three heartbeats, Melanie stared at him. Then she scoffed. "Don't be ridiculous."

"It's true." Adam stood, brushed off his muscled backside and looked around. "You weren't paying any attention, but when I first spotted the island we were still pretty far out. I could damn near see it from end to end, and not once did I see any sign of life. Not a kid, not a dog, not a single soul."

"You're just trying to scare me."

"Nope. The last thing I want is a hysterical woman on my hands." He peeled off his suit coat and shook it out, then tossed it onto a clump of dry, prickly-looking grass. He did the same with his shoes and socks. "I'm only hoping we'll be able to find some kind of food and water."

"Adam, stop it." She glared at him from under lowered

brows. Her heart raced; her stomach felt queasy. "There are no deserted islands in Florida anymore. It's a tourist mecca. This is just your way of being mean again."

He took two quick steps to her and caught her chin in his hand. "I'm a grown man, damn it. I don't run around trying to frighten women or be mean. Do you honestly think anyone on that boat will notice us missing? Do you think they'll even know where to look for us? How long do you think it'll be before we're missed?"

The second he touched her, her tongue became useless. She couldn't muster up a single word or protest. Her heartbeat slowed; her breath caught.

Damn, she felt vulnerable! She'd so wanted to make an impression on him after she saw him on the boat. She'd been planning and plotting on when she'd introduce herself, what she'd say, how she'd say it to let him know without a single doubt that she would no longer be bothered by him, that she was a woman now, totally immune to him.

But then she'd gone overboard, and he'd done the unexpected and dove in after her. She thought of how she'd acted in the water and wanted to dig a hole in the sand to hide. Now here she was, insulting him, baiting him, reacting to him.

She jerked her chin away. "I'm sorry."

"What?"

"I… No one will notice me missing. I came alone and I wasn't exactly friendly to anyone on the boat."

"You came alone?"

Oh, why did he have to focus on that one small tidbit? She hadn't even meant to admit that much. She put her chin in the air and said, "Yes. Alone."

He looked her over slowly from head to toe, made a grunting sound, then turned away and started unbuttoning his shirt.

"I figured you'd be married to some young yuppie executive type by now."

If all had gone as planned, she would have been. Thank God she'd called it off in time.

When Adam shrugged out of his shirt, at first all she could do was stare at his chest. Hard, lean, covered with a light dusting of hair a shade or two darker than his golden head, it was the type of chest female fantasies were made of. When his hands went to the buttons on his slacks, her mouth fell open, then snapped shut. In a croak, she asked, "What do you think you're doing?"

Without looking at her, he said, "You don't expect me to go exploring our little island in suit pants, do you?"

He didn't wait for an answer. The pants were shoved down, and she whirled around so fast her head swam. But she hadn't been quite quick enough. She saw snug cotton boxer briefs—wet briefs—molded closely to his lower body. The man was a total fiend.

"Adam," she said, doing her best to keep her tone calm and reasonable, "put your pants back on."

"No way. If you had any sense, you'd lose that skirt."

She clutched her skirts protectively to her body. "I will do no such thing!"

"Suit yourself. But I don't think it'll hold up long if you don't wash the salt water out of it and let it air dry."

He had a point, not that she intended to disrobe in front of him. It didn't matter that she wore matching shorts beneath the skirt and underwear under that. Her ex-fiancé had told her numerous times that she needed to put on weight, to gain some curves. And toward the end, she'd finally realized he didn't find her attractive at all. Oh, he put up a good front, and he tried. Jerry was always pleasant, mannerly, proper. That was one of the reasons she'd broken things off with him; he seemed more emotionless every day, like he had no depth, at least not where she was concerned.

She'd come here to rest, to get control of her emotions after the painful breakup. Ha! Controlling her emotions around Adam had always been impossible.

It was imperative she carry her own weight, that she prove to him her little display in the water was an aberration. She could and would fend for herself.

She was still figuring ways to do that when his warm breath touched the back of her neck. She hadn't even noticed him approaching!

"One thing hasn't changed, I see."

Melanie froze, not daring to move in case his mouth actually touched her skin—in which case she knew she'd likely faint. Her every nerve ending felt stretched tight with him so close. Even her fingertips tingled. "What?"

"You're still a shy little thing."

But she wasn't shy. She was just…affected by him. She'd always been affected by him. He made her nervous and tongue-tied and loopy. From the first day she'd seen him, he'd look at her and her stomach would do flips. Forcing herself to turn, she had her mouth open with a scathing retort when she remembered his state of undress.

Oh, my. Her lips wouldn't move. As to that, neither would her eyes; they stayed glued on the bare, very male body he presented. Her imagination hadn't done him justice.

Adam chucked her chin. "Come on. We'll walk along the shore a bit and see if we can find any signs of habitation."

He moved away from her, and she stared, heart racing, as he sauntered to his bag and picked it up. He left his discarded clothes lying amid the long, dry grass. As he went past her again, he whistled a jaunty tune.

If she'd found a rock, she'd have thrown it at his head.

Frustrated, annoyed and somewhat intrigued, Melanie hurried to catch up.

As Adam had said, many things had changed. But one thing that hadn't was his appeal. The man still had it in spades. And though she hated to admit it, she'd never been immune.

CHAPTER THREE

"If you're so sure we're alone, why drag along your bag?"

Adam smiled slightly to himself. Though she did her best to be cavalier, her voice shook. Good. Let her fret awhile. Misery loved company, and his mind was so jumbled at the moment, it was filled with the worst kind of misery.

He'd missed his meeting. Hiding his reaction from Mel wasn't easy, but he had no intention of letting her know how important the deal had been for him. Not only that, but it had taken mere moments in her company for him to revert to form, to become the taunting bully she'd always claimed him to be. He hadn't treated a woman with less than full respect and gentleness since he'd moved away from Brockton.

Except for now. By word and attitude he'd proved Mel right, that he hadn't really changed at all. And it made him madder than hell. "I have important stuff inside. Where I go, it goes."

His dark boxers were nearly dry now, but her long skirt was still dripping. He wished she'd lose it. One nice long look at her legs would make his outlook brighter. She was still so slender, so fragile. Seven years hadn't changed that, but emotionally, she was more sturdy. He laughed. Hell, she was almost mean, as she'd accused him of being.

"Why are you laughing?"

He slanted her a look. "Private joke." But while he was looking at her, he noticed how fair her skin was. "You got sunscreen on?"

She looked at her body, then crossed her arms over the delicate skin of her midriff. "I did have. But that was before our little dip in the ocean."

"Damn. Much as I hate to do this…" He stopped and set his bag on the sand, then knelt before it. "I have a shirt you can put on. I don't want to see you get burned."

"Playing hero again?"

His jaw locked for a second as her words hit him. He was so far from heroic it was laughable. She knew it too, and probably used the term as more of an insult than a compliment. He surveyed her smug little expression, then shook his head. "No, I just don't want to hear you whining later if your tender skin gets pink."

"I do not whine."

"The hell you don't."

She started to stalk away and he called out, "Just where do you think you're going, honey? If you get lost and a wild boar gets you, it's no sweat off my nose."

She halted in her tracks, then slowly turned to him. "There are no wild boars on a Florida island."

Shoving clothes aside, he lifted out the much acclaimed guidebook and shook it at her. "Says different in here!" So far, he really had no idea what the damn manual said. He hadn't had a chance to look it over completely.

She stomped back to him, kicking up sand along the way. She had the attitude of a very tiny, very female bull. "Let me see that."

He held it behind his back. "I don't think so. It's mine. In fact, I've got a lot of useful stuff here in my bag. Let's see—" He shoved the booklet under his backside so she couldn't get to it then began rummaging in his bag. "There's the shirt you could surely use to protect your delicate hide if only you'd stop being such a witch. Toothpaste and toothbrush. A few candy bars, gum, shampoo and soap. A razor." He looked at her and grinned his most evil grin. "Clean Skivvies and even a pack of condoms."

His evil grin was nothing compared to her aristocratic look of disdain. "Well, unless you intend to sweet-talk the boars, I seriously doubt you'll need the condoms."

"A smart man is always prepared."

"Then I'm so surprised you thought of it."

Her look was so snotty, he grinned, then actually laughed. "Damn, you're still a world-class snob."

She gasped at him. "I was *never* a snob!"

He held up one finger, interrupting her tirade. "But...you're a snob with nothing more than the clothes on your back. If you want to borrow anything I have, you better start being nice."

"Go to hell!"

He made an amused tsking sound. "Such language. Should I remind you, Mel, that there aren't any stores on a deserted island? Your charge cards won't do you much good."

"I don't even have my purse with me. Not that it matters, because we'll be rescued by dinnertime."

He shook his head in a pitying fashion. "You're still so naive."

"I was never a snob and I was never naive. You were always too busy provoking me to know me at all."

The words had a grain of truth, at least in regard to their earlier relationship, before high school. But he'd be damned if he'd let her make him feel bad now. "I was provoking because you were such a snob."

Her face colored in silent rage. "And you're a pessimist. Keep all your precious belongings. I won't need them."

Adam considered her stance; hands on hips, her hair a dark, glossy halo around her head, her wispy, flowery skirt. The island served as the perfect backdrop for her. She looked exotic and desirable and damn sexy. "Wanna bet?"

"What?"

He pursed his lips. "I'll make you a deal. You'll get my sincere apology if we're rescued by dinner."

"And if we're not?"

"Well, now, let's see." His gaze focused on her mouth, and his voice dropped slightly. "I always wondered what it would be like to kiss you."

She gasped; her cheeks turned hot for an entirely different reason. "I don't believe you."

"Oh, it's true. I wondered about it. A lot."

"Well, you can just go on wondering!"

And he would, he had no doubt of that. Even the seven years they'd been separated hadn't been enough to obliterate the fantasies he had about her. But now here was a chance to live them, at least to some degree. "Chicken?"

Her eyes darkened, brows drew together. "Of course not."

He stepped closer, whispering, "Then bet me."

"Jerk."

"And here I thought I was your hero."

She made a soft, growling sound, then gave an abrupt nod. "All right. But you'll be sorry when you lose."

"Will you be sorry, too?"

She turned her back on him. Smiling, Adam dug out the long-sleeved white dress shirt. Mel was stiff, nearly vibrating with anger. He should have been ashamed for taunting her, a gut reaction he thought he'd lost after high school, but instead, he was turned on. She seemed so sexy with her new outspoken manner.

"Here, let's get you covered up before you burn. It's the truth, I don't cotton to roasted woman. I'd rather kiss you tonight when you're not in pain from the sun." He tried his warmest, most sincere expression on her, the one that usually had women agreeing with his every word.

But when he reached to put the shirt on her, she stepped back and swallowed hard. "Adam, I don't think we should fight."

"Absolutely not." He reached for her again, and she caught his hand.

"In all seriousness, we could be stuck here for a few hours." Her expression was earnest, concerned.

"Could be." He wouldn't remind her again just how seriously they were stranded. Tonight, when he kissed her senseless, she'd finally accept the truth. The anticipation was almost enough to soften his disappointment over losing the deal. Almost.

"Could we call a truce?"

"Are you backing out of the bet?"

She sighed. "No."

"Then by all means, behold a peaceable man. Now put on the shirt." He slipped it around her, but he had to lean close to do so, and suddenly she gasped.

"Oh, my God! Your head."

He eyed her cautiously. "I know it hurts like the devil but it's still on my shoulders, isn't it?"

"You're bleeding!"

"Quit squawking, Mel. I'm fine. I just knocked my head on the slide when I went overboard."

"Here, sit down." She pushed at his shoulders and Adam

stared at her, not budging. Her tiny hands and puny strength were easy to ignore. But her sudden concern… He wasn't quite sure what to think of it. Over the years he'd imagined many things from Mel, but never genuine concern.

"Mel…"

"Melanie," she corrected, but this time without heat. "Now sit."

No woman other than his mother had ever pampered him, except in bed, so he sat and awaited a unique experience. His manly ego, however, insisted that he protest one last time. "I'm fine, Mel, really."

She leaned over him, and he could feel her soft breath on his shoulder, could smell the woman sweet scent of her. Her slender fingers touched, oh so gently, his scalp.

In hushed, pained tones, she whispered, "You've got a terrible gash, Adam."

He decided a little sympathy from her wouldn't be a bad thing. As long as he was going to let her believe he'd jumped overboard after her, he might as well go for broke. Besides, he would have come to her rescue—if he hadn't fallen in by accident. "It's not still bleeding, is it?"

"A little."

"Well, see then? It's almost stopped, so there's nothing to worry about. And after all that time in the ocean, it's been cleaned out good."

She didn't sound convinced. "I took first-aid classes in college. I think we need to put some pressure on it."

"Mel, my head hurts enough as it is without you playing doctor." He heard what he said, knew she'd heard it too, and grinned. "Then again…"

"Just be quiet, Adam." As she spoke, she came around him and opened his bag. "You must have something in here we could use as a bandage and wrap."

He caught her hands and pulled them away. "Quit rifling through my things!"

"Stop being such a baby!"

"I'm not…." He hesitated, caught by the worry in her gaze, the near desperation. She truly wanted to help him. *Mel Tucker was showing him tenderness.*

That fact left him a little shaky. "Oh, hell, go ahead then. Suit yourself. I can see you're going to be stubborn about this."

The first thing she pulled out of his bag was his business envelope, thickly padded and sealed. It held the contract of buying terms, a check, insurance papers. Everything he'd needed for his future. Now all wasted.

"What's this?"

He stared at the blazing sun and silently cursed the ocean, the weather and drunk captains. "Pretty much useless garbage at this point."

His tone was mean enough to put off more questions.

Of course, that didn't stop Mel. The rich lived by their own rules and seldom let anything stand in their way.

Still rummaging, she said, "It looks important."

"*Was* important. But I missed the deadline by now."

"Deadline for what? Oh, look. These will do nicely as a bandage."

Appalled, Adam growled, "I'm damn well not wearing my underwear on my head!"

"Oh, for goodness sake, I'll rip them up. They're white cotton and will work perfectly."

He shook his head. "Hell, no."

"Adam…"

"If you're so set on underwear, let's use yours."

Her eyes widened, and she sputtered. "I'm wearing mine!"

"So take them off."

She looked ready to smack him. "Mine won't do."

"Why not? You said underwear was perfect and I'd damn sure rather it be—"

"Mine aren't white and they aren't cotton," she blurted, then he watched, fascinated, as her face turned bright red.

He was still cad enough to love seeing a woman's blush, especially Mel's. "Do tell."

She wouldn't look at him. "Stop trying to distract me."

"I was distracting myself." Not that it would take much with her standing there still damp, her skin dewy, her skirt and halter clinging to her body. She was as thin as she'd been in high school, her ribs visible below the halter top, but she looked so soft, too, so damn female.

He cleared his throat. "All right. We'll skip undies altogether. Find something else. This'll do." He lifted out a black T-shirt he'd brought for the trip home, to wear with his jeans. Once the business meeting ended, he'd planned to get comfortable again. He positively hated suits.

Mel shook her head. "Black isn't good because it'll be harder to see if you're still bleeding."

"It's either this or your panties. Take your pick."

She took the T-shirt. "You always were a rotten bully, Adam Stone."

"So you ought to be used to it, right?" He was done trying to convince her he'd changed. What difference did it make, anyway? When all was said and done, they were still separated by a background that would never alter.

Adam drew his key ring from his bag. It had a small but lethally sharp pocketknife attached. He attacked the shirt with a vengeance.

Staring at the knife, Mel asked, "Why in the world are you carrying that?"

"Old instincts are hard to shake. I got the knife when I was sixteen, when we still lived by the river." He glanced at her, saw her appalled expression and shook his head. "I've never gutted anyone, honey. I've just kept it for protection. And because now I'm used to carrying it."

"Good grief, do you still have your leather jacket, too?"

He grinned. "As a matter of fact, yeah, I do. But it's too small for me to wear anymore. My mother bought me that jacket by taking in sewing. It means a hell of a lot to me. Of course, if she'd known what a redneck I felt like wearing it, she probably would have taken it back."

She laughed. "You did have your moments of mischief."

Adam tipped his head and studied her. "What about you?"

"What about me?"

He tweaked a dark, glossy curl by her ear. "You still got those Minnie Mouse combs you used to wear in your hair, one on each side?"

She looked surprised that he remembered; he could have told her there was little he'd ever forgotten, at least about her. He remembered the cute little dresses she used to wear, how serious she always looked, how alone.

His heart twisted in a familiar pang, and he cleared his throat. He didn't have the material things she'd had, but he'd had a close group of friends and always knew his family was there to give him as much moral support as he needed. "Do you still have them?"

She dipped her head to hide her face. "I do. I bought them myself when I turned fourteen. My mother thought they were frivolous, but I always loved them."

"Worth a lot, huh?"

"Worth a lot to me, but not to too many other people."

Adam felt like they were suddenly on dangerous ground. He knew Melanie had never had the best relationship with her parents. They'd loved her, there was never any doubt of that. But their expectations had always been pretty high. She wasn't allowed to be a regular kid, with regular faults. She was supposed to be better than that. Maybe those silly little combs had been her first attempt at independence.

Adam abruptly changed the subject. He didn't like seeing her so melancholy. He'd take her temper any day. "So what are we doing here? Do you want to use this damn shirt or not? Or are you just waiting for me to bleed to death."

"You said you weren't bleeding that much anymore!"

He shrugged, which only annoyed her more. He handed her the sliced-up T-shirt, then suffered through her efforts.

Actually *suffer* was a very apt word. Despite her new pique, she didn't hurt him. But she was so gentle when she cleaned away the rest of the sand and smoothed his hair, when she held the wadded bandage in place then wrapped a strip of the shirt around his forehead like a headband. Her scent enveloped him again, and twice he felt her breasts brush his shoulder.

Oh, hell. He was wearing no more than snug boxers, and his interest would be blatantly obvious if he didn't distract himself and quick.

"So what were you doing on this trip, all alone? Very few people vacation without a companion."

She carefully knotted the wrap. With a shrug in her tone, she said, "I'm used to being alone. And it makes it easier for me to think."

"To think about what?"

She finished with his bandage and sat back on her heels. The skirt pulled tight over her long thighs and smooth knees. That held his attention for several heartbeats, and when he finally looked at her face, he decided she looked uncertain. Adam thought she'd refuse to answer, but she lifted one shoulder and said, "About what to do with myself for the rest of my life."

"You couldn't figure that out back in Brockton?" Adam closed his bag and stood.

She stood also and dusted the sand off herself. "There were…distractions at home."

He took her hand with his free one and started them down the beach again. Mel didn't object, and he enjoyed touching her. Her fingers were so slender, her hand so tiny in his large one. "What kind of distractions?"

"Oh, family, friends…an ex-fiancé."

That last distraction caused his stomach to tighten. Trying to sound only mildly interested, he asked, "Family?"

"Surely you remember my mother and father. They're a bit…overwhelming. And they like to try to run my life."

"I remember they did run your life. They pretty much chose your friends, your clothes, your first car."

She nodded. "But that was before college. I came back a different woman."

She looked at him, and he could tell his reaction mattered to her. He smiled. "If what I've seen so far is evidence, I'd say you're very different."

"Yes." She let out a breath, satisfied. "But they didn't like it much. They're constantly trying to make my decisions for me, especially about who I marry. I needed time away from their campaigning."

"What about your friends?"

"They mean well, but they don't understand."

"Understand what?"

"Me." They walked several yards before she added, "They thought I should go back to my fiancé, that we'd make a perfect couple. Jerry is well established, influential. They all thought he worshiped me, but…"

Again his stomach clenched and his heart thumped awkwardly. The man she described was everything Adam would never be, the perfect cultured mate for a woman of her breeding. Adam had always known when Mel married, it would be to someone exactly like that.

He'd hated it then, and he hated it now.

The rain had stopped, but the humidity was almost choking. He felt he couldn't get a deep enough breath. "So what happened?"

"I didn't love him. And he didn't love me."

A warmth surged through Adam, making his muscles ripple. He clenched her hand a little tighter. "Your parents and your friends don't think love matters?"

"They thought I'd grow to love him."

She looked out over the ocean, avoiding his gaze. But Adam didn't mind. Just seeing her profile was nice. He liked the upward tilt of her nose, the way her long lashes cast shadows over her cheeks. He even liked her ears.

Damn. "Do you think it's possible you would have?"

Blue eyes darted his way, incredulous. "No. Not ever."

"Then you made the right decision."

"I know. But now what?" With her toes pointed, she kicked up sand and swung his hand just a little. "I mean, I need to find a job of some sort and get my life together."

Frowning, Adam asked, "You need to find work?"

Her eyes widened. "Oh! I don't mean that I'm broke or anything like that. But you see, Jerry is a lawyer, and I was his secretary. After I broke my engagement, it didn't seem right to work for him. And I wanted to do something new, anyway. Besides, work shouldn't only be about money."

Adam shook his head in disbelief. "Only the rich could have such an attitude."

"That's not true." She frowned at him. "Don't you want to enjoy your work? To have goals to reach for and take pride in? Don't you want to make a difference somehow?"

"I wanted to make a difference to my mother. She deserves

some peace now, some time to take it easy. And I wanted to give my brother a chance, lots of chances, to do the things I didn't get to do."

Very tentatively, she asked, "You say all that as if it's impossible now."

"No. I'll get to that point eventually. But it should have been today." He released her hand to run his fingers through his hair, only to encounter the makeshift bandage. His fist dropped to thump against his bare thigh. "If I hadn't gone overboard, I'd be on Marco Island right now, buying a small resort. My mother and Kyle are probably sitting by the phone, waiting for my call this very minute."

"Adam..."

He heard her concern but couldn't bear it if she felt sorry for him. He shook his head, dredging up lost control. "Forget it, Mel."

"But if you have the money to buy one resort, then surely you could just get another."

He laughed at her, more aware than ever of the differences in their outlooks. "This particular resort was dirt cheap because it needs a lot of work that Kyle and I could have done after it was ours. Unlike you or your family, I'm well used to working up a sweat. I could have turned the resort around. But the agent, Mr. Danvers, was clear that if I missed the deadline, it would be sold to the next bidder, who was only slightly below me. I scrambled around for two weeks getting things in order—only to fall off the goddamned boat."

Adam abruptly shut his mouth, disgusted with the situation and with himself. Why had he opened up to her like that? The details of his real estate deal were none of her business. Hell, he'd wanted to impress her, not drive home how shaky his financial position still was.

"Tell me about your family, Adam."

He scrubbed at his face, then twisted to see her. She knelt in the sand beside him, her expression sincere, curious. Adam shrugged. "Kyle is totally different from me, more like my mother. He smiles all the time, and nothing gets him down. When we were younger, and things got rough at home, I'd always end up in trouble, fighting with someone or mouthing off at school. Not Kyle. Everyone likes him."

"And your mother?"

"She's the strongest person I know." His eyes narrowed and he looked out at the endless expanse of sea. "Even when Dad died, she held up, doing what had to be done, getting through each day. As soon as I could make enough money, I moved them away from Brockton, so we could all have a new start. We didn't go far, even stayed in Ohio, but now they were looking forward to Florida." His jaw tightened and he threw a fistful of sand. "Damn, I hate to let them down."

Mel's hand touched his, and she whispered, "I'm sorry."

Her soft apology made him realize what a heel he'd been. It wasn't her fault he'd lost his balance, but he let her believe he'd jumped in to rescue her. Oh, hell.

"I fell in, Mel."

She touched his shoulder. "I know. Trying to save me."

He glared at her over his shoulder. "Didn't you hear me? I *fell* in. Yes, I made a grab for you, but no, I did not leap in to rescue you. Hell, that would have been an idiotic thing to do. If I hadn't lost my balance I would have just told the captain to turn the stupid boat around."

She looked confused. "You lied to me?"

"No, I didn't lie. You just assumed."

"And you didn't correct me!"

Shrugging, he said, "You were so anxious to…comfort me. I didn't want to miss the experience."

She fumed in impotent silence for three seconds, then kicked sand at him and stalked off.

"A repeat performance, Mel!" he shouted to her retreating back. "You keep playing the same scene—get mad and walk away. Only here, there's no place to walk to."

"Go to hell," she yelled without turning.

She took off at a furious trot, and she was nearly out of sight around a cove heavy with mangrove trees when Adam decided he'd have to apologize "Mel? Come on, Mel, wait up."

No answer. Grabbing his bag, he headed after her, calling her name. "Mel!"

The sun hung low in the sky, a heavy red ball turning the water in the cove crimson with its reflection.

He picked up his pace, his injured head pounding with every step, then almost ran into her when he rounded the bend she'd taken. "Damn it, you could have…"

His words dropped off. Ahead of them, some hundred yards up the beach, was a house. Well, sort of a house, more like a ratty shack. It was almost in the ocean because of the eroded shoreline. Exposed pilings beneath the structure showed how precariously it stood, and to Adam's mind exemplified the seriousness of their situation. If folks were anywhere about, they would have knocked such a dangerous eyesore down. Oh, they were stranded, all right. He wondered how often, if ever, people visited this damn island.

He took a step forward just as Mel took one back, closer to his side. "Do you think anyone is around?" she asked in a whisper, and he realized she was nervous. And in being nervous, she'd automatically come to him. The man.

He felt like Tarzan, ready to defend her against all predators. He wasn't rich, but for now, he was all she had. He grinned with the image. "Come on. Let's go exploring."

He led her to the front door of the house, but the steps were broken and separated from the main structure by the shift of the land. He set his bag on the sand and said in his best macho voice, "You probably should wait here."

"Adam, be careful." She fretted behind him, twisting her hands. "You don't know what could be inside there."

Wild boars? He grinned and glanced at her while shoving the door open—and got bombarded by a flurry of large flying insects.

Startled, Adam yelled, then fell backward into the sand, hitting his head once again.

CHAPTER FOUR

Melanie ran halfway down the beach before she realized what a coward she'd been. The bugs, giant roaches of some kind, were gone, their dark cloud moving far away.

Adam still lay where he'd landed, and she grew immediately concerned. She sprinted toward him. "Adam!" She came to a rushing halt beside his prone body, accidentally kicking sand over his chest and shoulders. He looked like a downed warrior in his headband and dark, snug underwear, with the rest of his magnificent, tanned body bare. She took a moment to observe him unaware, grew even more breathless, then shook herself.

Her pulse racing at Mach speed, she knelt gingerly beside him. "Adam?"

He groaned.

Her heart seemed to drop to the pit of her stomach. "Oh, thank God. Are you all right?" She cradled his head on her lap and touched his jaw. "Adam, can you answer me?"

He cocked one eye open, stared at her breast near to his face and closed his eye again. "Nice, Mel, real nice."

"Adam," she warned.

"No, don't slug me. There's already a rusty marching band

playing on my brain." He sighed, then added, "Oh, hell, I feel like a fool."

Stroking his jaw and chin, she asked, "Why?"

"It was just a few bugs, Mel."

"Ha! They were giant cockroach-looking bugs, and I almost fainted!"

"Yeah, well, having grown up by the river, I've seen plenty of bugs."

She shuddered. "Not me."

"I know." He made a smirking face, as if it was a crime not to have lived with bugs. Then he added, "But don't pass out on me here, because I'm not up to lugging your dead weight up and down this damn beach."

Only the very real pain she could see in his eyes kept her from dumping his head off her lap. That, and the picture in her mind of where Adam had lived. Once, when she'd been around sixteen, she'd snuck down by the river to spy on him. Driven by some inner demon, she'd wanted to look at him, to see him. He'd been especially provoking that day, and she'd had some far-fetched idea of finding out more about him so she'd be better prepared to deal with him.

She'd gotten the shock of her life.

The outside of the trailer had been as tidy as anyone could make it, almost hiding the fact that it was falling apart. Wildflowers had been planted around the skirt of the trailer in an attempt to hide holes. Melanie, in her misconceptions of the world, had wondered why they didn't move. It wasn't long after that she found out Adam's father had cancer, causing him to miss more and more work.

Some of the area residents had taken up a collection for the family, and she still remembered feeling ashamed when her parents donated so little, when she'd wanted to give so much.

It was no wonder he'd always resented her.

To hide her sudden discomfort and the pity she still felt, she quipped, "You know something, Stone? You've got worse mood swings than my mother when she went through menopause. And frankly, she was a royal bitch."

He chuckled. "That bad, huh? Well, considering I missed the most important meeting of my life, I spent an hour in the ocean using muscles I'd forgotten I had, my brains have been scrambled twice now, and I'm presently in a position I've fantasized over but can't do a damn thing about, then I'd say I'm justified."

Melanie's heart gave an excited stumble over his words. What had he fantasized? Certainly not about her. He'd never shown her anything but disdain. Sure, today he'd joked about kissing her, but that was just his way of making her uncomfortable. Yet the way he'd said it while eyeing her breasts…

Carefully, measuring every word, she said, "I can easily take care of your missed meeting, your muscles look…unforgettable to me, your head will feel better soon. Oh, and what did you fantasize about?"

Her nonchalance didn't fool him. He slowly sat up to face her, his large body too close, his gaze too intent on her face. She felt herself blushing without knowing why.

He worked his jaw in thought, then said, "I don't need you to do a damned thing about the missed meeting, so forget that. But I am glad you noticed my muscles—especially since I've more than noticed your soft little body. My head is going to fall off my shoulders long before it stops aching." He touched her cheek, the line of her jaw. "And you," he whispered. "I've fantasized about you, Mel, about touching you, kissing you." He leaned closer, his mouth only an inch away from hers. "Those last few years all I could think about was how damned exciting it would be to get you under me."

Oh, wow. Her vision clouded, and she had to part her lips

to breathe. The heat wasn't only surrounding her now, it was inside her, a part of her. No man had ever talked to her this way, not even Jerry, and she'd been engaged to him. It was exhilarating and stimulating and...this was Adam. She narrowed her gaze.

"Are you trying to humiliate me again?"

He drew back just a bit and stared at her. "Again?"

"Like in high school, when you asked me out. Oh, don't look so innocent! I know what would have happened if I'd been dumb enough to say yes. You'd have laughed and told everyone what a fool I was. That's the only reason you asked me in the first place, isn't it?"

He looked equal parts frustrated, angry and hot. "I asked you out because I wanted to."

"Oh, sure. And that's why you suggested we go driving instead of to a school dance or the movies where someone might have seen us."

"You're the one who would have cared, Mel. My reputation was already shot. Folks saw me as dirt poor, no-account, and a troublemaker."

"You were a troublemaker."

He ignored that little truism. "And you were the town princess, too good for the humble masses. Hell, your mommy and daddy had nothing but contempt for the rest of us, and they would have had me shot if they knew I'd asked you out." He shrugged, looking awkward for just a moment. "I figured you might go if no one would ever know about it."

She stared at him, appalled at his perceptions, feeling sick deep inside herself. He was right in predicting her parents' reactions. They wouldn't have been pleased. But to think of Adam as sincerely wanting to date her... Well, that would take a major attitude adjustment. He'd been so cocky back then, as if he'd been unaware of his poverty, of his social circumstances. He'd always seemed so self-contained, unaffected by others, especially by her.

Could he have felt as vulnerable as she did?

"Why?" She asked it simply, the question uppermost in her mind. "Why would you have wanted to go out with me?"

His expression became almost ruthless. With the black headband wrapped around his fair hair, his bare shoulders glistening in the hot evening sun, he looked like a savage.

His golden eyes glittered with intent, and then without a word he grabbed her by the back of the neck, pulled her closer and pressed his mouth to hers.

For a mere second he was still, the pressure firm. They both seemed frozen, afraid to move. Then he groaned and twisted and gathered her closer, his mouth opening, devouring. She felt the hot stroke of his tongue, urgent and deep, the sharp touch of his teeth, and she gave a small groan of her own.

His arms closed around her, bringing her as near as he could get her. Everything about him seemed to be hot and hard, like a steel inferno. Pressed against his damp chest, she felt every ragged breath he drew.

Being alone with Adam like this, hearing the things he claimed, was a fantasy come to life. As a young woman, she'd built a world around the idea of luring in the irresistible Adam Stone. Everything about him had excited her, and compared to him, other men had seemed lacking—including her fiancé. "Adam—"

His teeth nipped her earlobe and made her gasp. "Sh," he whispered, barely breathing the word so that all the fine hairs on her body stood at titillated attention. Her body felt ripe, hungry.

"Tell me that you want me, too, Mel."

Oh, she did. She really did. "We…we need to talk, Adam."

He leaned back to give her a warm smile, his gaze searching, pleased. "But you're not denying you want me."

She started to, only the words wouldn't come out, not with him looking at her that way. His hands stayed busy, slowly pushing the white shirt open and brushing over the exposed skin of her shoulders, arms and throat as if he couldn't quite touch her enough. Everywhere his fingers trailed, she felt gooseflesh rise, making her more sensitive. He appeared almost reverent, his gaze so hot she felt the touch of it against her skin.

She'd secretly dreamed of being with him like this, and she wanted so badly to give in. But she knew she'd caused him a lot of grief, and first she had to remedy that. She leaned away from the temptation he offered. "I want to buy the resort, Adam. I owe it to you."

Very slowly, he released her. His expression was cold, blank. "There was a bidder right behind me."

"So I'll make him an offer he can't refuse."

He jerked to his feet, then stared at her. "I don't want your charity, Mel."

"Charity?"

"I don't live on the riverbank anymore. I can damn well take care of myself, without your interference."

His attitude stunned her. "You're being unreasonable, Adam. I can afford to do this—"

"And I can't. Just like old times, huh?"

They stared at each other in heavy silence. He was so distant, so sarcastic, it was as if the delicious kiss had never happened. Melanie bit her lip to keep her emotions in check. His feelings were plain, but then, so were hers. She knew what she needed to do, she just didn't know how Adam would react. "You're a bullheaded jerk, Adam Stone."

He turned away to observe the shoreline. After several more

seconds, he said, "It's going to be dark soon. We should finish checking out the house to see if there's anything in there we can use."

The setting sun cast everything in shadow, lending an eerie quality to the island. Adam disappeared behind the house, and she didn't bother to follow him. How had everything changed so suddenly?

"I've found us some food."

She stared at him, carefully hiding her hurt. He held out two withered oranges.

"Behind the house." He watched her as he spoke, and she had the feeling he was trying to gauge her mood. "The orange tree isn't much to brag on, but next to that is a palm tree loaded with coconuts. We won't starve."

Fighting with him wouldn't solve anything, so she tried for a look of enthusiasm. "I can live with fruit."

He looked relieved, and even smiled at her. "They were probably planted by whoever used to live here. According to the guidebook, citrus trees are usually only on the mainland. There's even a wild strawberry patch here, though it looks like the bugs have gotten to most of them. And some thorny blackberries."

He dropped the fruit in the sand by her feet, then went around to lever himself into the front door again. Watching Adam climb wearing no more than form-fitting Skivvies was a unique experience. Muscles and tendons flexed and pulled tight across his back and shoulders. His thighs were long, athletic. She crept closer to the house to peek inside.

It had obviously been no more than a functional fishing cabin. There were no separate rooms, just a few dividing walls. At the back of the house were an old porcelain tub and toilet, a broken mirror still on the wall. Various broken tools, dishes and garbage littered the inside.

"It's not exactly cozy."

Adam snorted. "If it rains again, and it will, at least we'll be able to keep dry. And I think I might be able to drag that tub outside to collect the rainwater."

The tub was dirty, chipped and rusted. "Pray, for what?"

"To drink and bathe, sweetheart. Unfortunately, there's no catering service here, no ice machine right around the corner, no hot showers. Or haven't you accepted yet that we're stuck here?"

She really wanted to smack him. "We'll be rescued soon."

"Dream on." He began heaving at the tub. A large slithery snake glided from beneath and slipped across the dusty floor to disappear into a crack between the wall and the baseboard. It moved so quickly, neither of them had time to react. Adam turned to her, one brow raised, and she quickly ducked out of sight.

Sometimes, she thought, life was hardly fair. She'd come on this stupid trip to get away from meddling friends and family, stress and pressure. She'd wanted peace and quiet, but instead she'd gotten stranded on a damn bug-and-snake infested island with the one man who'd always made her crazy. Now it seemed that so many things she'd thought about Adam were wrong, but it didn't matter, because he still despised her inherited wealth.

"Come here and give me a hand."

Melanie turned, saw Adam struggling to lower the tub to the ground through the open doorway and applauded. "Bravo, Stone. Anything else I can do for you?"

He mumbled something she didn't hear and let the tub drop with a thud. After jumping off the doorstep, he dragged the tub straight past her and right into the ocean.

"Adam! What are you doing?" She envisioned him climbing inside the tub and somehow sailing away—without her.

But the tub immediately sank, and he only went out knee deep, just enough to swish the salty sea water inside it.

"I'm washing it. Something's been nesting inside it."

Shuddering in distaste, Melanie stood fretfully just outside the touch of the foaming tide and watched, praying no sharks would eat Adam, because she really didn't think she could stand being stranded alone.

But when he waded out and she saw that his snug boxer briefs were once again soaked and clinging to his very male body parts, she began to wonder if being stranded alone might be safer than being with Adam Stone.

The sun was nearly down, the air cooler, and Adam felt ready to burn up. On every imaginable level, he was painfully aware of Melanie. He could smell her warm, female scent, could hear her occasional movement, feel the touch of her gaze on his body. In a burst of frustration, he growled, "Stop ogling me."

Affronted, Melanie exclaimed, "I'm not!"

"Ha." He wanted an argument, a way to vent. When he'd kissed her, he'd nearly lost his mind, she tasted so good. He'd wanted nothing more than to lay her down in the sand and make love to her. Then she'd offered him money, and he'd gone cold inside. She couldn't know what it was like to take charity, to be dependent on others to get by. But he knew. And that was one more major difference between them.

She had spunk, he'd give her that. Most women would be carping and crying and complaining right about now. Their prospects for the coming night did not look good. But not Mel. No, she didn't complain, she just went on insisting everything was dandy in that damn annoying Pollyanna way she had of looking at everything. Even with bedraggled clothes and ruined makeup, she managed to appear regal and in control. She sat before him, her legs crossed just so, her shoulders straight.

She was staring at him again.

"Damn it, Mel." He dropped to his knees in front of her, at the end of his control. "Do you want me to pick up where we left off?"

She looked at his mouth, then slowly shook her head. "I want to talk to you."

"That again?" He plopped down, feeling the gritty sand on the back of his thighs, his palms. Damn sand everywhere. "All right. Let's get it over with."

She drew her knees up to her chest and carefully arranged her skirt over them. "Whether you deliberately jumped in to save me or not, the result was the same. You did get me to dry land, and I do owe you."

"That attitude ought to at least make our stay here interesting."

She drew a deep breath, and he had the feeling she was reaching for calm. "I intend to buy your resort, whether you like it or not."

He eyed her militant expression and shook his head. "No. Now would you like to wash all that paint off your face? It's pretty much a mess."

"Oh." She pressed her palms to her cheeks and looked a little embarrassed. He hoped that would be the end of it, that she'd get sidetracked with appearances and quit poking holes in his self-esteem.

Not Mel.

"I can wash up later."

"Not unless it rains again tonight. Already the puddles of fresh water are starting to disappear."

She blinked slowly, as if barely comprehending his words. "You expect me to wash my face in a puddle?"

"Well, honey, your options are somewhat limited right about now. It's either salt water, which is pretty sticky when it's drying, or a fresh rainwater puddle. The sand is clean, so the water is, too. And I can even loan you some of my soap—for a fee."

In the fading light, her pale blue eyes looked almost iridescent. He'd always thought she had the sexiest and most expressive eyes he'd ever seen. She didn't need makeup.

"What fee?"

"Another kiss, that's all." He could still taste her, and he wanted more.

"Bargaining away your goods? A real gentleman would just share."

"But we both know there's no real gentlemen on this island, don't we?" Provoking her seemed his only defense. If she was mad, she wouldn't talk about owing him. "Now what'll it be? You want the soap or not?"

Indignation made her eyes bright. "Oh, all right." Taking him by surprise, she leaned forward, grabbed his face in both hands and gave him a hard, dry smooch. He didn't even have time to pucker. "There. Now where's the soap?"

"That's it?" He had to fight to keep from laughing. Her averted gaze told him what that impromptu kiss had cost her in the way of nerve.

"That's it." She tried to look smug, but she avoided his gaze so the effect was minimal. "You didn't say what kind of kiss."

"I see I'll have to word myself more carefully in the future." Still smiling, Adam dug through his bag and pulled out the scented bar of green soap. It smelled like Brut cologne.

Melanie stared at it. "Is that all you have?"

"Sorry, but I didn't take into account feminine bathing preferences when packing it. It'll do the job. And you better hurry up before all the water either evaporates or sinks into the ground."

She took the soap and moved only a few feet away to where a shallow puddle had formed in the sand between some scrub grass and a young mangrove tree. On her knees, she bent forward and splashed her face. The position put her shapely rump up in the air, and Adam had to choke back several comments that tripped to the tip of his tongue.

Worse than that, he had to sit on his hands to keep from touching that sweet little bottom. He'd felt its softness when they were swimming to shore, had twice rested his head against her delicious buttocks. He'd had to fight the inclination to explore that area further while the opportunity presented itself. He'd even considered taking a few small nibbles, he'd always had a certain fondness for feminine posteriors, and everything about Melanie Tucker had always been a source of fascination.

She'd been too frightened of the ocean to notice his interest; he doubted that was the case now. But the woman obviously had no idea of her own charms. If she did, she sure wouldn't offer up such an irresistible temptation.

Hadn't her fiancé ever told her what a great bottom she had?

When she lingered, splashing again and again, he finally turned away. He wasn't into torture, and tonight his control seemed precarious, at best.

A few minutes later, face freshly scrubbed and even more appealing, Mel returned his soap to him. She sat beside him, looking more self-conscious than ever, but also a lot more determined. "Now, about the resort."

"Do you want a comb or some lotion?"

"Does the lotion smell like the soap?"

He grinned. "Sure does."

She stuck out her small hand, palm up.

Adam held the bottle out of reach. "You know you'll owe me again, only this time it'll be my choice."

She sighed. "And what exactly would your choice be?"

After looking her over from head to toe, he locked onto her gaze. Her eyes were wide and wary, and he thought he might be content to simply look at her all night. "It's a warm evening."

"Yes."

"I don't relish sleeping on this sand." He picked up a handful and let it sift through his fingers. "It sure as hell won't be very comfortable."

"We'll be rescued before it's a problem."

He grunted. Damn persistent witch. "Maybe, but if we're not, I want you to lose the skirt."

Her back snapped straight, and she glared at him. "This time you have to be joking."

"Nope." He enjoyed watching the flush bloom over her face and upper chest. He imagined her breasts rosy and warm, and shifted uncomfortably. "It's the only piece of material we have that's big enough to serve as a sheet. We can both snuggle up on it." When she looked furious, he asked softly, "What's the matter, Mel? If you're so sure we'll get rescued, then it won't be a problem."

He'd caught her and he knew it. His motives were twofold. If he could keep her mind on sex and off his personal business, she'd likely forget his financial confession. At the same time, he knew he'd gladly be stranded for a month if it meant he could fulfill his fantasy of being with her. Like an obsession that wouldn't go away, he wanted her as much now as he ever had. Maybe more, because he'd kissed her and knew how good she tasted, how perfect it had felt.

They had a staring contest going, one he knew he'd win because he enjoyed looking into her blue eyes.

"Oh, all right. But you're being outrageous and making me dislike you immensely."

He shrugged. "You've always disliked me. Not surprising. We're from different worlds."

Her mouth tightened. "I disliked you, Adam, not because you didn't have as much money as me. But because you were as provoking then as you are now."

Without a word, he handed her the lotion.

If she only knew how difficult it was for him to smell his favorite scent on her. It felt as if he'd branded her somehow, made her his by giving her his scent. It turned him on.

The entire atmosphere of the island was conducive to primal needs, reducing a man to his basic instincts. He wanted to protect her, provide for her. He wanted to claim her as his own in the most elemental way.

Damn, the coming night would be torture.

He was looking forward to it already.

CHAPTER FIVE

They had fruit for dinner, but Melanie could barely eat as she watched the island grow darker and darker. Nervousness set in whenever she thought of the night to come, of being alone with Adam on a deserted island.

After cracking a couple of coconuts open and using his knife to slice up several oranges, he'd gone back up the beach to fetch the clothes he'd left behind and the raft they'd floated in on. Adam made the decision that they should stay by the house in case it rained again, but for now, they remained outside.

The heat had settled in like a damp blanket. A slight, balmy breeze barely stirred the air, rustling the dry grasses and fringed palm leaves. She got to her feet to gather the remains of their meal and put the scraps out of the way in a tidy pile. She knew Adam watched her every move, could feel his hot gaze touching on her everywhere. Earlier, before the sun had gone, he'd entertained himself by perusing his damn *Key to the Keys,* where he'd found the idea for scraping the coconut shells clean and filling them with the remains of the rainwater.

She bent to rinse her hands in one of the few remaining puddles and nearly jumped out of her skin when he shifted.

"Mel."

She slowly closed her eyes at the husky way he'd said her name. She swallowed hard, then whispered, "Yes?"

A long moment of silence had her nerves pulled taut, when he finally said, "Come here."

With her back still to him, she sat on her heels, trying to calm her racing heart. Never had she been so conscious of another human being, but she should have suspected it would be this way. Good or bad, she'd always held a fascinated awareness of Adam that wouldn't go away, not even with the passing of seven years.

She was a grown woman, free to do as she pleased, and though she'd never really believed in casual sex, situations like this one just didn't happen often. And in truth, there was nothing casual in what she felt for Adam.

She turned her head to look at him. "Why?"

Lazily, his voice nearly drugged, he said, "You're keyed up. I can feel it. Come here and I'll comb your hair."

She lifted one hand to her tangled curls. That's all he wanted to do? He leaned against a palm tree, looking utterly relaxed, but she could feel his tension washing over her in waves. Her heartbeat doubled. "I…I can do it."

"I want to do it for you." When she started to protest, he said, "It's the price for using the comb. Now come here."

On legs that felt much too wobbly, she stood and walked to him until only a foot was between them. Adam took her hand, turned her around, then tugged her down between his thighs. Taking his time, he situated her just so. Melanie stared straight ahead at the silhouette of a palm tree against the dark gray sky. Adam's breath touched her neck when he whispered, "Relax, Mel. I won't hurt you. Ever."

She had no response to that. Her senses rioted, her mind numb against everything but the feel of his fingers in her hair, gently untangling every curl.

"I like your hair short."

Conversation. Innocuous, innocent conversation. She grasped it like a lifeline, trying to hide the mixed jumble of emotions she suffered. "I cut it after college. Jerry didn't like it. He thought it looked too unruly."

The comb stilled for the slightest moment, then Adam laid it aside. "You always had beautiful hair. I remember when you went from braids to barrettes to those pretty combs. I used to imagine your hair trailing over my chest."

"Adam…"

"And my stomach."

She bit her lip, the imagery crystal clear in her mind.

"Jerry must have been a damn fool."

Her heart was already racing when the weight of Adam's hands settled on her shoulders. "It's getting late."

Not knowing what to say to that, she simply nodded.

"No one's coming tonight to rescue us, honey."

She nodded again. Even if a rescue crew tried, finding them in the darkness would be nearly impossible.

"We had a deal."

There it was—the thing she had dreaded most, and yet strangely hungered for. At least it was dark enough that he wouldn't be able to see her clearly. She knew what she looked like, knew she was too thin, too gangly. A man like Adam, who'd had more than his fair share of feminine attention, might very well be disappointed. The thought made her stomach churn.

He stood and pulled her up with him, then stepped in front of her. Heat seemed to pour off him in waves, bringing with it his heady scent—not of the now familiar cologne, but of the man. Breathing deeply, she drew that scent into herself. She felt drunk with the pleasure and nervousness of the moment.

"Mel?" He touched her cheek, smoothed his hand over her skin. "It's okay, honey."

She nearly collapsed. He wasn't going to pressure her. It was still her choice, and for that reason more than any other, she wanted to prove herself. She'd made a deal and she would stick to it. But when her fingers went to the tie at her skirt, he brushed her hands away and did the unwrapping himself, gently easing the knot apart and revealing her with slow anticipation as if she were a long-awaited gift.

Holding the skirt open with clenched fists, Adam simply looked. Melanie was grateful for the added shadows of the trees behind them, but then Adam dropped the skirt and took her hand, easing her into the moonlight. She held her breath, keeping her head high, refusing to show her uncertainty. She locked her thighs and waited.

For long, agonizing moments, he stood there, saying nothing, barely breathing. When she saw the beginning of his slow smile, she almost crumbled inside. "Don't...don't you *dare* laugh at me, Adam Stone."

His eyes glittered in the darkness, and his hands cupped her hips, gently squeezing. "Honey, I'm so far from laughing right now, I couldn't even work up a chuckle." He gave her a light, barely there kiss on her lips, then dropped to his knees in front of her.

Alarmed, she started to step back, but he held onto her.

"This has been coming a long time, Mel." His fingers on her hips flexed, caressing her. "Damn, I've wanted you so long, I can't remember when I haven't wanted you."

"You...you didn't even *like* me."

"I liked you too much."

Not giving her time to mull that stark confession over, he slid his hot palms up and down the backs of her thighs. He made her knees weak, her stomach jumpy. "You're perfect,

Mel. Sleek and sexy." He glanced up at her, his expression fixed. "How the hell did you disguise yourself so well?"

He evidently didn't want an answer. He leaned forward and placed a warm, damp kiss on her navel. Stunned, she braced her hands on his shoulders and drew in a shaky breath. "Adam, I feel…funny." She could barely get the words out around the tightness in her throat.

"It's the coconut," he whispered, nibbling on her belly with his lips and rubbing his cheek against her. "It's an aphrodisiac."

"Don't…don't be ridiculous." She moaned when his hands glided higher, coasting over her bottom, then gripping her tight, pulling her closer to his kiss. His tongue dipped into her navel.

"True," he countered, concentrating his kisses over the low-riding waistband of her silky tap pants, "it's in the guidebook."

"Adam…"

"Aren't you turned on just a little, Mel?"

Oh, yes. But what she felt had nothing to do with coconut and everything to do with Adam Stone. It seemed he knew exactly how to touch her, where to kiss her, how to make her frantic with need. She'd pictured being with Adam many times, but she'd never imagined anything quite this intense.

Grasping her waist, he lowered her slowly, trailing kisses up her body as she sank onto her knees in the sand. His mouth lingered at her midriff; his tongue licked a hot path from rib to rib. He nudged aside the halter and placed damp, open-mouthed kisses on one tingling breast, only inches away from her painfully tight nipple. He nuzzled into her cleavage. "I'd like to eat you up from head to toe, Mel. You taste so damn good."

This time she couldn't stop the groan. Embarrassed by her unrestrained response, she tried to add a bit of jest to the moment. "Did…did you feed me the coconut on purpose?"

He drew the tender skin of her throat against his teeth, leaving his mark behind and eliciting another raw moan. "Right now, I'd do whatever it takes. God knows we'll never have another opportunity like this one."

He didn't say it, but she knew that once they were rescued, he'd consider their time at an end. If this was all she would ever have, she didn't want to waste it.

Both his hands cupped her head, and he gently touched his mouth to hers. "Tell me you want me, too, sweetheart."

She gasped out a resounding, "Yes."

Before the agreement had finished leaving her mouth, Adam devoured it, sucking it from her, his tongue searching for and finding hers. This wasn't to be a slow interlude, evidently, given his feverish pace. But she didn't mind. She felt ready to fracture with need. With each new touch, each deeper kiss, she wanted him more.

He pulled away to shake out her skirt across the sand. Then, staring into her eyes, he shoved down his boxers. Mel swayed on her knees, he was so perfect, so sexy.

Blindly, she reached out to cup him in her palms. He made a deep sound of pleasure and pain, fisted his hands on his thighs and tilted his head back. His eyes were tightly closed.

She wrapped her fingers around his throbbing erection and stroked. When her thumb glided over the tip of him, she found a drop of moisture. Fascinated, she gently spread it around and around, until his entire body trembled.

"Enough." He gripped her wrists and pulled her away. "I can't take it, Mel. Not yet. Maybe after…"

She started to protest, but he didn't give her time. His hands cupped her breasts; his thumbs brushed her nipples. When she groaned, he said, "You're wearing too many clothes, honey. I want to see you naked. I want to kiss you everywhere."

Everywhere? It took him mere seconds to untie her halter and bare her breasts. She felt another stab of vulnerability, until he bent to greedily suck one nipple. There were no preliminaries, no forewarnings. Just the hot, moist pull of his mouth and the rough stroke of his tongue. It was so intense she tried to draw away with a short, startled exclamation. But he held her close, his callused hands spread wide on her back, gently refusing to let her retreat.

After long minutes he released her, only to switch to her other nipple.

"Adam..."

"It's the coconut, sweetheart." He nipped her with his teeth, and she trembled, tangling her fingers in the silky hair over his nape, trying to bring his mouth to hers. But he didn't budge. "I intend to drink my fill, Mel, so quit fighting me."

His fill turned out to be long minutes of sheer agony. Before he finished she was spread on her back, half on, half off the skirt, and he had settled comfortably between her thighs. She couldn't keep her hips still, thrusting up against him, but that only seemed to encourage him, to make him more ruthless. When she tugged on his hair, hurting his injured head, he captured both her wrists in one hand and pinned her arms over her head.

Leaning back on his knees, his eyes glowing in the darkness, he whispered, "It feels like a lifetime I've been waiting to see you like this." The atmosphere vibrated with his potent sexuality, making her feel decadent and drunk with erotic need.

"I can't tell you how many times I imagined coming after you, forcing you to help me get over my obsession. I wanted you just like this, open to me, accepting me."

As he spoke, he kept her arms immobile, stroking his free hand slowly down her side, closer and closer to the notch of her thighs. Tingling from the inside out, she opened herself a little wider, making it easy for him, trying to hurry him.

"That's it, Mel. Show me that you want me."

"I do."

"Not enough. Not yet."

His long fingers slid over the soft material of her shorts, right where she needed his touch most. No man had ever done this to her, and it seemed so right that Adam would be the first to make her feel this way. She had the vague impression of knowing this was what she'd waited for. *He* was what she'd waited for.

"Please…" She felt so close to something she'd never experienced, and she desperately wanted it. She strained against him, lifting her hips as high as she could.

He pulled back. His eyes were midnight dark as he looked at her, seeing everything. With a slight shake of his head, he whispered, "Not yet, baby."

Gasping, she scrambled up and reached for him. Adam let her get as far as her knees, then caught the waistband of her shorts and started working them down. She tried to kiss him but he dodged her mouth, chuckling softly.

"It's okay, Mel. I promise. I'll take care of you."

"I want you to take care of me now."

He smiled, amused by her sudden lack of inhibition and uncharacteristic brazenness. "So impatient," he chided.

"You're the one who fed me the damn coconut!"

He slid her shorts and her panties down to her knees, then eased her onto her back to slip them the rest of the way off. He tossed them aside, and with a hand on each knee, spread her thighs wide. "Such long, sexy legs, Mel. Not at all what I imagined. Even better…" He bent to kiss the inside of one knee. "Hell, I'm glad I went overboard."

"Really?" She tried to keep her mind clear, to be coherent, but the cool brush of his silky hair on the sensitive inside of her thigh was startling. The fact that this was Adam, the town bad boy, the man who'd taken over her dreams, made it all the more incredible.

He kissed her belly a few inches below her belly button, then licked the spot. "Absolutely," he said with a throaty groan, then started licking his way downward.

"Adam."

His mouth closed over her, and she stiffened at the acute pleasure. Never in her wildest imagination had she been able to aptly prepare for such a thing. Her muscles went taut while her insides seemed fluid. His rasping tongue delved and stroked and licked, and when he slipped one long finger inside her she climaxed with a raw groan that ripped from her throat and echoed around the quiet island. Adam held her there, insatiable, refusing to let the pleasure dwindle until her body went utterly limp.

He released her, gently lowering her thighs and moving to her side. She felt so drained, she didn't at first realize that he had separated himself from her. Then she felt his hand cup her breast.

"Your heart is still pounding," he said with deep satisfaction.

"That's…that's good." A heartbeat, considering she felt like she'd died, was definitely a promising sign.

She could hear his smile in the way he spoke. "You didn't do a very good job of staying on the skirt. You're more in the sand than out of it."

What was he babbling about? What difference did it make if she was in the sand? Blindly, she reached out to him, wanting to draw him close again. He caught her hand and held it. "Mel, I lied about the coconut."

He obviously thought her beyond naive, bordering on stupid. But she played along. "No aphrodisiac?"

"Of course not. But you did want me."

Very slowly, his words sank in. She heard the wonder and

the insistence. She turned her head to face him. "I still do, Adam."

"Are you sure?"

He sounded uncertain, and for a man like Adam, that had to be unique. It was her turn to smile. Despite the lethargy that tried to rule her body, she rolled on top of him. He gladly went to his back and helped hold her in place, his hands firm on her bottom. She kissed his nose, his bristly chin. "No woman needs an aphrodisiac when you're around. You *breathe* and women want to jump your bones."

"You were never interested, Mel." He stroked her hair and gave her a slight smile. "No matter what I did, you managed to turn up your nose at me like I didn't exist."

Her eyes widened. "You really think that?" Then another thought invaded her fogged brain and she asked, "Do you mean to tell me you constantly provoked me just to get my attention?"

She might not have believed him, despite the recent display of his desire, if she hadn't seen the look in his eyes. But there was so much feeling there, so much raw emotion.

His hands cupped her head, his thumb brushed her cheek. "I'm sorry I was sometimes mean. As a kid, it seemed so damn unfair that you had everything, even things I hadn't dared dream of. You sort of represented everything that was missing in my life, all the stuff my parents worked so hard for but could never get."

She felt the prickle of tears and knew he wouldn't appreciate her sympathy. She swallowed hard.

"But somewhere along the way," he continued, "I started wanting you, not the material things you had. I'd stopped being mean by the time we were thirteen, Mel, but you didn't notice. You still avoided me." With a smile, he said, "You could get that pretty little nose so high in the air, I could have thrown myself at your feet and you wouldn't have seen me."

He was so wrong, but how could she explain all the various things he'd made her feel over the years? Yes, she'd often been angry at him, but she'd also felt alive whenever he was near. Adam never ignored her like the rest of the town did. He didn't give her only distant politeness. And he didn't hide what he felt behind proper manners, as her parents were wont to do. Her mother and father loved her, she'd never doubted that. But they considered an excess of emotion uncouth. They'd always been careful in how they expressed their feelings.

Not Adam. No, he teased and harassed and provoked—and she'd always responded to him, whether he knew it or not. In many ways, she'd equally dreaded and looked forward to her daily confrontations with him.

Twining her fingers in his chest hair, she said, "I was never…indifferent to you, Adam."

He gave her a crooked smile. "No, most times you hated me. And all I could think about was getting you out of your dainty little pants. Hell, there were days I'd get hard just seeing you in town or in school. You had a way of walking, like a queen, that drove me crazy. Even when I thought you were skinny—"

"I *am* skinny."

He shook his head. "No. You're thin, but you've got all the right curves in all the right places. If I'd known what you were hiding under those schoolgirl jumpers, I'd never have survived puberty."

She felt her cheeks heat, and Adam hugged her closer. His gaze was hot, probing. "I wanted you so bad, Mel, it's a wonder I survived. But I always knew you were out of bounds."

Daringly, she slipped her hand down his side to his hip. Hard muscle and bone moved as he shifted from her touch.

"I'm not out of bounds now." His eyes closed; his breathing came faster. Melanie leaned forward and kissed his chin. "Now, there's just you and me—and I want you."

He gripped her buttocks even tighter and rocked her against the long length of his erection. "I need to be inside you, sweetheart."

She wasn't experienced and couldn't tease as well as he. Already she wanted him again and felt no shame in admitting it. "Yes, please."

He laughed on a shaky breath. "You always were so damn proper."

"What we're doing now is far from proper, Adam Stone, and you know it."

His hands shifted, stroking her thighs. "All right, not proper. But you have to admit it feels damn right."

Nothing had ever felt more right in her entire life. Being with Adam seemed totally natural, because Adam was so natural. Loving him would be so easy. But nothing for the future had changed, and she doubted it ever would, not with the way Adam resented her background. But for right now, it just didn't matter.

Quickly rolling her onto her back, Adam sat up and reached for his bag. He lifted out a small foil pack and hastily tore it open with his teeth.

Melanie watched him in fascination. "Are you really such a hound dog that you carry condoms everywhere?"

Sitting by her side, he placed one hand on her belly and stroked. "Mel…I travel a lot, honey. And I avoid commitments like the plague."

Her eyes closed, both from the pain of his admission and the gentle stroking of his rough palm.

"I'm a man," he continued. His control seemed tightly leashed, but ready to break at any moment. "I enjoy sex, I won't lie about that. But as a rule, I don't believe in one-night stands."

She shifted, not really wanting details, unable to imagine him with someone else in just this way.

"Melanie, look at me."

She did, surprised by the use of her full name.

"I quit prowling after high school, sweetheart. But I am human, so I carry protection whether I plan on doing anything or not. I guess I'm old-fashioned enough to think if you make a baby, you should be a father, and I'm not ready to take a chance on that yet."

Melanie turned her face away. He couldn't have been more blunt, and while his words hurt, she understood. Adam had been given very little in life, and his attitude was actually commendable.

If only her heart weren't already involved.

"Mel?"

Choking back the hurt, she looked at him and smiled. "You talk too damn much, Stone, you know that?"

"And you're just a bit demanding." He pulled her on top of him again and situated her until she sat astride his hips. "I like it." Automatically, Melanie braced her hands on his chest and tightened her thighs. Slowly, he entered her.

She groaned at the incredible tightness.

"Mel?" His voice was strained, filled with disbelief.

"Not now, Adam." Later, when she could catch her breath, she'd explain to him why she'd waited so long to experience sex. But now the experiencing was at hand, and she didn't want to be distracted for a single moment.

Adam's chest rose and fell with his labored breaths. He pressed deeper. "Damn, you're snug." Every muscle in his arms and shoulders pulled taut with restraint.

She tipped her head back and concentrated on relaxing, on accepting him.

"Yeah. All the way, honey," he urged. "All the way…"

The natural resistance of her body gave way, and he buried himself completely inside her.

Mel dropped forward against his chest, overwhelmed with his size and strength. His fingers bit into her buttocks, holding her and his control tightly. Then he broke.

"I'm sorry," he growled through clenched teeth, even as he rolled her to her back. He thrust smoothly, deeply, lifting her hips high into the rhythm of his. Heat poured off his body.

Stunned, Melanie felt the pressure building again and she held on tight. His sudden fierceness fired her own. The friction was exquisite, the weight of his body on hers, his scent. As she started to climax, Adam pressed his face into the side of her neck and groaned out his own release.

Afterward they lay limp, both overheated, their limbs tangled. Melanie thought it was the most wondrous experience imaginable. Finally, as if the effort cost him, Adam shifted to her side, then tucked her close again. "Sleep."

She didn't need to be told twice. There in the tranquillity of the island, the moon shadows of palm leaves dancing over the white sand, the salty breeze from the ocean touching her skin, she felt more peace than she'd felt in all her life. Sleeping there with Adam was the easiest thing she'd ever done.

Loving, and leaving him, would be the hardest.

CHAPTER SIX

Adam opened his eyes, not certain what had awakened him, and squinted against the rising sunshine. He noticed several things at once. Melanie was no longer at his side, the day was hazy, promising rain, and a huge, smelly pelican stood over him, its expression rapt, staring at his naked body.

Adam quickly scrambled back, scraping his bare butt on the fine sand. The pelican boldly scrambled after him, keeping pace. Jumping to his feet, Adam tried to intimidate the bird by making shooing motions with his arms and yelling, "Scat!" The bird lifted its enormous wings and opened its baggy beak in a silent but alarming threat.

Adam froze. Where the hell was Melanie? Watching the bird with one eye, he called, "Mel!"

She stuck her head out of the empty shack. "You're awake!"

He didn't dare look away from the pelican. "I'm being attacked, damn it."

Dividing his glances between Mel and the bird, Adam caught the way Melanie stared, perusing his body in minute detail. A lesser man might have blushed, her look was so thorough. Of course, most men wouldn't have been preoccupied defending themselves against a curious bird.

Adam watched Mel leap nimbly out of the doorway and start toward them at an angle. She wore her halter and the silky tap pants and she was the sexiest thing he'd ever seen in his entire life.

His palms began to sweat.

"I think he might want food. I tossed some coconut and strawberries to him earlier, but he wouldn't go away."

Adam inched closer to her, intending to protect her with his body if need be. "I think they only eat fish."

The pelican didn't like him moving around and fanned his wings as a warning. Adam halted. He turned slightly to Mel, but she had her gaze directed on lower parts, which caused something of an immediate reaction in his body.

"Sweetheart, there's not a damn thing I'd like more this morning than to indulge your interest, but I don't want my eyes—or more important body parts—plucked at by our feathered guest while I'm distracted by you."

"Oh." She forced her attention to the bird. "He's kind of cute, isn't he?"

"You must be kidding."

The bird took a small, mean leap at Adam and he yelped, stumbling back. Being naked, he felt even more graceless than otherwise.

"Be still, Adam. You're frightening him."

She *had* to be kidding. "Honey, find me a rock."

Appalled, Melanie turned on him and pointed a finger. "Don't you dare!" The bird, startled by her command, turned to flee. But on his way, he snatched up her underpants, resting on a pile of palm leaves, and flew away with them.

Melanie's eyes were huge. "Now look what you've done!"

"Me?" Adam did his best not to laugh. And he couldn't very well hold a grudge against the bird. "You're the one who shouted. And for your information, I had no intention of hitting the damn bird with a rock, I just wanted to scare it away."

The bird soared down the island, out of sight. Hands on her hips, Melanie stared after it. "I washed out our stuff and left it on the leaves to dry. Now what will we do?"

"Our stuff?"

"Our…respective underthings."

Adam, having resisted her as long as he could, drew her close in the circle of his arms. "Why'd you leave me this morning?"

Mel toyed with the hair on his chest, avoiding his gaze. "I woke early so I decided to do some…stuff."

"What kind of stuff?" Already it was hard for him to carry on a conversation. She was soft and sweet and he knew her body well, knew how easily, how hotly, she responded to him. She'd combed her hair and made use of his toothpaste; he could smell the minty flavor on her breath. Her skin, sun-warmed and glowing, felt silky soft beneath his hands.

"I washed out our clothes, like I said. And I tidied up the shack in case we need to go in. The air smells rainy to me." She peeked at him, then away. "I also explored a little down the beach. A lot more of the same, except there's a mango tree there that has—"

Adam cut her off, his mood quickly changing when he thought of all the things that could have happened to her. "You took off down the beach without me?"

She looked surprised by his accusing tone. "So?"

Without even realizing it, he gripped her upper arms. "Mel, the sun's just coming up."

"There was enough light for me to see."

He wanted to shake her. "What would you have done if you'd run into another snake? Or a swarm of those damn beetles? What if you'd fallen and hit your head, or stepped on something sharp?"

She pulled away and stared at him. "I'm a big girl, Adam. I can take care of myself."

"Ha! Big girls don't go running screaming down the beach because of a little cockroach—"

"A swarm of huge cockroaches!"

"—and they aren't afraid to stick so much as a big toe in the ocean." He no sooner said it and saw her face blanch than he felt disgust for himself. Her fear of the water was real, if exaggerated, and he'd found it endearing, not something to ridicule her over. But he could tell by her quivering lip and rigid stance that he'd crossed the line.

He sighed. "Mel…"

She bit her lip to still it, and her hands fisted. After two deep breaths she very calmly, very coldly, said, "I am a coward and I freely admit it. I'm afraid of the water, or rather, things lurking in the water. But I can damn well carry my own weight here. I'm not the pampered little girl you remember. I do all the things normal women do, like go to college, work—even break engagements!"

"I didn't mean—"

That stubborn, adorable chin of hers lifted and she cut him off. "I cleaned out the shack so we can inhabit it, and yes, I did run into a few snakes. While I don't like them, I am quite capable of shooing them off with a long stick."

"Honey…"

"I also collected enough fruit for our breakfast and I got a dozen pricks on my fingers from my efforts." She thrust her hands in front of his face, glaring.

Smiling inside, Adam took her fingers and examined the small scratches. "Blackberry bushes?"

"And some of that stupid grass. It's as sharp as needles."

"You didn't need to do all that, babe. And I'm sorry I said anything about the water."

She jerked her hands away in renewed pique. "The point is, if I choose to go exploring, I will. I don't need your permission or your protection." Then she sneered, "Or are you going to lie some more about wild boars?"

"You read my *Key to the Keys?*"

She thumped him on the chest with one small fist. "I'm not an idiot, damn it! I don't need to read your dumb guidebook to know there aren't any wild boars here."

She was so adorable in her anger, and he was naked and hard. It was difficult to take part in the conversation when all he really wanted to do was lay her down and slide into her body again. Last night he'd tried to make her see how different she was from any other woman he'd been with. Sheer physical gratification couldn't compare with the deep, primal possessiveness he felt with her. But he knew by the look on her face she hadn't understood. She thought she was just one more woman in a long line of conquests. And this morning, being in a saner frame of mind, he wasn't about to tell her no other woman had mattered, not when he always pretended they were her. That was a little too heavy to lay on a woman after only one night.

"Mel, I don't want you wandering off alone because it isn't safe, boar or no boar. I have no idea what kinds of snakes are on the island, if they're poisonous or not. The shack looks ready to collapse, so until we can decide if it's safe enough to be in, I don't want either of us wandering off alone. Okay?"

His cajoling tone and apologetic expression must have gotten to her. "You're expressing yourself much better this time around, Stone."

He grinned. She obviously didn't know how badly it scared him to think of her getting hurt. "I'm naked, horny as hell, and you're running around in this sexy little outfit, looking good enough to be breakfast. How do you expect me to act?"

Her mouth opened and closed twice, then she looked down and started toying with his chest hair again. He liked her like this, all sweet and innocent and shy. His hands slid over her hips, appreciating the feel of her firm softness beneath the slippery material.

"I looked at you this morning."

Adam froze while kissing her neck. "Is that right?"

She nodded, bumping his chin. "You're very...sexy, too."

Grinning from ear to ear, he put one finger beneath her chin and lifted her face so he could see her eyes. "Am I hearing this right? You took advantage of my exhaustion to sate your curiosity on my poor body?"

A blush exploded on her cheeks and her long lashes drifted down to hide her expression, but she smiled. "Yes. And I enjoyed myself, too. You...affect me, Adam. Once I woke up and saw you, it was impossible to go back to sleep. I had to find something to do so I wouldn't attack you, but I knew you needed your rest after hurting your head."

"My head is fine, feeling better by the second." He kissed her long and deep, his tongue tasting her, enticing her. "You should have wakened me," he growled between nibbling on her lips.

"You're awake now."

"And you're overdressed." One small tug, and her halter dropped to her waist.

This time was no less frantic than the night before, and afterward, as they both lay sated and hot and damp from their exertions and the rising humidity, Adam frowned. He couldn't quite reconcile the way she made him feel, complete but still hungry, at peace but still turbulent. He'd always known there was something there, an irresistible chemistry that drew him in, but he'd thought it all one-sided. Now, seeing her naked beside him, panting for breath, her scream of pleasure at the time of her climax still ringing in his ears, he realized how wrong he'd been. She'd moved with him, kept pace with him, every step of the way.

Yet she'd been a virgin.

Laying a hand on her damp belly, relishing the fact that she still trembled, he said, "Tell me about yourself, Mel. What you've been up to."

She cocked one pale blue eye open to peer at him, and groaned. "I think you've killed me."

He laughed. "With pleasure." Leaning down to kiss her, he added, "You're one demanding little lady."

"You'd make me blush if I had the strength."

"You want me to show you exactly how much strength you still have?" He drifted his fingers down her belly.

Melanie caught his wrist and moaned. "No, I'll talk."

"Good. Start with this idiot fiancé of yours."

"He's not my fiancé, not anymore, and he's also not an idiot. In fact, he's very intelligent, successful—pretty special, really." She sighed, then tilted her head to the side to smile at him. "Jerry Marshall is actually considered quite a catch. He's not as tall as you, but he's handsome. Hair as black as my own, great teeth."

Adam made a sound of disgust. "I don't give a damn about his teeth. Why the hell haven't you slept with him?"

There was that seductive blush again, making his muscles twitch and his heart pound. When would her potent effect on him diminish? Never? He couldn't accept that prospect and determinedly pushed the problem from his mind. They were still eons apart, and he had a hell of a lot yet to accomplish before he could even begin to think of settling down, especially with a woman like Melanie Tucker.

But she'd given him her virginity. In too many ways to count, he felt she was his already.

"I don't know, Adam. The time just never seemed right." She wouldn't look at him, choosing to stare at the sky. "Jerry's practice kept him pretty busy, and our time together was usually spent at social gatherings or working. I guess I wasn't overly anxious to get intimate, and Jerry seemed content to wait."

"What an ass."

She smiled. "Well, I'd expect that attitude from a hound dog like you."

"I told you last night, I'm not nearly as insatiable as you want to think I am."

Her eyes widened and she leaned up far enough to look at their naked bodies. "Could have fooled me."

"It's different with you." He kissed her nose and spoke in a whisper. "You make me crazy." Maybe he was a hound dog, after all, because he sure as hell couldn't look at her, couldn't even think of her, without wanting her in the most elemental ways possible. "How long have you been broken up with this guy?"

"About a month." She cuddled closer and rested her head on his chest. "I wanted to get a different job, something more challenging. He didn't want me to. My parents agreed with him."

"What kind of job did you want?"

She tipped her head to look at him. "I don't know. Something fun, exciting. Working for Jerry was...well, it was boring."

"Maybe that's because Jerry was boring."

"Most women don't think so." She smiled slightly, then admitted, "I made a lot of money on the stock market, and by investing in real estate. I wanted to get more involved with that. I seem to have a knack for it."

"Real estate?" That was one of his big interests.

"Yes." She leaned on one elbow. "Adam, my money is all my own, separate from my parents."

That surprised him. Somehow he'd always figured she'd simply live off an inheritance, like every other pampered rich kid. "So you've made your own fortune?"

She nodded. "I have a way with numbers, and with property. Some day I'll inherit my parents' money, but for now, I don't want it or need it."

Ridiculously, he felt proud of her. She was more independent than he'd thought, and it pleased him. "Why not take what's coming to you? You get along with your folks, don't you?"

"Yes. I just like it better when I'm not answerable to anyone but myself." She turned her face toward him, and her smoky eyes nearly did him in. That is, until she spoke. "I want to buy your resort, Adam."

Her words felt like a punch to the chest, making him clench his teeth. After his mother had been forced to accept charity from the town to bury his father, he swore it would never happen again. Taking refuge from his painful memories, he moved on top of Melanie and parted her thighs.

She clung to him, accepting him. "Adam, please just let me explain what I—"

"Be quiet, Mel." He gently, inexorably pushed himself into her, his groan mingling with hers, their gazes locked.

Melanie waited until he was completely buried inside her, then whispered, "Adam, I've made up my mind. I'm buying the resort. From what you've said, it's a good deal, so—"

"Damn it." He began to thrust, and she held on tight, her fingertips digging deep into his shoulders. He wanted to drown out her words, the fact that she could do what he couldn't, that she had enough money and he still didn't. It proved her right; nothing and neither of them had really changed, after all. They were each older and wiser, but their placement in the world was the same; they were still at opposite ends of the scale.

All his life, he'd fought hard against a society that said if you were born with money, life was easy, but if you had to earn it, there was a whole new set of rules. He'd learned early on what the main rule was: those with money did as they pleased. Melanie included. She really didn't care what he wanted, she was just appeasing her ridiculous guilt.

Right now what he wanted most was for Melanie to give in to him, to be female to his male. At least in this he had the upper hand.

She quickened beneath him, and her teeth bit into the muscle on his shoulder. He flinched, and at the same time his touted control broke. He was a wild man—primal, complete.

Afterward, he didn't wait for his breathing to calm, for his heartbeat to slow. He came jerkily to his feet and stood looking down at her. So damn beautiful. So damn rich. Tears shone on her long black lashes, making her blue eyes liquid and bright. Her breasts shimmered with her gasping, ragged breaths.

He walked away, straight into the ocean until he stood waist deep. The water was cool, and with clouds covering the sun, he should have felt comfortable. Instead, he was stricken by the flash heat of anger and despair. He wanted to rail against the world. He hadn't used a condom that last time. And he wouldn't touch her again.

He thought of her, not more than two yards away, looking earthy, warm, satisfied, everything a woman—his woman—should be. He ground his teeth and reminded himself it wouldn't be for long. Surely they'd be missed soon and then someone would come for them. Someone had to rescue him, before he lost *everything*—his head, his heart, and his self-respect.

"She's such a damn tease," Adam accused.

Silence and a bold stare were the only reply from his feathered companion.

"Just look at her. She knows damn good and well I'm trying to be noble, trying to leave her alone, so what does she do? She starts flaunting, that's what!"

The bird waddled closer, as if enthralled by what Adam had to say. Adam shook his head. Leave it to Mel to befriend a big ugly bird. A bird who had stolen her panties.

She'd begun bribing the pelican two days ago, the same morning he'd sworn not to touch her again, by offering up a few colorful shells she'd found in the cove. Aladdin, named after the king of thieves, had swiped the shells and flown off, then returned later that day to steal again. He'd taken Adam's makeshift bandage when he'd pulled it off to dunk his head in the ocean, trying to cool down from the heat Mel generated, and the frustration of resisting her. He'd also stolen Adam's tie—and anything else he could get hold of.

Adam never complained to Melanie when she laughed at Aladdin's antics. He couldn't trust himself to talk to her much at all since deciding to leave her alone. Sleeping next to her for two nights without making love to her was the hardest thing he'd ever done.

He still held her; he'd done his best to comfort her and make her feel safe. Not that it had been necessary. She'd adapted better than he'd ever thought possible. Not once did she complain about the heat, or the lack of privacy, or sleeping in the open either on the sandy beach, or when it rained, in the ramshackle shack. She looked more enticing than ever with the touch of sun on her cheeks, and she never hesitated to give him hell when she thought he deserved it, which was most of the time. He admired her spunk and her capability.

He told himself it wouldn't be fair to make love to her now that he knew how innocent she was. She'd obviously been waiting for that one special man, and in spite of all the ways he'd improved his life, he was still leagues away from being Mr. Right.

Making love to her wouldn't be fair to him, either. Hell, given half a chance, he'd fall in love with her all over again, and then where would he be?

She had her heart set on buying the resort, on giving him back what he'd lost. She didn't doubt that she would succeed, which only proved again the differences between them. Mel knew her money would buy her whatever she wanted. It always had.

The pelican shuffled closer, keeping a watchful eye on Adam, who was keeping a watchful eye on Melanie. The rain, coming down in a fresh, warm shower, insulated them in the quiet eroticism of the island. Palms swayed under the gentle wind, the ocean looked agitated with its rippling surface, and Melanie, God love her free-spirited nature, reveled in it all. Little by little, she'd blossomed on the island, giving in to its erotic lure.

She'd taken his soap and shampoo and dashed into the rain, then proceeded to bathe, slowly, unselfconscious, fully aware that he sat in the doorway of the shack utterly spellbound. The first time she'd retreated down the beach to wash, but now she seemed determined to drive him insane. And she succeeded admirably.

Mel could sit on a rock to watch the sunset and he'd go crazy with lust. His need was so powerful, he hurt, but Adam wouldn't have looked away from her for all the resorts in Florida.

"Aw, hell," he blurted, making Aladdin jump warily. "Who am I fooling? I love her already. I never stopped loving her. Doubt I ever will. I'm fighting a losing battle here and I know it."

The pelican gave him a vague look of sympathy, then opened his wings wide...and snatched a sock from Adam's bag before soaring away.

Outraged, Adam stood and shook his fist at the bird. "I'm going to find a rock yet, you feathered bag of bones!"

On the beach, Melanie crossed her arms over her middle and laughed out loud. Her midnight hair hung in sodden ringlets around her face. And her body...damn, she'd finally slipped off her clothes. The bird was instantly forgotten. Nobility couldn't be expected to stand up to such provocation, could it?

With renewed purpose, Adam leapt off the stoop and headed in her direction. His fate was sealed, but fate had allotted him this special time with Melanie, and from now on he'd take advantage of every moment.

Melanie, aptly reading his intent, squealed and turned to run. Her long legs ate up the distance across the wet sand. The view from behind her was the stuff dreams were made of, so Adam let her stay two yards ahead of him.

Darting behind a squat palm tree, she playfully yelled, "What do you want, Stone?"

He paused several feet away, enjoying her antics. Anticipation would only make the conquest that much sweeter. After two days of deprivation, his body vibrated with lust, and the look he sent her was hot with need. "Come here, sweetheart."

"What's that?" she called, her eyes lit with laughter. "You want me to fix us some lunch?"

She could be such an imp. He'd never imagined this playful side to her. She'd always been so shy, so withdrawn. Of course, he'd never imagined she'd thrive so well on the bare existence of a deserted island, either.

Or that she'd willingly accept him as a lover.

He shook his head, watching her closely. "Yeah, I'm hungry, all right." Hooking his hands in his shorts, he began shoving the wet material down his hips.

She peeked around the tree at him and yelped. "Shall... shall I fix another fruit salad?"

Rain dribbled down her belly, caught in her feminine curls, then trailed down her thighs. He swallowed hard. "You can fix yourself right here." He pointed to the sand in front of him. "I'll take it from there."

"No strawberries? No coconut?"

As she spoke, she tried to inch away from the tree, preparing to run. Adam leapt out and caught her, hauling her close to his naked chest. With a startled squeal, she almost slipped away, then laughed hilariously when Adam hooked his leg behind hers and they both fell to the ground. Rain ran from his shoulders to her breasts. He stared hungrily at one stiff nipple. "I'm sick to death of fruit," he muttered, then drew her deep into the heat of his mouth.

Mel's fingers gripped his head, and she tugged until he lifted it enough to look at her. "I thought... I thought maybe you were sick of me."

"No!" He could see the confusion in her eyes, the vulnerability. He hadn't meant to hurt her. "I could never get my fill of you, Mel. I want you too much." He touched her mouth with his fingertips, then gruffly admitted, "Sometimes, when things were rough, dreaming of you like this was the only thing that got me through."

Even in the pouring rain, he could see her eyes fill with tears. "You don't want all of me."

They were both drenched, their skin slick. He moved silkily against her. "Yeah, I do. Every damn inch of you."

"No." He started to pull back, but her fingers gripped his hair and held him close. She gave him a swift, hard kiss. "You want my body, Adam, but not me, not who I am."

"You're not making any sense, Mel." But he was afraid he understood completely.

"You don't want my money. No, just listen!" She wrapped her slender thighs around his waist, holding him securely. "You resent who and what I am. If I even mention my money, you clam up and refuse to share yourself."

"Because I don't need your damn money!"

"Why?" she asked quietly. "Because it's mine? If I was a bank offering a low-interest loan, you wouldn't hesitate, would you? But my money is somehow considered tainted."

"Damn it, Melanie…"

"You're hanging onto the differences in our backgrounds, even though we've both changed."

"Don't you see, honey? Nothing's changed, not really. If we hadn't landed on this damn island, you'd never have given me the time of day."

"Adam." She said his name like a chastisement. "I know your life wasn't easy, but *I* didn't make it hard. In many ways, mine was difficult, too."

"Because of me."

"It doesn't matter now. If it wasn't for you, I would have drowned. Even if I'd made it to shore on my own, which is doubtful, the thought of being here alone terrifies me. But you've made it seem like an adventure. That's the way you are, Adam. You've been working all your life to save your mother and Kyle, and you *did* save me. You can deny it all you like, but you're still a hero. My hero. You saved me, and I owe you."

He hardened his heart against the plea in her eyes. When they got off the island and she was once again surrounded by her family and elite friends, she'd come to her senses. More likely than not, she'd be embarrassed over their shared intimacy, over her lack of inhibition with him.

Just thinking about it made his blood burn, and he stared at her. "All right, so I saved you. But you can forget the resort. I already consider myself fully and adequately paid." To emphasize his meaning, he thrust himself against her—and watched her expression crumble.

Adam rolled to his side, letting the rain lash his face and cool his shame while Melanie scrambled to her feet.

He heard her panting breaths over the downpour, could feel her tension. Her words were choked with tears when she shouted, "You're a mean, miserable bastard, Adam Stone!"

Adam flinched, but otherwise didn't move. What could he say? That she was right? There would be no explanations, no words to appease her. How could he explain what he didn't understand himself? He only knew he couldn't let himself get drawn in, because eventually, she'd realize the truth—that he was just a man, still working to get ahead and often failing.

He scrubbed at his face and silently accepted that the dream had ended.

Two seconds later Melanie let out a small screech and snatched up her shorts and halter. She darted behind a mangrove tree and frantically began to dress.

Alarmed, Adam jumped to his feet, expecting to see the wild boar he'd relentlessly teased her about.

What he saw instead was almost worse: a small fishing boat headed their way. At the helm, a hard-looking man who seemed impervious to the rain, stared toward them in disbelief. Though he was too far out to see them clearly, possessive rage washed through Adam. If the boat had shown up minutes earlier, its captain might have seen Mel naked.

The boat slowed and began idling toward the beach. Adam pulled on his sand-covered shorts and walked into the ocean to meet their rescuer.

CHAPTER SEVEN

"So you haven't spoken to her since this Flynn Ryder guy showed up, right?"

Adam gave a sigh of disgust as he and his younger brother, Kyle, rounded the corner of a heavily flowered courtyard and headed around the quaint building to the beach behind it. Tourists abounded at the newly opened resort, making Adam's temper burn. The resort should have been his. But the little witch had bought it back. For him.

Damn her.

He'd gone over the whole story a dozen times, but Kyle still hadn't run out of questions. "There was nothing to say after that. We both felt damn foolish for getting stranded in the first place. The shoaling around the island makes it dangerous for boats to get too close, so people don't visit it often. If it hadn't been for Flynn, who knows how long we might have been there? The idiots that lost us didn't even know we were missing, so nothing had been reported."

"Eventually I'd have figured things out and sent the cavalry," Kyle assured him. "But you never did say what Flynn was doing there."

No, he hadn't. Flynn Ryder evidently owned his own resort

on a neighboring island, but it was Aladdin leaving a trail of clothing around the area—specifically Melanie's panties—that had caused Flynn to investigate the smaller island. The minute Adam had explained they were both from Ohio, Flynn had nodded understanding and taken them to civilization.

Adam had felt like a complete fool over the whole thing, especially when Melanie told Flynn that Adam had saved her. Flynn had given him a skeptical look but hadn't bothered to comment. In fact, he'd said very little to Adam. But he'd talked up a storm with Melanie. Not that he had much choice. Melanie, deliberately provoking Adam, he was sure, had asked Flynn dozens of questions on the daily operations of owning a resort. Adam had considered throwing her overboard again. In the end, he'd simply ignored her.

Adam and Kyle stopped in a crowd of bikini-clad guests and looked around for a familiar dark head. The desk clerk had claimed she was out here—waiting.

"You're leaving something out, Adam."

Damn, sometimes his brother was too astute. Hedging, he asked, "Why do you think so?"

Kyle tapped the papers Adam clutched in one fist. "She bought you a resort. You're pissed off about it. She insisted on seeing you in person, and you're giving in. It doesn't take a genius to figure it out."

"Does it take a genius to figure out it's none of your business?"

"Why did you drag me along, then?"

Because he hadn't wanted to tempt fate by seeing her alone again. He felt terrible for the things he'd said, the way he'd treated her that last day. Once they'd reached a hotel and been given separate rooms, Adam had tried to contact her, to apologize and do the old see-ya-later routine. He hadn't wanted to part with hurt feelings, not when she meant so much to him.

And he'd wanted her to know how to reach him, just in case his forgetfulness with the condom became an issue. But she'd already checked out. And he'd been feeling sick ever since.

Then a week ago he'd gotten her damn letter saying she'd bought the resort back for him, just as she'd promised to do. She had to have paid considerably more than he would have, just to get the new owner to sell. And looking around, he could easily see all the extra money she'd invested already. In just over a month she'd made the place look stunning, much as he'd always envisioned it.

She'd done it all, and put his damn name on the deed.

The papers crumpled in his fist when he finally spotted her sitting at an outdoor bar situated ideally beneath a cluster of ripe palms. Her shapely bottom was perched on a bar stool, her long legs and smooth shoulders mostly bare. The dress she wore was tiny, snug, and matched the floral decor of the many patio tables and open umbrellas.

Where the hell had she gotten that getup? And since when did she flaunt herself for the masses, rather than for his private pleasure?

Kyle evidently followed his gaze, for he let loose with a long, low, admiring whistle. "Holy cow. That's Melanie Tucker, isn't it?"

Adam snapped his head around to stare at his brother. "You remember her?"

"I was only a couple grades behind her in school. And being the richest kid in town, she really stood out."

Adam thought it was more her eyes that made her noticeable, and when he looked at her, he saw those eyes staring directly at him. Slowly, she slid off the stool and started in his direction. She was barefoot, lightly tanned, her blue eyes looking bluer than ever.

His heart lodged in his throat, and he had to swallow hard

twice to regain his composure. Every muscle in his body twitched, and he struggled to relax. Which did nothing about the erection making his appreciation of her rather apparent. In his worn jeans, there was no way to hide it. He'd missed her so damn much.

"Adam." She stopped just a few inches from him and simply stood there, waiting.

Kyle stepped forward and extended his hand. "Miss Tucker. Nice to see you again."

She drew her gaze from Adam with an effort. "You're Kyle, Adam's younger brother, right?"

Adam listened with half an ear as the introductions commenced. She looked so good, and he'd been sick with missing her ever since he'd realized she was gone forever. Then he'd gotten the damn letter....

He came back to his senses in a flash and thrust the deed toward her. "I don't want this."

She smiled, lifting her chin high. "Tough. It's yours."

"Then I'll sell it and mail you back your check."

"You can't. We're co-owners. You might not have noticed or read all the small print given your...rather quick temper, but we have equal control of the resort."

"That's impossible."

"No, it's a fact. I told you, I have a knack for real estate, so I know what I'm doing. Everything's perfectly legal. And you were right, this place is wonderful. Much too good to pass up."

Kyle laughed, earning a glare from Adam. "Now, Adam, come on. I still don't understand why you're being so pig-headed about this."

Adam turned on his brother, deciding he was a safer target than Mel. He didn't have to fight the urge to kiss his brother. Through clenched teeth, he muttered, "We make our own way now, Kyle."

"No, *you* make our way. I haven't had a hell of a lot to do with it."

Adam drew back a step, scowling fiercely. "That's ridiculous. I'm your brother. Besides, you've been going to college."

Kyle turned to smile at Melanie. "Did you know he mostly paid my way through college? With what I made working part-time, it would have taken me years to pay back student loans. He also bought my mother a house. That's part of the reason he had to do some fancy financing to get the money together for this resort. If he didn't feel so responsible for us, he'd be rolling in dough."

"Kyle…"

Adam's warning went unheeded. "We're damn proud of him and all he's done. Even before Dad died, Adam's always been my hero."

There was that word again, making him edgy. He scowled at Kyle. "We're family. You've done plenty for me, too."

Kyle clapped Adam on the back. "He's always been one hell of a big brother. I was really looking forward to settling down here, soaking up some sun, using my degree in business to help get things going. But if he won't accept it…"

Mel's smile turned gentle and sweet. "I didn't know all that about Adam. But it doesn't surprise me. I think of him as a hero, too. After he rescued me from drowning, I knew he could do anything he set his mind to—which is why I didn't want him to miss this opportunity just because he likes to wallow in stubborn, misplaced pride."

Adam felt smothered in their collective praise. "For the last damn time, Mel, I *fell* in. I did not jump in after you!"

Very quietly, and with supreme confidence, she whispered, "But you would have."

How the hell was he supposed to argue with that? It was the truth, and he could see there was no point in denying it.

They stared at each other, both oblivious to the tourists milling around them. Kyle cleared his throat and said, "I think I'll just go look around a little."

Adam hadn't wanted to be left alone with Mel. Not that standing on a crowded beach was alone, but he felt totally apart from the others, as if only the two of them existed. He touched her cheek. "I'm sorry, babe. I know you mean well, but I can't accept."

"You gave me so much, Adam."

He smiled. "What? I let you use my shampoo and shared my toothbrush. It's hardly the same as a costly resort."

Melanie shook her head, and sunlight glinted off her dark hair. "No, don't you understand? You gave me your strength and self-confidence. All my life I've been sheltered and pampered, and men treated me like a glass doll. But you...you treat me like a woman." She nervously licked her lips. "You make me feel sexy."

"Aw, babe..."

"I might have shared my money, Adam, but that money hadn't made me happy. Knowing you wanted me, making love with you, even arguing with you, makes me happier than I thought possible. The best time I've ever had was being stranded with you."

"Honey, you were always sexy. Almost too much so."

She treated him to a crooked grin. "Since I walked out here this morning to wait for you, I've been hit on a dozen times."

Adam scowled, his gaze scanning the crowds. "Who hit on you?"

"It's not important. My point is—"

"The point is that you need more clothes on!"

"Adam, I'm covered far more than the women in their bathing suits. And besides, I like the way you looked at me when you saw me in this outfit."

Adam stepped closer and gave in to the urge to hold her, bringing her against his chest. "It's not the outfit, Mel, it's you. Even when you wore schoolgirl jumpers and penny loafers back in high school, you made me hard."

She blushed, but she also smiled. "You see? That's the most precious compliment I've ever gotten."

Adam rolled his eyes. "Your fiancé was an idiot."

"No." She licked her lips, and the vulnerability that sometimes clouded her eyes bit into his soul. "He wasn't an idiot, Adam. He just wasn't you."

It felt like she'd ripped his heart out. "Mel."

"And he didn't…love me."

The question was there in her beautiful blue eyes. Adam knew he owed it to her to tell her. What difference did her money make if he'd be miserable without her? In fact, he'd never felt so damn poor, so lacking in true wealth as he did when she'd left him without saying goodbye. He'd been an unhappy bastard ever since.

Before he could say anything, Kyle showed up, and he was grinning from ear to ear. "Adam, the place is perfect. Almost everything we would have done, she's taken care of. But there's still some things—"

Melanie spoke quickly. "—that could be improved on, only I've used up my savings. I need a partner to help me finish fixing things up." She drew a deep breath and clutched her hands together in front of her. "I know about buying property and what a good investment is. But I don't know much beyond that. I've got faith in this place, and I've done some cosmetic work, but there's still so much that has to be done. I can't…don't want to do it alone. So if you truly don't want to be partners with me, I'll sell you my shares of the resort. You can reimburse me over a period of time. I'll even make the interest rates fair, but I'd much rather—"

Very softly, Adam said, "I'd much rather marry you."

She let out her breath in a whoosh. "Marry me?"

Kyle grinned. "I knew it! She's the one you've always talked about. I could tell the minute you looked at her."

Adam nodded slowly, his gaze still locked with Melanie's. Melanie looked uncertain.

"Mom would harass him," Kyle explained, "about settling down, about giving her grandkids, but Adam always said he couldn't because he'd already met the most incredible woman, an icon that other women couldn't possibly measure up to."

"He said that…about me?"

Adam just smiled, watching his brother work. Kyle was smooth, much more so than Adam ever hoped to be. He could charm the socks off anyone, and though their mother didn't realize it, he was the real hound dog in the family. But Kyle was subtle, so the ladies usually didn't realize it until it was too late.

"Yeah. Adam always said you were an aristocrat and a little stuck up—"

"Hey!" Adam considered throwing his brother out to sea.

"But he made it sound real sexy." Kyle's eyes were bright with laughter.

"He did, huh?" Melanie looked unconvinced but open to suggestion.

"You betcha. So what do you think? You going to marry him so we can get this business settled?"

Melanie stared at Adam's chest. "Do you love me, Adam?"

He cupped her chin and tilted her face up. "Since I've been old enough to know what love is, you've been the one for me."

Tears welled in her eyes. "Me, too, though I didn't realize it. I just knew I watched for you and felt alive around you and that—"

"What?"

Mindful of Kyle's rapt attention, she tiptoed to whisper in his ear. "That I wanted you." She kissed his throat and wrapped her arms around him. "I knew I couldn't marry anyone else, not when all I could think of was you."

Adam dropped the deed so he could fill his hands with her. "I love you, Mel. I always have." He kissed her and vaguely heard the stirring of interest from the crowds watching them. His brother made the announcement that they were newly engaged, which earned a round of applause.

It was difficult, but Adam finally managed to pull his mouth away from hers. "Are there empty rooms inside?"

"Too many to count. I expect we need to work on that."

"I know one room we can fill right now."

She smiled at his deep, suggestive tone, and her cheeks turned pink. "I have one reserved just for us."

Adam felt like shouting, he was so happy. "So you'll marry me and put up with Kyle and welcome my mother?"

She grinned, trying for a look of indecision when her expressive eyes already showed how happy she felt. "Well, I suppose so, as long as you know my parents are rather curious about you, too. They'll want a big wedding, but they love me, so it shouldn't be too bad."

"I won't take money from them, sweetheart," he felt compelled to warn her.

She merely shrugged. "I told you I make my own money, and they've already accepted that, even if they're not happy about it. But you can plan on them pampering our babies. I figure with your strength of will, you'll be able to keep things balanced."

Adam nearly swallowed his tongue. "Are you...?"

"Not yet." She lifted her nose into the air. "But I want to be. And soon."

"I just love a bossy woman." Without warning he scooped

her into his arms and swung her in a circle. Kyle laughed when he said, "You heard the lady. I have work to do."

Kyle picked up the deed and shoved it into his pocket. "So we're keeping the place?" he shouted after his brother.

"Hell, yes." Adam grinned at Melanie. "I'm the richest man in the world. I can do anything."

* * * * *

CAUGHT IN THE ACT

CHAPTER ONE

Rain drubbed the window sluggishly, but Mick Dawson could still see out, still see all the different people milling around with colorful umbrellas and hats. He was so intent on watching for her he listened to the conversation with only half an ear. But then, half an ear was the most required when his friends got started on that particular topic.

"See that gorgeous blonde?" Josh Marshall said, deliberately baiting as usual. "The one who just came in? She's wearing a push-up bra."

"Is that right?" Zack Grange kept his tone dry. "How can you tell?"

"I know women." Josh's reply held an overdose of world-weary cynicism. "And I especially know women's breasts." He added, "At your age, I'd think you would, too."

"Yeah, and at your age," Zack retorted, "I'd have thought you'd outgrown your adolescent obsessions."

The three of them sat in the corner booth at Marco's, a casual Italian restaurant they'd first discovered five years ago. It was central to where they each worked, in the downtown area.

They came often, more so every year, it seemed, until now they met almost daily for lunch and often for dinner, too.

None of them was married. Josh remained a confirmed bachelor, Zack was now a widower and Mick…well, Mick hadn't met the right woman. His criteria were strict, but to his mind, marriage was forever. He'd seen the worst quite often, marriages made in hell and sustained with sarcasm and cheating and drink. He'd also witnessed that elusive best, unions overflowing with love and trust and support. No way would he settle for less than what he knew could and should be.

Because of their different jobs—each of them stressful—and their lack of romantic ties, meeting at Marco's was about as close to a domestic routine as the three men ever saw.

The restaurant served as a place for celebration—a promotion, a new house, whatever came up that seemed celebration-worthy. They also commiserated with each other there, as when Zack's young wife had died and he'd wanted to retreat from life, not seeing anyone, not doing anything except coddling his little girl. Or after Mick had gotten shot in the leg and missed several weeks of work, making him edgy.

Mick's life was all darkness and threats and caution. Ugly. Except here at Marco's, and with the people he trusted—his two friends, his family.

No one else. At least, not yet.

No woman had ever snagged his attention long enough to build a trust, certainly never for anything serious. Until now.

Now he was intrigued.

"Mick, tell this fool that breasts don't lift to the sun like a flower." Josh laughed at his own jest. "If they're damn near touching her chin, she's wearing a push-up bra."

Mick glanced at Zack and grinned. "Josh is an idiot where women are concerned—including his insane fascination with breasts, which, I agree, he should have outgrown years ago."

Josh shook his head in a pitying way. "Men do not outgrow their fascination with breasts. You two are just weird."

"A real woman," Mick told him, "would chew you up and spit you out."

"A real woman?" Zack asked, feigning confusion. "You mean someone with an IQ higher than ten? Why would Josh date anyone smarter than he is?"

Josh said, "Ha-ha. You're just jealous." He grinned and added, "Besides, the ladies have better things to do with their mouths when they're around me. Chewing is definitely out."

All three men laughed. "So," Josh said, "if you two abnormal specimens aren't turned on by a woman's breasts—which should be soft and natural, not shoved heavenward—then what does do it for you?"

Mick groaned. "Didn't we have this discussion back in high school?"

"Yeah, but it's still interesting."

"Bellies," Zack blurted.

Josh raised a brow. "Excuse me?"

For the moment, Mick felt content to just listen.

"I love a woman's belly." Zack leaned back, smiling to himself. "Not all muscled up the way some women want to do these days. Just a nice soft smooth woman's belly." He nodded, confirming his own conclusions. "Very sexy."

Josh considered that, then nodded, too. "Okay, I'll give you that one. Bellies are hot. But not belly button rings."

"No," Zack agreed. "A good belly doesn't need decoration."

"What about you, Mick?" Josh prodded. "Long legs? Great ass? What?"

Mick took another bite of his BLT, almost by rote, not because he was hungry. He considered his reaction when he'd seen *her* for the first time. What had he noticed? What had caught his eye and kept him so interested, to the point he almost felt obsessed?

He glanced out the dim window again. It was a miserable,

dank July day, breezy, with fat purple clouds hanging low in the sky.

She should be coming along any minute now.

He'd first noticed her at his old neighborhood. He'd been there to rent out the upstairs apartment of the building he still owned, the same building he'd once lived in as a child. There were a lot of…*unpleasant* memories for him there, along with a few special ones. He kept the building as a reminder to himself that his life had changed, *he* had changed, but he was still a product of his upbringing.

Evidently, she rented from the building next door, because she had come down the walkway to the street and headed toward the post office, letters in her hand. It worried Mick, because no one traipsed around unprotected in that area. To call it rough would be a gross understatement.

But there she'd been, strolling along without a care. He hadn't hesitated to follow her, making certain she remained safe, enjoying the back view of her as she strutted along, her stride long and sure and almost cocky.

The sun was blistering hot that day, shining down on her blue-black, shoulder-length hair, hair so silky it appeared fluid when she moved. Soft, light blue eyes looked beyond everything and everyone, including Mick, as if a great distraction held her. He'd been nearly spellbound by her tall, willowy body with its incredibly long, slim legs and broad, fragile shoulders. Strangely enough, even when she came back out of the post office and went past him, again oblivious to her surroundings, he hadn't noticed her breasts. All his attention had been on her face, with its strong jaw, straight nose, pale eyes.

Mick wondered for an instant what Josh would think of his oversight.

Because he wanted to meet her, wanted to get to know her and have sex with her until he passed out from sheer exhaustion, he wasn't about to discuss her with Josh or Zack. So he merely shrugged. "It's a combination of things, and it's different with every woman."

Before either Josh or Zack could respond to that obscure reply, Mick saw her. Blindly, he laid his sandwich aside and twisted in the booth to better see out the window. Regardless of the drizzling rain, the gray sky, he'd expected her. A little rain wouldn't chase her inside. No, not this lady. She jogged every day around the same time, the same place. Or at least she had for two weeks now. It felt like fate, seeing her first in an area where he owned property, and then here again, where he routinely visited.

Zack, being a reasonable sort, hadn't complained much when Mick had made him move so he'd have the window seat. Josh, though, was unreasonable, always. Outrageous bordering on obnoxious. He'd demanded, all with laughter and taunting grins, for Mick to admit who he was watching for. Mick had refused, but now it didn't matter.

The second he shifted his attention, going on alert, Josh noticed.

"Aha! There you go, Zack. I think we'll get to see this mystery lady any second now."

Mick told him, rather succinctly, what he could do with his speculations. But that didn't deter Josh; if anything, it made him more curious.

Both Josh and Zack twisted around, and they, too, watched through the window. The streets were crowded during the lunch hour. Open umbrellas jumped with the breeze as people milled up and down the sidewalk.

And there she was, weaving in and out of human traffic as she jogged, her head uncovered, her clothes better suited to a bright spring day than drizzling rain. Funny thing was, she went right past them, inky-black ponytail bouncing, rainwater dripping off her nose and darkening her sweatshirt, and still Josh and Zack looked, searching the crowds.

They hadn't realized she was the one.

Mick's body knew that she was. Just seeing her now, bedraggled and wet and distracted, he wanted her. His muscles felt tight, his blood hot, his flesh prickly. Damn, if just watching her jog did this to him, how would it feel to kiss her, touch her, to slide deep inside her and hear her moan out a climax?

He felt the stirrings of an erection and muttered a curse. Insanity, he decided, but it couldn't be helped.

To hide his reaction, he grinned and leaned into the corner of the booth. Now that she'd gone by, he could face Zack and Josh and still keep an eye on her for about half a mile on the long, straight street. He glanced, and saw there was almost no jiggle to her firm little butt in the skintight biker shorts. His large hands would cover that bottom completely, and he'd hold her still, keep her steady for his thrusts....

Josh interrupted his very interesting imagery. "So? What are we looking for?"

"Nothing now." Mick deliberately sipped his coffee, knowing he had to get control of himself. And he had to get her; maybe after he'd made love to her for no less than ten days, he'd be able to get her out of his system.

A comical look on his face, Josh stretched past Zack, nearly knocking his plate off the table, and pressed his nose to the window. He looked and looked and finally said, "Damn it, there's nothing, no one, out there worth staring at!"

Mick and Zack shared a look. Zack shrugged. "If you're only looking for breasts, that could be. Maybe Mick was looking for something else."

Josh frowned at Zack. "No way. You know he's straight. We've both seen him with women."

Mick spewed his coffee. Zack burst out laughing, and several women in the restaurant looked their way. They kept looking, smiling, flirting, and Mick shook his head. "You're drawing attention to yourself again, Josh."

"Me? I'm not the one laughing like an idiot."

"You don't need to laugh," Zack told him, "to be an idiot." Then slowly, as if speaking to a half-wit, he said, "I meant Mick was maybe looking at a woman who wasn't top-heavy. Just because it's your ultimate definition of what makes a woman, that doesn't mean the rest of us agree."

Josh studied Mick. "That right?"

"That you have strange ideas about women?" He took another sip of coffee and shrugged. "Yeah."

"I meant," Josh said, exasperated, "is she...lacking in the upper works?"

"As far as I can tell," Mick told him, a little annoyed and not sure why, "she's not lacking anywhere."

That only perplexed Josh more.

Mick again peeked out the window, and to his surprise, he saw her turn at the corner, cross the street and start back toward him. There was no more jiggle from her front than there'd been from her back. When she was just opposite the restaurant, she slowed and finally stopped. She rested her hands on her knees while she breathed deeply, heedless of the light rain and his avid attention.

When she straightened again, she stretched her arms high. Her shirt rose, showing a very sweet belly that Zack no doubt would have adored. Captivated, Mick continued to stare at her while a slow heat stirred deep inside him. She walked into the jewelry store located directly across from the restaurant, and Mick made up his mind.

Pushing aside his plate, he stood. So many times over the past few weeks he'd considered following her, initiating a conversation, introducing himself. He didn't want to rush her, but he'd dreamed about her twice, so he knew his fascination wasn't about to go away. Now seemed like as good a time as any to make his move. "I'll be back."

Josh and Zack stared at him, blank-faced. Mick was aware of a thread of urgency vibrating through his blood. It had been like that from the second he first saw her, and every moment after when he watched her. He couldn't put his finger on it, couldn't tell anyone outright what it was about her that appealed to him, what pushed him over the edge. He only knew he wanted her. *Bad.*

As he dodged cars and puddles in the roadway, and muddy, slick spots along the curb, he wondered—for about the hundredth time—if she'd been in the area awhile, or if she'd only recently moved in when he first saw her. He'd been buried in work for the past two months, putting in seventeen-hour days, so it was possible she'd been close by for longer than two weeks.

He could get another assignment any day, so he had to take advantage of the opportunity now.

He hoped like hell she was single. Since first seeing her, he'd studied her closely. There weren't any rings on her fingers, but then he knew women who didn't wear them, especially while jogging. Not once in the two weeks of his awareness had he seen her with anyone, definitely not a man, but that, too, could be a fluke.

Mick turned up the collar on his windbreaker and darted across the sidewalk, trying to keep as dry as possible. He didn't have to look behind him to know both Josh and Zack would be craning their necks, their noses pressed to the window, spying on him. It was totally unlike him to chase a woman.

It was totally unlike him to be interested enough to bother chasing.

Thunder boomed, echoing over the street and rattling windows just as he stepped through the jewelry store's ornate front door. Air-conditioning hit him, chilling his damp skin. He brushed his hair back from his forehead and looked around. Glass cases were everywhere, some large, some smaller to showcase a certain piece, and there, in the far corner, she stood. Dressed in her running wear she looked very out of place, conspicuous and unique in the upscale, glitzy store. She also looked sexy as the original sin with her skin dewy from the drizzle and sweat, her cheeks flushed from exertion, her hair as much out of the ponytail as in, wet and sleek.

Damn, he thought, annoyed with himself. She wasn't that pretty, was in fact kind of plain. She wore no makeup, but her lashes and brows were as dark as her hair. Her nails were short, clean. She had a nice body, strong and sleek, fine boned, but not overly curved, not typically sexy.

Not the type of body to make him sweat at the sight of her.

She didn't give out signals or flirt or even pay much attention to men, not that he'd noticed.

His eyes widened. God, maybe she didn't even like men. That'd be a kicker, one he wouldn't, couldn't accept. Not when the mere sight of her turned him on. He didn't just want her; he felt as if he had to have her, just as he had to sleep or eat. It was the damnedest feeling, and he wasn't happy with it or himself.

She didn't appear interested in any particular item as she moseyed from case to case, peering inside, then shaking her head and moving on. For the moment, Mick was content to watch her. He slipped his hands into his jeans pockets, then quickly pulled them out again when he realized that negligent pose might expose the weapon in the waistband holster at his back. Being off duty, he didn't need the gun, but he always carried it.

In this day and age, his cover wouldn't have been believable without it. Drug dealers, prostitutes, gamblers…they all expected you to be armed, and if you weren't, you were considered an idiot, or worse.

Usually, even when conditions didn't call for a weapon, he managed to smuggle in the Smith & Wesson 9 mm in an ankle holster. There were times, though, when he had to go without, leaving him feeling naked, and those were the times when he got most tense, when the adrenaline rush was all but blinding. He always wanted a woman afterward, a way to release all that pent-up energy.

He wanted a woman now.

He wanted her.

Moving closer, watching her, he was amazed that she didn't feel his attention, so acute that it had him half-hard again with expectation. It had always been his experience that blatant staring was felt like a stroke of ice. But then, she was a civilian, and he'd already noted the first day he saw her how heedless she could be of her surroundings. It amazed him sometimes that people could survive with so little caution.

The door chimed behind Mick and more people entered. Two men, dressed much like Mick in jeans and T-shirts, wearing sneakers, one in a ball cap. They appeared to be in their mid-thirties, clean, middle-class. As a cop, Mick automatically took in everyone and everything. He'd already noted the two salesladies, the older couple looking at cocktail rings for an anniversary. He picked up on actions and quiet dialogue and expressions.

Caution was as basic to him as breathing. And because he wasn't a civilian, wasn't oblivious, he immediately detected the sudden charge in the air despite the nonthreatening scene and apparently ordinary people. It had come in like the wind with the men, and Mick didn't like it worth a damn. He had a keen sixth sense, and he trusted it more than he trusted appearances.

The woman looked up, around, made brief eye contact with the two men who'd entered, then again with Mick. Their gazes locked and held for an instant, an instant that made his gut clench with awareness. She gave him a small smile, a simple, friendly smile that nonetheless heightened his tension, before she turned away again.

Senses on alert, Mick followed her, not too close, in no way obvious, but keeping her within reach. Because the shop was small and crowded with displays, the air thick and humid from the rain outside, he could detect her scent. It was earthy and rich, warm woman, damp skin and clean female sweat. His heart punched hard, a little fast; his sex thickened. He'd been too long without a woman, too long without any sexual relief. Sometimes being a contrary bastard was a real pain.

Her wet running shoes squeaked on the ceramic tile floor as she browsed, appearing to study the shop, not just the wares but the structure, the setup. Mick frowned as he watched her, further intrigued and a little distracted. Out of the corner of his eye he saw one of the men reach into his jacket pocket, and a silent alarm screamed inside Mick's head.

He jerked around, but not quickly enough.

"Everyone stay still and calm." The guy waved a SIG Sauer .45 around the room with menacing intent. "No one panic or do anything stupid," he said with a sneer, "and I won't have to kill anyone."

Damn, damn, damn. Mick took a quick, inconspicuous glance around. The elderly woman, clinging to her husband, looked ready to faint, while the salespeople stood motionless, frozen in horror. His movements so slight that no one paid him any mind, Mick edged closer to the woman he'd followed. She stared at the gunman, her blue eyes darker now with fascination, but he saw no real fear.

"We'll do our business," the guy in the ball cap said, "and then leave and no one will be hurt."

Mick didn't buy it for a second; the words sounded far too rehearsed, far from sincere. And there was an anticipatory expression on the man's face.

Things never worked out the easy way—not life, not love, sure as hell not an armed robbery.

The second man hitched his gun at the saleswoman. "You, come open the register and make it quick."

She balked, more out of surprise than rebellion. Mick had a similar sensation. They were surrounded by diamonds and gold of unbelievable value, yet this idiot wanted what little cash might be in the register? The robber had to realize that most sales would be handled with credit cards or checks; his demand didn't make sense.

Mick's hands twitched. He wanted to grab his gun; he wanted to be in control. Right now, control meant keeping everyone alive. It meant keeping *her* alive.

Without warning, the man who'd issued the order shouted, "*Now,* goddamn it!" and everyone jumped, the saleslady screeching and stumbling over her own feet as she rushed to obey.

A predictable panic reaction, Mick thought, to the threat of sudden violence, not something a robber intent on keeping things calm would have instigated. Mick's suspicions rose.

The older woman quietly wept, one saleslady turned white, the other shook so badly she had a hard time working the register. Before she could get it open, distant sirens broke the quiet, making both men curse hotly. Mick tensed, waiting for another outburst, for them to turn and run, for them to retaliate by shooting the saleslady. He'd learned early on that criminals did the most absurd and unaccountable things, often causing death without reason. He prepared himself for any reaction.

But what they did took him totally by surprise.

They didn't yell, didn't run. They focused their blame on the young woman next to Mick.

"Bitch," the guy in the ball cap snarled. "You set off an alarm."

Startled, she blinked, looked around, backed up two paces. "No," she breathed. It was the first time Mick had heard her voice, which quaked with fear, bewilderment. "I don't even know where—"

The man took aim at her and, without thinking, Mick blocked his path. Both gunmen froze at his audacity. He felt the woman's small hands against his back, clutching at his jacket. He felt her face press into his shoulder, was aware of her accelerated breathing, her trembling. She was deathly afraid, and anger surged in his blood.

His voice as low and calm as he could make it, Mick said, "She's a customer. She doesn't know where the alarm is."

He was ignored.

"Everybody get down!" As the guy in the ball cap yelled his order, a car screeched up in front of the shop, motor idling. The customers all dropped to the floor, panicked, including the woman at Mick's back. He felt her jerky movements, could hear her panting in terror.

Mick moved more slowly, his mind churning as he tried to buy himself some time. If he could get his gun… His elbow touched the woman's wrist, he was so close to her. She, like the others, had stretched out flat, covering her head with her arms, shaking. Mick kept himself balanced on his elbows, ready to move, watching without appearing to watch.

The sudden shattering of glass—again and again as each

case was destroyed—caused the older woman to wail, the saleslady to whimper. The woman next to Mick never made a sound. He wanted to look at her, to somehow reassure her, but he didn't dare take his attention off those weapons. The two men grabbed a few large items of jewelry, but it was as if they destroyed the store just for the sake of destruction.

It was by far the most pathetic, disorganized and unproductive robbery Mick had ever witnessed—and that made him more suspicious than anything else might have. By rights, they should have known where the most valuable items would be, and should have concentrated their sticky fingers there. Instead, they seemed to take whatever was at hand without thought to its worth. No one robbed a jewelry store without casing it first, without knowing what would be found inside and where.

The two men finally headed for the door. The tension tightened, grew painful, static crowding the air until it seemed impossible to breathe—and the bastard in the ball cap turned to fire.

Mick moved so fast, he barely had the thought of moving before he was over her, his arms covering her head, his muscular body completely blanketing her delicate one. Though she was tall for a woman, about five-nine, she was small boned and felt fragile to his six-three frame. He was plenty big enough, and more than determined enough, to be her protection.

She gasped at the feel of him on top of her and immediately stiffened, forcing her head up, twisting. "No! What are you doing?"

He jammed her head back down, then cursed when her cheek hit the hard tile floor. Knowing what she likely thought and wishing he could spare her, Mick said into her ear, "Be still."

She wiggled more furiously, trying to free herself, confused and frightened, unsure of his intent. "He's going to—" Mick began to explain, and then it was unnecessary.

The crack sounded loud and startling; the sudden pain in his right shoulder was a lick of pure fire. For only a moment, his arms tightened around her and he ground his teeth together. "Oh God," she whispered, trying to turn toward him.

Mick grunted, but didn't move. No, he wasn't about to move. For whatever reason, they wanted her dead, but they'd have to get through him first.

He felt the blood spreading on his back, sticky and warm; he was aware of the woman squirming beneath him, gasping, crying. But it wasn't until he heard the door open that he rolled and drew his gun at the same time. He blocked the awful pain, any distractions, and got off a clean shot through the glass door, clipping the man who'd tried to shoot her. The hollow-point bullet hit him high in the left thigh before he could get into the car. The leg crumpled beneath him and he went down in an awkward heap, howling in pain, grabbing for the open car door in desperation.

The car lurched away, spewing gravel and squealing tires, tossing the man back. The side of his head cracked solidly against the curb. He lay there unconscious, sprawled out like a wounded starfish.

Surging to his feet, Mick ran out the door. He spotted the car, drew careful aim and fired again. The back window exploded, but the car didn't slow. It careened around the corner on two wheels and disappeared.

Already the streets had filled with onlookers, people too damn stupid to stay inside and away from gunfire. Mick's arm rapidly went hot, cold and then numb; his fingers throbbed. His hand shook as he tried to hang on to his gun, to steady himself.

Josh and Zack appeared, having witnessed the tail end of

the robbery from the restaurant. Josh, smooth as silk, slipped the gun from Mick's hand and dropped it into his trouser pocket. They'd arrived just seconds before the police cars. More people from all over the street converged, whispering, curious. Josh caught Mick's upper arm and supported him. "Jesus, man. You're shot."

Zack came to his other side and yelled, "Someone call the paramedics. He needs an ambulance." That made Mick laugh, since Zack was an EMT. Zack shook his head wryly and pulled out his radio, putting in the call himself.

"Here, sit down," he said, and led Mick to the rain-wet curb.

"I don't want to sit in a damn puddle," Mick grumbled. "I'm fine." Fine enough that he wanted to find the woman. He looked around, and when he didn't immediately see her, terror started to take hold. He located the elderly couple leaning against the brick building. The old woman clung to her husband and cried, while he peered around in dismay and impotent anger. Mick saw the two salespeople, huddled together, dry-eyed but white as snow, apparently in shock. Cops swarmed everywhere, separating the witnesses so they couldn't share stories. Two police cars took off to give chase, while another radioed in the call. An officer headed Mick's way.

Where the hell is she?

When the cop reached him, frowning, his hand resting on his holster, Mick said quietly, "I'm Mick Dawson, Vice." He started to reach inside his jacket for his badge, but his arm wouldn't cooperate and he cursed.

Josh said, "I'll get it." He retrieved the badge and flipped it toward the officer, who nodded and yelled for someone to get a blanket.

Frustrated, Mick could do no more than stand there, getting weaker by the second, while Zack gave instructions into his radio and Josh more or less held him upright.

Zack told the officer, "The ambulance is on its way. I'm an EMT. I'll see to him until it gets here."

The officer, frowning in worry, handed Zack the blanket and then set off to clear the street.

Mick started to pull free, desperate to find the woman and make certain she was okay, but just then she stepped around the elderly couple. Her face, her beautiful face, was creased with worry, with disbelief. From a slight distance, they stared at each other, and there was no distraction in her gaze now, no oblivion. The horror of what had just happened darkened her eyes to midnight.

A bruise discolored her cheekbone from when he'd pushed her head down. His stomach cramped with that realization. She trembled all over, and Mick shook off Zack to go to her, needing to hold her, to apologize, though he didn't even know her name, had no idea who she was or why the robbers had wanted to kill her.

Zack, who'd been looking at the wound in his shoulder, drew him back. "Damn it, Mick, you're ready to drop."

Mick started to deny that, but then his legs gave out, and if it hadn't been for Josh and Zack supporting him, he'd have been sitting in the middle of the sidewalk instead of on the curb with a folded blanket beneath him. His vision swam, closed in.

"You're losing a lot of blood," Zack said in his calm, professional voice, but Mick heard the concern, the anger, as his friend began first aid.

"Don't let her get away." Mick meant to say it loud and clear, an order that couldn't be ignored. But the words emerged as a faint whisper, and that infuriated him. He'd finally met her—sort of—and he sounded weak, looked weak.

At the moment, he was weak. Too weak.

But she'd felt so good beneath him for that brief, charged moment, adding to his adrenaline rush, further arousing him though they'd been in the middle of a very dangerous situation. It was so absurd, but even as he'd braced for that bullet, he'd been aware of her under him, her ass cuddling his groin, her head fitting neatly under his chin.

He forced his head up and said again, trying for more than a whisper this time, "Don't let her get away."

He knew Josh heard him because he leaned closer. "Who?"

"In…the running clothes. Black hair." That was the very best description he could muster under the circumstances.

Josh looked up, eyes narrowed as he scanned the crowd and then settled on someone. He said, "You've got it, buddy. Now you just rest. I'll take care of it." He got to his feet and stalked forward purposefully, saying in a tone that brooked no argument, "Miss? I need to see you, please."

And Mick blacked out.

CHAPTER TWO

"Where is she?" The sound of his own voice, foggy and dark and thin, appalled him. Mick tried to clear his throat, but it was impossible.

"Shh," he heard Zack say. "Take it easy."

Mick struggled to open his eyes, then wished he hadn't. What the hell had they done to him? His shoulder didn't hurt, at least not at the moment, but he felt as if his brain might explode, and every muscle he possessed was sluggish, refusing to cooperate with his brain's commands.

More cautiously this time, he cracked his eyes open and found Zack on guard at his bedside. Where was Josh? Where was *she?*

"The woman?" he asked again, and he sounded like a dying frog.

Zack lifted a glass of water with a straw to Mick's mouth. He wanted to tell Zack to jam the straw in his ear, but he couldn't. He gave in to his thirst and took several quick sips. He started to move his arm, and fire burned down his side. *Now* his shoulder hurt. He ground his teeth, hissing for breath.

"The anesthesia is wearing off," Zack explained. "You'll be groggy a little longer, but overall you're fine. They left the bullet in—that's two for you now, right? Taking it out would only have caused more damage. You lost too much blood already."

Mick was still registering what Zack had said when his friend leaned forward and growled, not two inches from his nose, "You scared the hell out of me! Don't you know if you get shot you should stay down? Swinging your arm around that way just encouraged it to bleed more."

Mick grunted, as much from the pounding in his head as in reply. "Where the hell is she?"

Exasperated, Zack sighed. He didn't need to ask *She who?* "Josh has been keeping a close eye on her, since right before you passed out and bashed your damn head on the ground. Yeah, that's why your head feels like it's splitting. I'm surprised you don't have a concussion, as hard as you hit. If you didn't have to be so damn macho, if you'd just tell someone when you were ready to faint—"

"I did *not* faint." Mick's voice, his words, were gaining strength, and he grumbled, "I passed out from blood loss."

"Yeah, well, they look about the same when you drop right in the middle of a crowd."

It hurt, but Mick narrowed his eyes and said, "Zack? Come closer."

Zack, filled with new concern, leaned down close.

"Where the hell is she!"

Zack jerked back and grimaced. "All right, all right, you don't have to bust my eardrum. You said, all ominous cloak and dagger, 'Don't let her get away.' Neither Josh nor I knew if that meant she should be arrested, or if she was the lady you'd been watching for."

Mick jerked—and the sudden movement squeezed the breath right out of his lungs. Damn, he'd forgotten how badly a bullet hurt. Through clenched teeth, he snarled, "You didn't…?"

"Turn her over to the cops? Nope. They questioned her, of course, but Josh followed them to the station and then picked her up afterward. She's fine, just shook up and babbling about you being a hero—no surprise there, I suppose. She claims you took that bullet for her, and she wants to see you, overflowing with gratitude and all that, but, of course, since we didn't know what the hell was going on…"

"I'm going to kill you."

Zack grinned. "We collected her for you, but she's none too happy right now. Josh is more or less, er, detaining her. No, don't look like that. You know he wouldn't hurt her. But he's taxing himself; it's been over four hours, after all."

Four hours! Mick wanted to groan again, thinking of her waiting that long, Josh coercing her into hanging around….

"No," Zack said, correctly reading his mind, "she didn't want to leave, she wanted to see you. And she's not happy when she doesn't get what she wants. She's actually—" Zack coughed. "She's a very determined lady."

Zack looked at Mick's IV and added, "Evidently, she wants you."

That was a revelation, one he could easily live with. His head pounded, but Mick held back all wimpy sounds of distress and said, "Get her for me."

"Don't be an idiot! You're hardly in any shape to start getting acquainted." Zack stood, towering over the bed. "I assumed once you came to, you'd explain what the hell's going on, we could then explain it to her, and then we'd let the lady go home so you could get some rest."

"Do *not* let her leave here alone." Mick had awakened with a feeling of panic, again seeing that gun aimed at her—just her, no one else, and for no apparent reason. Until he figured things out, he wanted her watched. He wanted her protected.

It pissed him off royally that he had to ask others to do that for him.

"Mick, we can't just refuse to let her leave."

Giving Zack a sour look, Mick said, *"Get her."*

"Damn, you're insistent when you're injured."

"And I've heard more 'damns' from you in the last five minutes than I have since your daughter was born."

Zack shrugged. "Well, Dani isn't here to listen and emulate. Besides, it's not every day I see a friend shot."

"You say I need to recuperate, Zack?"

"That's right."

"So how is it going to help my recuperation when I get out of this bed and kick your sorry ass?"

Zack hesitated before giving in with a laugh. "I can't fight you now, because you're already down and I feel sorry for you. If I let you get up and attempt to hit me, you'd probably start bleeding all over the place again and rip your stitches, and I'd have to let you win." He held up both hands. "Stay put. I'll find out how soon you'll be moved to your room and when Delilah can join you."

Pain ripped through his shoulder as Mick did a double take. "Delilah?"

Zack stared. "Don't tell me you didn't even know her name."

"So?" Learning her name hadn't been his top priority. Touching her had, and he'd accomplished that while also protecting her. A nice start, except for the fact that someone wanted her dead, and had shot him trying to accomplish the deed. But he'd figure that one out eventually. In the meantime, he had no intention of letting anyone hurt her.

"So you took a bullet for a complete stranger?"

Very quietly, Mick asked, "Wouldn't you have done the same?"

And because Zack already had once, long ago, he turned and walked out.

The second Zack pushed aside the curtain and left, a nurse stepped in, ready to check Mick's vitals and reassure him. She lingered, and Mick couldn't help but smile at her, despite his discomfort and his current frazzled frame of mind. She was about five years older than he, putting her in her early thirties. She was attractive even in sensible white shoes and a smock. She smoothed his hair, her fingers gentle, while she explained that he'd be there overnight, but would likely leave in the morning, and that they'd put him in his own room very soon.

Still being polite, Mick was careful not to encourage her. He wanted to meet Delilah, wanted to talk to her, hear her voice when she wasn't frightened, see her smile again. She was the only woman he wanted at the moment, and he was relieved when the orderly showed up and announced it was time to take Mick to his room.

Any minute now he'd meet her, really meet her. And he promised himself that not long after that he'd kiss her…and more. He didn't know how he'd manage that, all things considered, but he would. He had to taste her, had to stake a claim in the best way known to man.

He discounted his wound. It wouldn't slow him down; he wouldn't let it slow him down.

He needed her.

"I'm capable of walking on my own."

Josh, the man "escorting" her to Mick's room, gave a disgruntled sigh and removed his hand from her arm. He'd been pushy and demanding, a total stranger insisting she follow his orders. She'd done so, once she realized he was a friend of the man who'd protected her.

But she didn't like him, and she definitely didn't like the

distrustful way he loomed over her. He pretended gentlemanly qualities, but she knew he held on to her so she couldn't get away. She'd already told him a dozen times that she had no intention of leaving.

Not that Josh paid any mind to what she had to say.

He had "slick" written all over him, from the way he held himself to the way he noticed every single female in the vicinity. She understood his type. Josh was one of those men who felt superior to women, but covered that nasty sentiment with charisma and a glib tongue. No doubt, given his good looks and outrageous confidence, women regularly encouraged him.

Del just wanted to get by him so she could meet the other man, the one who'd risked his life for her.

Josh slanted her one of his insulting, speculative looks. "I hope you don't go in there and give him any grief."

When she didn't answer him, he added, "He did save your sorry, ungrateful little butt, after all."

She could hardly ignore that! Del whirled and stuck a finger into his hard chest. "I know. I was *there,*" she snapped. Her control, her poise and any claim to ladylike behavior were long gone. Today had been the most bizarre and eventful day of her life. "You're the one who doesn't seem to understand that I need to see him, that I should have been there with him all along, to thank him—"

He glared at her, rubbed at his chest and walked away. Del had to hurry to catch up to him. A few seconds later they turned a corner, and Josh pushed a door open. "Here we go," he said. And then under his breath, but not much under, she heard him mutter, "Thank God."

Through the open doorway, Del could see the occupied hospital bed, and she drew up short. Heavy emotion dropped on her, making her feel sluggish in the brain—which was a first. Her breath caught. Her stomach flipped. Her heart fluttered.

He lay almost flat, his long, tall body stretching from one end of the narrow bed to the other. She remembered his height when he'd covered her, protecting her and all but dwarfing her despite her own height. She remembered the power of him, too, the vibrating tension and leashed strength.

His beautiful, dark brown hair now looked disheveled, spikey from the earlier rain and his injuries and… Her bottom lip quivered with her loss of composure.

He was the most beautiful man she'd ever seen, though she hadn't really seen him until he threw himself on top of her and saved her life. At first she'd thought he was with the robbers, and she'd known so much fear she'd actually tasted it.

Instead, he'd taken a bullet meant for her.

Her heart stuttered to a near stop. What kind of man did that? He didn't know her, owed her nothing. She'd barely noticed him in the store before that.

But when he'd chased the bad guys just like a disreputable Dirty Harry clone, she'd looked him over and hadn't been able to stop looking. He'd been all hard, flexing muscle, animal grace and speed.

Now he was flat on his back in a hospital bed. She sighed brokenly, choking on her emotions.

He turned his head at the sound she made, and those deep brown, all-consuming eyes warmed. A slight, heart-stopping smile curved one side of his mouth, and he looked sexy and compelling. In a deep, dark voice hoarse with pain, he whispered, "Hi."

Just like that her heart melted and sank into her toes. There was so much inflection, so much feeling, in that one simple hello. Vaguely, she heard Josh saying, "Delilah, meet Mick Dawson. Mick, Miss Delilah Piper."

Del paid no attention to Josh, her every thought and sense focused on the large dark man in the bed. In the bed because of *her*. No one had ever done anything even remotely like that for her. Her life in the past few years had been, by choice, a solitary one. Even before then, though, her relationships had been superficial and short-lived—nothing to inspire such protective instincts.

The reality of what he'd done, what he'd risked for her, threw Del off balance emotionally, just as the sight of him stirred her physically.

Without another thought, she moved straight to the bed. Mick looked at her, still smiling, but now with his eyes a bit wider, more alert, a little surprised. She sat near his hip and stroked his face. She *needed* to touch him, to feel the warmth of his skin, the lean hardness of his jaw…. Unable to help herself, she kissed him.

Against his lips, she said with heartfelt sincerity, "Thank you."

He started to say something, but she kissed him again. It felt…magically right; she could have gone on kissing him forever. His mouth was firm, dry. Five o'clock shadow covered his jaw, rasping against her fingertips, thrilling her with the masculinity of it. Heat, scented by his body, lifted off him in waves, encompassing her and soothing her. He tasted good, felt good, smelled good.

A little breathless, bewildered by it all, Del said, "I'm so sorry. It should be me in that bed."

"No!" His good arm came up, his hand, incredibly large and rough, clasped her shoulder, and he levered her away. For a man in a sickbed, he had surprising strength and was far too quick.

And he looked angry. And protective.

Excitement skittered down her spine, while tenderness welled in her chest.

The door opened again and Zack, the man who was a little nicer than Josh, started in. He jerked to a halt when he saw them both on the bed, nose-to-nose. Startled, Zack began to backpedal, only to change his mind once more when he spotted Josh standing in the corner, smirking.

"Uh, Mick?" Zack sounded ridiculously cheerful and vastly amused. "I see you're feeling...better."

Josh chuckled. "I imagine he feels just fine right about now, since she's in here."

Slowly, not wanting to upset Mick, Del stood and cast a quick glare at both men. In her fascination with Mick, she'd all but forgotten them and how they'd bulldozed her, refusing her every request, evading her questions.

"I'd have been with you sooner, but they wouldn't let me," she said to Mick, feeling piqued all over again. "I didn't know what was going on or why—"

"Only family could see him before he got to his room," Zack said, some of his cheerfulness dwindling.

Del had heard the same lame explanation at least ten times, yet Zack had pretty much stayed with Mick, except for when he'd taken a turn guarding her so Josh could look in on him. They were friends, not family, or so they'd told her, so their excuses held no weight. They'd insisted she come to the hospital, insisted she wait around, and then they'd refused to let her do anything useful—like see Mick and thank Mick and...

She brushed her stringy bangs out of her face, still annoyed, still frustrated. "You could have taken my suggestion and told them I was his wife. Then they'd have let me in."

Josh choked; Zack raised one eyebrow and looked at Mick. Mick grinned, then reached out for her hand with his good arm, which meant stretching across the bed. When she took his hand, he said, "I'm sorry you were worried." And in a quieter tone, "Are you all right?"

Dismissing the other two men, she again sat on the bed. She wanted to kiss him some more, but his friends were standing there, not only ogling them, but bristling like overprotective bulldogs. Besides, after her run through the rain, and the burglary, she probably wasn't all that appealing.

"I'm fine."

Mick touched her bruised cheek with gentle fingertips. His eyes were nearly black with concern. "Damn, I'm sorry about that."

His tone made her heart beat faster, made her skin flush and her insides warm. They'd only just met, but she felt as if she'd known him forever.

Catching his wrist, she turned his hand and kissed his palm. Again he looked surprised, and if she didn't miss her guess, aroused. His eyes were hot, his cheekbones slashed with color. He stared at her mouth.

Was it possible he felt the same incredible chemistry?

Del had to clear her throat to say, "You saved me. I'm sorry I freaked. I thought…well, at first I thought you were with them and you intended to…"

"I know." He continued to stare at her mouth, which made her belly quiver, her nerves jump. "I'm sorry I scared you."

The irony didn't escape her. Here he was, in bed, wounded, and he kept apologizing to her. She'd never met a man like him. "You kept me alive," she stressed, which discounted any side effects, such as a small bruise, as unimportant. "I'm the one who's sorry. Well, not sorry that I'm alive, but sorry that you got hurt in the process."

"It's just a flesh wound."

Zack coughed and Josh snorted.

She looked at his two friends, then peered at Mick suspiciously. Was it worse than she thought? But the nurse had told her he'd be okay.

Her ire resurfaced and she said to Mick, "I wanted to come in and see you, but they wouldn't let me. Waiting was awful. When we found out how long it would be, I planned to go home and shower and change, and try to make myself presentable, so when you came to I wouldn't be such a sight, but he—" she directed a stiff finger at Josh "—wouldn't be at all reasonable about any of it."

"Don't blame Josh," Mick said, smiling just a bit. "I asked him to keep you around."

"You did?"

"I was afraid you'd disappear and I wouldn't get to see you again."

His words were so sweet, she forgot about her sweat and ruined clothes and stringy hair. "I wouldn't have done that, I swear! I would have come right back."

Again she leaned down and kissed him, but this time he was ready for her and actually kissed her back. His tongue stroked past her lips for just a heartbeat, then retreated. Her breath caught and she sighed. *Oh wow.*

With a numb mind and tingling lips, she heard him rumble in a low voice, "I want to see you, Delilah."

She lowered her voice to a mere whisper. "I want to see you, too. I just wish I'd had time to clean up. I'm all sweaty and I have mud on my feet and my clothes are limp and wrinkled. I smell like a wet dog."

His hot gaze moved from her eyes to her mouth and back again, his expression devouring. "You smell like a woman."

She almost slid right off the side of the bed. Much more of that and she'd be sweating again, that or she'd self-combust.

He was just so darn sexy! The dark beard shadow covering the lower part of his face made him look dangerous.

After witnessing him in action that afternoon, she knew he *was* dangerous. His brows were thick, his lashes sinfully long, his high-bridged nose narrow and straight, his mouth delicious. And those dark eyes… This man had singled her out and risked his life to save her. It was beyond comprehension.

It was the most exciting thing that had ever happened to her.

Only a thin hospital gown and a sheet concealed his entire gorgeous, hard body from her. She looked him over, saw the width of his chest, the length of his legs. His feet tented the sheet, and as her attention slid back up his body, she noticed something else was beginning to tent, as well.

She returned her gaze to his, saw the burning intensity there, and froze. He wasn't embarrassed and made no attempt to conceal his growing erection.

Using his left hand, Mick lifted her fingers and caressed them gently. His eyes were direct, unapologetic, and when she glanced at the other two men, it was to see them looking out the window, at the ceiling, anywhere but at the bed.

She was unimpressed with their show of discretion after everything they'd already put her through. It didn't matter that they'd directed their attention elsewhere; they were still in the room, their presence noticeable. They'd more or less forced her to stay, at Mick's request, but it was obvious they still didn't want her alone with him.

If they'd really been polite, if they'd trusted her at all, they'd have left the room. But no, they weren't ready to budge an inch. She supposed they didn't know her well enough to trust her and, after all, he'd just been shot, but still…

Mick looked vital and strong and all-male, and his effect on her was beyond description. She'd long since decided men weren't worth the effort, but oh, she hadn't met this man yet.

"Are you sure you're going to be okay?" She gripped his hand hard, trying to accustom herself to the unfamiliar feelings of tenderness and worry and explosive desire. It had been forever since she'd felt so much awareness for a man. Well, actually, she'd never felt it—not like this. Which was the main reason she seldom dated anymore. Men didn't appreciate her emotional distance.

She felt far from emotionally distant now. "The nurse said you'd be fine, but…"

"Yeah." His voice was rich with promise. "I should be out of here soon."

"Tomorrow," Zack said, still keeping his eyes averted, "as long as you agree to take it easy. They'll send you home with antibiotics and painkillers, but knowing you—"

A noise in the hall alerted them to more visitors. Mick released his hold on Del and bunched the blankets over his lap to hide his partial erection just seconds before a man and woman pushed through the door. They entered in a rush, heading straight for Mick.

Not being much of a people person, Del faded aside, inching into the corner opposite Zack and Josh. Mick frowned in displeasure at her retreat, and Josh said, "No worries. I've got it covered." When he moved to stand between Del and the door, Del realized he meant that he'd continue to keep her around.

As if she'd leave now!

Del's attention snagged on the pretty blonde woman now hovering over the bed, kissing the top of Mick's head, his high cheekbone, his chin. "Thank God you're all right!"

The woman's lips were all over Mick, and Del didn't like it at all. But she knew she had no right to complain.

"I made Dane drive like a demon to get us here."

"Angel," Mick protested, all the while grinning widely so

that Del knew he didn't really mind her attention at all, "you didn't need to rush. I'm fine."

Del wondered if Angel was her name or an endearment.

The woman pressed her cheek to Mick's. "But you were shot!"

Zack laughed. "I told you on the phone he'd be all right."

"I had to see for myself."

Josh crossed his arms over his chest and smiled. It was apparent to Del that they all knew each other, that these were more of Mick's friends. These people Josh trusted; she could see that.

Feeling like an outsider, or worse, an interloper, Del frowned.

"According to the doctor," Josh said, addressing Angel, "he'll need some babysitting."

Zack nodded. "Luckily the bullet hit at a tangential entry. It was expended enough that the force didn't carry it into the chest cavity, which could have injured his lung, or in a through-and-through injury that could have caused more damage to his arm."

"Yeah," Mick mumbled, tongue in cheek, "I'm real lucky."

Del's heart ached for him. This was the most she'd heard, and it hadn't been revealed for her benefit. Rather, the information was for the new arrivals, especially the woman with the lips.

The female who was trusted.

It all sounded so horrendous, worse than Del had imagined. If the shooter had stepped just a little bit closer, if his aim had been a little higher… She closed her eyes, fighting back a wave of renewed fear and impossible guilt. Mick could so easily have been killed.

Her eyes snapped opened when she heard Angel say, "You'll come home with me, of course."

Del had no real rights to jealousy or possessiveness, but she felt them just the same. Who was this beautiful woman who felt free to kiss and touch Mick?

And then the thought intruded: was he married?

Del's stomach knotted. She tried to see Mick's hand, but couldn't with both people crowded near his bed.

The man with Angel said, "The kids would love a chance to fetch and carry for you. They adore you, you know that."

With incredible relief, Del realized that if they had kids, they must be a couple. Which meant Mick was safe from any romantic entanglement with Angel.

Del was just beginning to relax again, feeling on safer ground, when yet another couple pushed through the door. This woman was lovely, too, but the man with her held her close to his side, leaving no doubt that they were together. He was large and dark and so intense he looked like Satan himself. Del stared, but no one else seemed alarmed.

Mick even rolled his eyes. "Angel, did you drag Alec and Celia down here, too?"

Angel touched his face. "They were visiting when we got the news. Of course they insisted on coming."

The room was all but bursting with large men. Josh and Zack were big enough, but their physical presence was nothing compared to Dane's and Alec's, both of whom were in their prime and exuding power.

And Mick, even flat on his back and wounded, was a masculine presence impossible to ignore. He had an edge of iron control, of leadership, that couldn't be quelled by an injury. All in all, the men made an impressive group. Del expected the walls to start dripping testosterone any moment.

She watched them all, memorizing names and studying faces as they shared familiar greetings. The women were all-smiles, and even Dane looked somewhat jovial. Alec, however, looked capable of any number of nefarious deeds.

Just as Del thought it, she saw his piercing gaze sweep over Mick from head to toe, and he grinned a surprisingly beautiful grin, making his black eyes glitter and causing Del to do an awed double take.

"I knew you wouldn't go much longer," Alec drawled, and even his deep voice sounded scary to Del, "without getting yourself shot again. It's a nasty habit."

"I'll try real hard to keep that in mind," Mick said.

"Zack tells me you got shot on purpose this time." Alec crossed his massive arms. "At least I try to avoid it when possible, and when Celia isn't around."

Celia, slim and elegant, leaned over Mick's bed and kissed his forehead. To Del's way of thinking, there was far too much kissing going on, and far too many visitors. At this rate, she'd never get him alone.

But that concern was secondary to another. Judging by what Alec had said, this wasn't the first time Mick had been shot. Del looked at Josh and Zack, to judge their reactions to that news. Their expressions were impassive, leading her to believe they already knew Mick had been shot before this.

"Don't let Alec tease you, sweetie," Celia said. "He's glad I got him shot. Otherwise we'd never have ended up together."

Alec looked very dubious at her statement, whereas Del was completely floored. What in the world did these men do that they took turns catching bullets?

Celia continued, saying, "If you stay with Angel, then we can visit you."

Del knew that any second now Mick would agree to Angel's offer, and then she'd lose her chance. She took a deep breath, unglued her feet and tongue, and declared, "I'm taking him home with me."

The room fell silent, and as one, all eyes shifted her way. The women and two men stared, as if seeing her for the first time.

Mick smiled.

Under so much scrutiny, Del squirmed. Thanks to the rain and her long jog and the events at the jewelry store, she looked like something out of a circus sideshow. But determination filled her. She wasn't a coward and she wouldn't start acting like one now.

Moving out of the corner, she edged in around Angel, who kept kissing Mick's forehead. Del got as close to him as she could, then stated again, "I'll take care of him." She made her voice strong, resolute.

Angel blinked, looked at the other people, then back at Del. "You will?"

"Yes. After all," Del explained, "it's my fault he's hurt."

Everyone's gaze shifted from her to Mick. Expressions varied from male amusement, astonishment and fascination, to female speculation.

Del wanted to wince, to close her ears so she wouldn't have to hear what Mick might reply to her appalling assumption. They were strangers in every sense of the word, but he'd claimed to want to see her again. What better opportunity would there be than for her to take him home? She'd never played nurse to anyone before, but how hard could it be?

She stood by his bed, refusing to budge, blocking Angel and her lips, in particular, and waited in agony.

Expectation hung in the air, along with a good dose of confusion.

Mick grinned, managed a one-shoulder shrug and addressed all six people at once. "There you go. Looks like it's all taken care of."

"What do you know about her?"

Josh looked down at Angel and shrugged. They stood in the hallway outside Mick's door, which was as far as Angel would go. "Not a damn thing," he said, "except that Mick is in a bad way."

Angel pressed a hand to her chest, looking as if she'd taken the bullet herself. "The wound?"

Josh knew how close she was to Mick—practically a surrogate mom even though only nine years separated them. Mick's real mother, from what he understood, had been plagued by too many personal weaknesses. She'd died long ago, and Angel and Dane's family had become Mick's. "I'm sorry, I meant that he's been acting...infatuated."

Relieved, Angel bent a chastising look on him. "Mick is a grown man, a very levelheaded man. He doesn't get infatuated."

Josh knew that, which only made it more baffling. Beautiful women flirted with Mick and he hardly noticed. But this one... Josh shook his head. "Call it what you want, but today he chased her down, took a bullet for her without even knowing her name. And according to Zack, the first thing he asked about, even before he got his eyes open, was Delilah."

A slow smile spread over Angel's face. "This is wonderful!"

"Did you hear me?" Beyond respecting her a great deal, Josh knew Angel was one of the chew-'em-up-and-spit-'em-out women Mick had mentioned during their lunch, so he carefully measured his words. "Today, just a few minutes ago, is the first time he officially met her. Before that, he just watched her jog every day." Josh thought about Mick's preoccupation with Delilah and added, "She's not even all that eye-catching."

Angel smacked him on the shoulder. Not hard, but it still stung.

He refused to rub it.

"Looks are nothing, and you should know it by now. Besides, I think she's cute."

Dane, carrying two colas, strolled up behind her. He handed one to his wife and asked, "Who's cute?"

"Mick's woman."

Grinning, Dane said, "That little dynamo in there telling him she won't leave now that he's awake, not even to go home and get a change of clothes? And if she does leave, she absolutely will not take a bodyguard with her?" Dane laughed as he sipped his drink. "Both Alec and I offered, at Mick's insistence. Alec even promised her we wouldn't leave him alone, that one of us would be sure to stay with him until she returned. But she's not convinced. If anything, that seemed to have the opposite effect on her."

"I wonder why."

"Because she likes being difficult," Josh pointed out, disgruntled.

Dane grinned. "Actually, I believe she's jealous of Angel."

Angel frowned. "Of me? But Mick and I are like…"

"You don't have to convince me," Dane told her. "But then I know you both well. She doesn't."

"Why would she need a bodyguard?" Angel asked, changing the subject. Dane spent a few minutes explaining about the bizarre aspects of the robbery, and Mick's concerns.

"For whatever reason, I don't think Mick has told her that he's a cop," Dane said. "He tried telling her she could be in danger, but she's blowing the whole thing off as nothing more than a fluke, or a coincidence. I get the feeling he'll have his hands full with that one."

Josh glared toward the closed door. "After spending several hours with her today, I can tell you that she's about the most contrary woman I've ever met. All she did was bitch at me."

Dane raised both brows. "Let me guess, you tried treating her as you do most women, flirting, teasing—"

"Condescending," Angel added.

"I was charming!"

"—and," Dane continued, "she was too smart to fall for it."

"She wants to do things her own way," Josh grumbled, still amazed that she'd taken exception to his manner, "and damn the consequences. She's far too...independent and stubborn for my tastes."

Barely stifling a chuckle, Dane clapped him on the shoulder. "It's good for you, teach you a little humility around the ladies."

Josh wasn't interested in learning humility, thank you very much. He and the ladies got along just fine. Delilah Piper— well, she was just an aberration, a woman who couldn't be swayed with sound male logic, smiles or compliments. In fact, she'd been rude enough to scoff at his compliments, as if she'd known they were false, which, of course, she hadn't because he was damn good at flattery when he chose to be.

Josh felt renewed pique; no woman had ever scoffed at him before. "Do you want me to go drag her out of there?"

Dane's expression filled with anticipation. "Oh yeah, I'd love to see you try."

True, Josh thought. Knowing her—and, after spending hours closed up with her in the waiting room, he did indeed feel that he knew her—she'd probably kick him someplace dirty. His groin ached just thinking about it. She'd threatened to do him in once today already, when he wouldn't agree to label her Mick's wife, just so she could sneak in and see him sooner. Obstinate woman.

And besides, brute force wasn't something he'd ever used on a female. He'd only been mouthing off because he'd used up his other tricks on her without success. "I'll see if I can dredge up some diplomacy," he told Angel and Dane, and sauntered into the room with all the enthusiasm of a man headed to the gallows.

One look at Delilah and he was again filled with confusion. What was it about her that had Mick going gaga? The woman was...*lanky.* That's the only word he could think of that described her. Her arms and legs were long, her body slim, her breasts small. She appeared delicate when he knew she was anything but.

He had, however, noticed that she had a very nice tush, not that it made up for the rest of it.

And now she watched him, on alert, as if he had no right to be in the room seeing one of his best friends. His gaze met Alec's and Alec shrugged. Celia stared wide-eyed.

None of them were used to Mick being thwarted. Most times, he told people what needed to be done and they did it. Mick had an air about him that demanded obedience. Women especially went out of their way to make him happy. Not that Mick took advantage of his appeal to women. Just the opposite, he seemed unaware of how they gravitated to him and he was the most discriminating male Josh had ever known. Beautiful women came on to him, but more often than not, Mick showed no interest at all.

Until now.

According to Angel, Mick had been that way since he was sixteen. Always a take-charge guy, always irresistible, but at the moment he looked ready to pull his hair out.

With flagging patience, Mick said, "I want you to be comfortable, Delilah. Go home and take the shower you mentioned earlier. Change your clothes if you want, get something to eat."

"I'm not hungry and I'm used to the clothes now." Her every word exuded stubbornness, though an edge of desperation could be heard, too.

Alec and Celia stood at the foot of the bed. Celia shook her head and Alec narrowed his eyes in contemplation.

Mick looked tired and frustrated and pained as he said, "I don't need you to babysit me, Delilah."

Josh decided enough was enough. Mick wasn't in top fighting form or the conversation never would have gone on for so long. He hated seeing his friend this way, wounded and weak.

Josh had handled plenty of women in his day. This one was no different—at least not in the most important ways.

"Of course you need a damn babysitter." Josh leaned against the wall, ready to take on Delilah and win. "Good God, Mick, you were dumb enough to get shot in the first place, then dumb enough to pass out. I can understand why she doesn't trust you now to do as the doctors and nurses tell you. You'd probably yank out your IV, wouldn't you? Or get up and parade around the room until you keeled over again. If she doesn't stay right here like a good little mother hen to make sure you behave yourself, you might even—"

Predictably enough, Miss Delilah exploded. She went stiff as a spike, sputtered, then practically shouted, "Don't you talk to him like that, Josh!"

Celia jumped a good foot at Del's explosive outburst. Alec coughed to cover a laugh. Zack, always laid-back and calm, watched the drama unfold with interest. But then Zack knew Josh and likely suspected his motives.

"Well," Josh reasoned, extravagant for the sake of their audience, "why would you refuse to go home and change out of your rumpled clothes unless you didn't trust him to act intelligently?"

Delilah fried him with a look before bending down to Mick. She said very sweetly, "I'll be right back."

When she stalked around the bed, both Celia and Alec scurried to get out of her way. Josh didn't know if it was the scent of mud and sweat that motivated them, or the intent look on her face.

As she passed Josh, she snagged his shirtfront and dragged him out after her. Biting back a victorious laugh, Josh looked over his shoulder in time to see Mick chuckling. Josh sent him a salute.

Once in the hallway, Delilah rounded on him. She opened her mouth to speak, but he beat her to it. "You need to shower. I can see sweat stains under your arms, and I can smell you."

Her face flaming with color, she kept her gaze glued on Josh, then turned her head the tiniest bit and sniffed. She wrinkled her nose and frowned.

Josh almost laughed. Truth was, Delilah smelled kinda nice, like shampoo and lotion and woman, not that he'd ever tell her that. Calmly now, because he didn't want to offend her, he said, "Mick needs you here. I know that. Hell, you're all he's talked about since he came to."

"Really?" She looked skeptical, and hopeful.

"Yep." Seeing her uncertainty, Josh softened. Most of her aggression had been on Mick's behalf, so he couldn't really hold it against her. "He'll be uneasy if he thinks he's imposing. You don't know him like I do. He's not used to relying on anyone. Do you really want to start a relationship that way?"

She stared down at her muddy sneakers and mumbled, "No."

Such a small voice for Delilah! And he noticed she didn't deny the relationship part. Good. At least that meant she was as interested as Mick. Josh would hate to think his friend was the only one smitten.

"He also doesn't want you to be alone. He doesn't worry about women often, so you could show a little gratitude and go easy on him."

Seconds ticked by before she finally admitted, "I didn't—don't—know those men." She looked at him, her eyes troubled. "And I don't want a total stranger waiting around on me while I shower and change. I don't like to impose on others, either."

Josh wanted to curse, to end this awful day by heading home and phoning a reasonable woman, a doting woman who'd give him the comfort of her body and her feminine concern. He did not want to spend more time with this particular woman, who treated him as an asexual nuisance.

But he knew what he needed to do. He drew in a breath and made the ultimate sacrifice. "All right. Then let me take you home. You can do what needs to be done, then I'll bring you back. You can stay until visiting hours are over. I know he'd appreciate that."

As if he hadn't made the grand offer, she said, "Maybe Zack could drive me home?"

If it wasn't for Mick... Josh drew a deep breath and reached for control. "Zack can't. He has a four-year-old daughter and he needs to get home to her."

"Oh." Delilah eyed him, apparently liking his plan as little as he did. "I suppose Dane or Alec would be okay...."

He should have said fine, should have let Mick deal with her. Instead, he heard himself say, "Dane and Alec just drove two hours to get here, and I'm sure they'd like to spend their time visiting Mick, not chauffeuring your stubborn butt around town."

Stiffening, she said, "I could take a bus...."

"And Mick would still worry. Someone shot at you today, lady." From what Josh understood, someone had singled her out as a victim. It didn't make sense, and he understood Mick's concern. "You witnessed a burglary and it doesn't matter that you told the police you didn't recognize anyone, that you have no idea what's going on, it's still strange."

She didn't relent, and he said, his patience at an end, "Hell, I promise not to speak to you, all right? I won't even look at you if it'll make you happy."

Using both hands, she covered her face. Her normally proud, straight shoulders hunched and she turned partially away.

Thinking she was about to cry, Josh froze. Damn, but he couldn't deal with weeping women. There was nothing he hated more, nothing that made him feel more helpless. His stomach tightened, cramped. Delilah acted tough and talked tough, but she was still female, delicately built, and she'd been through an ordeal.

But she didn't so much as sniffle. "I don't mean to be nasty," she said from behind her fingers. Her voice was miserable but strong, and devoid of tears. "It's just..." She hesitated for a long minute, then dropped her hands and sighed. "I feel so responsible."

Josh's hostility and impatience melted away. She'd been involved in a robbery, shot at, stuck in the hospital all day in wet, grubby clothes with total strangers. If he'd known her longer, he'd have offered her a hug. But he'd just met her—and so had Mick. Josh was still worried. It wasn't like Mick to fall so hard so fast. He'd never even seen Mick trip. On rare occasions, Mick dated, and then moved on.

Josh couldn't think of a single female, other than family, who Mick would have invited to stay at the hospital with him. Not only would he have found it an intrusion, he was far too private to want anyone around him when he wasn't up to full speed.

In his line of work, Mick naturally had to be careful, and that caution had carried over into other aspects of his life. Or perhaps it had always been there, left over from a less-than-wonderful childhood. But whatever the reason, Josh could tell that for this woman, Mick was throwing caution to the wind.

Settling for a friendly arm around her shoulders, Josh steered her back toward the hospital room. "The last thing Mick would want is for you to feel bad. About anything. As to responsibility, it sure as hell isn't *your* fault those idiots showed up and started shooting. Okay?"

"Thanks." She nodded, and even managed a small smile for him. Josh was struck by that smile, and for the first time, he had an inkling of what Mick felt.

They walked through the door, and she seemed to forget all about Josh the second her gaze landed on Mick. Nonplussed, he watched her hurry back to Mick's bedside. "Josh is going to drive me home, but I'll be right back."

Mick's surprise at the quick turnaround was plain to see as he looked from Josh to Delilah and back again. Josh winked. Oh yeah, he'd have fun ribbing them later with this one. He'd gotten her to do what the rest of them couldn't. He hadn't lost his touch, after all.

"Don't worry, Mick," Josh said, feeling in good humor for the first time since the shooting, "I'll keep a real close eye on her."

That earned him a frown from both Delilah and Mick. Delilah apparently didn't think she needed to be watched, and Mick obviously didn't want any male looking at her too closely. Jealousy, Josh decided, and was glad he'd never suffered such a miserable emotion.

"You really don't have to rush," Mick told Delilah after

dragging his attention away from Josh. But it was plain to Josh that Mick wanted her back where he could be the one keeping an eye on her, protecting her, not any other man, not even a friend he trusted. He was also in pain and doing his best to hide it. Damn stubborn fool.

Delilah glanced around the room. "Will your visitors stay all night?"

"No," Mick said, making the decision before anyone else could answer.

Alec coughed again. Celia rushed to assure her. "We'll be at a nearby hotel for the night, but we'll stay here until you get back. How's that?"

As if it was up to her, Delilah nodded. "That'd be perfect. Thank you." Then she bent to kiss Mick again. "I'm going to give my cell phone number to the nurse, just in case." She turned to Josh. "Are you ready?"

"I'll be right there."

She looked suspicious at his delay, but didn't question him on it. She turned and moseyed out.

The door had barely closed before Angel and Dane came back in. Angel propped her hands on her hips and said, "Now that she's not within hearing distance, tell me the truth. Does your shoulder hurt?"

With a crooked grin, Mick admitted, "Hell, yes." Then he turned to Zack. "If you could see about some pain medicine…?"

"The doctor ordered it for when you woke up, but you were too bullheaded to take it."

"It would've made me sleepy."

Josh shook his head. "And God forbid he miss a single second of Delilah Piper's visit."

Zack, always something of a peacemaker as well as an EMT, laughed. "I'll go get your nurse and she can take care of you."

Josh walked over to the bed, where both Dane and Alec now hovered. Josh knew they were dying for some answers. Together the two men ran a private investigations firm, and they could sniff out trouble without even trying.

"The other men got away. The police are still looking, but they haven't turned up anyone."

Mick's curse was especially foul. "What about the one I shot? Did they find out anything from him?"

"The idiot had ID on him. He's Rudy Glasgow, and he's still unconscious." Josh knew that despite Mick's injuries, he'd want to know it all. Still, he hesitated before saying, "It doesn't look good."

Mick dropped back onto the pillow with an aggrieved sigh. "I know my shot to his leg didn't put him under. Was it the head wound from when he fell?"

"Yeah. You two mirror each other—both shot, both with conked heads. Only his was worse. He rattled something in his skull and the docs don't know when he'll come to, which means they don't know when he'll be able to answer questions, if ever. You were lucky that you landed more on Zack than the concrete when you fell."

Not amused, Mick cursed again.

"I also turned your gun over to the officer first on the scene. He insisted, of course, and with you passed out cold..." Josh shrugged.

"That's standard procedure," Mick assured him, not worried. "I'll be issued a new one."

Josh nodded. "I notified your sergeant and he's getting in touch with Internal Affairs."

"Which means I'll have to see the damn psychiatrist, too." He groaned.

"Just procedure?" Josh asked, though he already knew any

shooting required a follow-up visit with the shrink, just to keep the officers healthy in mind and body.

"Yeah." Mick looked weary beyond belief. "When she leaves here tonight—"

Dane held up a hand. "We won't let anything happen to her. I promise."

And Josh assumed that meant one or both of them would be tailing her the rest of the night, even after she finished her hospital visit. Delilah wouldn't like it if she knew. But then, Dane and Alec were damn good, so she wouldn't find out unless they wanted her to know.

Alec looked thoughtful, and with his intense, dark features, the look was almost menacing. It had taken Josh some time to get used to him. "So you think the robbery was a sham? Just an excuse to shoot her?"

"They aimed for her head," Mick rumbled in disgust, describing how he'd covered her, and the shooter's angle. He gave details he hadn't given when Delilah was in the room. "They didn't threaten anyone else. Hell, they didn't even look at anyone else."

"But why her?" Dane asked.

"I haven't got a clue. Far as I can figure, she was just a customer, like the other two in the shop."

Though Mick said it, he didn't look quite convinced. Josh didn't like any of it, especially since his friend seemed determined to be in the middle of it all. "I'd better get out there or she'll leave without me."

"She doesn't have a car here, does she?" Mick asked, concerned over the possibility.

"No, but believe me, that wouldn't stop her. Prepare yourself, Mick, because she's about the most obstinate, bullheaded woman I've ever run across." He squeezed Mick's left shoulder. "Take it easy while we're gone."

"You won't let her out of your sight?"

"Just when she showers." He grinned at Mick's warning growl. It amused the hell out of him how possessive his friend had gotten, and how quickly. "Quit worrying. I'll bring her back safe and sound."

CHAPTER THREE

Mick watched Josh go, and though he trusted Josh implicitly, he cursed the injury that kept him confined to bed. "She could have been killed today."

Angel sat beside him on the narrow mattress. "Is that why you agreed to go home with her? So you can protect her?"

He nodded, but he saw that both Alec and Dane knew his reasons were more varied than that. And more territorial, more sexual. Protecting wasn't the only activity he had in mind. He'd never burned for a woman before, but now he felt like an inferno ready to combust.

Why the hell would someone want her dead?

Mick remembered the way she'd been looking the place over, the way she'd initially smiled at the men—a smile he'd considered merely polite, stranger to stranger.

Zack came back in, the nurse trailing him. She gave Mick a dose of morphine through his IV, and seconds later the discomfort receded and lethargy settled in.

Mick relished the relief from the searing pain, even while he fought to stay awake and sharp enough to think.

"Relax," Dane ordered him.

"I have to figure out what's going on." A vague sense of impending doom, of limited time plagued him.

Dane shook his head. "No. You're in no shape to start snooping around. Let it go for now. The bastard who shot you isn't going anywhere, and he won't stay out forever. When he comes to, you can question him. Or better yet, let someone else do it."

"No." Even with the morphine clouding his mind, Mick knew he wasn't about to pass up the opportunity to get some answers. "I need to call my sergeant, to tell him I want to stay advised. And I need to talk to the head nurse. I need to—"

Angel pressed her fingers over his mouth. "You need to sleep. I have a feeling when Delilah gets back, you'll be determined to stay awake and alert."

Alec cocked a brow while cuddling Celia to his side. "He wouldn't want to miss a minute of that, as Josh said."

Mick relaxed, thinking of Delilah's emotional strength, her boldness, how she'd kissed him, her taste, her heat. They were right—he didn't want to miss that. In the next instant, he fell asleep.

Mick woke to the sound of quiet tapping. The room was dim, with only one light glowing in the corner. The curtains were all closed, but he could tell it was night. He'd probably slept another four hours or so, and it enraged him. There was a lot to consider, a lot to do, not the least of which would be getting to know Delilah.

The tapping continued, light and quick. He bit back a groan as he turned his head on the soft pillow and zeroed in on the source. There, sprawled in the room's only chair, a laptop resting across her thighs, was Delilah.

God, she was lovely.

A nurse had evidently brought her a pillow and blanket in

an effort to help make her comfortable. The padded lounge chair could have served as a bed in a pinch. Delilah had the back reclined, the pillow behind her shoulders, the blanket thrown over the arm of the chair.

Her rich dark hair, freshly washed, swung loose and silky around her shoulders. The light from the laptop cast a soft blue halo around her. Her eyes looked mysterious, purposeful, as she typed away. Mick watched her, aware of the acceleration in his pulse, the expanding sexual tension.

She'd changed into a pair of baggy jeans and a miniscule, snowy-white, cropped T-shirt. Her sandals were off, tucked beneath the chair, her bare feet propped on the edge of the counter in front of the window. Two flowering plants now sat there, no doubt from Angel and Celia.

Delilah's slim legs seemed to go on forever, and Mick, still only half-awake, pictured them around his hips, hugging him tight while he rode her, long and slow and so damn deep. He visually followed the trail of those incredibly long legs, and when he came to her hips he imagined them lifted by his hands, her legs sprawled wide while he tasted her, licked her and made her scream out a climax.

A groan broke free from him and Delilah jumped, nearly dumping her laptop. "Mick!"

Heat throbbed just below his skin. He was so aroused he hurt, but he'd done nothing more than look at her and give his imagination free rein. What would it be like to actually have her?

He swallowed and said with a drawling, raw deliberation, "I don't suppose you'd like to give me another kiss?"

Slowly, her gaze glued to his, she set the laptop on the floor and stood. "I didn't mean to be so brazen earlier. I just…it amazed me that anyone would do what you did."

"So you kissed me?"

Arching one dark brow, she half laughed. "I wanted to devour you, actually."

The shadows in the room did interesting things to her body. "Do you always say exactly what you think?"

She shrugged. "I guess so. I know I shouldn't, but I'm out of practice when it comes to this sort of thing."

"You can say whatever you want to me, okay?"

She nodded. "You saved my life, and you got hurt in the bargain. I saw you and I just...wanted to kiss you."

That didn't sound right to Mick. "So it was about gratitude?"

"Yes...no. I'm not sure." She made a helpless gesture, then shifted her feet and tucked her silky hair behind her ear. "The thing is, touching you seems...right."

He understood that. Touching her seemed right, too. Hell, devouring her seemed right. He'd have gladly gotten started right that minute, but she stood there, waiting, uncertain, very different now that they were alone. She wasn't as defensive, and there was no reason for her to be protective.

No woman had ever been protective of him. Except Angel, but that was back when he'd been a boy. With Delilah it felt different.

"Everyone else has left?"

"Yes. Angel and Celia gave me the number of the hotel where they're staying so you could call if you needed them. The man, Alec, said you had his cell number if you wanted to make sure he was on duty. Whatever that means."

Mick nodded, understanding perfectly. Alec would wait and watch for Delilah to leave. He'd protect her until Mick could take over. There wasn't a more capable or harder man than Alec Sharpe. Knowing he'd keep his eye on Delilah gave Mick a new measure of relief.

When he didn't speak, she gestured at the flowers and said, "The women bought these in the gift shop."

"That's just like them."

She fidgeted. "They're…friends of yours?"

"More like family. As close as family can be without all the baggage."

"Oh." A mix of emotions crossed her features—confusion and relief. "Josh and Zack said they'd be in touch in the morning."

"I figured as much." She stood there before him, barefoot and fidgety, and Mick used the opportunity to look at her. The loose jeans hung low on her slim hips, showing a strip of pale belly between the waistband and the hem of her shirt. He saw the barest hint of her navel, enough to fire his blood, to make his mouth go dry.

He glanced at her breasts and found himself smiling. She was indeed small, but still so damn sexy he ached all the way down to his toes. As he stared, her nipples tightened, pushing him over the edge.

He needed her closer. Because she looked uncertain, he asked, "You didn't like kissing me?"

"I did!" she blurted, then bit her bottom lip. She twined her fingers together and shifted her bare feet again. "I just didn't want you to think that, you know, just because you were nice enough to save me that you had to…"

"Had to what?" Inside, he grinned, knowing what she thought, but in the mood to tease her.

"You know. Be sexual with me." His gaze shot to her face and she rushed to add, "I wasn't sure if you felt the same way I did. I mean, you're incredible. Gorgeous and sexy and hard and…what woman wouldn't want you? But I'm just me. I didn't know if you wanted to—"

Just that quickly, his humor fled. "I want to."

"You do?"

He was hard, and there wasn't a damn thing he could do about it. "Come here, Delilah."

As if reassured, she strode to the bed and sat beside him, this time to his left. "You want me to kiss you again?"

Unwilling to rush her or scare her off, he didn't move. He wanted her to be as free as she'd first been, taking what she wanted from him, when she wanted it. Was there a better male fantasy than having a bold woman who knew her own mind and went after what she needed?

Holding himself still, Mick said softly, "I'd love for you to kiss me again."

"You don't need anything first?" She searched his face, looking him over, he assumed, for signs of discomfort. "A drink? More pain medicine?"

I need you. "No."

Tentatively, she laid a hand on his chest. "You're so warm," she whispered, her fingers lightly caressing, edging under the loose neckline of the hospital gown. "I watched you sleep for a while and it made me nuts." She glanced at him, meeting his gaze. "You even look good when you sleep. I had to get out my laptop to keep busy, just so I wouldn't end up touching you. I didn't want to wake you."

Mick had no response to that, other than a rush of heat. The thought of her watching him and wanting him fed his awareness of her, making it more acute.

She touched his throat, then slid her slender fingers over his uninjured shoulder. "I think," she whispered, watching the progress of her hand, "that you're about the sexiest man I've ever seen."

If they'd been anywhere other than a hospital room, he'd have pulled her under him. He shifted, felt the pain deep in his shoulder and cursed.

She quickly pulled away, then poured him a drink of water and lifted the straw to his mouth. "Shh. This will help."

Getting her under him would help, but he didn't say so. He drank deeply, hoping the icy water would cool his urgency, return a measure of his control. It was insane to want a woman this way.

After setting the paper cup aside, Delilah again rested her hand on his chest. Her gaze locked with his. "Your heart is racing."

"I'm horny," he explained, because anything more eloquent was beyond him while she continued to touch him.

Her light blue eyes twinkled and her lush lips curled into a satisfied feminine smile. "No sex for you, at least not until you're healed."

That "not until" stipulation—which pretty much guaranteed he'd eventually have her—about stopped his heart. Without another word she leaned down and touched her mouth to his. She was gone before Mick could respond.

Her blue eyes were warmer, softer, and he rumbled, "Again."

She looked at his mouth, bent, stroked his bottom lip with her hot little tongue. "Do you like that?" she breathed.

He groaned.

Still so close he tasted her breath, she asked, "You're not married or anything, are you?"

"No."

"At first, I was afraid Angel or Celia—"

"No." Using his left hand, he touched her hair. Warmth, softness. "I love your hair." He tangled his fingers in the silky mass and brought her mouth back flush with his.

"Thank you," she murmured, and obligingly gave him the longer kiss he wanted.

Dull pain pushed at Mick, but he blocked it from his

mind. It was nothing compared to the feel of her. "Open your mouth."

She did, then accepted the slow, deliberate thrust of his tongue. He stroked deep, taking her mouth, exploring all the textures and heat, and the taste that was uniquely Delilah.

They both groaned.

Delilah pulled back. She touched his jaw and asked, "Did I hurt you?"

He had to stop this or he'd lose it completely. "Of course not."

"I'm not married or anything, either."

Mick, still on the verge of a meltdown, managed to lift a brow at that candid disclosure, and she shrugged. "I just thought you should know," she said, her words coming in soft, uneven pants, "being as we're...well, doing this."

"This?" She stayed close and the scent of her, lighter now and touched with lotion and powder, filled him. He wanted to wrap himself in it, wanted to hold her close to his body until their scents mingled.

"The whole sex thing." She drew a breath, but kept her gaze steady, unwavering. "I assume that's where we're headed. I mean, I'll have you all to myself in my apartment and I want you. I assume you want me, too."

He could hardly believe what she'd just said. No woman had ever come right out and so boldly stated her intentions to have an affair with him. Women sometimes chased him, but they were subtle, never so up-front with their motives. They teased, flirted, advanced and retreated.

They didn't advance and advance.

"What is it you do?" she asked, unconcerned with his be-mused astonishment—maybe even unaware that she'd aston-ished him. "I've never known anyone who carried a gun and shot people."

He should have been prepared for that, because he knew she'd ask. But he was still stuck on that affair statement, attempting to get his head back together—a near impossible feat because all he could think about now was starting that damn affair. The sooner the better.

"Mick?"

He wanted to tell her the truth, but he knew nothing about her except that she evidently had an enemy, someone who wanted her dead, someone who would have succeeded if that bullet hadn't been sidetracked by his shoulder. He also knew she was eccentric, a woman heedless of her surroundings, honest to a fault, brazen and stubborn one minute, shy and uncertain the next. And he knew she wanted him, not as much as he wanted her, but enough.

His innate caution warned him against going too fast. Thinking of Dane and Alec, he lied. "I'm a private investigator."

Her eyes widened with unrestrained excitement. "Seriously?"

She looked so comically surprised, he grinned. "Yeah." Starting things off with a lie wasn't the best course of action, but he had few choices until he found out what was going on. If all went as planned, he'd be able to tell her the truth soon enough. She'd understand his reasoning and forgive his deception. He'd see to it.

"Wow." She settled on the side of his bed, her hip against his, her hand still resting on his chest. "I could use you for research."

Mick did a double take, momentarily getting his mind off the idea of pulling her down on the narrow bed beside him. "Research for what?"

She shrugged in the direction of the laptop. "I'm a writer.

I'm always looking for easy ways to research. From the horse's mouth is always the easiest."

A writer? Now, somehow that fit. The creative types were always a bit different, as far as he knew. "What do you write?"

"Mysteries." She waggled her eyebrows. "Fun stuff. Whodunits with a few laughs and some racy romance thrown in."

It was Mick's turn to say, "Wow." Then he added, "Have you ever been published?"

"Well, yeah." She seemed to consider that a stupid question.

She'd said it so casually, as if it were nothing. He'd never met a novelist before, and now he planned to sleep with one. "How many books have you done?"

"I've had four published so far, with two more in the works." She nodded toward her laptop. "I'm working under a deadline right now."

"How old are you?" Mick didn't think she looked old enough to have one book published, much less four. He'd always pictured writers as more seasoned, scholarly types.

His question made her grin. "Twenty-five, almost twenty-six. I sold my first book when I was twenty-three."

Mick eyed her anew. A mystery writer. He had to shake his head at the novelty of it. And here he'd claimed to be a PI. A match made in heaven. "I'll be damned," he said, still dealing with his amazement. "Maybe I could read one sometime?"

"Sure. I'll show them to you when we get to my apartment. By the way, I drove myself here so I could take us both home tomorrow. Your friend Josh was pretty ticked off about it. He was going to tattle, and you should have seen his face when we found you asleep. He looked so frustrated, I thought his head would explode. Of course, for that one, it might be an improvement."

Mick closed his eyes. Some maniac had tried to kill her,

and here she'd been on the road alone again, vulnerable. He could just imagine Josh's frustration. "Delilah."

"Del."

"Excuse me?" He opened his eyes again and stared at her. Hard.

"If we're going to be friends, you may as well call me what everyone else does."

"And everyone else calls you...*Del?*" It sounded like a man's name to Mick.

She shrugged. "It's what I've always gone by. Only my father called me Delilah, usually if he was angry, and he died a few years ago. Now I only use my full name when I write."

Mick wondered how her father had died, if she had any other family left.

He shook off his distraction. He'd have time to ask her about her family later. Keeping his tone stern, he said, "Josh was right to be angry. Someone tried to shoot you today. You shouldn't be alone, not until I—" He pulled back on that, quickly saying instead, "Until the police can figure out what's going on."

She flapped her hand at him, waving away his concerns, then let it settle on his abdomen. He nearly shot off the bed. Every muscle in his body clenched and his cock throbbed. He'd never been in such a bad way before.

If she moved her fingers just a few inches lower, she could make him feel so much better. He closed his eyes against the image of her soft hand holding him, stroking him. Too fast, he was moving way too fast.

"I don't think," she murmured, watching her hand on his body, "that they were really shooting at me. Why would they?" She looked up at him, her hand thankfully still. "I mean, they aimed at me, but I think it was just a random thought. They were criminals and they got thwarted because the police showed up, and they were mad, so they wanted to shoot someone."

Nearly choking on an odd combination of explosive desire, frustration and protectiveness, Mick asked, "And you think they chose you, a woman who didn't have a thing to do with anything, a woman just visiting the store? They didn't look rattled or frenzied. They looked like they meant to shoot you—you specifically—before they took off."

Her fingers spread wide and her brow furrowed. "I don't know. I didn't notice anything like that."

Her baby finger was a quarter inch from the head of his penis. His body strained, fighting against his control. He *needed* to lift his hips, to thrust into her hand.

"You," he rasped, "are the person they accused of setting off an alarm, when you hadn't moved and weren't anywhere near anything that could have triggered an alarm."

That made him think of something else, and he forced himself to concentrate on things other than her touch. "How did the cops know? Did anyone tell you?"

She stared blankly at his bandaged shoulder, deep in thought. "The officer who questioned me said someone on the street noticed the guns when he was walking by, and he used his cell phone to call them."

"Honey, listen to me." Mick put his left hand on her bare waist, between the bottom of her shirt and the top of her jeans. Her skin was smooth and warm, her muscles taut. "Did you recognize either of them? Was there anything at all familiar about them?"

"No, of course not." She looked at her hand on his abdomen, then at his erection. He read her thoughts as if she'd spoken them aloud. Instinctively, he tightened, which brought forth a moan of pain from both physical discomfort and sharp anticipation.

"You're in a bad way," she said in a hushed, husky tone filled with understanding and her own measure of need.

He wanted to howl. He wanted to ask her to go ahead and stroke him, hard and fast, that she use her mouth…

"Delilah…"

"Del," she whispered, and started to glide her hand lower.

Using his left hand, Mick caught her wrist. His hold was tight, too tight, but he felt stretched so taut he was ready to snap. "I'm in worse than a bad way," he rasped. "I'm on the very edge, and if you touch me I won't be able to control myself."

She tilted her head, staring at him as if she didn't quite grasp his meaning.

"I'll come," he said bluntly, then watched for her reaction.

She stayed still, but probably only because he held her slender wrist in an iron grip, refusing to let her move.

"This is difficult for me," he explained, watching her, needing her to understand. He felt more tension than he had at fifteen, when he'd seen his first fully naked female, there for the taking. He'd lost control then; he was ready to lose control now. He ground his teeth and insisted, "I'm not usually like this."

Her eyes, warm and heavy-lidded, looked him over. "You're hurt, in bed. This is a strange situation."

"It has nothing to do with any of that and everything to do with you. I want you bad, and have since the first time I saw you."

He could tell that admission pleased her. "Today?" she asked.

Gently, he lifted her hand away from his body so he could carry on a coherent conversation. He brought her hand to his chest and kept it there. "I saw you two weeks ago, near a building I own. You were heading to the post office."

Her frown reappeared. "I never noticed you," she said. Then, chagrined, she added, "I was probably plotting, and I don't pay much attention then. My mind tends to wander."

He thought about how she'd been examining the jewelry store, studying it, prowling from one corner to the other. "Plotting...what?"

"My book, of course."

She said it as if it should have been obvious to him.

"So," she asked, "you saw me a few weeks ago?"

"And many times since then. I eat at Marco's a lot, and you—"

"Jog by there a lot." Her smile was very sweet. "Whenever I have a deadline, I need to get outside at least once a day to clear my head so I can really think and plot. So I jog. But I've never noticed you before."

"I've watched you almost every day. Today when I saw you actually stop and go into the jewelry store, I decided it was time to introduce myself."

Her countenance darkened. "Instead you saved my life."

They stared at each other. The air was charged, until a nurse started backing in, dragging a cart with her.

Delilah moved so fast, Mick was stunned. She snagged the pillow from her chair and dropped it over his lap. To the nurse she said, "Time to check him again?"

The nurse looked over her shoulder and smiled. "I'll only be a minute." Then she turned to Mick. "For an injured man, you're about the healthiest thing I've ever seen."

Mick was in no mood for small talk. "Is that right?" he asked, while watching Delilah.

"Yep. Great lungs, great reflexes. The epitome of health. I wish everyone would take such good care of their bodies."

Delilah made a choking sound at that observation. "I'll, uh, just get out of your way." She tapped a few buttons on her laptop, closed it and set it on the window ledge. She picked up a large tote from the floor and swung the strap over her shoulder, saying to Mick, "I'm going to run down to the coffee shop and grab a bite to eat. Do you want anything? You slept through dinner."

The nurse said, "We can still get him a tray."

Delilah leaned close and whispered, "It was nasty-looking stuff. I'd pass if I was you."

The nurse heard and grinned. "The coffee shop has pretty good sandwiches and chips and desserts. You're not on a restricted diet, so if something sounds good…"

Delilah started out. "I'll surprise you."

"Delilah—"

"Del," she said, then added, "Don't worry. I'll be right back. We'll pretend we're having a picnic."

And before he could warn her to be cautious, she was gone. Mick sank back against the pillows, the ache in his shoulder receding to no more than a dull, annoying throb. The nurse offered him more pain medication, but he passed. He needed all his wits about him to deal with Delilah Piper. Otherwise, he thought, grinning shamelessly, she'd probably take sexual advantage of him in his weakened physical shape.

He could hardly wait.

The nurse finished her poking and prodding, changed his bandage, and then, at his request, handed him the phone.

He called Josh. A woman answered—no surprise there—and Mick heard her grumbling, heard the squeaking of bedsprings, before Josh came on the line.

"You're either feeling much better or much worse if you're making a call."

"Much better," Mick told him, and he knew it was only a partial lie. "Can you bring me a change of clothes tomorrow? The nurse said I should be ready to get out of here by eleven."

"Sure thing, but it'll have to be early. I'm on duty starting at eight."

As a fireman, Josh worked varying hours, usually four days on, four days off. On his off days—today being one—he spent a lot of time with women.

Zack, an EMT stationed right next door to the fire department, was just the opposite. He spent all his spare time with his daughter and only rarely made time for women, and then only when his hormones refused to let him put it off any longer.

"If it's inconvenient, I can ask Zack."

"It's no problem. I'd planned to check up on you anyway, just to make sure your little woman hadn't done you in."

"You don't like her?" Mick asked, not really caring, but curious all the same. Personally, he found everything about Delilah unique and enticing, even her damned stubbornness, which had earlier about driven him nuts.

"She's…different."

True enough, Mick thought.

"And she took exception to me right off the bat."

Mick grinned. That was probably a first for Josh.

"She's not like other women, and she'll take some getting used to. But it appears she's as nuts about you as you are about her, and I suppose that's all that really matters." There was a muffled sound as someone snatched the receiver away from Josh and he apparently wrestled it back. Mick heard him growl, "Just hang on. I'll only be a minute."

Chuckling, Mick said, "I won't keep you."

"S'no problem. She'll wait. So, what's it to be? Jeans? And I guess some type of button shirt?"

"That'd be easiest. I'm sure you can find your way around my house."

A feminine whisper, insistent and imploring, sounded in the background. Mick grinned again. "G'night, Josh."

"Hey, before you go, you should know that Alec is hanging around, waiting to take care of things for you."

Mick appreciated the subtle way Josh explained that with his lady friend listening. "Thanks. I'll ring him next."

He disconnected his call with Josh and punched in Alec's number. He imagined Delilah would return any minute, and he wanted to make sure things were set first.

"Sharpe."

"It's me, Alec. Where are you?"

"Hanging out in the parking lot."

"Damn, I hate to do that to you."

He could hear the smile in Alec's tone when he said, "Celia's with me. It's no problem."

That made Mick smile, too. He could just imagine the two of them necking like teenagers. Alec was still a bad ass of the first order, but with Celia, he was a pussycat. "Why don't you head out and I'll call you when she decides to leave?"

The door opened and Delilah came through, her arms laden with paper bags and disposable cups of steaming liquid. Mick eyed her cautiously, not sure how much she'd heard.

She set everything down and turned to him with a smile. "Is that Josh?"

"No, it's, uh, Alec." He could hear Alec laughing in his ear. He knew they all appreciated the unique effect Delilah had on him.

"Alec?" That surprised her, he could tell, but not for long. "Well, tell him to go home and go to bed. I'm not leaving tonight, so I don't need a bodyguard."

Mick scowled. "Delilah…"

"Del." She sat on the side of the bed and took the phone

from his hand, then said into the receiver, "I'm going to stay the night. But thanks for thinking of me, anyway."

And then she hung up.

CHAPTER FOUR

At ten o'clock, the doctor gave Mick the okay to leave, together with a long list of instructions. Del listened intently and felt confident that she could take care of everything that needed to be done.

Angel and Celia, along with their husbands, had come and gone already. They'd been there since early morning, but because Delilah now realized that they were in fact Mick's family, she enjoyed the attention they lavished on him. He treated both women with an avuncular ease, not with the heated awareness he'd shown her.

Unfortunately, Josh had shown up, too, at the crack of dawn. She'd been asleep when he'd arrived, and was forced to awaken to his scowling face. He'd seemed suspicious of her overnight stay, as if he thought she might have molested Mick in his sleep. Stupid man.

Though Josh was uncommonly handsome, and could be witty when he chose to be, she wasn't at all certain she liked him. Whenever he looked at her, his demeanor plainly said he found her lacking. He distrusted her interest in Mick, and showed confusion at Mick's interest in her.

Nevertheless, she did appreciate his friendship with Mick.

Willingly, he'd brought Mick clothes to wear home, then insisted she leave the room while he helped Mick dress. She would have stubbornly refused—*she* wanted to help him dress!—except Mick had wanted her to leave, too.

Delilah had already washed her face and brushed her hair and teeth while his family visited. They'd shown up just as Josh was leaving, and she couldn't help but feel a twinge of poignant sadness, seeing how loved he was. He had a good family, loyal friends, and she envied him that.

Hoping to make a better impression on them today than she had yesterday, she'd applied a little makeup and exchanged her slept-in T-shirt for a dark-rose tank top. Though the hospital was cool, out the window she could already see heat rising off the blacktop in the parking lot.

Now that they were alone again, Mick paced around the room, waiting for an orderly to bring a wheelchair. To Del's discerning eye, he looked ruggedly handsome with his morning whiskers and tired eyes. He also looked a little shaky. She wanted to coddle him, but she'd already figured out that he wasn't a man used to relying on others.

"Does your family live close?"

He glanced up at her, clearly distracted. With his arm in a sling and his eyes narrowed, he looked like a wounded pirate. "A coupla hours away. They'll be back over the weekend, I'm sure." His dark gaze sharpened. "Will that be a problem?"

"To have them visit? Of course not. For as long as you stay with me, I want you to be completely comfortable. It'll be your home, too."

He looked undecided, as if there was more he wanted to say, then he just shook his head. "We need to come to a few understandings."

"Oh?" Seeing Mick flat on his back in bed was one thing. Him standing straight and tall—all six feet three inches of him, moving around the room with flexing muscle and barely leashed impatience—was another. He was an intimidating sight. An arousing sight.

"I want a few promises from you." He stalked toward her, as if ready to pounce, and she felt her heart tripping.

She was a tall woman, meeting many men eye-to-eye. Not so with Mick. He looked down at her, his dark eyes drawing her in, and without thought Del went on tiptoe and touched her mouth to his.

He froze for a beat, then slanted his head to better fit their mouths together, and caught her with his good arm at the same time. He carefully gathered her close, his large hand sliding up her back to her nape and holding her immobile.

Del was acutely aware of his arm in the sling between their bodies. Her breast brushed against the stiff cotton restraint and she shuddered, trying to keep space between them so she wouldn't inadvertently hurt him.

"Relax," he whispered, and then his hand left her neck to coast down her spine, down and down until he was squeezing her bottom, cuddling, drawing her up and in until her pelvis nudged his groin. He made a rough sound of pleasure.

Del pulled her mouth away and rested her forehead on his chest. "This is incredible," she groaned.

"I know." He kissed her temple and asked, "How many bedrooms do you have?"

Her nerve endings jumped with excitement. "I have two, but I was thinking we'd—"

The orderly pushed into the room with the wheelchair and gave them a cheery greeting.

Del felt heat flood her face, more so when Mick gave her a scorching look of understanding. He started to pick up the small bag of items he had to take home, but Del rushed to beat him to it.

"You just sit," she said, trying to regain some composure, "and I'll get this." Mick kept her so flustered, she could barely think, and she almost left her laptop behind. Without preamble, the orderly plopped nearly everything into Mick's lap and started out the door. Del hustled after them.

"It's stupid to ride in a wheelchair when I'm perfectly capable of walking."

"And smooching," the orderly said in agreement, even more cheerful now that he knew what he'd interrupted. "But it's hospital policy."

Mick stayed silent until they got into the car and were on their way. He seemed inordinately alert, watching everything and everyone, and he soon had Del on edge.

"Do all PIs act like you?"

Mick didn't bother to glance her way when he said, "Yeah."

"Are you going to do this the whole time you're with me?"

Again, he said, "Yeah." But then he turned to face her. "You were shot at, Delilah. I wish I could blow it off as bad luck on your part—being in the wrong place at the wrong time—but I can't. Not yet. Not until the police have a chance to talk to the guy I shot, and that can't happen until he comes to."

She bit her lip. "Do you think he'll die?"

"I doubt it." He turned to look back out the window, hiding his expression from her, but she heard the contempt in his tone when he added, "But don't feel bad if he does."

"I wouldn't. I mean, I don't. He could have killed someone."

"That's about it."

Given his surly tone, she decided a change of topic was in order. They stopped at a light and she looked Mick over. His hair was thick and shiny and a little too long. The whiskers on his face, combined with the tiredness of his eyes, made her heart swell. Today he wore the softest, most well-worn jeans she'd ever seen on a man. They hugged his thick thighs and his heavy groin and his lean hips and tight buttocks.

Her pulse leaped at the thought of that gorgeous body beneath the clothes. Tonight, she'd get to see all of him. She'd make sure of it. She was so wrapped up in those thoughts, she almost missed the light turning green.

She eased the car forward, while her thoughts stayed attuned to Mick.

The shirt Josh had brought him was snowy-white cotton, buttoned down the front, and looked just as soft as the jeans. The thick bandage on his shoulder could be seen beneath, as could the heavy muscles of his chest, his biceps. "The doctor says you can shower," she told him with a croak in her voice. "But he doesn't want you to soak."

"Right now, a shower will feel like heaven."

"Will you need anything in particular? I could run by your place after I drop you off and pick you up anything you need."

"Josh grabbed me a change of socks and boxers. Angel's taking care of the rest later today. For now, whatever soap and shampoo you have will work." He glanced at her, smiling just a bit. "Do you use scented stuff?"

"No."

His eyes went almost black. "Good. I love the way you smell. I'm glad it's you and not from a bottle."

Del tightened her hands on the wheel. Boy, much more of that and she wouldn't make it home. Luckily, he stayed silent for the rest of the ride, and Del didn't bother trying to draw him out again. Her heart couldn't take his idea of casual conversation.

She pulled up to the garage in front of her building. She had to pay extra to park her car there, but she knew if she left it on the street, it'd likely get stripped. She said as much to Mick as she turned off the ignition.

"Yeah, I know. I told you I own that building next door, right?"

Del rushed around to his door to help him—and got a disgruntled frown for her efforts. He was suddenly in an oddly defensive mood, and she didn't understand him.

"You told me. I wasn't sure if you meant the building to the left or the right."

He grunted. The building to the left was a shambles. His building was nicely maintained. "Alec used to rent from me, before he married Celia. The agency where he works is located between here and where he lives now."

Del cocked a brow. "If he doesn't live *here* now, why did he follow us?"

Mick jerked around. Wary, he asked, "What are you talking about?"

She rolled her eyes. "Your friend is pretty hard to miss, looking like Satan and all. I saw him a few cars behind us. I suppose this is more of your protection?"

Tilting his head back, Mick stared at the heavens. "Something like that." When he looked at her, she could almost feel his resolve. "I don't have a gun right now. The cops confiscated it as evidence."

Del gasped. "They're not going to accuse you of anything, are they?"

"No, it's routine to take any weapon used in a shooting. I'll get another one before the day is out, but until then, I wanted someone armed to keep an eye on things."

Fascinating. He spoke about guns with the same disregard that she gave to groceries. "This is all really extreme, you know."

"It's all really necessary, as far as I'm concerned." Then he added, "Trust me, honey. This is what I do, and I'm not willing to take any chances with you."

That sounded nice, as if he might be starting to like her. But maybe, Del thought, all private detectives were as cautious as Mick. She had no comparisons to go by; she'd never known a PI before.

Shrugging, she decided not to fight what she couldn't change, and hefted out her laptop. She put the leather strap of the carrying case over her shoulder along with her tote, and then reached inside for his bag.

Mick caught her shoulder with his left hand. "Something we need to clear up."

Del peeked up at him. He looked too serious, almost grim. Getting to know this man, with all the twists and turns of his personality, would be exhilarating. "Yes?"

He relieved her of his bag, then her laptop, holding both casually in his left hand as if they weighed no more than a feather pillow. "I'm not an invalid."

Her temper sparked. "No, of course not. But you are wounded and you're not supposed to strain yourself."

Without warning, he leaned down and gave her a loud, smacking kiss. His expression was amused and chagrined and determined. "It doesn't strain me, I promise."

"But you can only use the one arm."

Slow and wicked, his grin spread. "I can do a lot," he whispered in a rough drawl, "with one arm."

Her stomach curled at the way he said that and what she knew he inferred. She cleared her throat. "I see."

"Good. Now lead the way."

She didn't want to. She wanted to insist that he let her help him. He'd done enough already, more than enough. Too much. The man had a bullet in him, thanks to her.

She turned and marched toward the front stairs. The entry

door was old and heavy, and she hurried to open it, anxious to get Mick settled inside.

Together they climbed the steep stairs to the upper landing, where she used her key on both of the locks for her apartment door, one of them a dead bolt. Being a runner, she made the climb with ease, breathing as normally as ever when she reached the top. She half expected Mick, with his injuries and his load, to huff at least a bit, but he didn't.

He did, however, keep a vigilant watch. "I'm relieved to see the landlord keeps the place secure. Not all the buildings in this area are safe."

Del looked at him over her shoulder as she reached inside and flipped a wall switch. She didn't tell him that she'd had the dead bolt installed recently. The front door opened directly into her living room, and one switch turned on both end-table lamps. She said only, "I'm not an idiot. I wouldn't endanger myself."

She tossed her tote onto the oversize leather sofa to her right and reached for her laptop. Mick, who'd been looking around, taking in her modest apartment, held it out of reach, lifting it over his head as if he didn't have a bullet in his other arm, as if the pain wasn't plain on his face. His strength amazed her.

"Where do you want it?"

Sighing, Del pointed to her desk in the corner, where a half wall separated her kitchen area from the rest of the room. Her desk was the only modern, truly functional piece of furniture she had. A computer occupied the center of the tiered piece, with a fax machine, a printer and a copier close at hand. There were file folders and papers stacked everywhere, notes, magazines, interviews she hadn't yet put into the file cabinet behind the desk. Reference books littered the floor.

Mick lifted a brow and boldly glanced at her papers as he set the laptop down.

His curiosity would have to be appeased another time, Del decided. She took his arm and steered him toward the narrow hallway on the opposite side of the room. "The bathroom is this way. You can shower while I change the sheets. Are you hungry?"

He'd never admit it, she knew, but he looked ready to drop, pain tightening his mouth and darkening his eyes. Twice she'd seen him rub at his temples when he didn't know she was looking. The doctor had told her that he was as likely to have headaches from his fall as pain from his wound. Del had a hunch the two were combining against him.

"After you finish," she said gently, but with as much authority as she could summon, "you'll need to take your medicine."

Mick stopped in the bathroom doorway and caught her chin with his hand. His gaze burned, touching on her mouth, her throat, her breasts. "After I finish," he said, his fingertips tenderly caressing her skin, "I intend to see about you."

Her knees almost went weak. "Me?" It was a dumb question; she knew exactly what he meant.

Nodding slowly, he said, "All that teasing you've been doing, all that talk about starting an affair, and your bold touching. I'm beyond ready."

She really did need to learn a little discretion, she thought, now wishing she hadn't told him all her intentions. But she was used to going after what she wanted, and he'd been irresistible, a man unlike any she'd ever known. Everything about him turned her on, from the protectiveness she'd never received before, to his strength and intensity, to his rough velvet voice and drool-worthy bod. The man was sexy emotionally and physically, and she wanted him.

She caught his wrist and kissed his palm. "Mick, you need to rest. There'll be plenty of time for…"

He carried her hand to the thick erection testing the worn

material of his jeans. Her heart dropped to her stomach, then shot into her throat.

"You think," he whispered roughly, his eyes closing at the feel of her hand on him, "that I can rest with that? The answer is no."

Her palm tingled and of their own accord her fingers began to curl around him. He lifted her hand away, leaned down and kissed her. "I just need fifteen minutes to shower and shave."

Carrying his bag into the room with him, he turned and closed the door, leaving Del standing there with her lips parted and her eyes glazed and her muscles quivering. She sucked in a breath and let her head drop forward to the door, bracing herself there until she stopped trembling.

His effect on her was startling, almost too much to bear. She'd given up on men as too much trouble, with not enough payoff. But with a mere look, Mick could make her hot, and when he touched her, or she touched him, the need was overwhelming.

She heard the shower start and realized she hadn't reminded him to be careful. She leaned close and said loudly, "Don't soak your shoulder! The doctor said that was a no-no."

Just as loudly, he retorted, "I was there, Delilah, remember?" And then she heard the rustling of the shower curtain and knew he was naked, knew he was wet….

She turned and hurried away.

When he'd answered her, he'd sounded distinctly irritable. Well, hell. Heaven knew, he was likely to be doubly so when he found out she had no intention of making love with him today. It would be too much for him, and there was a good chance he'd injure his shoulder anew.

No, she couldn't let him do that.

She also couldn't let him go unsatisfied. She closed her eyes, feeling wicked and sinful and anxious. There was only one thing to do. Granted, *she* was likely to end up the frustrated one, but that was a small price to pay to a man who'd played her hero, a man who'd saved her life. And she had no doubt he'd make it up to her later. She may not have known him long, but she knew that much about him already. The man wanted her—more than any man ever had.

It was a heady feeling. She liked it.

She especially liked him.

Mick found her in the kitchen, staring into her refrigerator as if pondering what to fix. A glass of iced tea sat on the counter.

He shook his head, not yet announcing himself. Foolish woman. How could she possibly think he'd want food when she stood there looking more than edible? Oh yeah, he wanted to eat her up. And he would, slowly and with great relish. "Delilah."

She whirled around, first appearing guilty, then abashed when she saw his naked chest. He'd done no more than pull on snug cotton boxers; he had no need of the sling right now, though he kept his right arm slightly elevated to relieve his shoulder of pressure. The bandages there were made to withstand showers and would dry soon.

Any clothes he would have put on would just be coming off again, so he hadn't bothered with them, either. By look and deed she'd made her willingness, her own desire, clear. It didn't matter that he hardly knew her, not when everything about her felt so right.

He braced his feet apart and let her look her fill.

Her eyes widened and then traveled the length of him. Twice. She touched her throat. "If I looked as good as you, I'd have skipped the boxers."

Though he appreciated the sentiment, Mick was too far gone with lust to manage a grin. "Want me to take them off?"

She shook her head and said, "Yes. But not yet. If you were naked now, I'd forget you're hurt and do something I'd regret."

"Like what?" She continued to stand there, her gaze returning again and again to his straining hard-on, which the snug cotton boxers did nothing to hide.

"Like throwing you down on the floor and having my way with you."

He did grin this time. "The bed is right around the corner. Why don't we go there now?"

Just that easily, he saw her resolve form, harden. He may have only known her a day, but he already knew that look.

"You need to take your medicine. Good as you look, I can see that you hurt."

The pain in his shoulder and head were nothing, certainly not enough to make him want to wait another day to have her. "I'll take a pill after I've sated myself with you."

Her gaze locked on his. "Oh boy, you don't pull any punches, do you?"

"From what I remember last night in the hospital, neither do you." And to encourage her, he added, "But I like it when you speak your mind."

She nodded. "Okay, yes, I want you to sate yourself with me. I want to sate myself with you, too." Her expression was one of worry, regret. "But I figure that'd probably take me hours, maybe even days, so we should maybe put it off until you're not likely to die on me."

Damn, her brazen words mixed with the sweetness of her expression and the obvious worry she felt for him was an aphrodisiac that fired his blood. She was a mix of contradictions, always unique, sometimes pushy and too stubborn. Mick took two long steps toward her, ignored the continual throbbing in his shoulder and head, and gathered her close.

He wasn't prepared for her stiffened arms, which carefully pushed him back again. Shakily, she said, "We have to make a deal."

The need stalled, replaced by innate suspicion. What possible deal could she need to make at this moment? Thoughts flew through his head as he remembered numerous deals offered to him by prostitutes, drug dealers, gamblers, people from his youth and the people he now came into contact with every day of his life.

He also thought about the robbery, about her uncommon interest in the jewelry store, her interest in him, her willingness to bring a near stranger into her home and have sex with him.

By nature, he was overly cautious. From his upbringing, and then working undercover, he'd become suspicious of almost everyone and everything.

Because of his background, he often doubted the sincerity of women in general.

Dropping his hands so he wouldn't accidentally hurt her with his anger, Mick growled, "What kind of deal?"

She blinked, confused by his temper. Carefully, her words no more than a whisper of sound, she explained, "I can't stand seeing you in pain. I want you to take your medicine first, then we'll go to bed."

Mick made sure no reaction showed on his face, but once again she'd managed to take him off guard. Her deal was for him, not for her. "The medicine makes me too groggy."

"Not for fifteen minutes or more. I've watched you after you take it. It doesn't kick in right away, and you only go to sleep when you let yourself."

Still not touching her, he said, "What I have in mind will take more than fifteen minutes."

She inhaled sharply at his words, then touched him, her hand opening on his chest, her fingers splayed, sifting through his body hair. The reflexive clench of his muscles brought a sharp ache to his temples, his shoulder.

"You're welcome to stay here until you're completely recovered," she said, still stroking him with what seemed like acute awe, probably attempting to soothe him, when in fact each glide of her delicate fingers over his muscles wound him that much tighter. "There'll be plenty of time for both of us to indulge ourselves."

He didn't answer right away, trying to figure her out in the middle of an intense arousal that kept rational thought just out of reach.

"Please," she added, both hands now sliding up to his shoulders. One edged the bandage that came over his shoulder from the back. "I won't be able to enjoy myself for fear of hurting you."

He didn't want that. He fully intended for her to experience more than mere enjoyment. He wanted her ripe with pleasure, numb with it. He wanted to give her the kind of explosive release she'd have only with him.

Yet, she was right. In his present condition, it wasn't likely to happen. With her insistence, she was probably helping him to save face.

Mick brought her close and said against her hair, "I'm sorry. I'm not used to wanting a woman quite this much." He wasn't used to wanting to *trust* a woman, either. But he wanted to trust Delilah. He wanted to involve himself with every aspect of her life. He needed to tie her to him in some way.

Nodding, she said, "I know the feeling. You blow my socks off."

He tilted her back so he could see her face. Her honesty humbled him, and pleased him.

"We haven't discussed it," he said, thinking now was as good a time as any, "but I want you to know the nurse was right, I come with a clean bill of health—in all ways. Not only have I always been discriminating, but I'm very cautious, too."

That brought a beautiful smile to her face. "Same here. I can't claim to have been a recluse, but I haven't met many men that I wanted to get involved with. Not like this, not enough to let them interrupt my life. And men take exception to that. They don't like to be neatly compartmentalized."

"Is that right?"

She nodded. "You may not have noticed, but I get really wrapped up in my work, and most of the time I'm not even aware of men around me. At least, not for long."

Mick grinned. "I noticed. At first I wondered if maybe you were a lesbian."

Her mouth opened, then closed. She frowned at him, her pale blue eyes burning bright. "I'm not."

His grin widened. "I noticed that, too."

Still scowling, she said, "Not that there's anything wrong with—"

"Of course not. But I have to tell you how glad I am that you're interested in men."

"I'm interested in *you*."

He appreciated her clarification. "Which means I'm one lucky bastard."

She snorted. "If you were so lucky, you wouldn't have gotten shot." She turned and grabbed up the pills. "Take these."

He downed them in one gulp, washing the bitter taste away with sweetened tea.

"Are you hungry? You really didn't eat that much yesterday, and you hardly touched your breakfast."

He'd been too caught up in his thoughts, in mentally organizing all the things that had to be done that day, to concern himself with breakfast. And the truth was, he felt hollow down to his toes. He could probably eat two meals, but not yet. "No. I just want you. And now that I've swallowed the damn pills, time's wasting."

Her eyes warmed, the vivid blue darkening. She took his hand and turned to lead him down the hall. Without looking at him, she said, "Let me see if I can help you to sleep soundly for a few hours."

It took a great deal of resolve not to turn her against the wall and enter her right there, standing up, without the benefit of a soft mattress. At twenty-six, he'd known lust, but he'd never known anything like this, an all-encompassing need to devour a particular woman.

Her bedroom was small, holding a bed that would barely accommodate his size. The beige spread was tossed half off the bottom of the mattress, pooling on the floor and showing matching beige sheets. Across from it sat a triple dresser with a mirror, the top cluttered with papers and candles and receipts.

A wooden rocker sat in front of one window. The other window held an air conditioner, softly humming on low, keeping the room pleasantly cool. Over the bed a ceiling fan slowly whirled, barely stirring the air but making the room comfortable.

The building didn't have central air, of course. None of the buildings on her street did. Some of them didn't have heat, either. Thankfully, Delilah's apartment building was kept up, just as Mick kept up his building next door. And she wasn't on the first floor, so she could open her windows without fear of intruders.

Her bedroom wasn't what you'd call neat, not with laundry piled on the chair and shoes tossed haphazardly over her closet floor, but it was orderly. He had the distinct impression Delilah could walk into this room and find anything she needed without effort.

She went straight to the bed and propped up the pillows. "Sit here."

Bemused, Mick allowed her to take control. She always seemed less reserved when she was the aggressor, as if taking control gave her more confidence. He wanted her without inhibitions, so he gladly let her lead.

He settled himself, easing his injured shoulder back against the headboard. Delilah stood in front of him and unsnapped her jeans. The sound of her zipper sliding down nearly stopped his heart. Transfixed, he watched her disrobing in front of him. There was no false modesty, no timidity, but no real brazenness, either. She revealed her body with a no-nonsense acceptance that touched his heart; she wouldn't flaunt, but neither would she cower. Mick tightened his fists in the bottom sheet and held himself still.

He'd been half-afraid he was rushing her, moving too fast. But judging by her willingness now, she was finally as ready as him.

But then, he'd been ready from the first moment he saw her.

CHAPTER FIVE

Delilah's jeans dropped, and she smiled at him as she stepped away from them, using one foot to nudge them aside. "I'm not as perfect as you," she stated, again with that simple acceptance of her own perceptions, "but somehow I have a feeling that won't bother you."

Oh, he was plenty bothered, on the point of going insane. Her comments weren't geared toward gaining compliments, but he could only give her the truth. "You're the sexiest woman I've ever seen."

Her mouth twitched and then she laughed. "Yeah, right. With small boobs and a straight waist and gangly limbs?"

He wanted to correct her, to point out everything he found enticing, yet when she caught the hem of her tank top and tugged it over her head, he went mute. His heart struck his rib cage, his breath caught.

The bra she wore had no shoulder straps, and the cups only half covered her. When she flipped her hair back, he could have sworn he saw the edge of a mauve nipple.

He swallowed hard. "This is insane. Come here."

"In a minute. Don't you want me naked?" she teased.

"God, yes." He shifted his legs. He was uncomfortable,

drawn tight, ready to come from just the sight of her. "I want to touch you, too." *And taste you and bury myself deep.*

Reaching behind her back, she unhooked her bra and let it drop. Her breasts were round and firm, with small, tightly puckered nipples now darkened with desire.

She left her miniscule panties on and walked toward him, her gait long and sure and purposeful. Without reserve, she climbed into the bed and straddled his lap. Mick groaned as her rounded bottom nestled on his thighs and her breasts came even with his face. He reached for her.

"Shh," she said, catching his right arm and holding it still. "Let me. You just sit back and relax."

Blood rushed through his head. He gritted his teeth and nodded. He didn't tell her that relaxing was out of the question.

"Tell me what you want." As she spoke, she looked at him and touched him, and his vision narrowed to only her.

"I want to taste you."

Her eyes smoldered, encouraging him even as her hands attempted to ease him. It was a wasted effort. Each soft stroke of her hands—over his chest, his uninjured shoulder, his waist, his throat—inflamed him.

He saw the pulse fluttering in her throat when she asked huskily, "Where?"

"Everywhere, but for now, I want your nipples."

Her thighs tightened around his, giving her away. She wasn't nearly as detached or in control as she pretended. He didn't quite understand her forceful determination, but he knew at least part of it was inspired by reciprocal lust.

She drew a shaky breath and slowly, so slowly the anticipation damn near killed him, she leaned forward.

Mick struggled to stay calm. He couldn't stop himself from bending his knees, forcing her farther forward, couldn't stop the flexing of his cock against her tantalizing ass. But he made certain to gently kiss the rounded softness of her breasts, to nuzzle against her until she moaned. He teased her, licking close to her nipple but not quite letting his tongue touch it.

She twisted, attempting to hurry him, but Mick held himself in check. She needed to catch up to him—if that was possible.

With a rough, impatient sound, she finally murmured, "Mick, please…"

He placed a wet, soft kiss directly over her nipple, briefly drawing her into the heat of his mouth with a gentle suction, and then releasing her. It wasn't easy, considering he wanted to feast on her.

She moved against him, one small jerk on his thighs before she stopped herself. Panting, she said, "I like that."

"I thought you would." He did it again, then again and again until she gasped for breath, until her hands settled in his hair and her nipples were tight wet peaks. Likely with more force than she realized, she brought his mouth to her breast, saying without words that she now needed more.

And he suckled her, strong and deep and long.

The combined sensations rocked him: the taste and feel of her on his tongue as his mouth tugged at her, the heat of her sex pressing insistently against his abdomen, her scent and softness and her unique determination.

The physical bombardment on his senses was enough, leaving him confused and wild with need. But the emotional storm also overwhelmed him. He wanted to consume her savagely, brand her as his own, hear her cries and feel the bite of her nails. And he wanted to hold her gently to his heart, to let her feel protected and know that he'd take care of her. Basic, elemental instincts rolled through him in a way he'd never felt before.

As he continued to tongue and suck, her back arched and she released a ragged moan. Then she moved against his thighs, a riding motion that rubbed the damp silk of her panties along the length of his shaft.

He replaced his mouth with his fingers and said harshly, "Kiss me, Delilah."

She did, stealing his breath as her tongue licked in to tease his. As wild and out of control as he felt, she was more so.

"Let's get these panties off you," he murmured, knowing he couldn't last much longer.

She pulled away, trembling, gasping for breath. Her head dropped forward. After a moment, she dipped down and kissed his throat, her mouth open and hot and wet. Mick wanted to protest, but he loved the feel of her mouth on him.

The pills had muddled his mind some and it took more effort than he could dredge up to stop her as she sank lower, biting at his chest, hotly licking his own nipples, tasting and teasing him.

His arm hurt like a son of a bitch and his head continued to throb dully, but raging lust and crushing need overrode it all. Using his good arm, he tangled his fingers in her silky hair, letting it slide over his chest and then his abdomen as she moved lower and lower down the length of his body.

When her tongue dipped into his navel, he nearly shouted with the pleasure of it. "God, Delilah," he managed to rasp, "baby, you have to stop."

She ignored him. Her hand crept up his tensed thigh, higher and higher until she cuddled his testicles for a brief, heart-stopping moment before grasping his erection and slowly stroking.

He stiffened, all sensation, hot and thick, rushing into his groin. Her mouth, still gentle but hungry, kissed him through the cotton boxers, and the pleasure-pain was so excruciating it blocked everything else.

He cursed, feeling himself sinking, out of control. He had to stop her, but he didn't want to. He wanted her to—

As if she'd read his mind, she eased the boxers down.

"No," Mick protested with a long groan, knowing he sounded less than convincing. The damn pills had melted away his determination, made him forget all his plans. He could only focus on Delilah, on what she did, how she touched him.

"I've been thinking about this all day," she breathed.

He opened his eyes, needing to watch. The look on her face mirrored his own emotions of fire, need, possession. She watched her hand driving him to distraction, her grip firm, her thumb curling over the end of his erection with each long stroke, pushing him closer and closer....

Mick felt a surge of release and desperately fought it off, but she saw the drop of fluid at the head of his penis and leaned forward.

He shuddered, cursed, held his breath—then shouted in reaction when her mouth closed over him, not tentatively, as he'd expected, but sliding wetly down the length of him, taking all of him in, sucking.

Maybe if he hadn't taken the damn pills, maybe if it had been any woman other than her, he could have controlled himself.

But from the moment he'd seen her he'd wanted her, and he couldn't hold back, couldn't stop himself from coming. His fingers knotted in her hair and he held her head to him, not that it was necessary because she didn't pull away. She drew him deeper and made a low sound of pleasure that he felt in his soul. He tightened, surged, and experienced the strongest release of his entire life. He growled with the force of it, his body taut, arching, his mind going blank.

His only realization in that turbulent moment of rioting

sensation was that no other man would ever touch her; she was his, and he intended to keep her.

Mick didn't sleep long this time, probably no more than an hour, but he awoke half-frozen. The air conditioner, on the highest setting, hummed loudly, and the ceiling fan whirled overhead. He felt his hair blowing, felt his skin prickle with goose bumps.

He'd passed out just as she'd left him, half propped against the headboard, his legs now limp, his shoulder cushioned by a soft pillow. At least she'd pulled the spread up to his waist, he thought, a bit disgruntled.

He felt like an idiot as he looked around and realized the room was empty. He cursed. Then cursed again when he pushed the spread away and became racked with chills. It was like sleeping on the wing of an airplane, for crying out loud!

He swung his legs to the floor, stood—and nearly fell. Weakness had invaded every muscle. The pain pills had no effect on his aches, not after that mind-grinding orgasm, where every muscle in his body, clear down to the soles of his feet, had knotted in pulsating pleasure. She'd wrung him out—no doubt that had been her intent.

He grunted, unable to believe what she'd done, and unwilling to accept that after she'd done it, he'd had the gall to fall asleep.

If the room hadn't felt like a meat locker, he'd probably have been hot with embarrassment.

He glanced down at his boxers, still around his thighs, and shook his head. It was too much, far too much.

He straightened his underwear, whipped the spread off the bed and around his shoulders to ward off the cold, then went to the window to turn the unit down. The air conditioner sputtered and died with a sigh.

Forcing himself forward on shaky limbs, Mick left the bedroom. The apartment was quiet, other than the rattling of pans in the kitchen area. On his way down the hall, he decided to take the offense. Delilah knew he'd wanted to make love to her, but she'd taken the choice away from him. *How* she'd taken it away had been beyond incredible, but still, she needed to know that he wouldn't be so easily manipulated. Not ever again.

He was appalled that he'd proved so easy this time. But then, maybe that's why she'd given him the pills, to weaken his resolve. He'd be sure to ask her that.

When he reached the arched kitchen doorway, she had her back to him, stirring a pan of something on the stove. Whatever she was cooking smelled good, as did the coffee in the coffeemaker. She'd pulled her tank top back on, but not her jeans, and the sight of her bottom in the silky panties did a lot to obliterate his other concerns.

Before he got distracted, he asked, "Did you talk me into the pain pills so you could keep us from having sex?"

She yelped, dropped her stirring spoon and jerked around to face him. Their gazes locked.

The sight of her face made his mind go blank, his heart trip. *She'd been crying.*

"Delilah?" he asked around a sudden lump of emotion. Damn, that bothered him. He didn't get lumps of emotion. In his job, he saw the worst life had to offer and he handled it dispassionately, with a distance that could be applauded. Always, from the time he'd been a young boy, he'd kept his emotions in check.

But God, she looked like hell with her eyes swollen and wet, her cheeks blotchy, her nose red. Seeing her made his heart thump.

She bit her bottom lip and turned to the stove again. He heard her sniff. "Yes."

Mick shook his head. He wanted to hold her, to comfort her. Yet she'd turned her back on him. "Yes what?"

"Yes, I gave you the pills so you wouldn't complain when I…eased you. It was the only thing I could think of. I didn't want you to strain yourself, and the doctor said it was too soon for you to have sex."

Talking with Delilah was like wading through syrup. He kept getting stuck, but damn, it was sweet. He cleared his throat, forcing the emotion away so he could think and react clearly. He slowly approached her and stood at her back, close enough to breathe in her sexy scent and see the enormous pot of spaghetti sauce she stirred. "You spoke with the doctor about us having sex?" Her initiative amazed him—and aroused him.

"Yes. Right after I bought the condoms."

Mick paused. *Bought the condoms?* Before he could ask, she said, "I snuck them into the bedroom, in the nightstand drawer, just in case you didn't go to sleep after you came."

She spoke as bluntly as any man, but then, she'd done that from the first, speaking her mind with candor. Unlike other women he knew, she didn't measure her words. She was so female she made him crazy, yet she didn't always act female. Damn if that didn't arouse him, too.

Hell, everything she did aroused him. Just moments before he'd thought himself fully satisfied, but now… "The hospital sells rubbers?"

She glanced at him over her shoulder, and he watched one fat tear track down her cheek. "Yeah, of course they do. It's a hospital, and they understand about unnecessary risks."

She'd managed to distract him, after all.

Mick shook his head and wrapped one arm around her

waist. Resting his chin on top of her head, he asked, "Why are you crying, sweetheart? Did I hurt you?"

"Of course not." She leaned into him, then pushed back with a frown. "You're shivering." Twisting, she put her hand to his forehead in a maternal gesture of concern. "Are you sick?"

"Just cold." He turned her back around and laced his hands over her middle. Her bottom pressed into his groin. "The room was like ice."

She nodded. "I figured you'd like it cold. Most men get warmer than women, right?"

He had no idea, but he doubted any man would relish the igloo accommodations she'd provided him. She'd obviously had some sexual experience, and she was comfortable with her body, with her sexuality. But she was far from knowledge-able about the opposite sex. Mick shook his head at the added contradictions. "Why are you crying?"

She shrugged and leaned back against him. "I'm just a little sad. I'm sorry you have to see me like this. I'm a terrible crier. Very ugly. The news just took me by surprise."

"What news?" He rubbed his chin against her hair, spread his hand over her belly. He loved the feel of her, her softness, her sleekness. She was so feminine, but not in a frail way.

"A guy I know died. I just read it in the paper."

Mick stiffened, caught between conflicting reactions. He wanted to comfort her from any upset, and he wanted to jealously demand information about the guy who'd made her cry. He must have been important to her to bring on the tears.

It shouldn't have mattered. They'd only just officially met, and hadn't officially consummated their relationship yet. But it did matter. A lot.

"Who was he?" Mick asked, keeping her pressed into him by his hand on her belly.

After a long, shuddering sigh, she put the spoon down and turned into his arms. Her face nuzzled into his chest and she whispered, "Just a guy who helped me with research." He felt her wet cheek on his pec muscle and groaned.

"I'm sorta known for my research methods, you know," she continued. "They've become part of my publicity." She leaned back to stare up at him earnestly, and in case he hadn't understood, she clarified. "For my books, I mean."

"How is research a publicity stunt?"

She lifted one shoulder. "People are amazed by the strangest things. But whenever I write about something in a book, I try to experience it first so that I get it right. When I can't experience it, I try to talk to someone who has."

"So what type of research did this guy help you with?" Mick hoped like hell it wasn't a love scene. He could handle anything but that.

Turning away, she reached for a napkin and mopped her eyes. Mick heard another loud sniff. "He was a small-time criminal. I had a scene in my book where a guy stole a car. I couldn't really steal a car—" she glanced at him and added "—not without getting arrested, I'm sure."

"Better not to try it," he agreed, smiling.

"That's what I figured. So I hired this guy, and he took me through all the ins and outs of car theft. For a criminal he was a really nice guy."

Mick glanced at the coffeepot. "Mind if I have a cup?"

"Oh, of course." But she didn't let him get it himself. "Sit down and I'll pour it for you."

Since his knees were still shaking, Mick sat. More than most things, he hated being weak, and for now there was nothing he could do about it. He pulled out a chair at the black, wrought-iron parlor table and gratefully dropped into it.

"Cream or sugar?"

"Black, please."

She set the steaming mug in front of him. His first sip made his body hair stand on end, and he nearly spat it back out. His throat raw, he rasped, "Damn, that's strong."

Delilah didn't take his comment as a complaint. She smiled, looking adorable in her skimpy top and panties, her nose bright red. "I figured you being a man and all, you'd want it strong."

It was a wonder new hair hadn't sprouted on his body. He coughed, and because he didn't want to hurt her feelings, he said, "I think I'll take the cream and sugar, after all."

She happily got them for him, then went back to the stove to check her sauce. To Mick, it looked like there was enough to feed an army. Hopefully, she didn't expect him to eat it all—because he was a man.

Making sure she didn't notice all the sugar he dumped into his coffee, he asked, "So where did a nice woman like you meet a car thief?"

"In prison."

The mouthful of coffee—still too bitter to enjoy—got spewed across the table. He continued to choke as Delilah grabbed up a dish towel and patted his back.

"Mick! Are you all right?"

He wheezed, trying to regain his breath enough to speak. With his eyes squeezed shut, he finally demanded, "What the hell were you doing in prison?"

Tilting her head, she smiled. Given her swollen eyes and the tear tracks on her cheeks, it didn't have the usual effect on his libido. "More research." She chuckled. "You didn't think I meant I'd been serving time, did you?"

Actually, he had, but he wasn't dumb enough to say so. Relief warred with confusion. "Of course not. But can you explain all this research for me?"

She pulled out her own chair at the table. "Okay, but don't

let me forget the spaghetti sauce. Your friends are coming over for dinner and I want to impress them."

"Josh and Zack?"

She snorted. "I meant your other friends, the ones you said were like family."

"Dane and Angel are staying for dinner?" He didn't like putting her out, especially since she was so upset.

"I invited them. Angel called and said she had your things, and wanted to know when it'd be a good time to drop them off. I know she's still worried about you, and she doesn't exactly trust me, so I thought this would be a way to make her feel better."

Cautiously, Mick asked, "What makes you think Angel doesn't trust you?"

Del made a face. "I'm not dumb."

Mick let that go. He'd have to talk to Angel first to see what had been said. He knew Angel would never insult Delilah, but she was protective. "Why do you want to impress them?"

"They're like your family. I like you, so of course I want them to like me."

Mick almost told her it didn't matter what anyone else thought, that he intended to make her a part of his life. But he'd never gotten so deeply involved with a woman, and to do so now, at Mach speed, was just plain foolish. He liked her, all her quirks and unique qualities. He liked her different way of viewing things and her outspokenness mixed with occasional glimpses of uncertainty. And God knew, the sexual chemistry between them was explosive.

But most of her background was still a mystery to him. So he forced himself to be cautious, to go slow. He tucked a tendril of her silky hair behind her ear and asked, "Are you sure you're up to a dinner party?"

"Why wouldn't I be? You're the one who got shot."

"*You* were the target. And you've been crying."

She waved that away, ignoring his first comment and only responding to his second. "I'm overly emotional about the people I care for. There aren't that many. Being a writer keeps me isolated, so I don't get into the social swing of things often. Neddie became a friend as well as a teacher. We had a lot of fun hot-wiring my car."

This time Mick just stared. She gave an impatient sigh and went on. "It's true. We were alike in a lot of ways, reacting to our place in society. Neddie became a misguided criminal, just trying to fit in. I became a writer."

"It's hardly the same thing."

"Of course not. I just meant that we understood each other. Neddie was wrong, and he knew that. But he always said he never hurt anyone who didn't deserve to be hurt. Anything he did, he did among other criminals, including stealing cars. And from what he told me, I believe him."

"Criminals always have excuses, Delilah."

"Well, he was a nice criminal, okay? And very patient. We took my car to a deserted lot and practiced on it for hours. Once I got the hang of it, Neddie timed me."

Mick's left hand, resting on the tabletop, curled into a fist. "You went to a deserted lot with a convict?"

"Can you imagine how the cops might have reacted if they'd seen me hot-wiring a car around here?"

She needed a keeper. *She needed him.* He drew a calming breath, something he found himself doing often around her. "Back up and tell me what you were doing in prison."

"I had a character in a book who had spent a good portion of his life in prison. I couldn't very well write that without knowing what the inside of a prison was really like."

"Ever heard of research books?" he asked dryly.

She laughed. Though he knew her humor was aimed at

him, he was glad to see her mood lightening. "I use research books when I have to. But I think it's always better to get firsthand, in-person information whenever I can."

"You said that's part of your promotion?"

"Yep. It didn't start out that way. But then this one reporter got wind of it when my last book hit the *New York Times* bestseller list. She interviewed me and asked me all kinds of questions about my research, and since then the media is real accommodating. They always make a fuss about my way of researching."

His head throbbed. "Media?"

"Yeah. Silly, huh?"

His tongue felt on fire as he sputtered, "You're a celebrity."

Delilah wrinkled her nose and with a note of dismissal said, "To some people, I guess."

"You do this often?"

She shrugged. "Often enough. I was on a talk show once, and not too long ago I got featured on the news."

"The news?"

"About my newest book, and my research for it. It was fun."

In that moment, a thousand questions went through his mind. What the hell was a celebrity doing living in this neighborhood? How much money could she possibly make and what other types of research had she done?

Could any of that have to do with the incident at the jewelry store?

Before he could start on his interrogation, and that's what it would have been because he fully intended to get a lot of answers, she said, "We better get a move on. Everyone will be showing up in about half an hour. I still need to shower and change and make the bed and boil the spaghetti and fix a salad—"

Mick caught her hand as she rose. He tugged her between his legs. "I can help."

This time her laughter had the desired effect. He got hard as a stone. "Mick," she said playfully, and cupped his neck in both hands. "I think I can handle a shower on my own."

Damn, that brought an irresistible image to his mind. Delilah naked and wet, water streaming down her body, over her belly and between her thighs....

He released her hand and curled his arm around her waist, keeping her close when she tried to impatiently edge away. "I meant," he said, his voice now hoarse, "that I can handle spaghetti or a salad."

"No," she said in that unrelenting tone he already recognized. Delilah was used to making all the decisions, and used to holding her ground.

He'd have to work on that flaw.

She leaned down and quickly kissed him. "Not one-armed, you can't, and the doc specifically said you shouldn't use your right arm."

Mick was ready to explain a few things to her, but she added, her voice sweet and cajoling, "Please, Mick. Just let me take care of you, okay?"

He opened his hand on the small of her back, then slipped it down her spine to her bottom. He filled his palm with one firm cheek. "All right," he agreed. "But on one condition."

Her eyes narrowed. "What?"

"Tonight, after everyone is gone..." He let his fingers drift lower, pressing in to touch the heat of her, pleased with her gasp and small moan. "Tonight you'll let me show you exactly what I *can* do with one good arm."

Breathless, she said, "Sex is—"

"I know, not on the agenda." His fingers caressed her. "But I can return your favor of today."

Her lips parted, her eyes glittered and her cheeks looked warm. Several heartbeats went by, then she whispered, "Yes, okay."

Mick felt like a conquering warrior now that she'd given in to him at least a little. He grinned and smacked her butt. "I'm glad you can see reason. Now go get your shower. I'll pull on my jeans and park myself in front of the TV."

"And you won't lift a finger?"

He stood, kissed her forehead and replied, "Not until tonight."

With a comical look on her face, she turned the sauce down to warm and left the room. Mick flexed his aching shoulder, winced and decided to make a fresh pot of coffee while Delilah was otherwise occupied. He could only imagine Dane's expression if he took a gulp of that thick, bitter brew. It would probably prove amusing, but then Mick would have to drink it, too, which would negate all the fun.

So far, her coffee, her air-conditioning and her lack of discretion in dangerous situations were the only things he had trouble with. Those things aside, Delilah Piper was one hell of a woman. With each passing minute, he fell a little harder.

CHAPTER SIX

It turned out to be a hectic evening, and Delilah was glad to see it winding down. Not only had Dane and Angel come to dinner, but Alec and Celia had called, and she'd invited them along. She figured she might as well get the family gathering over with. She was used to people not understanding her, to assumptions that her preoccupation with her stories was sheer daydreaming, motivated by lack of intelligence or attention.

She wasn't used to caring, to going out of her way to be accepted, and she'd felt on edge. Added to that was her urge to write. She had a deadline looming, and her mind kept wandering to her story.

Then Zack had dropped in with his four-year-old daughter, Dani. She was about the cutest thing Delilah had ever seen, and strangely enough, writing took second place to other thoughts. Dani had blue eyes like her father's, but her hair was blond and curly, and she had dimples when she smiled.

It took only a moment for Del to see that the little girl adored Mick. With her father's admonition to be careful of Mick's injury, she'd rushed to him, climbed into his lap and kissed his cheek as if he were a favorite uncle. Then she'd given him three more kisses to "make him all better." Mick had claimed to feel much improved on the spot, which prompted Dani into giggles.

Something about seeing Mick with a little girl in his arms made Del's heart swell. It was an incongruous sight, Mick so strong and darkly handsome, holding such a delicate, fair child. But it also looked very right, as if Mick were made to be a father.

Del frowned at that. Their relationship, started only a day before, hardly warranted thoughts of parenthood. She shook off the strange aberration and concentrated on being a perfect host.

She wasn't used to entertaining and she definitely wasn't used to so much company. But she didn't resent the intrusion on her writing time. In fact, it was all really nice.

During dinner, Josh phoned, and minutes later another man called for Mick, though he didn't introduce himself and Mick didn't tell her who it was. During his whispered conversation, she saw Alec and Dane share a look.

Her small apartment felt like Grand Central Station. Celia kept watching her closely, as if she was waiting for something, though Delilah had no idea what. Both she and Angel were cautiously nice.

Other than Mick, Del hadn't entertained a man in ages. And she'd never entertained a man's family before now. She had no idea if she was doing things right.

Mick caught her alone in the kitchen getting ready to make more coffee. He wore the sling again, but he still managed to drag her close for a kiss.

"Dinner was great."

He sounded sincere, and she smiled against his mouth. "Thank you." It had been a guessing game, trying to figure out how much sauce and spaghetti to make. After she'd done her best calculation, she'd doubled it for good measure. And that was a good thing, because the men had eaten far more than she'd ever anticipated. "Everyone is so nice. I like them."

"Even Zack?"

"His daughter is wonderful."

Mick laughed at that careful evasion. "You still holding a grudge?"

That sounded infantile, so she shook her head. "No, of course not. I understand why they were so protective of you."

"They were protective of *you,* Delilah."

She didn't agree, but saw no point in arguing. "I suppose for Zack to have such a sweet daughter, he must be a good father."

"He is that." Mick stroked her hair, then added, "Zack likes you. He told me so."

Staring at his chest, Del asked, "What about the others?"

He tipped up her chin. "Angel is cautious because I don't normally get involved with women."

Del wasn't at all certain she understood that. "You're not a virgin."

He choked on a laugh. "No."

"Then what do you mean—"

"I mean I'm real choosy. I already told you that, right?"

"The same is true for me, but maybe for different reasons. I've never had much time for men."

"You're making time for me."

There was no denying that. But Mick was…different. Well worth any effort.

"And," he added, still explaining Angel's reserve, "we've been moving pretty fast."

Delilah chewed over that obvious bit of information. "She's afraid I'll hurt you."

His eyes warmed, and his hand on her cheek was so gentle. "She's afraid you could, and that's a first." He kissed her again. Then once more. "Damn, I have to quit that or they'll wonder what we're doing in here."

She didn't want him to quit. "We're just kissing."

"I want to do a lot more."

So did she. "Tonight, I wouldn't mind—"

His hold tightened. "Tonight," he growled, "it's your turn."

Her heart tripped. She was still aroused from the afternoon. She'd been aroused since the second she saw Mick in that hospital bed.

Knowing he wanted to touch her and…do things to her made her whole body feel tight and too hot and somehow empty. Sighing shakily, she said, "All right."

"An agreeable woman," he teased, and took her mouth with a kiss that curled her toes and made her breasts tingle.

A knock sounded on the wall behind them. Mick lifted his head and turned.

Del groaned, then went on tiptoe to peek over his shoulder. Celia stood there smiling. Alec stood next to her, looking amused.

"I—I was just about to make more coffee," Del stammered.

"Why don't you let Alec do that?" Mick suggested, putting his good arm around her shoulder.

That idea didn't sit right. "But he's a guest."

Alec raised a brow and gave Mick a curious glance. "I don't mind. Coffee is my specialty. Besides, I think my wife is dying to ask you something."

Celia elbowed him, then stepped closer. She looked anxious, her hands clasped together, and she kept glancing from Del to Mick and back again. Finally she blurted, "Are you *the* Delilah Piper? I mean, I saw some books on your shelves and I know it seems crazy, but…"

Mick looked at Del with surprise, and Celia stood there holding her breath. "That's me," Del said.

Mick frowned. "You've heard of her, Celia?"

"Are you kidding? She's fabulous! One of my favorite authors."

That got Del's attention. "Thank you. You've read me?"

Celia rushed closer. "Each and every one. Ohmigosh, that last one had me on the edge of my seat. When the car went off the bridge into that river…" She shivered, as if remembering the scene.

"I did that, you know," Del told her. When Celia stared wide-eyed, Del nodded. "It's true. Of course, I took some lessons first, so I wouldn't drown myself, but then we found this old bridge that no one uses anymore, and the instructor and I took the car right off the side."

Beside her, Mick growled, "What the hell are you talking about?"

And in an awed whisper, Celia said, "Angel didn't believe me that it was you. I mean, that you're the author who really did all those things."

"The coffee will be done in a minute," Alec said, interrupting another angry outburst from Mick. "Why don't we go back in the living room and Celia can grill you like I know she's dying to?"

Del loved talking about her work, and she allowed herself to be tugged into the room. Mick held her hand tight, and as soon as her backside found a couch cushion, he demanded, "What the hell do you mean, you drove your car off a bridge?"

Angel gasped. "Then it's true? It's really you?"

Mick didn't give her a chance to answer. "Delilah, what's going on? What are they talking about?"

"You don't know?" Alec asked, then shared a look with Dane. To Del, all those shared looks felt like a conspiracy. Regardless of her attempts, she was still an outsider in their group.

"Know what?" Mick's gaze narrowed on Del, dark and

almost…predatory. A hush fell, everyone watching with expectation.

Del turned in her seat to face Mick, unsure of his sudden change in mood. He sounded angry for some reason, and he looked more than a little disturbed.

Maybe he needed another pain pill, though he kept refusing them. "I explained how I do my research, and about the interviews, Mick."

"You said you visited a prison, not that you drove your car into a river."

She took exception to his tone, especially in front of their guests. She wanted the visit to go well, not be ruined by an argument.

Attempting to sound reasonable in the face of his growing ire, she explained, "I knew what I was doing. I took diving lessons and a class that teaches you how to keep from panicking. I learned all kinds of neat things. You see, under murky river water you sometimes get disoriented because it's so dark." She shivered. "Really nasty, if you want the truth. But if you let out just a little of your breath, the bubbles will rise and show you the way to the surface."

Mick groaned.

"Also, if you stay calm, your heartbeat is slower and you use less oxygen, so you can hold your breath longer. I wasn't very good at that part of it, though. I couldn't hold my breath long at all. Still, it was pretty exciting to—"

"Drive your car," Mick rasped in an ominous voice, "deliberately off a bridge?"

Del frowned. Unlike Angel and Celia, Mick didn't seem at all impressed with her career. Not that she expected or needed him to be impressed. In fact, it was kind of refreshing that he didn't seem in awe.

She was used to a variety of reactions, most of them gush-ing, some fascinated, even disbelieving. But not angry. That was a reaction she'd never encountered. "It was kind of neat."

"Neat?"

That one word held a wealth of scorn and incredulity. Del lost her temper, too. "I may have done a lot of...eccentric things, but it's my life and I can damn well—"

"What other eccentric things?" he demanded. "What else have you done?"

She heard Dane mutter something, and Alec chuckle in return. Those two seemed to find everything amusing, and this time Del had the distinct impression they were laughing at her, or rather her predicament.

Indignant, she gave them each a look of censure, not that it had any visible effect; Dane winked at her, and Alec continued to smile. *Men,* she thought, and decided to ignore their misplaced humor.

Though her heart hurt and embarrassment threatened, Del stood and walked to her bookcase. She pulled out her first book and addressed the women, while deliberately disregarding the men—Mick especially. "For this story I learned skydiving."

"I've always wanted to try that," Dane admitted.

Despite her resolve to ignore him, Del glanced his way. "I learned how to do it without a chute. Another jumper passed me one in midair."

Mick closed his eyes and groaned. He definitely sounded in pain this time.

"For heaven's sake," Del said, thoroughly exasperated. "I *had* a chute! I just pretended I didn't. And there were plenty of other people jumping with me, trained for that sort of thing. Rescue jumpers were there in case something went wrong. Besides, we practiced a lot first in simulated jumps before I actually did it."

Angel piped up and said, "I remember the villain in that book had to steal a chute off another man. That man almost died, but being the male protagonist, he didn't."

"I never kill the male leads." She looked at Mick. "That would ruin the romance aspect of the books."

He groaned again.

Celia, like a true adventurer at heart, asked, "Did you take a chute off someone else?"

Alec immediately hauled her to his side and wrapped his brawny arm around her shoulders. "Don't even think it," he warned, and he looked deadly serious, his expression fierce. Celia just smiled.

"I didn't want to go that far," Del said, a little distracted. It fascinated her the way Celia and Alec interacted. He looked so savage, so menacing, yet Celia wasn't the least threatened by him. Just the opposite; Celia cuddled closer. "I learned how to put a chute on in the air."

Mick bolted to his feet. He looked ready for a full-fledged rage. The only other time she'd seen him like that was the day of the robbery, when he'd rolled to his feet after being shot, and raced out the door. That day his eyes had been nearly black with rage—as they were now. His jaw had been clenched tight, too—as it was now.

She wasn't quite sure what to make of him.

Lifting her chin, Del pulled another book off the shelf. "In this one, I learned how to navigate through an underwater cave."

"That was the creepiest scene," Celia whispered. "There were sharks and poisonous snakes. It gave me nightmares." Then she added, "It was also my favorite book."

Del went to her desk, pulled out a pen and signed both books. She handed one to Celia and one to Angel. "Here, a gift."

Celia clutched the book to her chest. For a long moment she was speechless, then she blurted, "Thank you!"

Angel looked amazed. "You don't have to do this."

Del shrugged. "I get some copies for my own use." She hoped to change the subject so Mick would quit scowling. It didn't work.

Attempting a relationship was hard work. Now she remembered why she'd never much bothered. Of course, that was before Mick, with guys who were easy to dismiss.

She couldn't dismiss Mick.

Angel scooted to the edge of her seat. "Where do you get your ideas?"

She'd been waiting for that question; without fail, it always got asked. She smiled, then for almost half an hour answered questions and explained about her work and laughed and had fun. Mick didn't appreciate hearing about her research techniques, but the women, especially Celia, hung on her every word.

When Del admitted that she had a looming deadline and intended to put in a few hours of writing that night, Alec pushed to his feet. "We need to be heading home. It's getting late and Celia—" he gave his wife a cautious look "—is getting ideas."

Dane also stood, saying in an aside to Del, "Alec is a worrier."

Del looked at the big dark Alec, towering protectively over his petite blond wife. He looked like a marauder, not a worrier. "If you say so."

Angel leaned against Dane and sighed. "We'll let you get to your work."

Del blushed. "I didn't mean to run everyone off."

"Not at all. Dinner was wonderful and the company was

even better. But the kids will be getting antsy at their grand-
mother's."

"You have children?"

"We have two," Angel told her. "Grayson, who's twelve,
and Kara just turned ten."

"Our Tucker is nine now," Celia said, "and looks just like
his daddy."

Alec's frown lifted into a smile of pride. "The kids would
love to meet you, Delilah."

Mick forestalled Del's reply by saying, "I'll tell you all about
them tonight."

Del seemed to be the only person who heard his lingering
undertone of annoyance.

Angel bent a fond look on Mick. "He does love talking
about the kids, so prepare yourself."

"That's because they worship him," Dane added. "It's almost nauseating how they fawn all over him. Especially Kara.
The boys aren't quite as bad as she is. But as you probably noticed with Zack's daughter, females love Mick."

Angel elbowed Dane hard, which made him grin and kiss
her mouth. Del had already noticed what an affectionate bunch
they were, always touching and teasing and kissing.

Mick obviously loved these people, and they loved him, but
now, rather than making her feel excluded, the sight of them
all together touched her heart and made her yearn for things
she'd never considered before. They were wonderful people.

At the moment, though, Mick was busy throwing them
all out.

Del watched as Mick herded everyone toward the door. She
had the distinct feeling he wanted privacy so he could yell at
her. Not that she'd let him. No one had yelled at her since she
was a little girl, and she wasn't about to let Mick start now.

Celia surprised her by giving her a hug and telling her she'd cherish the book. Del felt a little silly. It was only a book, but she enjoyed Celia's enthusiasm.

Angel followed suit and hugged Del, too, whispering in her ear, "It's so nice to see Mick confused by a woman." She leaned back and grinned. "Thank you for taking such good care of him."

"My pleasure."

Angel's mouth quirked. "I can see that it is."

Mick stood at the door until everyone had gone. Del didn't wait around for him to start complaining or questioning her. She gathered up the coffee cups and carried them to the kitchen.

He stepped up close behind her. "Delilah."

She could feel the tension emanating off him in waves. It made her tense, too. "Call me Del."

Her hands shook. She refused to turn and face him, choosing instead to rinse out the cups and put them in the dishwasher.

He ignored her order. "Why," he asked in a barely audible growl, "do you do all this crazy stuff?"

"You mean like bringing strange men home to my place? I was just wondering the same thing."

She'd meant to distract him from his grievances, but her ploy didn't work.

"Hell, yes, that's part of it. Don't you have any sense of self-preservation at all?"

She tightened her hands on the edge of the counter. "I learn what I need to know and I don't take unnecessary risks."

He stepped closer, crowding her against the sink. His anger was there, pulsing between them. But there was something else, something more. Her skin prickled with awareness as she felt his erection nestle against her bottom. Her breath caught.

"Tell me why you do it, babe."

She swallowed hard. "The media claims I do it because I like writing about heroes, about guys who can win against all odds, solve twisted mysteries and get the bad guy every time. They psychoanalyze that I'm setting myself up as a heroine."

"Are you?"

"No." It was difficult to think with him so close, and so aroused. "My parents say I've always been too creative and too frenetic. I'm not content to sit idle."

His hot breath touched the side of her throat as he spoke. "I can see that." He nuzzled her, making the fine hairs on her nape tingle, her breasts swell. "You've got more energy than any woman I've ever met. And you don't think about things, you just act."

"You're...you're complaining?" His words sounded disgruntled, but his touch was so gentle, so exciting.

His good arm came around her waist and squeezed her. "The things you've claimed to do are insane, Delilah."

"Look who's talking! A man who deliberately takes a bullet in the back." She forced enough room between them so that she could turn and face him. Her hand trembled from a mix of anger and excitement as she reached up and touched his jaw. "What if that bullet had hit something vital? A lung or your heart or your spine? You could have been killed."

"I'm trained to react."

She snorted at that bit of idiocy. "They don't train you to get shot, do they? I thought PIs did sleuthing, not gunplay."

He looked away from her gaze and focused instead on her mouth. "We do what we have to do."

"And that includes nearly getting killed for a stranger? At least I take every precaution when I do my research."

His eyes, when they met hers again, were so dark, so intense that Del felt consumed by him. "I couldn't bear the thought of that bullet hurting your soft skin," he whispered. He leaned lower and kissed her, tiny biting kisses from her throat to her ear, to where her neck met her shoulder.

Del shivered, then forced herself back in control. "I can't change who I am, Mick. This is what I do, what I enjoy doing."

He pressed his face into her throat and simply held her. It was a tender, possessive embrace and made her heart rap hard. "Not since before Angel married Dane have I felt the need to protect someone."

She slipped her fingers through his silky hair, over his neck and the hard joint of his shoulder. "I don't need you to protect me," she assured him softly. Then, touching the bulky bandage on his back, she added, "I don't even want you to try to protect me. Especially not when you get hurt in the bargain."

His head lifted and he stared at her hard. "*Tough*. We've forged a bond, you and I, whether you like it or not." He tangled his hand in her hair and tipped her head back. "You *did* take me in, not just into your home but into your bed. If you didn't mean it, you shouldn't have started it."

"Mean it?" She found it hard to breathe with him watching her so intently, as if he could see her soul. "What... what does that mean?"

"It means you're mine now."

He continued to study her, probably waiting for her to refute his claim, but Del had no intention of doing so. No one had ever wanted to protect her. No one had ever wanted to claim her.

She swallowed. "I was going to clean the kitchen—"

"Leave it," Mick ordered.

"—but I'd rather go to bed with you."

His jaw hardened and his pupils flared. He caught the back of her head and drew her up for his kiss. He tasted so good, and she leaned into him until she heard him groan.

"Mick…" Very gently, she pushed him back. "You should take your medicine."

"Not this time, sweetheart."

"Your shoulder—"

"Will be fine. I promise." He took her hand and started toward the bedroom.

Del admitted to herself that she wanted to let him have his way. Never in her life had she felt so hungry for a man. Never had a man been so hungry for her.

The bedroom door closed behind them and Mick leaned against it. "In the morning," he said, "we're going to talk. Without distractions."

Del had no problem with that plan. "You'll tell me more about the kids and how you and Angel met and about your background?"

There was only a slight hesitation before he nodded. "All right."

"I'm curious about you, Mick."

His gaze moved over her, hot and anxious. "We haven't had much time for talking, but we'll catch up. For now…"

"For now, I want what you want."

He pushed away from the door, his smile slow and lazy. Hot.

"As long as you don't hurt yourself," she qualified.

Mick again caught the back of her neck and lifted her to her tiptoes. Against her mouth he said, "You can help me out by taking your clothes off."

She smiled. "And yours, too?"

"God, yes."

Mick knew he should have put off the lovemaking in favor of getting a few things straightened out, but he seemed to have little control around her. That in itself was a worry. He was used to an icy indifference in most situations, an iron discipline that never wavered.

Especially where women were concerned.

Too many things didn't add up, and now that he understood the lengths she went to for research—his blood nearly froze every time he thought of it—new questions were beginning to surface about the robbery. He couldn't let lust make him lose sight of the possibilities.

She kicked out of her sandals while unbuttoning her blouse, and his discipline shattered. She didn't undress slowly to tease him. Rather she tore her clothes off as if she felt the same burning urgency as he.

Mick braced his feet apart to keep himself steady while she stripped bare. Her frenzy fired his own.

Tomorrow they would talk. But tonight, he'd make her his in every way.

CHAPTER SEVEN

In no time, Delilah stood before him wearing only a lacy bra and skimpy panties. He was so hard he hurt. He could feel the hot pulse of blood through his veins, the heavy, rhythmic beating of his heart.

Slowly, savoring the moment, Mick walked to her. With just his fingertips he touched one taut nipple straining against her bra. "Don't move," he whispered, and bent to take her in his mouth.

Her moan was raw and real and satisfying. Mick took his time, suckling her, teasing with the tip of his tongue, the edge of his teeth. He felt the heat rising from her slim body, her restless movements, her heavy hot breath.

"Mick, please." Against his instructions, she tangled her fingers in his hair and tugged. He straightened and began working his own buttons loose.

He held her gaze as he asked, "Are you wet for me right now, Delilah?"

Her pupils dilated, she shook her head. "I don't know."

"Check for me."

Her lips parted. "But…"

"Put your fingers between your legs," he urged, "and tell me what you feel."

Her pulse thrummed wildly in her throat. She swallowed hard, her gaze locked with his, and when her hand moved between her thighs, Mick had to bite back a groan. He locked his knees against the wash of raging lust.

"I...I'm swollen. And hot."

Triumph exploded through him. "And?"

Trembling, she whispered, "And wet."

He cursed low. The damn shirt pulled at his shoulder as he tried to wrest it off. Delilah stepped up to him, her entire body quivering. "Let me."

With gentle hands she eased the shirt from him, then went to her knees to work on his jeans. *Not this time,* he told himself, seeing her on her knees, knowing how ready she was for him.

He let her get his jeans unsnapped and unzipped, then he stepped away. "Stand up, Delilah."

"But—"

"It's your turn tonight, remember?"

Staring at his erection, she licked her lips with blatant insinuation and said, "I know."

Mick laughed, a harsh, hoarse sound. She looked as if she wanted to make a feast of him, and that nearly cost him his control. "You are such a tease." Then, with more command in his tone, he said, "I want you to finish stripping, then sit in the chair."

Startled, she cautiously stood and looked over her shoulder. The chair was piled with clothes, positioned in front of the window. Her bewildered gaze met his. "The chair?"

"That's right." He looked at her breasts, straining against the lace. "Take off your bra. I want to see your nipples."

She glanced again at that straight-backed, hard-seated chair. A shiver ran through her before she reached behind herself to unhook her bra. The position thrust her breasts out more. Mick hardened his resolve, doing his best to remain unaffected by the luscious sight of her. Looking at him, Delilah dropped the bra. Her breasts rose and fell with her accelerated breathing.

"Now the panties," he said, feeling sweat dampen his back and shoulders. His hands shook with the need to touch her, but instead he went to the chair and removed the clothes, dropping them onto the floor. He turned to face Delilah—and she was breathtakingly naked.

As if she was overwhelmed, her head hung slightly forward, her hair shielding her expression. Her long legs were pressed together, her knees locked. Her hands flexed, opening and closing in small, nervous movements.

Mick was caught between wanting to stand there and look at her forever, and needing to be inside her now, this very instant.

Her nipples had flushed a dark rose, puckered tight. The black curls between her thighs looked silky, shielding her secrets.

"Don't be shy with me, Delilah."

Her head lifted, their gazes clashed. "I want to throw you down on the carpet. I want to strip your jeans off you and taste you again." She licked her lips, panting. "I don't understand it, but I'm not shy with you at all. I just want you. A lot."

Mick held out his hand. "Then come here. Let me help you."

She strode to him, her small breasts jiggling, her silky dark hair swaying. He caught her and held her away, but tipped up her chin so that she looked at him. "I want you to sit in that chair and let me pleasure you."

She blinked hard and a slightly worried frown pulled at her brow. "Couldn't we just—"

"No." Mick moved her to the chair and urged her onto the hard seat. He smiled at the way she sat so straight and proper, her spine erect, her knees together and her hands in her lap. But not for long.

Going down on one knee, he sat back on his haunches. "Open your legs as wide as you can, Delilah."

Her shoulders stiffened and color rushed into her face. "What are you going to do?" she asked, both breathless and excited.

"I'm going to kiss you." He glanced at her face, then back to her sex. "Here." Pressing his fingers between her thighs, he cupped her in his warm palm and felt her spontaneous jerk. Though she was tense, her breathing suspended, he could feel her, soft and wet, just as she'd said.

Shifting slightly, he stroked her, his fingertips opening her more, touching her distended clitoris. "Relax for me," he murmured.

Instinctively, she curled forward before catching herself and, with some effort, leaned back in the chair. She took several deep breaths, and her thighs went limp, yielding to him as he pressed her legs wide. "Scoot to the edge of the seat."

Her head tipped back and her eyes closed. He saw her throat move as she swallowed audibly. "Mick, I feel... exposed."

"You are exposed," he whispered, watching as she slid forward in a delectable sprawl. "I wish I had two good arms right now so I could touch you everywhere."

Her eyes snapped open. "You're not hurting, are you?"

"Shh. I'm fine." He moved between her thighs and leaned forward to kiss her mouth, taking his time, enjoying her while he breathed in the spicy scent of her arousal. She curled her fingers around his upper arms and held on, making no move to push him away.

He could feel her impatience and drove her as far as he could, wanting her to remember this night forever. When she couldn't stop squirming beneath him, he cuddled her breast in his left hand. He wanted to hold both breasts, but his right arm and shoulder felt numb with pain.

He teased her nipple, stroking with his thumb and carefully tugging until her back arched. "Give me your other breast."

Her eyes slowly opened. "What?"

"I want you in my mouth."

Understanding dawned and her look turned equally hot and gentle. She cupped her breast and raised it high. At the same time her other hand went to the back of his head and brought him forward.

At the sight of her offering herself so sweetly, Mick growled. He kissed her softly at first, plucking with his lips, lapping with his tongue. She moaned, pressing herself into him, and he suckled greedily, unable to get enough of her taste, her incredible scent. Delilah moaned and writhed and managed to raise herself enough to rub against the fly of his jeans.

Mick cursed the injury that kept him from taking her in all the ways he wanted.

"Mick!" She cried out, straining against him.

It was too much. He moved back and opened her legs even more. Her pink flesh glistened, wet and ready, and he leaned forward to taste her deeply, his left hand curving around her bottom and holding her still.

Delilah raised her hands and covered her own breasts, crying, moving with his mouth. He loved the taste of her, so hot and sweet. He pressed his tongue into her, slow and deep, then stabbed with quick motions, swirled and licked and teased, and when he knew she was near, when he felt the tremors going through her slender thighs, her belly, he caught her clitoris and drew on her gently.

Her contractions were so strong she nearly escaped him. Fingers biting deep into her soft ass, he held her close and did his best to block the pain of his injury, enhanced by her thrashing.

With one long, last, shuddering moan, she stilled. Her breathing remained ragged, loud, and she seemed boneless in the narrow chair, her long limbs sprawled for him, around him. Her hands dropped to her sides.

Shaken, Mick put his good arm behind her and rested his face on her belly. Though he stayed perfectly still, which eased his physical aches, his mind still reeled and his emotions rioted.

Damn, he thought. This level of connection was more than he'd expected, more than he'd even known existed.

It scared him spitless, because he wasn't a hundred percent sure he could trust in it, in her. He just knew he wanted her now, and he couldn't bear the thought of any other man with her like this.

His arm tightened and he forced himself to say lightly, "You okay, sweetheart?"

"Maybe."

He raised up to smile at her. "The taste of you is enough to make me insane."

Her eyes remained closed, but she smiled. She took several deep breaths to calm her racing heart and said, "Know what I'm thinking?"

He lightly kissed her belly button, then nuzzled the soft skin of her stomach. "Vague, soft, happy thoughts, I hope."

"I'm thinking I want you inside me."

Mick clenched his jaw. He wanted to be inside her, but he didn't see how he could. Much as he hated to admit it, he wasn't invincible. His arm hurt like a son of a bitch, more so with every breath.

Her position in the chair had taken a lot of the physical

stress off his arm and shoulder, but her soft moans had caused his muscles to tighten, to flex, and now his pain felt very real.

Delilah sat up. She cupped his face in her hands and said, "Did I tell you I took riding lessons?"

His shoulder screamed a warning, but his erection was more than willing to listen. "On a wild stallion, no doubt?"

Her smile was still softened by her climax. "No. As a little girl, my parents gave me riding lessons. C'mon." She pushed at him gently until he moved back and gave her room to stand. She reached a hand down to him, and with a laugh, Mick came to his feet.

"First," she said, "a pain pill for you. And no arguing. I promise to make it worth your while."

Mick pulled her up short. "You don't have to do this, sweetheart."

"But I want to." Her expression clearly showed her confusion. "I'm not doing you a favor by making love to you. What you just did…it was so wonderful. I had no idea."

Mick wanted to know which part had surprised her, but he kept quiet.

"The only thing is that now I feel empty." She flattened her hands on his chest and stared up at him. "I meant it when I said I want you inside me."

Holding her gaze, he slid his hand down her belly. "My fingers would probably do," he said, and matching actions to words, he pressed two fingers deep inside her.

"Oh, God." Still sensitive from her climax, she dropped her head forward and curled her hands, clutching at him. They both breathed hard. "That's…that's wonderful," she whispered, delighting him with her honesty, her openness.

Her hand moved down his body and curled around his hard-on.

Mick had to fight to keep from coming the second she

touched him. He felt primed to the max, and her hand was so soft and feminine. "Delilah," he warned, closing both hands around her shoulders.

"This," she whispered in a sultry voice that coasted over him like rough velvet, "will feel even better."

He had to laugh, though it sounded more like an agonized groan.

She released him, patted his butt and said, "Now quit trying to distract me." Taking his hand again, she led him toward the kitchen, where she kept the pain pills. "I have the feeling you like to control everyone and everything, but I've been on my own too long for that nonsense."

She wasn't looking at him, so it felt safe to smile. She was the most endearing woman he'd ever met.

Her insight was also uncanny. It was true he liked to have control, but more than that was the fact he wanted to take care of her, protect her. He'd never even come close to feeling that with any woman other than Angel, and then it had been a clear-cut feeling. They'd both been going through bad times and had quickly learned to trust each other, to help each other. They were friends and there'd been no confusing possessiveness or lust or this irrational need to make her a part of him, to somehow meld her body and soul with his own.

He loved Angel, just as he loved Dane and their children, and by extension Alec and Celia and Tucker. He'd protect any one of them with his life, but that instinct had never been put to the test. Dane and Alec were more than capable of taking care of their own, so Mick's sense of protectiveness was blunted by their presence.

Not so with Delilah. There was nothing and no one to soften the raw edge of volatile emotions consuming him.

He knew it was too much, too strong and overwhelming.

It put him at risk, a risk he'd never faced before because he'd never met a woman who hit him so hard on a gut level.

He had absolutely no idea how to deal with her.

She stopped beside the kitchen counter, unmindful of her nudity, although Mick relished the sight of her under the bright fluorescent lights. While she filled a glass with water, he looked her over. Her shiny dark hair was mussed, half hanging over her brow, framing those incredible, bright blue eyes. Her lips were still slightly reddened from her climax, her cheeks still flushed.

Her nipples still tight.

He sucked in a breath and accepted the pill she handed him, tossing it back and washing it down with the entire glass of cold water. Delilah stepped behind him and peered at his shoulder.

"I think we should change the bandage."

He didn't want her taking care of him, and turned to face her. "It's fine."

She propped her hands on her slim hips and frowned up at him. He'd never had a naked woman remonstrate with him before. It put a new slant on things.

"I'm changing your bandage, Mick." When he started to speak, she interrupted, saying, "It's early yet and I have a feeling you won't be falling asleep despite the pain pill."

"God, I hope not." He still smarted over the fact that he'd fallen asleep on her earlier.

"Then that means, being as you're so determined and you refuse to listen to common sense or a doctor's orders, we'll be making love for some time yet. You need to be comfortable and relaxed so that you don't hurt yourself."

He gave her a lazy smile, eyeing the glossy dark curls over her mound and the long length of her legs, now braced apart as if for battle. "Relaxed, huh? You think your lovemaking is so boring I'll be able to just sit back and yawn?"

Her eyes got heavy, her smile wicked. "I think you need to let me handle things. It'll be a novel experience for you. I'll be gentle...but thorough. I promise."

He must be getting used to her, Mick thought, because her boldness didn't shock him at all, it just fired his lust. He shook his head, but heard himself say, "All right."

Her soft smile broke into a triumphant grin and she turned, giving him a view of her saucy behind as she marched away. Crooking one finger, she called back to him, "Come along, now. I'll see to everything."

He was in so deep he could barely breathe, and strangely enough, he didn't give a damn. Everything would work out, he'd see to it.

Later.

Del couldn't remember ever having so much fun. Mick was astounding, giving over to her and trusting her. At least as far as his body was concerned. His thoughts were still a secret, but she understood that. Her life wasn't one she openly discussed, either. Not that it had been bad, only that it had been different, and not many people understood her or her choices.

At the moment, she had Mick stretched out on his back, a pillow cushioning his head, his shoulder freshly bandaged. Together they had showered, touching and teasing anew, then taking turns drying each other. While she'd brushed her teeth, he'd commented on her body, complimenting her in the most outrageous ways.

She returned the favor, savoring the sight of him naked at her sink, his razor and aftershave there as if they'd always been a part of her home, as if they, as well as he, belonged with her.

He had an incredible physique, tall and strong and wholly

masculine. While he brushed his teeth with amazing dexterity, considering he used his left hand, she watched the play of muscles in his shoulders and biceps. Still damp from the shower, his dark hair clung in curls to his nape and temples. Her blood raced at the beauty of him.

There wasn't a single flaw to his body—except for that obscene bullet wound.

Her heart nearly broke at the sight of it, and without thinking, she'd moved to kiss him above and below his stitches, where dark bruises marred his olive skin.

His groan, one of mingled awareness and physical pleasure, encouraged her. He'd braced his hands on the sink and allowed her to do as she pleased—and she pleased quite a bit.

After that, she'd spent a good fifteen minutes just touching him, caressing his aching muscles and hopefully massaging away some of the pain and stiffness from the injury.

Even with his head dropped forward and his body totally relaxed, Mick still looked so powerful, so strong and capable. It made her stomach jumpy to know he wanted *her,* desired *her.*

Had nearly died for her.

He grew impatient with the subtle touches and teased, "Is it your plan to taunt me all night? Because I'm a hair away from taking control again."

She laughed at him, then squealed as he hurried her to the bed. She had to regain the upper hand so he didn't do more damage to his injury, and it took her several minutes to convince him that she needed to wrap his shoulder again.

He'd finally given in, but only because she let him touch her anywhere he wanted while she saw to that chore. It was apparent that, even though she lacked his physical beauty, Mick felt the same fascination for her body that she felt for his.

Now he reclined in her bed, his eyes dark and hot, watching her as she leaned over to the nightstand and withdrew a condom.

"I hate to sound unsophisticated," she said, "but I've never put a rubber on a guy before. Tell me if I do it wrong."

He didn't reply, merely watched her as she tore the small package open and reached for him. She felt the subtle clenching of his muscles, the heat rising off him in waves. She glanced at his jaw and found it locked hard.

"Like this, right?" she asked, knowing she was pushing him, and enjoying it.

"Good enough," he growled, and his abdomen tensed as she slid the condom over the head of his penis and then midway down its length.

Del surveyed her handiwork. "Not bad," she announced, trying to drag out the anticipation as long as she could. It wasn't easy; already her hands were shaking and a weakness seemed to have invaded her bones. Mick was thick and hot and silky in her hand.

"I've always been really careful," she whispered, trying to regain lost control, "about protection. Not that I'd mind having children someday, but not until I meet the right man."

His body taut and expectant, Mick rasped, "I want kids someday, too."

Del soothed him, stroking his right arm, his chest and shoulders. She met his smoldering gaze and asked, "With the right woman?"

"Yes."

Sliding her leg over his hips, she positioned herself. "Well, this woman is going to make you crazy with pleasure tonight."

His back arched. "I'll get my turn," he told her.

She laughed. "Not until the doctor says you're able." Slowly, so slowly every nerve ending sparked, she lowered herself. He'd barely penetrated at all, just the thick head of his penis inside her, her inner muscles gripping and quivering around him, when she stopped with a gasp. "It's…it's been so long for me," she muttered, trying to explain, her words broken and breathless and fast. Already she felt stretched, uncomfortably tight, yet tantalized. "I'm…I'm not at all sure."

Mick strained beneath her, sweat dampening his forehead, his chest. Delilah knew she couldn't wait any longer or he'd hurt himself. Swallowing back her own discomfort and uncertainty, she braced her hands on his chest, drew a deep breath and pressed down until he was fully, completely inside her.

An explosive curse broke from Mick. She whimpered in response. For long moments, neither of them moved except for a slight trembling of rigid muscles and a spontaneous flexing of sexes as they each struggled to adjust.

Forcing her head up, Delilah looked at Mick through a sweltering haze of sensations. "Are you…all right?"

"No." His left hand lifted, spread wide over her hip. "I need you to move, baby."

Del licked her lips. "It's just that you're…bigger than I thought."

Without his permission, his hips rose, pressing into her, deepening his penetration. "I can't do this," he groaned.

And Delilah's heart tumbled over.

"Mick." Leaning down, she kissed his mouth, his throat, licked at his salty skin. Very gently, subtly, she rocked her hips. His fingers contracted on her flesh, biting hard as he urged her to continue.

She slid up, her wetness making it easy and smooth, then all the way down again, harder and faster with each turn. Suddenly, despite his injury, Mick gripped her hips in both hands and pumped into her, holding her tight to him, not letting her retreat. He looked feral and explosive and so sexy she felt her own climax begin.

This was what she'd wanted, him filling her, his body a part of hers, wild and real with no reserve between them. She tipped her head back and cried out her pleasure, then heard Mick's answering moan of completion.

A few seconds later his fingers went lax and she lowered herself to nestle against him. He grunted, and she mumbled, "Did I hurt you?"

It took him a little while to answer, but she didn't mind. She felt the bellowing of his chest beneath her ear, felt his sex still deep within her. "Mick?"

Using his left hand, he smoothed her bottom. "I'm feeling no pain. Even my brain is numb."

She didn't want to, but she raised herself to her elbows. "Will it hurt you if I sleep here with you?"

His dark eyes opened. "It'd kill me," he said huskily, "if you didn't."

Tears clung to her lashes. She hurried to blink them away and sat up more. After a deep, calming breath that helped to chase away the excess emotion, she said, "I'm ready for bed. You?"

The way he looked at her told her she hadn't fooled him one bit. He knew she was mired in sentiment, that making love with him had thrown her for a loop. She'd had sex in the past, but this wasn't sex. This was… She wasn't sure what to call it. Sex had been easy to give up, but she couldn't imagine giving up Mick.

More tears clouded her vision, but he didn't seem to mind. In fact, he looked…satisfied.

Del snorted at herself as she swiped at her eyes. He'd come, so of course he was satisfied. "I'll just get rid of the condom and turn on the air conditioner and—"

Mick moved out of her reach. "I can take care of myself,

thank you, and I'll set the air conditioner. I'd like to wake up without hypothermia."

"I set it too cold?" She watched him climb from the bed, and was gratified to see he shook just a bit, too.

He stood in front of her and touched her chin. There was a silly smile on his face, in contrast to the male triumph in his dark gaze. "Yeah. You set it too cold," he agreed. "I'm a man, not a polar bear."

Then he went down the hall to the bathroom. Del stood there, bemused, until she heard the water turn off and the toilet flush.

She rushed to straighten the bedclothes and reposition Mick's pillow. She'd sleep on his left side, to keep from injuring his shoulder, she decided.

He walked into her room, as comfortable with his nudity as she was. After setting the air conditioner a tiny bit higher, he got into bed as if sleeping with her were nothing. She wasn't sure if she liked that or not, considering it seemed like a very big something to her. But then he turned off the light and settled back, and when she crawled in next to him, he put his arm around her, drawing her close. The darkness added a new level of intimacy, filling her with contentment.

Her mind peaceful, her body sated, she kissed his chest and asked, "Will you tell me if you get uncomfortable during the night?"

"No." She pushed up to frown at him, but he only laughed and pressed her face back to his chest. "Shh. Go to sleep, Delilah. You've worn me out and I need to recoup so I can get even tomorrow morning."

Feeling smug, she said, "You'll have to wait to even the score. I have to go out in the morning."

His arm tightened. "Where to?"

"Neddie's funeral is tomorrow."

"Neddie?"

Because she'd already told Mick all about him, she sighed. "Neddie Moran, the man who helped me with my research."

A volatile silence followed her statement, then seemed to detonate. Mick turned, pinning her beneath him in one hard, fast movement, his expression furious. "Neddie *Moran* is the criminal who taught you how to steal cars?"

Watching him warily, she said, "Yeah, so?" He'd sounded ready to fall asleep one moment, then outraged the next. "Mick, you're going to hurt your arm."

For some reason, he looked astounded that she would even mention his arm. He jerked around and flipped the light back on. "Forget the morning. We've got to do some talking right now."

"We do?" Del scooted up in the bed and pulled the sheet over her breasts.

"Damn right we do. Do you know how Neddie Moran died?"

"He drowned."

"He didn't just drown. Someone else drowned him." Mick drew a breath. "Sweetheart, he was murdered."

CHAPTER EIGHT

Mick awoke to an empty bed. Again.

This time, in light of everything he now knew, fear hit him before anything else. He glanced at the bedside clock. Three-thirty. They'd finished their talk almost four hours ago. Where the hell was she in the middle of the night?

He was out of the bed and heading for the door on silent feet before he'd even given himself time to think about it. The reality of her association with known criminals had his skin prickling with unease, his every sense on alert.

She saw no connection between Neddie's recent death and her own very near escape from death.

Mick, however, was positive that the two events were in some way related. She'd associated with Moran, formed a strange friendship even, and now the man was dead. It had been tricky, telling her what he knew of Moran's death without telling her how he knew, or giving away confidential information. The death was still under investigation, but thanks to reporters, it was public knowledge that Neddie had been drowned in the river, so Mick had no problem sharing those details.

Not that they'd swayed her. The most he'd been able to

get out of her was a promise that she'd let him escort her to the funeral. Mick planned to avoid even that, using a deception to keep her away, while he had men checking into any possible associations between Neddie and the robbers at the jewelry store. He didn't like himself for it, but he felt it necessary to protect her.

Hours of talking to her had proved that reason and logic wouldn't work. Not with Delilah Piper, and definitely not when she felt an obligation to a friend.

Mick went only a few steps down the hallway before he saw the dim blue light of her computer shining in the otherwise dark apartment. He heard the light tapping of her fingers on the keyboard, and peered around the hallway corner.

Sitting there in front of her computer, her glossy hair mussed, a T-shirt her only clothing, Delilah looked totally absorbed in her writing. Mick leaned against the wall and watched her, aware of a strange twisting in his heart.

Never had he allowed himself to consider hearth and home and a family of his own. He'd become so discriminating with women, so particular, that he'd doubted any woman would have ever appealed to him on that level.

But standing in a dark hallway looking at Delilah, he felt a contentment unlike anything he'd ever known. She was a woman of constant change and contradictions. She made him hot with her careless, comfortable air, and she kept his emotions turbulent with her daring and her stubbornness. And now that he'd laughed and argued and made love with her, he couldn't imagine not having her in his life.

Insane, he insisted to himself. But his pulse continued to riot and his lungs constricted, and only a small part of that reaction was due to lust. Hell, he shouldn't even have felt lust. It hadn't been that long since she'd wrung him out.

But he looked down at himself and, sure enough, he was already semihard. What could you do with a woman who affected you so strongly, except keep her close and make sure she didn't have the chance to affect any other man the same way?

Delilah paused, bit her lip, stared at nothing in particular and then smiled and began typing again. Mick shook his head. She amazed him, amused him, and she turned his libido red-hot.

Not wanting to startle her, he said softly, "Am I interrupting?"

She glanced up, then held one finger in the air, indicating she needed him to wait.

He should have been annoyed. They'd finished making love for the first time and she'd sneaked away to write, and now had the gall to make him wait. He smiled. No woman had ever treated him as she did, and damned if he didn't like it. Probably because her reactions, her responses, were all so real. Delilah didn't have a deceptive bone in her body. She said what she thought, did as she pleased, and that meant she could be trusted—the most appealing factor of all.

Mick sidled closer and stood behind her. He moved her heavy hair off her nape and used his thumbs to stroke her.

Delilah froze, then twisted to face him. "Um…I can't write with you there."

"Why not?"

She frowned, then turned off her monitor. Shadows closed in around them. "It makes me jittery for anyone to look over my shoulder. I don't want you to read anything out of context and think it's lame."

"I wasn't reading," he explained, still holding her neck easily between his hands. "I was considering the possibility of dragging you back to bed."

Delilah faced the computer again, her hands in her lap, her head bent forward. Finally she said, "I'm running behind, Mick. I need to finish up this scene, okay?"

"It's almost morning."

"I know. But the scene is there now, in my head." She twisted again, this time in a rush. "I'm sorry. I know this probably seems odd to you. But writers write…whenever. And I do have a deadline that is quickly closing in." She shrugged. "I've never had anyone live with me, so I've never had to not write when I wanted to. Know what I mean?"

Mick grinned. She meant that she didn't want him to interfere with her writing, but was trying to be tactful. He said only, "How long do you think you'll be?"

Again she shrugged. "I don't know. As long as the words are coming, I want to keep at it. Once this scene's done, I'll have some free time before I need to start the next one."

A thought occurred to Mick: if she stayed up all night writing, perhaps she'd forget about the damn funeral, and he wouldn't have to deceive her. "Okay, sweetheart. You take your time, okay?"

"You don't mind?"

"Of course not. There'll be times when I'll be gone all night working." Even in the dim shadows, he saw her scowl and had to fight from laughing out loud. "I'm sure you'll be understanding, too, won't you?" he teased.

Very grudgingly, she muttered, "I guess."

"Then I'll see you in the morning."

She continued to stare up at him. "Since you're here anyway, will you give me a good-night kiss?"

"My pleasure." Mick made it a kiss to singe her eyebrows—and felt himself burned instead. In that moment, he wondered if he'd ever get enough, if a lifetime of tasting and touching her would ever satisfy him.

He had his doubts.

"Wow," she said when he lifted his mouth. "You think I can work a kiss like that in with a murder scene?"

Mick stared at her blankly and she waved her hand toward the computer. "That's where I'm at in the book. All your talk about Neddie and connections and conspiracies gave me an idea for the murder scene. Do you think my hero would stop in the middle of trying to chase down the escaping madman to kiss the heroine?"

Mick shook his head. "If the heroine was you, I'm sure of it."

He saw the white flash of her teeth, then heard her chuckle. "You're outrageous. Now go on before I totally lose my train of thought and end up with them making love in the middle of the street instead of doing the responsible thing."

Thinking of the "responsible thing," Mick pushed any remnants of guilt from his mind. He'd do whatever was necessary to protect her. "Take as long as you need," he said. "Good night."

As soon as he turned away, he heard the tapping on her keyboard resume. Madmen and making love and responsibility. Somehow they were all tied together with Delilah, and probably with her research pal, Neddie Moran, and the shooter, Rudy Glasgow, and the robbery.

All Mick had to do was find out how.

His mind filled with possibilities, both intimate and protective, so it was no wonder he slept fitfully. He had just awakened again when he felt Delilah slipping into bed beside him. He glanced at the clock and saw that it was only an hour or so until dawn.

Turning toward her, he slid his good arm beneath her head and murmured sleepily, "Did you finish your scene?"

"Yes." She snuggled down, fitting herself to him as if they'd been doing this for most of their lives. That's how it was with Delilah, natural and comfortable and *right*. Her hand settled on his chest, her fingers twining in his body hair, caressing. "I'm sorry I woke you."

"You didn't." Mick pressed his mouth to her crown, drawing in the sweet scent of shampoo and Delilah. "I've been thinking."

"You should have been sleeping."

"I'll sleep with you." He felt her smile against his chest. "What were you doing in the jewelry store, honey?"

Startled, she looked up at him, then with a shrug, nuzzled into his side again. "I was researching."

Their voices were both low, mere whispers over the hum of the air conditioner and the lazily twirling ceiling fan.

"What kind of research?"

Her fingertips sought and found his nipple, toying with him, making him stiffen even while half-asleep. "In this book," she whispered, "the hero has to break into a jewelry store and steal something that the madman is after, before he can get it. So I was trying to see how I'd break into that store if I was a madman."

Mick chuckled. "Neddie couldn't tell you how to do that, huh?"

"He told me a lot of things, gave me a lot of ideas, but not details on a robbery." She pressed her face against Mick in a show of emotion. "I'd contacted him about it, and even left a message, but he hadn't returned my call. I realize now that he probably couldn't."

Shit. If she'd left a message on a machine, then that could be the link that had led them to her. Mick squeezed her closer. No way in hell would he let anyone hurt her. "What exactly did you say on the message?"

"Mick." She rose up on one elbow to look at him. "I do like talking to you in the middle of the night like this, but—"

"Actually, it's morning," he said softly, pushing a curl away from her face.

"That's my point. I really would like to get some sleep."

He chuckled. "No sparing my tender sensibilities, huh?" That made her frown with concern, and he added quickly, "I'm just teasing."

"Are you sure? Because I guess I could stay awake and talk more about this if you really wanted to."

"Actually," he murmured against her mouth, "I was thinking about sports."

She again pushed away, peering at him through the dark with interest. "Are you an athlete?"

Snorting, he said, "Hell, no."

"You don't like sports?"

"I have no idea. I just never played any."

"But all little boys play baseball and football and—"

"I didn't."

She seemed to have forgotten all about sleeping, and her frown was back. "Well, why not?"

He didn't want to talk about his childhood, about his mother's shortcomings. Not now. Preferably not ever. "I was thinking about a sport you taught me."

Despite his best effort, there was an edge to his tone, a deliberately forceful change of subject that she picked up on. She might often be obtuse to her surroundings, but Mick found she was very attuned to him. It unsettled him, and turned him on.

She cupped his jaw in a gesture so tender, his heart ached.

"What," she asked, lightly touching the corner of his mouth, "have I taught you?"

"Riding." He rasped the word, forcing it past an emotional lump in his throat, desperate to change his ache to a physical one, one that she could easily appease.

In the next instant, Delilah kissed him—everywhere. The emotional and the physical commingled, a variety of needs that stirred him on every plane.

After she rolled the condom onto him, she mounted him with a smile and leaned down to kiss his mouth. She slid her body onto his with a snug, wet fit, and whispered wickedly, "Giddyap."

Delilah groaned as she managed to get one eye open. Her entire body ached in places she hadn't known she had. And her butt was cold.

She forced her head up and saw that Mick had kicked the covers to the bottom of the bed. Her front, curled into his side, was warm enough. But her behind faced the air conditioner and was numb with cold.

When she looked Mick over, gloriously naked, she quickly heated. Until she noticed the alarm clock.

"Noon!"

Beside her, Mick groaned and he, too, opened one eye. "What is it?"

"I overslept!"

"Don't worry about it," he mumbled, and tried to draw her close again.

"But Neddie's funeral! I'll never make it now." She couldn't be sure, but Mick looked very satisfied over the situation. Del frowned. "Did you keep me awake all night on purpose?"

Both eyes opened and he stared at her breasts. "Yeah."

"Mick!"

"I'm not into making love with comatose women, so of course I had to keep you awake."

"Oh." She subsided, but only a little. "That wasn't what I meant."

"All I did," he informed her, reaching out to smooth his hand over her hip, then her belly, "was mention riding." He glanced up, his dark eyes unwavering. "You're the one who did the rest."

Because he was right, and because his hand felt too good on her body even now, she flushed. "I feel terrible," she admitted.

Mick cupped his fingers between her legs, fondling, seeking. His voice morning-rough, he crooned, "I think you feel very nice."

She frowned at him and said, "I'm sore, so forget it."

His smile made him look like a pirate. A dark sexy pirate, set on pillaging. "I'll be understanding," he promised, "and run you a nice hot bath. I'll even get the coffee." Then he added deliberately, "But forgetting about it is impossible."

"Mick." She said his name on a sigh.

His tone, his look, turned serious. "You're about all I can think of these days."

She melted. And she wasn't that sore, she decided. But he'd taken her words to heart and slid out of the bed. He stretched, careful of his wounded shoulder, and she sighed yet again at the sight of him. *Much more of this,* she thought, shaking her head, *and I'll begin sounding like a wounded coyote.*

"Since it's already too late to make the funeral, would you like to come with me today?" He looked expectant—and just a bit too watchful.

"Where are you going?" she asked.

"I need to set up something with a therapist for my shoulder."

"I thought the doctor said to give it two weeks first."

Mick shook his head. "I can't wait that long." He flexed his right arm, winced, and added, "I don't like being less than a hundred percent."

He started out of the room and she scurried after him. He detoured into the bathroom, so she had to pull back. Damn, he shouldn't be pushing himself. But how could she stop him? He far outweighed her and had double the stubbornness she possessed.

She waited in the hallway until she heard the bathwater start. She called through the door, "Mick?"

The door opened and he snagged her, pulling her inside. He looped his left arm around her waist, kissed her pursed mouth and said, "You soak while I get coffee. I'll shower when you're done."

"You're supposed to be resting!" she said, trying for a stern expression.

"Making coffee won't tax my meager strength, I promise." He kissed her nose and swatted her on the behind left-handed. "Now, soak."

"Take your medicine!" she yelled to his back.

She was submerged in the hot water, letting it ease her aches and pains, when Mick came in carrying two mugs of steaming coffee. To her disappointment, he'd pulled on jeans, and she frowned at him. "No fair me being naked and you being dressed."

He handed her a cup of coffee. "It's the only way I can guarantee we'll make it out of here today." He grinned and added, "Otherwise I'm likely to join you in the tub. You're a helluva temptation."

She ignored his outrageous compliment and sipped—and moaned with pure, unadulterated pleasure. "Oh, that's good."

"Just what I wanted to hear. I'll take over all the coffee duties."

"You could just show me how to do it."

"I'm not quite that trusting."

Wondering just how trusting he might be, she splashed him. "So you're saying you don't like my coffee, either?"

"I had a hairless chest before drinking it."

Del tried to feign insult, but she ended up laughing instead. "Okay, so I made it stronger for you. I thought all men wanted their coffee strong and black."

He nodded. "So you know a lot of men with iron stomachs, impervious to the cold, fearless and reckless and invincible?"

"No, but that's how I write them," she teased.

Sounding far too serious, he asked, "Is that the kind of man you were looking for?"

Del considered getting serious, too. She considered telling him he was exactly what she'd been looking for, even though she hadn't realized it until she met him. Instead, she shook her head. "I know the difference between reality and fiction, but I don't have much experience with men's preferences. And for the record, I wasn't looking. I didn't really think there was room in my life for a man, not since I've kinda thrown myself into my writing."

Mick put the toilet lid down and sat. "You really enjoy writing, don't you?"

Her need to write wasn't always a pleasant one. "I suppose it's a love-hate relationship. I feel the craving to write almost all the time. Sometimes it's inconvenient. People think I'm dumb because I plot a lot. They consider it daydreaming, and write me off as being too fanciful. But I doubt I'd feel like me if I wasn't writing."

She hesitated, then tilted her head to look at him. "I hope you can understand. There'll be a lot of times when I'm trying to listen, but my mind will go off track. And I get up a lot at night to write. It seems like as soon as I try to sleep, my brain starts churning and I just can't shut down."

"I'll persevere."

"It doesn't mean I'm not aware of you. It doesn't mean you're not important."

"I understand."

His acceptance was just a tad too quick, making her suspicious. "Do you? Not many guys I've dated have."

He gave her a measuring look, then asked, "Have you dated many?"

"Sure. In my younger days, when I was curious about things."

"Things?"

She grinned. "Sexual things, though the sex was never enough to keep me…engaged for long. I outgrew my curiosity and my fascination with men. These days, writing is more interesting, and more important than any guy—especially when I have a deadline, which I almost always do." She thought about that, and added softly, "Of course, those guys weren't as important as you."

Mick looked down at his coffee cup for a long moment. "Because I protected you?"

"Partly," she agreed. "No one has ever tried to protect me before. You blew me away, putting yourself in line for a bullet."

"What about your folks? Surely they're protective."

"I guess." She idly soaped her arm, thinking about her family. "They're wonderful, and they love me, but with two older, more serious brothers, I'm kind of the odd duck."

Mick didn't say anything to that, just continued to encourage her with his silent attention.

"You can imagine how they all reacted when I told them I wanted to be a writer." She laughed, remembering. "They told me to get serious, and when they saw that I *was* serious, they worried. Especially whenever I did research. Now, though, they're really pretty proud."

"Are you close with them?"

"Oh, sure. And my brothers are great. They're both married and have kids and houses. They still worry on occasion, but meeting you would probably fix that."

Mick went still. "Did you want me to meet them?"

She'd rushed things, she realized, and said, "Not yet."

He frowned. "You said I'm different than the other guys you dated."

"Well...yeah. I never invited any of them to move in with me."

"How am I different?"

She shook her head, lost to rational explanations when it came to her response to him. "I don't know. Everything just feels different with you, sort of sharper edged. Better. I hope that doesn't alarm you. I mean, I won't start pushing for more."

Mick set his coffee aside and stripped off his jeans. "What if I push for more?"

Del felt her mouth fall open as he stepped into the tub behind her, forcing her to move up while the water sloshed inside the tub and over the sides. His hairy legs went around her, and he tugged her back into his chest. Against her ear, he whispered, "Delilah?"

"Then…" She swallowed, trying to get her thoughts collected. "Then I guess we'll just take it one step at a time."

He cupped his hand and poured water over her breasts. "Are you still sore?"

Her heart swelled and her stomach curled in anticipation. She leaned back, closed her eyes and whispered breathlessly, "No."

CHAPTER NINE

They settled into a nice routine. Mick didn't want Delilah in his house, where she might see evidence of him being a cop, so he had Josh and Zack alternately bring him more clothes as he needed them. Now her closet was filled with his things.

A dozen times he thought of telling her the truth, of explaining why he'd started the deception in the first place. But he'd only known her a little over a week, and working undercover made him more cautious than not.

Their relationship grew every day. He'd have a chance to tell her everything eventually.

Meeting with his sergeant had been difficult. Mick had set it up so that Angel and Dane would be visiting when Josh came by. They drove out for pickup pizza, and Mick slipped away to meet with the sergeant. He got a new gun, which he hid away, and an update on the robbery—which wasn't promising, since they hadn't discovered anything new.

He'd eventually have to see the shrink, as policy dictated anytime a shooting occurred. But under the circumstances, the sergeant was willing to give him more time for that.

Though he could have driven himself, Mick claimed soreness to keep Delilah with him when he went to physical ther-

LORI FOSTER

apy. She took her laptop and wrote in the waiting room while he went through a series of increasingly difficult exercises meant to bring him back to full strength. It was slow going, and frustrating, to say the least, but he knew it wouldn't be much longer before he could make love to her as he wanted to, without concern for his injury.

Often he woke at night to an empty bed, and he'd hear her in the other room, tapping away at her keyboard. Rather than go back to sleep, he usually waited for her, and they'd make love when she crawled back in beside him.

Her unusual routine suited him just fine.

There didn't seem to be any dwindling of the devastating chemistry between them, but little by little they were both less alarmed by it, and now they wallowed in the near-violent sensations. Delilah proved inventive and curious, and she had no shyness with his body, taking everything she wanted and giving back as much in return.

Ten days had passed before his sergeant called and told him Rudy Glasgow was finally awake and coherent and ready to talk. But strangely enough, he only wanted to talk to Mick. He'd actually awakened from his coma a few days earlier, but had remained stubbornly silent and still too weak to leave the hospital. There'd been no sign of the other men, but Mick wasn't giving up, and neither was the police department.

His sergeant told him to give Detective Faradon, the lead investigator for the case, a call. Mick peeked in at Delilah, saw she was totally engrossed in her story, and punched in the numbers.

He spoke briefly with Faradon before requesting that the detective use Delilah's number only for emergencies. "Anytime you need to get in touch with me, just call my place and leave a message. I'll check the calls often."

"Running a secret life?" Faradon asked.

Mick ground his teeth together. He didn't want Faradon to know that he was still keeping secrets from Delilah. "I don't want her to overhear anything," he said as an excuse. "It could taint the case if she learned of anything important."

"Just telling you is risky," Faradon agreed. "We're only keeping you informed because you were shot, which makes you damned involved, from where I sit."

"Thanks." Mick rubbed the back of his neck. "I'm glad you understand. So, you got a pen handy?" He recited his home number to Faradon, then they briefly discussed the condition of the man in the hospital before hanging up.

Now all Mick needed was an excuse to get away from Delilah. He didn't want her to know that he'd be talking with Rudy Glasgow, yet he'd made such an issue of going nowhere without her, she was bound to be suspicious if he tried to leave on his own now.

As usual, she sat at her computer working when he finished making lunch and approached her. She was nearing the end of the book, and according to her, that's when she got most involved with the story. She had to tie up loose ends and wrap up the novel with a punch. Mick considered the way her mind worked, conjuring up so many twisted mysteries, and he shook his head. "Hungry?"

Glancing up, she asked, "Who was on the phone?"

Mick stalled, then said, "Just a friend."

"Josh? Zack?"

He hated lying to her, and often he didn't even need to. She hesitated to pry, so if he just shook his head, she'd let it go at that. Sometimes it seemed to him that Delilah went out of her way to give him his privacy, to not push. That bugged him, since it took all his concentration to keep from pushing her. She came to him willingly, accepted him in all ways, but there were still pieces of her that remained hidden. It made him nuts.

Instead of answering her specific question, he asked, "What do you have planned today?"

She accepted the sandwich he handed her and took a healthy bite while shrugging. "Writing. More writing. I hope to finish this weekend. Why? Did you need me to take you somewhere?"

It amused Mick to see how she dug into her sandwich. Sometimes when she wrote she forgot everything else, including food. When her hands began to shake, then she'd remember and grab a bite to eat.

Other times she did nothing but eat while writing. She kept a variety of snacks in her desk drawer—white-chocolate pretzels, caramels, peanuts, chips. She shoveled food away like a linebacker, yet she stayed so slim, even delicate. Her metabolism astounded him.

Settling his hip on the edge of her desk, Mick shook his head. "No, I don't want to interrupt you today. Looks like it's going well."

"It is. I've thought about this scene for ages. It's a fun one to write. Really gruesome."

He laughed at that. "Then you stay home and finish up, but I do need to go out for just a little while."

"Without me?"

"Unheard of, I know, especially with how I've depended on you." He studied her face, seeing the hurt and something more. "You don't really mind, do you?"

She hedged, saying, "Why do you need to go out?"

Going with a sudden inspiration, he touched the end of her nose and smiled. "It's a surprise."

She flopped back in her seat and gave him a mock frown. "Not fair. What kind of surprise?"

"Now if I told you that, it wouldn't be much of a surprise, would it?"

She hesitated, fiddling with the crust on her sandwich. "You don't need to buy me things, you know."

He nodded gravely, playfully matching her mood. "I know."

She didn't look appeased by his response. "You sure you're okay to be on your own?"

"I'm a big boy, Delilah."

"Ha! Don't I know it." Her lecherous grin had him laughing again.

Damn, how he loved her shifting moods, how he loved…

Oh no. He pulled up short on his wayward thoughts, frowning at himself for letting such a deep insinuation intrude. He'd known her all of ten days—if he disregarded the two weeks prior to their formal meeting. He cared about her, more so every hour. No denying that. And he was drawn to her on the most elemental levels.

But it was far too soon to be thinking beyond that. Far, far too soon.

She mistook his frown and sighed. "Okay, I won't play mother hen, but please don't overdo it. It hasn't even been two weeks since you were shot."

Glad of the misunderstanding, he nodded. "Cross my heart."

Mick was ready to leave ten minutes later. He reminded Delilah to keep her door locked and not to let anyone in when he wasn't there. She was still skeptical about any personal threat, but she placated him by agreeing. She had few visitors, other than his friends, but she received mail from her publisher and agent regularly. She promised Mick she would be extra careful, and he finally left.

He was anxious to get some answers, anxious to face the man who'd put a bullet in his back.

The man who'd tried to kill Delilah.

The thought burned Mick, put a fire in his gut and a vibrating tension in his muscles. His sergeant had warned him not to overstep himself, to keep his cool, and Mick had agreed, even knowing it wouldn't be easy. The case was out of his hands, turned over to Homicide, and they could have refused to keep him involved. But they'd agreed to let him in to talk to Rudy Glasgow, in hopes he'd be able to get additional information.

Knowing Delilah would stay in her apartment alone all day made it easier to be away from her. She'd said she intended to write, and Mick believed her. Once she got involved with her stories, not much, including him, could pull her away.

He found her intensity rather endearing.

An around-the-clock watch had been placed on Rudy's room, even while he'd been unconscious. As Mick approached, the present guard came to his feet and set his magazine aside. Glancing down, Mick saw it was a periodical on martial arts. He smiled.

"Dawson, with City Vice." Mick held out his credentials for the guard to verify.

He nodded. "I was told to expect you."

"Has anyone else been in to see him? Has he talked to anyone else?"

The young officer rubbed the back of his neck. "Far as I know, he made a call to his lawyer and told the lead investigator that he'd speak with you. That's it."

"He called a lawyer?"

"Almost first thing after waking up. I heard he was real insistent about it."

Mick supposed that with an attempted-murder charge on Glasgow's head, getting a lawyer would be a huge consideration. "He's doing okay now? They expect a full recovery?"

"Yeah. He's a bit weak and shaky yet, and his leg is still healing, so they're planning to keep him another day or so, but then they'll ship him out." The guard grunted. "If you ask me, he's ready to go now, just dragging it out for the sake of a cushy bed."

Mick didn't doubt the probability of that. He pulled the door open.

The room was similar to the one he'd stayed in, only the shades were tightly drawn to keep it dim, and the TV played loudly. Mick took it all in with a single glance, then lounged against the wall. "You wanted to see me, Glasgow?"

Rudy Glasgow glanced over at him. His face was pale, his eyes shadowed, testimony to his physical state. It didn't move Mick one bit.

Rudy studied Mick for a long minute before grinning and motioning him closer. "I won't bite. Hell, even if I did, I doubt you'd feel it, I'm so damn weak."

Mick refused to respond to that prompt. He went straight to the matter most important to him. "Why'd you try to shoot her, Glasgow?"

He had to shout to be heard over the television, and it annoyed him. Rudy had soft sheets under him, plump pillows behind his head, a mostly eaten meal still on the tray beside his bed. Except for his elevated leg, wrapped in gauze where the bullet had struck, and the guard outside his door, he seemed to be pampered.

It grated that a criminal—an attempted murderer—should be treated so gently.

With a long, lethal look, Rudy said, "That bullet may have crippled me for life."

Mick bared his teeth. "No shit? That's the best news I've had all day."

"Screw you," Rudy suddenly said, lifting himself forward in a surge of anger. He kept his tone low, his voice a growl barely audible over the sound of the TV. His right hand twisted the sheet at his side.

Mick raised a brow, glad to see he'd riled the man. In his experience, information was always more forthcoming when your adversary was upset.

The information he got wasn't quite what he'd been expecting.

Slowly, by tiny degrees, Rudy's hand opened and he rested back on his pillows. He breathed deeply, as if that small fit of temper had taxed him, then a sardonic light entered his tired eyes and he actually chuckled. "But then," he said, "she's already doing that, isn't she?"

"Doing what?"

"Screwing you." He laughed again.

Feigning ignorance, Mick asked, "What the hell are you talking about?"

His laugh was bitter and mean. "That double-crossing bitch you protected. Oh, she covered her ass real good, I'll give her that."

Impatient, Mick barked, "Turn that damn television down. I can barely hear you."

"You heard me just fine, but I'll keep the set on so no one else hears. This conversation is between me and you. What you do with it after that is your own business."

"You planning on telling me something important, is that it?"

"Damn right. You," Rudy rasped, and thrust a finger at Mick, "are making cozy with an accomplice."

"Is that so?" Mick forced himself to speak casually, though a tightness invaded his chest. "And who would it be?"

"The woman you protected!"

"The woman *you* tried to kill?"

"She had it coming!"

Finally, Mick thought, finally he'd get some answers. He summoned a pose of boredom, when inside he seethed with anticipation—and something else, something damn close to dread. He blocked it; *he had to know.* "How do you figure that?"

"Because she was in on the robbery."

Mick laughed, though he didn't feel even an ounce of humor.

Rudy seemed beside himself. "Why the hell else did you think she was there?"

Mick stayed silent, not about to encourage him.

The man smirked. "My lawyer has been in contact with her, you know. He told me that she's got you moved in and under her spell. She even bragged to him that you wouldn't prosecute her, not while she's keeping you happy in bed."

"You expect me to believe this?" Mick knew Delilah hadn't talked to any lawyers. He'd been with her twenty-four-seven. Protecting her, he thought… No, he wouldn't let doubts intrude because of this scum! Delilah was an open, trusting woman. A gentle woman.

Who drove her car into rivers and learned how to hot-wire cars. A woman who kept company with criminals…

Mick shook his head. He knew every damn call she'd gotten. From her agent, her editor… But then, he'd just taken her word on that, when the strangers had called and she'd excused herself for a private conversation.

"You know she's a damn publicity hound," Rudy continued. "Don't you read at all? This is her biggest stunt yet, though we sure as hell didn't know about her twisted ending until we heard the cops coming. Then we realized she'd tipped them off. There was no other way they could have known we'd be there."

Icy dread climbed Mick's spine, chilling him on the inside, making his voice brisk. "A passerby claims to have seen you through the front window, and he called the police on his cell phone."

Rudy waved that away. "She set the whole thing up, including the guy who placed the call. Think about it—what was she doing there when she didn't buy anything? And why the hell would a real successful writer live in that dump she calls home?"

Mick had often wondered the same thing himself. But what did he know about a writer's salary, successful or otherwise? And for that matter, what did Glasgow know about how Delilah lived?

Feeling edgier by the second, Mick demanded, "Why tell me this?"

"Why?" Again Rudy leaned forward, and this time he shook a fist. "Because I'll be damned if I'll sit here and rot while she goes scot-free!"

"So you think I'll go to the police and have them arrest her? That I'll ask to have her prosecuted?"

"Cut the crap. You don't need to go to the cops because you *are* a cop. I know it, and more importantly, *she* knows it, regardless of your lame act about being a PI."

Mick's heart thudded to a standstill. How did this man know what he'd said to Delilah, unless Delilah had told him? Feeling as if a fist was tightening around his windpipe, he managed to say, "A cop?"

"That's right. You must really think she's stupid, but believe me, she's a clever one. She hadn't counted on you being in the jewelry store that day. She'd told us she just wanted to take part in the robbery, to experience it because of her twisted way of researching things. We'd get the goods and she'd get her insight. She promised to pay us nicely for our trouble.

"But then I guess she decided it'd work out better for her if she got rid of us. If anyone got wise to what really happened, she'd be off the hook. It would have been our word against hers, and she's fast becoming a celebrity, while we all have records. Without any proof to back us, she'd have walked away with a ton of fresh publicity, and we'd all have done time."

"You still don't have any proof—or are you stupid enough to think I'm going to believe you?" Mick had bluffed with the best of them, and right now he felt as if he'd gambled with his heart.

"Just hear me out."

"Not if you're only going to spout bullshit."

Again, Rudy's hands fisted in the sheets, and his face turned an angry red. "When she realized I knew the truth about how she'd set us up, she saw you as a way out. I bet she came on real strong, didn't she? I can tell by your expression she did." Rudy laughed. "She figures you'll protect her, but I want you to see justice done. That's what cops do, right? They arrest the criminals."

Mick narrowed his eyes. "Or shoot them in the leg."

"Bastard!"

His shout was so loud, the guard stuck his head in the door. "Everything okay in here?"

Mick didn't even look at him. "Get out."

Holding up his hands, the guard said, "Just checking," and backed away, letting the door hiss shut behind him.

Mick took a step forward. His heart hammered, but he kept his expression impassive, blank. "Give me one good reason why I shouldn't take you apart."

"Why the hell would I lie? And think about it—how would I know all this otherwise?"

"Your buddies who got loose?" He stood right next to the bed now, staring down at Rudy, fighting the urge to do him more damage. "We haven't rounded them up yet—but we will."

Rudy groaned, but more out of frustration than pain. "Believe me, they're long gone. Not a speck of loyalty in their veins. No, the only one I've spoken with is my lawyer, and he gave me some gritty details that just about pushed me over the edge."

Mick didn't want to hear any details. "Give me the lawyer's name."

"Not yet." Rudy absently massaged his leg. With deep satisfaction, Mick watched the pain cloud his face. "Not until she gets what she deserves."

"Why would she tell the lawyer anything? It would only incriminate her."

The man shook his head. "He's in love with her. He would never do anything to hurt her, including sharing this information with you. He only told me because he wanted me to understand that she had no intention of getting involved in this mess, that I couldn't count on her to help me out."

"Ah." Mick made a tsking sound of false sympathy. "So you have no one to corroborate this ridiculous tale, huh? Too bad." The sarcasm didn't work as well as he'd hoped; he still felt ready to shout with rage. The *ridiculous* tale was far too close to sounding plausible to suit him.

"I don't need anyone to confirm my story. You already know it's true."

"Not so," he lied. "I don't believe anything repeated by an attempted murderer and bungling thief."

The man looked dumbstruck, then florid with rage. "She really did get to you, didn't she? I understand she wore you out that first night, drugged you, then used her mouth to put you to sleep. But you're a good sport. I mean, you paid her back in kind, right, once you'd gotten a little rest and your friends had all gone home?" Rudy jeered, his voice grating down Mick's spine. "For a wounded man, you were tireless, I'll give you that. But then with her in the saddle, what man wouldn't be?"

A red haze of pain and anger nearly blinded him. "You son of a bitch." Mick grabbed him by his hospital gown and twisted, lifting him a good six inches off the mattress. Disappointment threatened to buckle his knees. He had begun trusting her, caring about her, even lo—

No! None of that mattered now. The only way Rudy could have known the intimate details of Mick's first night with Delilah, especially the playful reference to riding, was if she'd told someone.

And why would she do that unless what Glasgow said was true? He couldn't believe he'd let his lust for her override his professional instincts.

Anguish tore through Mick, obliterating his reason, filling him with bitter regret.

On the heels of those overwhelming sensations was refreshing fury, a reaction he knew how to deal with, an emotion that gave him back his breath—and his strength. He let the rage overtake him.

He released Rudy with a wrenching motion that made the man choke and hold his throat.

Mick backed away, knowing he'd gone over the edge. He wouldn't let her hurt him like this. He wouldn't let her make him forget his duty, his responsibilities.

Goddamn it, he'd been the worst kind of fool, but no more. He didn't verify or deny Rudy's claims, he simply turned on his heel and walked out, but he heard Rudy alternately gasping and laughing behind him.

Hot purpose drove Mick, made his steps long and hard and impatient.

The guard tried to speak to him, but Mick's throat was all but closed, his thoughts, his feelings agitated, even violent. He had to collect himself, get himself under control.

And he had to see the lead investigator on the case. He had evidence to share—and he wouldn't feel sane until he did.

Delilah heard the knock and left her desk. Mindful of her promise to Mick, she asked, "Who is it?"

"Josh," a voice called back, and, leaving the chain on the door, she cracked it open.

Not only Josh stood there, but Zack, too. They made a mismatched pair, she thought, seeing them both smile at her. Josh with his dark green eyes and blond hair always reminded her of a slick cover model. He had cockiness stamped all over him, and he knew his effect on women. She shook her head. His effect was wasted on her. She had eyes only for Mick, and she liked it that way.

"Can we come in?" Zack asked.

If Josh looked like a model for *Playgirl,* then Zack, with his kind blue eyes and bone-straight, light brown hair, looked like a model for the Sunday ads, maybe for comfy house slippers. He looked warm and cozy, like a man meant for a family.

Josh was excitement. Zack was comfort.

Mick was both those things and more. He was everything. Too quickly, he'd become so important to her.

She held the door open so they could enter. "Mick's not here."

They both drew up short, and Josh, in the rear, almost ran into Zack. "What do you mean, he's not here?"

Delilah shrugged. "He said he had a surprise something or other to do and left at lunchtime, almost four hours ago. He didn't want me to go along."

They shared a look. "You promised to stay in?" Josh guessed.

She shrugged. "I had writing to do, anyway. But this over-protectiveness is getting absurd." She gave them both pointed looks to let them know they were grouped in with the over-protective absurdity. After all, they backed Mick up every time he warned her to be cautious. She wondered how they thought she'd lived this long without them all looking over her shoulder, protecting her every step of the way.

Zack put his arm around her. They were both overly fa-miliar, treating her now as if she and Mick were a longtime couple. They'd come around almost every other day, and had learned to make themselves at home. "Grant the guy the right to worry."

"He doesn't return the favor." She didn't mean to sound complaining, but it sure came out that way.

"Meaning?" Zack asked in a gentle tone.

"Meaning he doesn't want me to ever worry and he looks annoyed if I do."

Josh dropped onto her couch. "'Course he would. He's a guy."

Del warned him with a look. "Your sexist attitude is going to get you into trouble someday." At first Josh's attitude had rubbed her the wrong way, but now she accepted him, even liked him. In small doses.

Zack nodded. "I've told him the same, but this time he's right. Mick can take care of himself."

She laughed at them. They saw everything in black-and-white, especially where men and their roles in life were con-cerned. Men were supposed to protect, to defend, to cherish. Even Josh, with his variety of girlfriends, treated them all as special. And Zack made his beautiful little girl the center of his life.

That thought brought another, and she asked, "Where's Dani?" She enjoyed visiting with the child. Dani wasn't the average four-year-old. She was too precocious, too aware of her surroundings.

"Gone to the movies with a neighbor and her daughter. She said to give you a hug from her." So saying, Zack pulled Del close and squeezed her, rocking back and forth.

She laughed and pushed herself away. Never in her life had she been touched so much. Her parents, once they'd realized she was different, had given her space—not necessarily space she wanted, but evidently space they needed. They hadn't known how to deal with her, so they'd dealt with her less.

Not so with these guys. The less they understood her, the more determined they were to figure her out. And in the process, they coddled and cuddled her a lot. They made her laugh, made her exasperated, made her feel important, wanted.

She enjoyed it all, the intimate, hot touching she and Mick shared, the friendly touching and camaraderie she got from Mick's friends, and the emotional touching, the acceptance, the welcome. Not a day went by that she didn't hear from one or another of Mick's family or friends.

It had never occurred to her how isolated she'd become. She wrote in a void, emerging only for research and publicity. But then Mick had saved her life, and in the process, changed it irrevocably.

"When do you expect him back?" Josh asked, even as he picked up the TV remote control and started looking for a sports channel.

Zack turned the television off. "Dolt, did you consider that she might be busy?"

Josh glanced at her. "You busy?"

Feeling rather conspicuous now, Del gestured at her desk,

littered with small sticky notes and research files. "I was just writing the last chapter."

"Then we can hang out and wait for Mick?"

Zack groaned. "Writing is work to her, you idiot. How can she work if you're here disrupting her?"

Josh looked totally bemused by the idea that he might be a bother to anyone, and Del relented. "Not at all," she said. "I'll enjoy the company. I really don't know how much longer Mick will be, though." She glanced at the wall clock and saw it was nearly five. "I thought he'd be back by now."

Zack glared at Josh, which made Josh raise his brows in a *what?* expression, before asking, "You're sure you don't mind?"

"I've been writing all day. My legs are cramped." Then a thought hit her and she said, "I haven't been out running once since Mick moved in. I miss it."

Again they shared a look, and it was Josh who said, "It's not safe for you to be out traipsing around until they catch those other guys."

"Yeah, right," she scoffed. "Who's to say they'll ever catch them? Am I supposed to stay cooped up forever?" Josh opened his mouth and she rushed to say, "Don't answer that! I know what *you* think already."

He grinned shamelessly. "I was just going to say to wait until Mick is completely healed and I'm sure he'll run with you. In the park. Or someplace else that's safe."

"But not here," Zack added.

"No, not here."

Del sat down on the couch next to Josh. "Why not here?"

Josh frowned, measuring his words. "Being the intense writerly type that you are, you may not have noticed, but this area is pretty hazardous."

"Hazardous how?"

He glanced at Zack for help. Zack sat on her other side. "Unsavory types live around here."

"Really?"

"Well, yeah...you never noticed?"

She chuckled at his disbelief. "Of course I did. I also noticed the variety of people who live here, old and young, black and white and Hispanic, male and female, friendly and hostile. I love the atmosphere, the constant chaos. No matter what time of night I'm up to write, there's something going on outside. People feed my inspiration, and I write better in places like this."

Zack reached over and tweaked a tendril of her hair. "You're a nut, sweetheart."

She swatted at him, laughing.

Josh agreed. "Most women I know want to avoid the criminal element as much as possible. You're the first person I've heard who wants to embrace it."

"I write about the criminal element, remember? Most of my mysteries revolve around a villain. Besides, I go where my villains go. And that makes for some fun travel."

"Yeah?"

"Yup. I love moving."

They were just getting into that discussion when Del's doorbell rang. She glanced at both Zack and Josh, then started to get to her feet.

Josh stopped her with a hand on her arm. "Mick?"

Shaking her head, she said, "Not unless he lost his key."

Zack moved past them both. "I'll get it."

Del smiled at their determination in keeping her safe. She didn't bother telling them that she received a lot of special delivery packages from her editor. No, she just sat back and indulged them in their maleness.

When Zack opened the door, she saw two people there, a

man and a woman dressed in suits. The woman gave a faint, stony smile. "Is Ms. Delilah Piper in, please?"

"Who's calling?" Zack asked suspiciously. At the same time, Del stood to better see.

The woman looked past him. "Ms. Piper?"

"That's right." Del started toward the door, but Josh kept pace at her side.

The woman flipped open her bag to display a shiny, very official badge. "I'm Detective Darney, with the city police department. This is Detective Breer. Would you mind coming with us to answer some questions?"

Josh bristled, eyeing the badges as if to verify their authenticity. "What's this about?"

At his tone, the male officer spoke up. "She's wanted downtown for questioning. That's all...for now."

Confused, Del asked, "Questioning about what?"

Both Josh and Zack flanked her, and Del appreciated their solid, comforting presence. She felt off balance and a little frightened.

Detective Breer ignored Josh and faced Del instead. "For possible involvement in the jewelry store robbery," he intoned, his voice so deep Del felt her skin prickle.

"What?" She thought she shouted the word, but it came out as only a vague, rusty whisper.

Detective Darney looked sympathetic. "You've been named as an accomplice," she gently explained. "But before any charges are filed, we'd like to talk to you."

Del had no idea what to do; she'd never faced a situation like this! She turned to Josh with a blank stare, hoping for direction. He looked furious and concerned. "Don't worry, sweetheart. We'll be right behind you."

"Mick..."

Zack gave her a squeeze. "We'll get hold of him. I promise."

She nodded, reached for her purse, and then Detective Darney had her arm, leading her out the door.

CHAPTER TEN

At least they hadn't handcuffed her, Del thought with a struggling sense of humor to temper her despair. Her throat felt tight, her chest hurt and her stomach was queasy. She almost faltered as she was led through double glass doors and into a long corridor, but the police station wasn't a place to make a scene.

Detective Darney's heels tapped on the tile floor on one side of her, while Breer's heavy steps echoed as solid thuds on the other. They had her caged in—guarding against her escape? Absurd, almost as absurd as the interrogation room where they stopped.

Detective Breer pulled a chair out for her. "Would you like a cup of coffee?"

Numbness seeping in, Del shook her head. The proffered courtesies, in light of the situation, were almost laughable. She drooped down into the chair.

The plastic-covered seat squeaked beneath her. Her blouse stuck to her back from the heat and her tension, forcing her to lean forward. Sweat gathered between her breasts. The unmarked car she'd ridden in had icy-cold air-conditioning, but this room was hot, stuffy, closing in on her. Suffocating.

Once while doing research, she'd been in a room just like this. She knew the procedure and the protocol, and tried to calm herself with the fact that she knew what to expect, though she'd certainly never thought she'd find herself in the position of being an actual suspect.

Still, she wouldn't panic. It was all a misunderstanding. And thinking that, she said, "If you get hold of Mick Dawson, he could explain to you that I was just a victim."

As if she'd summoned him, Mick strode in. He had another man behind him, and both of them wore frowns, but Mick's was darker, and very grim. Del didn't understand, and she couldn't stop herself from saying in some surprise, "Mick!" and then, as relief washed over her, "Thank God you're here."

His black-eyed glance lacked any emotion as he took a seat at the end of the table—a good distance from where she sat.

Anxiety smothered her. Mouth dry, pulse racing, Del looked down the expanse of the table to Mick. It meant something, that awful distance he'd instigated, but for the life of her, she couldn't imagine what. When he'd left her at the apartment that afternoon, everything had been fine.

He'd even told her he planned to get her a surprise gift.

Thinking this wasn't exactly the surprise she'd hoped for, Del twittered nervously. The silly sound just sort of escaped on its own, a girlish giggle, a forerunner to hysteria, making her edgier. She slapped a hand over her mouth. She didn't un-derstand...any of it.

She swallowed hard and reached for composure. "What's going on?"

The man who'd entered with Mick held out his hand. He was large and beefy, and had salt-and-pepper hair neatly trimmed above his elongated ears. Watery, pale blue eyes were closely spaced to an overlarge nose. His suit fit his square frame loosely, and a wrinkled tie hung crooked around his neck.

He looked like a wonderful character, Del thought, someone she could put into a book. She knew she shouldn't be thinking such inane thoughts at the moment, but all other thoughts cut like tiny razors, and her mind naturally shied away from them.

She couldn't bring herself to accept the man's hand.

He eased back, putting his hand in his pocket. The other held a clipboard. "Ms. Piper, I'm Detective Faradon, lead investigator on the robbery you were involved in." He checked his clipboard, then rattled off the date and time and location.

Del concentrated on finding her breath and centering her thoughts. She had to deal with this—whatever it might be. "Could you please tell me what this is all about?"

Rather than sit, Faradon propped his hip on the edge of the table. Del expected the table to collapse under his weight, but it held.

She skipped another glance at Mick. He was staring at her with such stony concentration that it struck her like a physical blow, forcing her to flinch away.

The other two detectives watched her as well. It was like being on display, or caught in a hangman's noose, and it hurt.

"Ms. Piper, are you acquainted with Rudy Glasgow?"

She shook her head, then stopped abruptly. "Yes, he's the man in the hospital, the man Mick shot."

"So you do know him?"

"I know of him." Her heart beat too hard, too fast. "I've read the accounts since the shooting. His name has been in the papers. He's…he's unconscious."

"Not anymore." The man surveyed her through lowered, bushy brows. His expression turned speculative, calculating. Finally, he said, "He claims to know you."

Forgetting her sweaty blouse, Del dropped back hard in

her chair. Her spine offered less support than an overcooked noodle. "He's wrong," she replied flatly.

"He claims," the man continued, glancing at his clipboard, "that you set the whole thing up as a publicity stunt."

Del's gaze shot to Mick and locked with his. Neither of them blinked. Dear God, surely he didn't believe such an idiotic story.

She shook her head. "No."

"That's it?" Mick asked, his voice harsh and loud in the closed room. "No other explanations?"

Del searched his beautiful face, his once gentle face, and her heart crumbled. The flat, compressed line of his mouth, his locked jaw and dark flinty brown eyes showed his distaste. *For her.*

Del winced with a very real pain. *He'd already found her guilty in his mind.* She wanted to reach out to him, to touch him, but she couldn't. She didn't think he'd let her.

"Mick?" she whispered.

His expression hardened even more and he looked away.

It hurt worse than anything she'd ever felt. She murmured to his averted face, "I can't believe you just did that. I...I really can't."

He gave her another sharp look, but this time she dismissed him.

Looking down at her hands, Del said, "I don't know Rudy Glasgow, and I didn't set up the robbery for a publicity stunt. I don't do that."

"You have been known," Detective Breer pointed out, "for your extravagant research tactics."

"Tactics that have never hurt anyone or broken any laws." She felt hollow, stiff. Wounded. "I was there that day, as I've already said, to see how a robber would set things up, but—"

"Isn't that something of a coincidence," Detective Darney

asked, her voice soft in comparison to the men's, "that a robbery would take place while you were doing your research for a robbery?"

"Yes." Del's stomach churned with an awful dread. "It's an incredible coincidence."

"You've spoken with him."

Del jumped at the lash of Mick's accusation. She didn't quite look at him when she asked in a small voice, "Who?"

He rounded the table until he faced her from the other side, giving her no choice but to meet his gaze. "Glasgow. I saw him today." He slashed a hand through the air, impatient, provoked. "He knows *things*."

"What kind of things?"

After glancing at the other people in the room, Mick narrowed his eyes on her. "Things you and I have done. Intimate details that he couldn't have guessed at."

Detective Darney turned away. The men stared at her, their attention burning hot. Embarrassment hit her first, then a wave of remorse for what Mick had clearly thrown away.

And finally her temper ignited in scalding sensation. It chased away the numbness and burned away the hurt. Her heart raced, her pulse pounded.

Very slowly, she came to her feet. "I haven't spoken to anyone about anything we've done."

"He knew it all, Delilah. He knew *details*."

She stared over his shoulder, her mind racing as the ramifications of that sank in. "Then he…he found out some other way."

"How?"

"It's not my job to figure it out." She turned pointedly to Faradon. Sweat gathered at the base of her spine. She itched from the prickling of fear, mortification, loss and anger.

"All of you," she said, addressing the whole room, "you are

looking at the wrong person. I don't know Rudy Glasgow. I haven't spoken with him."

"You've told no one?"

She glanced at Mick, overcome with sadness. His distrust would not be easy to forgive, and he would be impossible to forget. But she had no choice now. "What we've done, Mick... well, it was special to me." She got choked up and despised herself for the weakness. She wasn't used to declaring herself in front of a crowd, especially a hostile crowd. And she didn't delude herself; this crowd was hostile. They'd already condemned her.

She cleared her throat and made a last stab to reach him. "I would never have discussed our personal situation with anyone, much less the man who shot you."

For a long, sizzling moment, Mick stared at her, and she held herself still, hoping he'd smile, that he'd tell her he believed her. That he'd apologize.

He jerked away, cursing softly. His back to her, Mick ran a rough hand through his hair, and Del found herself stupidly concerned for his injury. She could feel his tension, his anger.

She ignored everyone else in the room. At the moment, the only one who mattered was Mick. What the others thought could be straightened out later. She said steadily, "If you just think about it, you'll know I couldn't have done that. That I wouldn't have done anything like that. You know me."

"Barely," he said, still not facing her.

She wavered on her feet. That he could say such a thing after everything they'd done together, after everything she'd felt for him...

She called herself a fool, even as she begged, "Don't do this."

His gaze cut toward her, accusing. "He said you were counting on our relationship to keep you safe from the law."

Mick's insinuation was clear. He chose to believe a man

who'd shot him in the back, rather than her. Del forced herself to straighten. Later, she'd have to decide how to deal with her broken heart.

Right now, she had to figure out what to do to make the detectives believe her. That had to be her top priority.

But how? She looked around at them—and saw pity from the lead investigator, interest from Detective Breer and understanding from Detective Darney. Del hated it all, and accepted that they all considered her guilty.

"Are you arresting me?" She was proud of her steady voice, the strength in her demand.

Faradon tapped his clipboard against the table. "Not just yet. But I don't want you to leave town."

"Fine." Del turned to walk out on wobbly legs, but he stopped her.

"Ms. Piper?"

She froze.

"I may have more questions later. I trust you'll cooperate with me?"

She turned to face him. "The man wanted to kill me—or so everyone keeps telling me. Now that he's come up with this outrageous tale meant to incriminate me personally, I have to believe it was a deliberate act against *me*. Of course I want him convicted and his cohorts found. I'll help you any way I can."

Looking a little bemused by that heartfelt speech, Faradon murmured dryly, "Thank you."

Del pushed the door open and walked out. Her neck hurt, her stomach coiled. Tears burned behind her eyes, and she fought them back.

She wanted to run, as fast as her legs could carry her. Just as she hadn't known such wonderful elation existed until she'd met Mick, she hadn't known anyone had the power to hurt her so badly.

But she held her dignity intact and walked, head held high, back down the long corridor. She was more than a little aware of Detectives Breer and Darney following behind her.

When she reached the front desk, Josh and Zack stood there, impatient and worried. Zack reached for her first, pulling her into a warm, tight embrace that was just what she needed, but not who she needed it from.

"Hey," he said, squeezing her a bit tighter, "are you okay? You're shaking."

Swallowing back a choking sob, she nodded against his chest and allowed herself the luxury of being held by him for one moment more. Then she pushed away.

Josh touched her cheek. "Mick didn't return my page yet."

It took two attempts before the words would come out. "No need to page him. He's here."

Josh and Zack frowned, their expressions mirroring each other. The irony struck her, and she almost laughed. Not only would Mick not help her, but... "He was the one," she said, trying for a note of self-mockery in place of desperation, "who evidently brought the new evidence to the police."

Josh didn't appear convinced. "Honey, are you all right?"

"No, no I'm not." Any second now she was going to throw up. Not because of Rudy or the robbery. She was innocent, and sooner or later they'd all realize it.

No, she was sick at heart, and sick inside, because she loved a man who'd just turned his back on her, and she had no idea how she was going to recover.

A deep breath, then another, didn't really help. "Being that you're Mick's friends, not really mine, and being that he now thinks I'm a... Well, I'm not sure what he thinks." She shook her head, understanding now why he'd kept his thoughts so private—because he'd never trusted her. "All I know is that it's ugly, that everything has changed, and I have no doubt you'll both back him up as you always do. So—" she fashioned a smile out of her stiff lips and tried not to notice the concern in their eyes, the caring "—I guess this is goodbye. It's been swell, guys."

She hurried out front, with both of them rushing behind her. A taxi rounded the corner onto the adjacent street, and she jogged across the parking lot to hail it, just wanting to escape, to be alone—as she'd accustomed herself to being. She had the cab door open when Josh grabbed her arm.

"Delilah, wait."

She looked up at him—and saw Mick standing in the station doorway. "He can explain," she said, tears filling her eyes to the point where everything blurred. "Goodbye."

Josh had no choice but to release her. She didn't look back to see them talking. She knew what Mick would tell them, what he believed, and she couldn't bear to see them turn on her, too. She'd finally gotten comfortable with them, accepted them as a part of her life, a disruptive, unruly, fun part.

And now it was over.

She dropped her head forward and covered her face. *How?* she wondered, wishing she could understand what had happened, how it had all gone so wrong in the blink of an afternoon.

The man Mick had shot was no longer unconscious. And he'd told Mick something, found some way to convince him that she was involved. Mick had said he knew personal things, intimate things. That had to mean details of their lovemaking.

Judging by the way Mick had looked at her, *he* hadn't told a soul, so he'd assumed that she had done the blabbing. To a criminal. To a man who'd tried to kill her and had shot him.

And then the shock of it hit her. She felt chilled to the bone, shivering with realization, revulsion.

The cabby pulled up to her apartment, and Del handed him

a twenty, not even thinking about getting change, or how much she'd tipped him. She stumbled to the steps leading to her apartment and stared up at the front door.

There was only one thing for her to do.

She had to leave.

Mick hated to admit it, but he was relieved to see that Josh and Zack had followed Delilah to the station. That meant she hadn't been alone when the detectives took her. He'd regretted sending for her almost immediately, but then he had a lot of regrets, and they all centered around her. He had to stop thinking with his emotions and start using his head instead.

He turned to Josh as he approached, but wasn't prepared for the solid pop in the left arm his friend delivered.

"Ow, goddamn it!" Awkwardly, he rubbed his arm and glared at Josh. "That hurt."

"Good." Josh looked ready to take another swing, this one at Mick's head. "What the hell did you do to her?"

"To Delilah?"

Zack rolled his eyes. "No, to Queen Elizabeth. Of course to Delilah. She came out of here nearly in tears."

"Not *nearly* in tears," Josh accused, his nostrils flared like a charging bull. "She was crying, damn it."

Mick hurt from his hair to his toenails, and not all of it was physical. The idea of Delilah crying only added to his pain, making it more acute when he'd thought he couldn't hurt any worse. Dully, wishing he could undo the past, or somehow change it, he said, "She's not who you think she is."

Zack went very still, then stiffened. "What did you do?"

To see his two best friends rallying to her defense added one more bruise to his already battered conscience. He'd wanted them to accept her, and vice versa. But now it hardly mattered.

In the briefest terms possible, Mick explained the situation.

He hated going through it again, hated rehashing all the ways he'd been duped, all the ways she had lied.

When he finished, Josh popped him again.

Mick squared off, unwilling to let Josh's hostility continue. "Will you quit that!"

Pushing himself between them, Zack said, "Josh has a point."

"A point?" Mick stared at him, incredulous. "All he did was hit me!"

"Because you needed to be hit," Zack explained, always the cool one, always the peacemaker. "Jesus, man, you don't know anything about women. I realize you don't date much—"

"Look who's talking."

"—but I figured you'd have picked up some things just from being around Josh, if only by osmosis."

"I know more than I care to," Mick grumbled in return. He knew that he was a lousy judge of character, that he'd allowed his gonads to overrule his good sense. That few people could be trusted, but he was too damn stupid to learn that lesson.

"Not," Josh said, pressing forward again, "by a long shot."

Mick was amazed by Josh's red-eyed, aggressive attitude, which went well beyond defensive friendship for Delilah. *He was acting territorial.* Mick closed the space between them in a heartbeat. "What the hell does she mean to *you?*"

"More than she does to you, obviously!"

Again, Zack wedged into the middle, chest to chest with Mick, forcefully moving him a few feet away from Josh. "Quit baiting him, Josh. And Mick, he's right. Why the hell didn't you talk to her privately?"

"I'm a cop," he reminded them, with an enormous dose of sarcasm and a chip on his shoulder so large his knees almost gave out. "I'm supposed to bring in the criminals." No sooner did the words leave his mouth than he winced. He sounded just like Rudy.

Josh shook his head and all but shouted, "You're also in love, you ass."

Mick stared at him, and wondered if he could reach him before Zack intervened. Probably not, judging by Zack's watchful attention. Mick settled for saying, "Go screw yourself."

"Oh yeah, that'll fix things." Josh threw up his hands. "Do you have any idea how rare a woman like Delilah is?"

Possessiveness bristled along his nerve endings, despite what had just transpired in the interrogation room. "Not more than a few days ago, you were calling her strange!"

"Strange, unique, rare." Josh shrugged. "But that was ten days ago, before I really knew her."

"You're keeping count!"

"She's damn special."

Zack nodded. "Very special."

"Did either of you hear me?" Mick demanded in a shout, so frazzled and confused he knew his hair should be standing on end. "She's dealing with Rudy. She was in on the whole thing."

Zack leveled him with a pitying look. "I don't believe it."

"Neither do I," Josh added. "If you'd talked to her privately, maybe she could have explained."

"She had a chance to explain in there," Mick roared, stabbing a finger toward the station, "and all she did was deny any connection to him."

"Maybe because she has no connection, and maybe because you threw her for one hell of a loop." Josh squeezed his eyes shut. "God, she looked so hurt, it's breaking my damn heart, and I'm not the one in love with her."

Zack raised a brow over that, but refrained from saying anything.

"She's crazy about you, Mick. She trusted you." Disgust filled Josh's tone. "And you just tossed her to the wolves."

Mick looked away from the accusation in Josh's eyes. "All I did was have her questioned."

"All you did," Josh said, grabbing him by his shirtfront and shaking him, "is show her that you don't care two cents for her feelings, that you don't trust her and that you'll gladly believe a man capable of murder rather than hear her side of things."

Put that way... Mick shook Josh off and paced across the parking lot. Heat rose from the blacktop in waves, adding to his frustration, making him sweat.

His first sight of Delilah in the interrogation room had showed her to be wilted, stunned. By the time she'd walked out she'd mustered up a bit of stiff-backed pride. But the incredible vibrancy that he'd thought an integral part of her had been gone. He shook his head, wanting to dispel the image of her beautiful blue eyes clouded with distress. "I was...sick when I got done talking to Rudy."

"Sick and stupid," Josh sneered.

Zack grabbed Josh. "Will you knock it off! This isn't helping, and to be frank, I'm beginning to be a bit suspicious of your interest myself."

Josh glared at him, then at Mick's questioning gaze. Finally, he shrugged. "If Mick wasn't interested in her, I'd have been hot on her trail. So what?"

Already on a short fuse, Mick exploded. "You miserable son of a—"

This time Zack had to leap between them, shoving at both men hard to keep them from coming to blows. "You're both causing a scene, damn it!"

Around Zack's body, Josh taunted, "What's it matter to you, buddy? You just threw her away." And then, as if that wasn't enough to curdle Mick's blood, he added, "I think I'll go *console* her."

Another struggle ensued, while Zack did his best to keep the two of them apart. Josh, muttering a sound of disgust, finally gave up and stepped away. "Fine, you still want her? Well then, go after her. But *listen* to her. And don't you dare make her cry again."

Mick, red in the neck and teeth gnashing, subsided as well. He didn't really want to take his rage out on a friend. It took him several moments, but he finally got the words out. "You honestly think there might be another explanation?"

They both nodded at him. Josh said, "I believe in her. She may be good at coming up with elaborate plots for her books, but she'd never hurt someone she cared about."

Mick wondered if, after what he'd just put her through, he could still be counted among those she cared for.

"And no way," Zack added, "would she take a chance on innocent people getting caught in the cross fire just for publicity."

Mick groaned, hearing the ring of truth in their words. Josh walked away from them both and went to stand near a telephone pole. Zack squeezed Mick's uninjured shoulder. "Yep, I'm afraid you might have blown it. Better to get there as quick as you can and start your apologies. If you give her too much time to consider what you've done, she may not be able to forgive you."

Mick stared at his feet. "I can't imagine what explanation there could be. Rudy knew things that no one should have known."

"It would be easy enough for him to guess that you were sleeping together. That doesn't take an Einstein."

"He knew...details. Specific details that went beyond—"

"I understand," Zack rushed to say, before Mick could

stumble on. But Mick noticed there was a gleam of curiosity in his eyes, too.

He straightened. "I'll give her a chance to talk to me, one on one. And I hope like hell you're right, that she can clear this all up."

"Ha. I think you better do more than that. You better get down on your knees."

Mick glared at him, but as he walked away, he didn't rule out the possibility of begging. He'd never felt so miserable in his life—not when Angel had been threatened and he knew he couldn't protect her, not even when his mother had died in a stranger's shack, an empty whiskey bottle beside her. No, the thought of losing Delilah was a gnawing ache that kept expanding and sharpening until his guts felt on fire and his chest threatened to explode.

Even if she had been in on the scheme, he didn't want to lose her. He'd find a way to keep her out of jail, keep her straight, even if that meant keeping her in bed, under him, from now on.

Before he reached his car, he was running.

It occurred to him with a blinding flash of insight that if his friends were right, if Delilah was in fact innocent, he'd just left her alone and vulnerable. Anything could happen to her.

He stepped on the gas and made it to her apartment in record time.

Josh saw Zack glaring at him and he grinned, though his grin felt more sickly than not. "What?"

"Don't use that innocent tone on me. What the hell were you thinking?"

Forcing a chuckle, Josh shook his head. "I just worked him into a lather. He needed to be shook up or he'd have stood around here pondering all the possibilities, and by the time he realized we were right, it would have been too late. I saved him some time and heartache, that's all."

"So everything was an act? You're not hung up on her?"

Josh winked, and lied through his teeth. "Not at all. You know I like to play the field."

"Huh. I know you've never had a woman show complete and utter disinterest in you before."

"True." Delilah had gone from not noticing him, to grudgingly accepting him as Mick's friend, to displaying a fondness that bordered on sisterly. From the start, she'd made her preferences known, and it had been Mick all the way. Josh laughed. "I tell ya, I can live without it ever happening again."

Zack turned to look at the road. "I hope Mick doesn't kill himself getting over there."

"I just thought of something," Josh said, and reached for the cell phone clipped to his belt. "Since we both know Delilah didn't have any part of sharing that information, someone must have been spying on them."

"But how?" Zack asked. "Mick claims it was very personal in-the-bedroom stuff."

Josh grinned. "Yeah, I wish he'd elaborated on that." Zack laughed, never guessing exactly how big a lie that was. The last thing Josh wanted to hear was the personal sexual details between them. It ate him up.

Delilah, with her contrary ways and openness and brutal honesty, had stolen a piece of his heart. It was the damnedest thing he'd ever experienced, and while he was thrilled all to hell and back for Mick, he couldn't help wishing that he'd found her first.

He shook off his melancholy. Right now, all he wanted was for Mick and Delilah to be happy, and that meant Mick had to get her to forgive him. To that end, Josh wanted to figure out what had gone wrong.

"You think someone could have seen in through the bedroom window somehow?"

"I don't know," Josh admitted, "but I know who could find out."

Awareness lit Zack's eyes. "Alec?"

"You betcha." He punched in a series of numbers and waited until the call was answered. "Alec Sharpe, please. Yeah, it's an emergency."

Only a few seconds passed before Alec took the phone. "Sharpe here."

It would have taken far too long to explain, so Josh merely said, "Hey, Alec, this is Josh. Mick is kind of in trouble and you need to get over to Delilah's apartment."

To Josh's surprise, Alec didn't ask any questions, didn't ask for details of any kind. He said only, "I'm on my way," and the line went dead.

Zack looked at Josh as he closed the cell phone. "Well?"

Josh shrugged. "He, uh, he doesn't say much, does he? But he's heading over there now." He glanced at his watch. "Figuring he was at the office, I think it'll take him about forty-five minutes."

Zack frowned in thought. "With what I've heard about Alec, I wouldn't be surprised if he made it in thirty."

Then they stared at each other. Josh shifted, looked up at the broiling afternoon sun and then the glare off his car's windshield. He propped his hands on his hips and tilted his head at Zack. "You got anywhere you need to be?"

After glancing at his watch, Zack said, "Not for a few more hours. Dani was going to the pizza parlor after the movie."

They'd been friends so long, they often shared thoughts

without words being spoken. "Think we should?" Josh asked.

Neither one answered, then in unison they said, "We should."

CHAPTER ELEVEN

Mick sat out front for several minutes, stewing in his own misgivings. He hated to admit how much he hoped, prayed, that Delilah could come up with an alternate explanation. Even now he wanted to hold her, to tuck her close and tell her everything would be all right, that he'd keep her safe and keep scum like Glasgow away from her.

He groaned. It was entirely possible that she'd set up the whole robbery, that he'd gotten shot because of her.

It was even probable, given the facts at hand.

Cowardly bastard, he accused himself, and jerked his car door open. He'd face the outcome, whatever it might be, just as he'd faced everything in his life, good and bad.

He took the concrete steps two at a time. The long flight of stairs leading to the upper level didn't slow him down, either. He bounded up them, anxious to speak to Delilah, to figure things out.

He started to knock, then decided to use the key she'd given him. She might refuse to let him in under the circumstances, so he unlocked the door and stepped quietly inside.

The apartment was silent, causing his instincts to scream. Mick reached to the small of his back and pulled out his gun.

He'd armed himself right after seeing Rudy in the hospital. He hadn't worn the gun before that because he hadn't wanted to make Delilah suspicious, and he was only a mediocre shot with his left hand. But he'd felt naked without it.

Every light in her apartment blazed, and things were scattered everywhere—boxes on the floor, cushions pulled loose from the sofa.

Fear for her clawed at him. Mick crept forward, away from the open door, then quickly ducked as the chopping block from the kitchen whooshed past him, barely missing his head. It fell to the floor with a clatter, the wood neatly splitting down the middle. He whirled and aimed.

Thrown off balance by the impetus of the attack, a small body tumbled forward and landed against his chest, warm and familiar. Mick automatically raised his gun to the ceiling while catching her.

He and Delilah stared at each other.

Slowly, Mick lowered his arm to his side, watching her warily. She stepped back and away from him, then covered her mouth, breathing hard. "Ohmigod." Her fingers over her open mouth trembled. She shook her head. "I'm sorry. I didn't know it was you."

All color had leached from her face. Her eyes appeared huge and distressed. Everything inside Mick melted, all the suspicions and the worry and the anger temporarily replaced by the need to protect her. "Are you all right?"

Seconds ticked by while they stared at each other. She shook her head again. "No."

That was all she said before turning away and heading for her bedroom. Obviously, no one else was in the apartment, given the way she went about her business.

Mick followed her into her room, and the first thing he saw was the suitcase opened on the bed, partially packed.

His knees locked; his healing shoulder pounded with a renewed ache. "You going somewhere?"

She didn't look at him again, though her face remained pale and he could see her hands trembling. "Yes."

His throat tightened. "Where?"

"I can't tell you in here."

A frown pulled at his brows. "In here in the bedroom?" he asked, perplexed by her odd behavior.

She shifted impatiently. "No, here in my apartment."

"You heard what Faradon told you." He strode toward her, uncertain but determined. He wouldn't let her get away from him. "You're not to leave."

Her scathing glance stopped him in his tracks. "I can't very well stay here. But don't worry. I'm not skipping town. I'll still be around for you to persecute."

"Prosecute," he corrected automatically, then caught himself, realizing she'd said it on purpose. He clenched his teeth, counting to ten. Attempting a softer, more reasonable tone, he said, "I don't want to prosecute or persecute you, babe."

She went to her dresser, picked up an armload of items and dropped them haphazardly into the suitcase. "Get out of my way," she said as she started past him to the hallway. "What are you doing here, anyway? And why are you creeping around with your gun out? Were you going to shoot me?"

She didn't wait for an answer to that outrageous insult, but marched into the hall.

"You know damn good and well I wouldn't shoot you! I wouldn't do anything to—"

"Hurt me?" She stopped abruptly. "It's a little too late to make that claim, isn't it?"

"Delilah…"

In a hurry to finish packing, she rushed off. Was she leaving her apartment rather than throw him out? Did she think he intended to stay with her still?

Actually, he hadn't thought that far ahead, but the idea of leaving her, of not having her next to him at night, her soft body his to touch, her gentle breath warming him, gave him a lost, sick feeling in the pit of his stomach.

He put his gun away, then knotted his hands to keep from reaching for her. She looked...breakable. Fragile.

She stopped in the middle of the floor, as if uncertain what to do next. Her gaze landed on her computer, and she dove toward it with a purpose, quickly pulling cords and disconnecting the monitor.

Mick used that opportunity to clasp her shoulders. Touching her made him feel better. "Delilah, listen to me."

She jerked away so violently, she almost lost her balance. "Don't touch me," she said in alarm, her eyes huge and round and filled with wariness. "Don't you ever touch me again."

They watched each other in silence. Mick was the first to finally speak. "Tell me what's going on."

For a long minute, she stared at her hands. "All right." She took a deep breath, met his gaze defiantly. "I fell in love with you. I trusted you. I knew it was too soon for that, but I couldn't seem to stop it. And you've broken my heart. I really don't think I can ever forgive you."

Her words were damn difficult to take, filling him with elation—because she loved him—and the heavy weight of sadness, because he didn't know if he could do anything about it. He chose his words carefully, watching her, gauging her reaction. "Because I turned you in?"

Her eyes closed and a tiny, very sad smile appeared. "No, because you'd think that about me at all." She looked at him again. "Here I was, letting myself go crazy for you, and you hadn't really learned anything about me at all."

The need to hold her was a live thing. He barely resisted it. "Can we back up just a bit?" When she didn't answer, he asked, "Why are you in such an all-fired hurry to leave now?"

She gave a broken sigh. "And here I thought you were so smart. Smart and brave and honorable." She reached for his hands and enfolded them in her own. Leaning so close he thought she would kiss him, she whispered near his ear, "I didn't tell anyone anything. I figure you didn't, either. That means my place has to be bugged."

Mick stood there, stupefied, watching her lean back, watching her wait for his reaction. Bugged?

A stillness settled over him, slowing his heartbeat, squeezing his lungs. *Of course her place was bugged.*

But it would have to be worse than that. Just listening wouldn't have given anyone such specific details of their first night together. No, that was something that had to be seen, too.

Almost in slow motion, Mick looked around, heart pounding with acceptance. He caught Delilah by the shoulders. "Come on."

"Where?"

"To my car. I want you out of here."

She dug in her heels, resisting his efforts. "I'm not your responsibility anymore. I can take care of myself, just like I've always done."

"We can't talk here," he insisted.

And she added with a note of sadness, "We don't need to talk anywhere. We're through."

He hadn't been willing to accept that when he'd thought her an accomplice; no way in hell would he accept it knowing she was innocent and in danger. And he didn't doubt her now, not at all. Maybe he was too anxious to find an alternate explanation, one that didn't incriminate her in any way.

But this time he was going by his heart, by his guts, not by his damn pride or his conscience.

He gripped her shoulders tighter, opened his mouth—and heard someone say, "Am I interrupting?"

They both whipped around, and Mick shoved Delilah behind him. Alec lounged in the doorway, one black brow quirked in question, his equally black eyes speculative.

Mick caught Delilah's hand, dragged her resisting behind him, and stepped out into the hallway. Without a word, Alec followed. They moved to a corner and there, where no one could possibly hear, Mick asked, "What the hell are you doing here?"

"Josh called and said you needed my help." He looked at Delilah, his gaze speculative. "What's going on?"

"Damn." Mick quickly explained the possibilities to Alec. Several times Delilah tried to wiggle her hand away from him, but he held tight, and she seemed reluctant to make a scene.

Alec didn't appear the least surprised by any of it, but then he was a specialist when it came to espionage equipment. "Probably a Minicam," he said. He put his large hand on the side of Delilah's neck and bent to look her in the eyes. "You okay?"

She didn't so much as glance at Mick. "I'll survive."

Alec considered that, holding her gaze for a stretch of time, then shook his head. "I think you should go on home with Mick. Let me check things over here and... No?"

She shook her head. "I'm not going home with Mick."

"Yes, you are," Mick told her. "Alec, I just need a sec to talk to her."

Her gaze glued to Alec's, Delilah bared her teeth in what she probably thought looked like a confident smile, but instead showed her tension. "I'm *not* going home with Mick."

Alec raised his brows, waiting for Mick's response. He was

saved from that fate when pounding footsteps sounded on the stairs. They all moved at once, Mick again shoving Delilah behind him while drawing his gun, and Alec stationing himself in front of them both.

Josh and Zack skittered to a halt at the sight of them blocking the hallway.

"Uh, we decided you could use some backup," Josh explained.

Mick growled, knowing Josh thought he couldn't apologize to Delilah correctly on his own.

Delilah mistook him, though. From behind Mick she muttered meanly, "Some watchdog you are if you need those two."

Mick turned to frown at her.

Alec sighed.

More footsteps sounded. Dane, gun in hand and arm extended, reached the top of the stairs in a crouch. Everyone blinked at him.

Alec said, "You got my message."

"Yeah." Dane came to his feet and tucked the gun away in a shoulder holster. "What's going on?"

Delilah stepped around Mick, glaring at all five men. "Do you all run around town armed?"

Josh and Zack shook their heads. "Of course not."

Alec, Dane and Mick said at the same time, "Yeah."

She turned away in exasperation. "I need to finish packing."

"Packing?" Josh asked, his tone filled with alarm.

"You're going somewhere?" Zack tried to step in front of her.

Alec caught her by the back of her shirt, then quickly held up both hands when she rounded on him. "Don't slug me, just listen up, okay? You can be pissed off at Mick all you want. Hell, I would be, too."

"Me, too," Josh and Zack said almost in unison, earning Mick's glare.

"But," Alec continued, "you have to think here. Don't go putting yourself in danger just to spite yourself. I don't know where you intended to go, but with everything we've just found out, even you have to realize you need someone who can protect you."

Dane crowded closer. "Just what the hell is going on?"

Mick groaned. "God, I'm getting tired of explaining this."

"Then let me." Delilah drew herself up, and she wore the meanest expression Mick had ever seen. It relieved him, because at least some of the shock, some of the hurt, had been replaced. "Mick went to the hospital to see Rudy Glasgow."

"He's awake?" Dane asked.

"Yeah," Mick said. "Unfortunately, he is."

"While there," Delilah continued, "Rudy convinced him that I was part of his little gang, a criminal to be arrested."

Her tone was so nasty, the men all held perfectly still as if frozen by her censure.

"You see, Rudy knew personal stuff—and no, none of you need details—about what we'd done here in the apartment."

"In the bedroom," Zack supplied, earning a hot glare from Delilah.

"So, of course," she practically sneered, "Mick had to believe the worst about me."

Mick swallowed hard. She'd have them all lynching him before she finished. Already Josh was seething again, and Zack kept giving him reproachful looks. Dane and Alec just seemed resigned. "Delilah—"

"He convinced his connections in the police department to have me picked up for *questioning*."

Everyone looked at everyone else. Dane ventured, "Connections?"

Mick shook his head. "Never mind." Delilah didn't yet know he was a cop, and he had a feeling now wasn't a good time to tell her. He had enough amends to make without confessing his own deception.

"She thinks her apartment is bugged," Alec finished for her, cutting to the chase, "which would explain things."

"Ah." Dane nodded. "That'd make sense, I guess."

"It explains it better than thinking she had a hand in that damned robbery," Josh pointed out unnecessarily.

Zack elbowed him hard.

Defensive, Delilah crossed her arms over her middle and repeated, "I am not going home with Mick. I can take care of myself."

"You know," Alec said, his lowered brows making him look more than a little fierce, "this could have all been a ploy. Why tell Mick you were involved unless someone wanted him to get angry with you, to walk away from you?"

"Which would leave you alone and unprotected," Dane finished for him. He nodded. "Someone wants to get to her, but that's impossible with Mick watching over her. So they instigated this little separation."

Still determined, Delilah said, "I have a deadline."

"Good Lord," Mick muttered, unable to believe she'd be concerned with that now.

"I don't have time to debate with you. I just want to get settled down and finish my work."

"Someone is after you, damn it!"

Even when Mick shouted at her, she didn't meet his gaze. She stared down at her feet and said, "I'll be very careful."

She turned toward the apartment door, and again she got pulled up short. Josh, standing tall and resolute beside her, held her arm. "If you don't want to go home with Mick, come to my place."

Raging jealousy shot through Mick. Growling, he took an aggressive step forward, and both Alec and Dane flattened a hand on his chest, stalling him.

Delilah smiled in regret. "I can't do that, Josh. I'd drive you crazy in an hour."

"Not so."

She shook her head stubbornly. "No, it's out of the question. I wouldn't consider imposing on you."

"Then come home with me," Zack said. "Dani would love to have you there."

"No," she answered gently, looking a little amazed by the offers. "I don't sleep regular hours, and I'd be disruptive and—"

Dane shrugged. "You know you're welcome to our place, or to Alec's."

Alec nodded. "Absolutely."

"But either way, Delilah," Dane continued, "you can't be alone. It isn't safe."

Mouth open, she shook her head. "I don't believe this. You people hardly know me. You can't really want me underfoot. And if there is some type of danger, I could be bringing it to your homes!" She shook her head again, more violently this time, as if making a point. "No, I could never do that."

Dane turned to Mick. "Why don't you go in with Alec and look around? I'd like to speak to Delilah alone a second."

"About what?" Mick asked suspiciously, afraid Dane might bury him further. He was beyond pleased that everyone had jumped to her defense, had rushed to assist her, but he'd have been happier if she'd had no alternative but to give him another chance.

"About life and love and reality."

Josh grinned. "Can I listen in?"

"No." Dane caught Delilah's arm and dragged her toward the steps. "This'll only take a minute."

Delilah went grudgingly. Truth was, she didn't know what to do. Her only plan had been to get out of the apartment. She felt…dirty. Not just from Mick's impossible and hurtful accusation, but by the sickening possibility that someone had been watching her, someone had seen her making love to Mick. She shuddered with revulsion.

Dane put his arm around her shoulders and stopped at the landing at the bottom of the stairs. It was slightly cooler here, but not much. She felt hot and irritable and irrevocably wounded.

"You asked why any of us would want to take you in."

"I've never known people like you," she admitted, glad for something to think about besides the invasion of her privacy.

"We'd do it for Mick. We love him, and it's obvious you're important to him. He'd go out of his head if he screwed up this badly and something happened to you. I don't want to see him hurt that way. He's been hurt enough in his life."

The thought of Mick suffering because of her made her sadder than ever. Damn it all, she still loved him—and that was sheer stupidity on her part. Nursing her hurt, she said, "Yeah, he cares so much he thinks I'd get him shot."

"Men in love do stupid things. Our brains get all muddled. It's not what we expect, and we don't know how to deal with it."

"He's not in love."

"Wanna bet?"

"He's never said so."

"In words, maybe. But from the start he's been fascinated with you."

She scoffed, and Dane added gently, "Delilah, he took a bullet for you."

She shrugged off that irrefutable fact. When he'd thrown himself on top of her, he hadn't even known her name, so he couldn't have had feelings for her then. And since then…well, since then everything had been too fast. She was confused, so no doubt he was, too. "Mick is a hero," she reasoned. "He'd do that for anyone."

Dane laughed. "I agree, he's pretty damn heroic. But he's still human, so you have to allow him some human faults. Like bad judgment on occasion, and jumping to conclusions. And acting before he's really thought things out—which is what I think happened today."

"Do you have any idea how badly it hurts for him to think that of me?" Her heart, once full to bursting with love for Mick, now felt cold and hard, a dull ache in her chest.

"Yeah, I do. I made the same mistake with my own wife once."

That got her attention. Delilah stared at him, fascinated.

"It's a long story," Dane said, "and I won't bore you with the details now, but I let her think I was my deceased twin, because I thought she'd had a hand in trying to murder him."

Delilah felt her mouth drop open, her eyes widen. "That sounds more outrageous than the stuff I put in my books."

Dane winced. "I know." Then he smiled. "I fell in love with Angel before I got around to telling her the truth. When it all came out in the open, she hated me. Or at least I thought she did. *She* certainly thought she did. Circumstances not a lot different from what you're dealing with now kept her with me. And it gave us a chance to work things out."

"You think I should go home with Mick so he can make amends?"

"I think you should give your relationship every chance

to work out the ugly mistakes. It's not like you two met under normal circumstances. You've been shot at, he's been wounded, someone is obviously after you for some reason— that's enough in itself to make any relationship difficult."

"I guess."

Dane hugged her close. "One more thing. Mick wouldn't risk his life for just anyone. From what he said, he was already mesmerized by you before the shooting. He'd watched you, and thought about you. I understand it happens that way sometimes."

She rubbed her face, so tired and washed-out and confused she could barely order her thoughts enough to keep talking. "I don't know."

"You're feeling muddled, too," Dane pointed out, while gently rubbing her back. "All the more reason you should give things a chance. Go to his place, rest up, talk. I'm not saying to forgive him tonight, but at least let the opportunity exist for him to make it up to you. Give him a chance to explain. Who knows? Maybe he'll say something profound and you'll be able to forgive him."

They heard a noise and looked up the stairs. Mick stood at the top. Had he heard their conversation? His gaze on Del, he said, "We found something."

"We'll be right there." Dane put his arm around her and started her walking. "It's been a rough day. Wouldn't you like to go sit down and let your mind rest for a few minutes?"

Mick waited for them, watching Del closely with his intense, probing gaze. He almost seemed to be holding his breath, he stayed so still.

"Delilah?"

The gentleness, the hope in the way he whispered her name, broke Del's resolve. She nodded. "I'll go with you."

He let out his breath in a rush.

"But this doesn't mean I forgive you."

He nodded. "I haven't forgiven myself. For now I just want to get you settled and know you're safe." Then to Dane he said, "It's an optic fiber Minicam. High-tech stuff, run from the apartment next door."

Dane halted in midstep. "Next door?"

"Led in through the vents on the connecting walls." He glanced at Del, and she could feel his suppressed rage. He held himself in check for her, but he was more furious than she'd ever seen him. "Which included all the rooms except the kitchen and the bathroom."

Thinking of the eyes that had been on her, watching her while she wrote, slept, while she made love with Mick, made her stomach lurch. In the next instant Mick was there, gathering her close despite the trouble between them. "I'll find them, babe, I swear."

Giving herself a brief respite from her pride, Del rested her head on his shoulder. God, it felt good to have him hold her again.

When Dane went ahead into her apartment, Mick led her toward Josh and Zack. He touched her chin, bringing her gaze up to his. "I think it'd be best if you waited in my car. I'll only be a minute."

Josh threw his arm around her shoulder—and Mick promptly removed it. He said under his breath, "You've pushed enough today, Josh."

Josh just grinned, and Del had no idea what they were going on about.

"Have you ever noticed the neighbors next door?" Alec asked Del as he reentered the hall.

She gathered her scattered emotions. Now was no time to fall apart. "I know most everyone else in the building, but I thought that apartment was vacant."

"Does your landlord live here?"

"Afraid not." She wrung her hands, still shaken by having her worst suspicions confirmed. "I can call him if you want to check it out."

Mick shook his head. "We'll need to notify Faradon. He'll get a search warrant."

Del looked from one male face to another. "So what do we do now?"

"We get you settled and safe." Mick's eyes narrowed. "And then I'm going to see Rudy again."

CHAPTER TWELVE

Delilah waited inside Mick's house while he carried in her computer equipment, which she'd insisted on bringing along. Alec had checked the hardware and software for bugs and declared everything clean, so there was no reason for her to miss her deadline.

A severe headache left her somewhat nauseous, but she wasn't sure what to do. She'd never been in Mick's home before. Whenever he'd needed something, she'd offered to bring him home, but he'd always gotten someone else to take care of it.

Now she realized why. He hadn't wanted her inside his personal domain. That would have been too close to suit him. He wanted to keep her as distant as he could while still being intimate with her. And she, like a fool, had given him the perfect opportunity by moving him into her apartment.

"Where would you like me to put it?"

She turned to see Mick standing in the doorway, his arms filled with her monitor and keyboard, watching her. Josh and Zack stood behind him, loaded down with more equipment.

Del glanced around and shrugged. "I guess the bar counter would work as well as anywhere."

Mick didn't move, even though Zack and Josh were making impatient noises behind him. "You can use my desk."

"No, thanks." She walked away. The last thing she wanted was to further invade his privacy.

Almost an hour passed before they had her settled in. Dane had trailed them during the move, watching to make certain they weren't followed. The whole thing seemed very cloak-and-dagger to Del. Despite her profession, she'd never expected to be on the receiving end of a real mystery. Mysteries were figments of her imagination, not reality.

Mick's house, moderate in size, probably forty years old, had a quaint coziness about it. Del stood at the kitchen sink looking out the window. His backyard faced a cul-de-sac, and some distance away she could see a pool filled with playing children, another family grilling out on their patio. It all seemed so…domestic. Hard to believe she was here because someone wanted her dead.

Zack slipped his arms around her and rested his chin on top of her head. "You'll be all right."

She patted his hands where they crisscrossed her waist. One thing she'd realized through all this was that Josh and Zack were now her friends, too. She cherished that fact. "You think so?"

"I know there's no way in hell Mick's going to let anything happen to you."

She laughed at that. "Oh, I dunno. He just might decide I'm a criminal again and hand me over to them."

"Nope, ain't gonna happen. You've thrown him for a loop is all, and believe me, that's not easy to do." He kissed her temple, then asked, "Did I ever tell you how hard it was to make friends with him?"

She shook her head.

"He was so closed off, so damned isolated from everyone and everything. Because the fire department and the life squad are located right next door to each other, Josh and I were friends before we ever met Mick. But we all ate at Marco's and every day we'd see Mick sitting there alone. He'd just eat and leave."

It wasn't a pleasant image, his self-imposed isolation, and Del's heart softened in spite of her efforts to the contrary.

"One day some guys came in drunk and started causing problems." Del heard an odd note of enthusiasm in Zack's tone. "They were loud, disruptive, making a mess and scaring off customers. It was interesting, watching Mick go on alert, seeing how he took it all in and waited to make a move, without even appearing to notice. A waitress asked the men to leave, and one of the guys stood and took an aggressive stance. There were four of them, but Mick never hesitated to jump to her defense.

"He told the guy—nicely—to back off. A punch was thrown, and within seconds, Mick had the guy flattened. The others tried to rush him, three against one, but Mick didn't have any problem handling them." Zack chuckled. "He sure got Josh's respect that day."

"You two didn't help him?"

"He didn't give us a chance," Zack claimed defensively. "At least not with the actual fight. But afterward Josh insisted on buying him a drink—*insist* being the operative word, because Mick was hell-bent on keeping to himself—and the rest is history. It still took us half a year to get him to loosen up, to finally realize we weren't in cahoots with the bad guys. But we've been pretty close ever since."

"You're saying Mick doesn't come by trust easily?"

"You have to get him there kicking and screaming."

She smiled, thinking that a pretty apt picture. "Why?"

"Now that's something you'll have to ask Mick."

"I'm glad you're not telling *all* my secrets, Zack."

Zack gave Del a reassuring squeeze and turned to face Mick with a grin. "Just trying to help out."

Josh stood next to Mick. "Good luck. I just got read the riot act for that very same thing."

"You," Zack said, "had it coming."

Mick actually smiled. "You know, Zack, sometimes it's hard as hell to tell whose side you're on."

"I'm on the side of the right and just." He saluted Mick. "I suppose you're ready for us to make our exit?"

"I wouldn't be that rude."

Josh snorted. "He told me to get the hell out." So saying, Josh went to Del and hugged her right off her feet. "If he gives you any problems, call me."

Over Josh's shoulder, Del saw Mick's expression harden, and she quickly disengaged herself. "I'll be fine."

Josh teased, "But just in case…"

Zack grabbed him by the back of his shirt and dragged him away. "I need to get home for Dani, so we'll see you both later. Mick, if you need anything, just let us know."

Mick didn't answer; he was too busy watching Del.

She shifted uncomfortably, then heard the front door close. *Now what?* she wondered.

Mick came a step closer to her. She felt hemmed in by his imposing silence and the cold sink at her back.

She wasn't sure what she expected, but he only said, "You look exhausted. Why don't you take a warm shower while I hook up all your computer stuff? Or are you hungry? I can fix you something to eat."

She shook her head, very unsure of herself and the situation. "A shower sounds nice. But I…I don't know where it is."

Appearing pained, he closed his eyes, then opened them with a rueful sigh. "I'll show you around."

It was a two-bedroom house with hardwood floors and a small cream-and-black tiled bathroom. He showed her his bedroom, his air watchful, then the guest bedroom across the narrow hallway. Del peeked into both rooms.

His dark gaze pierced her careful reserve. "You can use whichever room you want." Unnamed emotions deepened his voice.

"Where will you sleep?"

"Wherever you want me to."

Well, heck. That put the decision back on her, and she felt too unsteady to force the issue at the moment. She gestured toward the smaller room. "I'll use this one."

With no inflection whatsoever, Mick said, "All right. I'll put your things in there." He led her back into the bathroom. "Towels are in the linen closet right here, and shampoo and stuff is already on the tub ledge."

He started to turn away and she reached for him. The muscles in his forearm tightened when her hand closed around his wrist. "Mick?"

He looked from her hand to her face. "Yeah?"

Del wanted to groan. He was so stiff, so…formal. She had a feeling he was trying not to pressure her, but she wished he would… No, she didn't know what she wanted.

"Is there any chance they know where you live?"

"No. We weren't followed today. Dane made sure of that, and I trust him. And only my closest friends, and the people I work with, have my address."

"But…"

In the briefest of touches, his fingertips grazed her cheek. "I've got a lot of explaining to do, honey. I wanted to wait until I got you here, so you couldn't change your mind about staying with me. But now I think I have to come clean."

Del stiffened. "If you're going to hurt me again, Mick Dawson—"

"No." His fingers tunneled into her hair, stroking her warmly. "I swear, I'll do my best never to hurt you again. But what I have to say will probably make you madder than hell."

She could deal with mad, she supposed. "All right."

"Take your shower, get comfortable, then we'll sit down and lay everything out in the open."

She wasn't at all sure she liked the sound of that, but figured he was right. From here on out, she wanted, demanded, honesty. If he couldn't give her that, they had nothing.

Mick gave a satisfied nod. He'd managed to accomplish a lot while she showered. But then, she'd stayed in there forever. Too many times to count he'd wanted to check on her, to make sure she wasn't crying or upset, but he knew getting too close to her while she was naked and wet would be his downfall.

So he clenched his teeth and worked. He had her computer, printer and fax machine all set up in a neat little organized corner. He'd given her his own padded desk chair, and taken one from the dinette set for himself. He'd hung her clothes in the closet, changed the sheets on the guest bed—a bed that had never been used. Canned chicken noodle soup simmered on the stove.

He'd called his sergeant and explained things, and spoken with both Faradon and Dane. Unfortunately, the apartment next to Del's was indeed empty, but they had been able to get some fingerprints. Running them would take some time.

Mick had just finished cutting two sandwiches into halves when Delilah walked in.

Her wet hair was combed straight back from her forehead and she'd pulled on loose shorts and a T-shirt. Barefoot as usual, she padded toward him and pulled out a chair. "I hadn't realized I was hungry, but the soup smells good."

Mick was so tense even his knuckles hurt as he put some soup in a bowl and set it before her. They ate in silence. When she was almost finished, he said, "I'm not a private investigator."

Her head lifted, her eyes wide and cautious. "You're not?"

Because he couldn't stop himself, Mick pushed his bowl aside and took her hand. "At first I lied out of necessity. I can't tell everyone the truth, that's just a fact of my job. Why I continued to let you believe the lie, I'm not sure. I told myself that we didn't know each other well enough. Too many things didn't add up." He met her beautiful blue eyes and admitted, "Actually, I think I was just afraid."

"Of me?"

He looked down at their clasped hands. She was so small boned, so delicate despite her height. She had a willowy appearance, and he wanted nothing more than to protect and cherish her. "It isn't easy to admit, but you scare the hell out of me."

Time stretched taut while she pondered those words. She turned her hand in his and returned his hold. After taking a deep breath, she said, "Okay, so what do you really do?"

"I'm a cop. I work undercover."

She stared at him, silent.

"I'd just finished a bust when I met you, which is a good thing, since I don't have a medical release to get back to work yet, and I hate turning over a case to someone new. It screws up the work that's already been done."

Still holding his hand, Delilah rested her free arm on the table and leaned forward, her animosity and distrust replaced by curiosity. "That's why you were armed?"

"Dane and Alec really are PIs. But yeah, I never go anywhere without my gun. Used to be a gun would make you stick out as a cop, but these days *not* having a gun would be a bigger giveaway. The world has turned into a nasty place."

She chewed her bottom lip. "What you do, is it dangerous?"

"Sometimes." Lying to her was no longer an option. "I mostly deal with prostitutes and drugs and gambling. Because of what I do, I live well away from where I work."

"I noticed."

Of course she had. Delilah was no dummy, he thought with a sense of pride. Even more encouraging was the fact that she hadn't yet pulled away from him. He took hope. "Rudy knew I was a cop. He said you knew and had told him."

He felt her slight emotional withdrawal when she stated, "But now you know that isn't true."

He rubbed his thumb over her knuckles, trying to soothe her. "I assume he heard me on the phone, talking to my sarge while I was at your apartment."

"Where was I?"

"The shower, the bed, involved in writing."

"Oh."

"Delilah…I'm sorry."

"No, I understand."

"Do you? Because I sure as hell don't." Self-disgust rose in his throat. "That first night I spent with you, I should have told you the truth."

"As I remember it, that first night I was too busy seducing you," she said, her tone lighter, more accepting.

"And here I thought I was the seducer."

Her face suddenly paled and she swallowed. "All the while, someone watched us."

"Don't think about that." Mick wanted to pull her into his lap, to hold her close. Instead, he redirected her thoughts. "If one of Rudy's cohorts did hear me, they still wouldn't know I was undercover. The station protects my identity."

Mick could see her researcher's mind at work. She frowned thoughtfully and said, "I think I understand how all this works, although I've never interviewed an undercover officer before."

"Now's your chance," he teased, so relieved that she wasn't angry, he almost felt weak.

"You drive your personal car to the station, but then trade up for an undercover car?"

"Not exactly. No uniforms ever know who's undercover. There's a special place where we switch cars, provided by the city. Once a car gets burnt up—"

"Burnt up?"

"Recognized." She nodded and he continued. "Then we get a new car."

"Something old and disreputable?" she asked, her nose wrinkling at the thought even as her eyes lit up with interest.

He shrugged. "Sometimes. But sometimes we get a fancy car. You never know. It depends on the case."

"You work with a partner?"

"Not exactly, but no one ever works without backup. We all carry pagers and cell phones—another common tool among criminals, thankfully. If something goes wrong, we have special codes we can dial to get help fast."

They talked for over an hour. Delilah surprised him with her understanding. But then maybe it was just her desire to learn about his profession that swayed her. He told her about how wires could be detected with special devices that ran through TVs. If the TV reception got wavy, meaning it had picked up the wire's reception, a perp might know he'd been set up, and things could get hazardous real quick.

Mick told her about his jump-out bag. It held a mask to cover his face when he made arrests, so the perps wouldn't recognize him. And about his vest, which he wore even when it was ninety degrees outside. He described the SIG Sauer guns some punks carried, and the hollow-point bullets used to make a bigger wound.

Everything he told her, no matter how gruesome, only made her curious for more. In so many ways she delighted him, excited him, alternately brought forth his lust and his protectiveness.

When she started yawning, Mick stood to put their bowls in the dishwasher. "I think it's time for you to get some rest. After everything I put you through today, you have to be exhausted."

He turned to see her rubbing her eyes tiredly. "I'm wiped out." But she didn't stand, didn't make a move to go to bed. She just stared at her hands.

Mick closed the dishwasher and stood at her side. "You don't have to be nervous here, Delilah. My house is secure, and Faradon has someone driving by every fifteen minutes. You're safe."

"I know." Still she didn't move.

Mick knelt down beside her. "What can I do?" he asked. He searched her face, and wished like hell he had some answers. "I know I can't make up for not trusting you, but I'll do whatever you need me to."

She stared at his hand on her knee. "You don't owe me. What you did...it's understandable. I just wish you'd talked to me first. Together we might have..."

"I'm a bastard, I know." He worked his jaw, then pointed out, "You haven't yelled at me at all."

Her slender shoulder lifted in a halfhearted shrug. "At first I was too devastated to yell. Then too hurt. Now...well, now I understand."

"I'd feel better if you'd yell."

Her soft mouth curled at his words, which weren't quite facetious. "There's no point to it."

And Mick had to wonder if that meant she considered him a lost cause, not worth the effort of a good yell.

Time, he'd have to give her time. "Come on. I think I'm ready for bed, too."

Looking at him through her inky lashes, she stood. He couldn't decipher her mood, and hated the helplessness he felt.

They went down the hall together, and Mick allowed himself to hold her for just a moment. He kissed her forehead and stepped away. "If you need anything, or want anything, I'm right next door."

She nodded. "Good night."

Mick stared at that damn closed door for far too long before taking himself off to bed. He doubted he'd get any sleep, and in fact, he wasn't tired at all. His body hummed with tension, with leftover adrenaline.

He left his door ajar so he'd hear her if she called out. Lying there in the darkness, he went over all the possibilities, but couldn't come up with a good reason why Rudy would want her dead.

It had to be linked to Neddie Moran somehow. It was just too much of a coincidence for her to have known Neddie before he was killed, and for Neddie's death to have taken place so close to the attempt on her life.

Mick turned to the bedside table and picked up the phone. Hitting the lighted numbers, he called Faradon.

"It better be important," Faradon grumbled. It sounded to Mick like the man was eating, but then Faradon probably ate a lot. He was as big as a bear.

"Did you find any connection between Neddie Moran and Rudy Glasgow yet?"

"Nope, not a thing so far. But then it could be Neddie knew

one of the other guys, and without their names, we're lost. The prints'll probably help. Don't worry, we'll keep digging. We're bound to turn up something soon."

Frustrated, Mick had just replaced the receiver into the cradle and settled back when his door squeaked open.

Delilah's silhouette was outlined by the faint light coming through his windows. "Mick?"

Mick's body thrummed to life as he propped himself up on one elbow. Unless his eyes deceived him, she wore only a T-shirt. He forced the raw hunger from his tone and asked as gently as possible, "You okay, babe?"

She crept closer, hesitated. "I don't want to sleep alone."

Those softly spoken words had a startling effect on his libido, an even bigger effect on his heart. Mick lifted his sheet, inviting her into his bed.

She hurried the rest of the way to him and slipped in by his side. For a second, she kept a slight distance between them. Mick didn't move, didn't breathe, and then she turned to him and gripped him tight, and all the pent-up tension inside him exploded.

"Christ, I'm sorry, so damn sorry," he murmured into her hair. His hold was tight and infinitely gentle.

Del cuddled closer, comforted by his scent, the warmth of his skin.... "You're not wearing anything?"

He stilled, then said, "I can put something on if you want."

"No." She loved touching him, and she needed the feel of him right now. All of him. The hair on his chest provided a nice cushion for her cheek, and she nuzzled into him. "Just hold me, okay?"

He turned to face her, drew her closer into his body so that he surrounded her, protected her. Always. Del felt a fat tear sting the corner of her eye. God, he was always trying to protect her.

"Does it bother you?" she whispered into the darkness, into the safety of his nearness.

"Hell, yes." His large hand opened on the back of her head, his rough fingertips sinking in to cradle her scalp, massage, soothe. "When I think of those bastards looking at you, I want to kill them. I *could* kill them."

Del sniffed and laughed and continued to cry softly. She was so damned confused. "No," she chided, wanting to hear him, to borrow some of his strength. "I meant does it bother you that they saw *you*. Your privacy was invaded as much as mine."

"I hadn't thought about it," he said. "At first I was just blind with…"

"Rage? Because you thought I had lied to you?"

He shook his head, then nuzzled her shoulder and squeezed her until she squeaked. "I hate to admit it," he rumbled against her throat, "but you deserve the truth. Ugly as it might be, regardless of how damn asinine I feel about it."

"The truth?"

"It wasn't rage I felt first, but this awful drowning hurt." He pressed his mouth to the skin of her throat, her shoulder. "There aren't many people in this world who could hurt me. But thinking that you'd used me, that you were laughing at me…it knocked my legs out from under me. It was all I could do to get the hell out of Rudy's hospital room without ripping him apart."

Del turned her face to his. "I'm sorry," she said very softly, and meant it.

"Oh God, don't. Don't apologize to me!" He sat up and switched on a light, shocking her, making her blink against the glare of it. "You should slap my face, Delilah. Or curse me or…hell, I don't know what. But don't apologize."

She looked up at him, her eyes welling with emotion, and his expression crumbled.

"Oh, babe, no, don't cry."

That got her laughing again, a wobbly, pathetic laugh. "Don't apologize, don't cry." She sniffed, and gratefully accepted the tissue he handed to her. She blew hard before continuing. "I've thought about it, and I can see why you believed Rudy. We haven't really known each other that long, not long enough for unconditional trust."

She scooted up to sit against the headboard. "Trust doesn't really come easy to me, either."

"Tell me what to do," Mick said, touching her cheek to remove one lingering tear. "Tell me how to prove to you that I *do* trust you."

She blinked. "Do you?"

He settled himself beside her, and their shoulders touched. Del had the sheet to her chin, but Mick barely had it covering his lap. Even now, in a vortex of emotions, he stole her breath away. He folded his hands over his abdomen and stared at the far wall.

"Damn right I trust you," he said. "I think it was myself I didn't trust all along. But you…almost from the minute I saw you, I wanted you. You drew me like no one ever had, and that shook me because I wasn't used to anyone affecting me like that." He glanced down at her. "It's scary the way you make me feel."

Del lifted her left arm over her shoulder and curled into his side again. "Okay?"

His arm tightened. "Better than okay."

"Will you tell me about your childhood?" She felt him stiffen, felt the stillness that came over him, body and mind.

"Why do you want to know?"

"To try to understand. I've gotten the impression it wasn't great, but that kid's a part of you."

"No."

"You can't run away from your past, Mick. All you can do is deal with it."

"I've dealt with it," he muttered.

Del knew she was pushing, but it was important to her to know all of him, the good and the bad. "Then you shouldn't have any problem sharing with me." To force the issue, she added, "Since you trust me."

"That has nothing to do with trust."

"Of course it does!" Again she twisted to look at him, but he pressed her head back to his shoulder. Del grinned. "You know, even Neddie trusted me enough to confide in me. He told me about his past and things he'd done, things he regretted."

This time Mick turned her face up to him. His fingers were hard, firm on her chin. "What things did he tell you?"

"You first."

"Delilah…"

She only raised a brow, waiting.

He sighed, gave a slight shake of his head and then kissed her forehead. He settled back, and though his pose was relaxed, she felt the rigid way he held himself. "Family services took me away from my mother twice. The first time it happened, I was about five. She'd gone out partying and hadn't come back, and a neighbor reported her."

Covering her shock and her sympathy, Del asked, "How long was she gone?"

"All weekend. In those days, other than her disappearing every now and then, it wasn't so bad. The house stayed kinda picked up and she had a regular job and she still seemed to… like me."

Seemed to like me. Del's heart cried out at the hurt he must have felt. She smoothed her hand over his chest and kept quiet.

"They gave me back to her easy enough, and I was glad. Sometimes being with her was rough, but it was nothing compared to not knowing what would happen, or being stuck with strangers. My mother promised to take some classes, to get into rehab for her drinking, and voilà—I was back home."

"Were things any better then?"

He laughed. "They got worse, actually. She was embarrassed that her neighbors knew I'd been taken away, so we moved. She got a new boyfriend and started drinking even more, but she was careful to put on a good show for the folks who checked up on her. It was another couple of years before things really went down the toilet."

Del cringed at the idea of something worse than a mother neglecting her son for an entire weekend, but again she kept silent, wanting him to talk.

"My mother had an affinity for drink first, and men second. She moved them in and out of our house, but none of them ever contributed, and most of them didn't care to see me too often. Until I was about twelve, I tried to just stay out of sight. But then her liver went bad and she got really sick, and the guy who was with her at the time took her to the hospital. She had to stay awhile, and he skipped out, so family services had me again. That was the worst. I mean, at five I probably needed looking after. But at twelve? I'd have been fine on my own, and when they finally let her out of the hospital I knew I had to take over or I'd get taken away from her for good. Not that I'd have missed her much, but…" He shrugged.

"The familiar," Del said, "is almost always easier than the unfamiliar."

"Yeah." He smoothed his fingers up and down her bare arm for a few minutes, thinking. "I was bigger than her by then, so she couldn't close me off in my room anymore or use threats against me. I could outrun her, and smacking me hurt her worse than it did me. So I told her how things were going to be."

Del shivered at the harshness of those words, at the awful reality he'd faced at such a young age. "At twelve years old, you took charge?"

"Damn right. And she listened, and did as I said, because she knew otherwise I could get her arrested."

"How?"

"She had men in the house who were thieves and cons. She'd done a lot of stupid stuff while drunk, including pros- tituting herself for drinks, gambling with money we didn't have, accepting stolen goods in exchange for a room—usually to someone busy dodging the law. Our television, and for a while our car, were both stolen."

Del wondered if that was why he'd chosen to work Vice, because he'd already seen the other side of it.

"A lot of the men would make big promises, some even to me. They'd talk about taking care of her, buying things, but they all lied. Family services lied, too, always telling me things would get better. And she was the worst of all— she lied every damn time she said she loved me. After that, she'd always tell me not to say anything to anyone because she'd be taken away and I'd be left all alone." He laughed, a rough, humorless sound. "I knew it was bullshit all along. Whatever maternal instincts she'd had got drowned in a bot- tle early on. By the time I was twelve, she'd already pretty much wiped her hands of me, but my new conditions really finished things off."

He drew a long breath. "She did as I told her, and she hated me in the bargain."

Del hugged him tight. "What, exactly, did you tell her to do, Mick?"

CHAPTER THIRTEEN

"We sold our house, which we were about to lose anyway, since she missed more and more work from drinking and couldn't make the payments. I didn't want to end up on the street, and neither did she. I checked around and found an apartment building—the one right next door to where you rent. It was a terrible area even then, but I used the money we made off the house to buy it, and the rent from the other apartments was income. I was in charge, taking applications from renters, collecting the rent, running ads when necessary."

"You did all that at twelve?"

"There weren't a lot of choices." He smiled down at her. "But it wasn't bad. Hell, it was the best it had been for a while. She stayed drunk and ran around with every Tom in town, but she knew better than to screw with the bill money. When I got old enough, I got a job and that helped, too."

"When did you meet Angel?"

His gaze brightened with a smile of genuine warmth. "She moved in when I was sixteen. Her first son, Grayson, was just a little-bitty squirt, and she'd been in a car wreck and was barely able to get around herself. I helped her out, and she started tutoring me in the school subjects I had problems with.

Angel was…she was the type of woman I hadn't seen before. She didn't lie or make things up. If something needed to be done, she found a way to do it."

Del felt more tears gather and quickly swiped them away. "I know she loves you."

"Yeah. She does. She thinks of herself as a big sister, or a surrogate mother, I guess." Mick reached over and tweaked Del's nose. "Now, you talk about a role model, that's Dane. Alec, too. They're both great guys."

She caught his hand and held it to her cheek. "They say the same about you."

Del kissed his palm, and he asked, "Delilah, will you forgive me?"

She hesitated to be totally honest with him. She knew that she loved Mick, and she'd rather die than hurt him. But the night was quiet, the light low, and he deserved the truth. "I can forgive you, because I understand." *I love you too much not to.* "But I don't know that I'll ever feel the same again."

He went rigid. "What does that mean, Delilah?"

She wished he hadn't turned the light on. She'd have preferred the concealing darkness, which made confessions so much easier. "Since the day I met you, I've seen you as bigger than life, a knight in shining armor, fearless."

He snorted. "That's nonsense. Hell, I just told you, *you* scare the hell out of me."

She shook her head; nothing really scared Mick, she knew. And she certainly didn't have that type of power over him. If she had, he wouldn't have turned on her so easily. "I write about heroes every day, but I didn't know they existed. I didn't think any man would deliberately risk his life to keep someone else safe. I didn't know a stranger would risk his life, not for me."

He frowned over that.

"I saw you as…" she shrugged helplessly "…the best of everything."

Mick shoved away the sheet and stood. Gloriously naked, he stalked to the window and looked out at the black, balmy night. A large oak blocked what little moonlight there might have been. No leaves stirred; all was silent except for the bumping of her heart.

The faint light from the bedside lamp threw a glow along one side of his body, causing shadows to dip and swell over his muscles and bones, exaggerating his strength, which she already knew to be considerable. She wanted to touch him everywhere. She wanted to eat him up. And nothing, not even her hurt, could change that.

"I come from nothing, Delilah." His voice broke the night, harsh and raw. "For most of my life, I was nothing. Despite how they feel about it, I'm like a stray that Angel dragged home and everyone accepted. I owe Angel and Dane and their whole goddamn family for showing me what family is, for letting me know how a real life could be, and for helping me to get that life. I owe them for who I am now. But if you stripped them away and left me with just myself, with just the bare bones of *me,* I'd be back at square one. And that sure as hell isn't a white knight."

"No!" She struggled to her knees, clutching the sheet to her throat. "You are who you are, Mick Dawson, a strong, capable man with or without anyone else."

He whirled around. *"I am not a damn hero."*

He looked livid, his eyes red, his nostrils flaring. Del stared.

"Don't you dare put me on some fucking pedestal," he growled, "because I'm guaranteed to fall off. I'm human, and I blunder my way through life just like everyone else."

When she remained silent, wide-eyed and stunned, he stomped back to the bed, caught her upper arms and lifted her from the mattress, causing her sheet to fall. She worried for his injured shoulder, and his injured soul.

"You thought I was impervious to cold, too, that I had insides made of iron."

Del sputtered. "Don't bring up my coffee now!"

"You don't know what I go through, how I fight every day to make sure I stay deserving."

Deserving of what? she wanted to ask, but she couldn't. "Mick…"

"To a lot of people, right and wrong are clear-cut values. But not to me. I force those ideologies into the front of my mind all the time—that a woman strung out on drugs is wrong, not just desperate. That a young man with a gun is a criminal, not a kid trying to survive. I don't even know what a white knight is, but I know what the rules tell me, and I follow those rules to the letter."

Del swallowed her hurt. Looking at him, seeing his pain, hurt even more. "Did those rules tell you to protect me when you knew it might get you killed?"

His jaw clenched; his entire body tightened. But his hands didn't hurt her. She knew without a doubt that Mick would never, ever physically hurt her.

"An officer has to take action when he sees a civilian threatened."

She barely heard what he said. "Did those rules insist you turn me in because you thought I was breaking the law? Or did you do that because you thought I'd used you?"

He tipped his head back and groaned. "Both."

"Mick?" She needed to touch him, to soothe him, but his hold didn't allow for that. So she gave him the only words she knew that might help. "I forgive you."

His gaze jerked to hers, hot, burning, filled with relief, with satisfaction, greed, elation.

She saw the pulse racing in his strong throat, saw the muscles in his shoulders quiver, saw the glaze of relief in his eyes.

"I want you," he groaned. "More than I've ever wanted anything. More than I wanted my mother to care, more than I wanted Angel to be safe." He shook her slightly. "More than I want my next breath. But I'm just me, and if you try to make me more than that we'll both be disappointed."

Del licked her lips. It sounded to her like he loved her, though he hadn't quite said so. "Do you want me now?"

He lifted her a few inches more until his mouth ground down on hers, bending her head back. His tongue thrust deep. Her body came into stark contact with his, making her aware of all his hard angles and firm muscles, and the long, hard length of his throbbing erection.

Just as quickly his kiss eased and he gentled his hold. His velvet tongue licked, teased, then slowly withdrew. "I'm sorry," he murmured against her mouth, nibbling on her lips, softening them. *"I need you."*

"Your shoulder," she said in alarm, fearing he'd hurt himself.

And Mick groaned again, a sound of half humor, half awe. "Even when I act like a marauding bastard, you don't put me in my place." His expression was less strained, and a half smile curled his mouth. "You're something else, Delilah Piper, you know that?"

"Something good?" she asked.

He smoothed her hair, stroked her lips with his thumb. "Something wonderful," he whispered, and then he kissed her again, this time with such sweetness, such love, she didn't even need to hear him speak the words. She couldn't resist him. He'd tell her what she wanted to hear sooner or later, but for tonight she had him, she had his confidences, and that was more than enough.

★ ★ ★

The second Mick awoke, he knew the other side of the bed was empty. He sat up in a rush, panic closing in—and saw Delilah sitting in the chair by the window. He eased back, but his heart continued to stutter and his stomach still cramped. "You couldn't sleep?"

A dark shadow made up her form in the gray, predawn light, and still he sensed her smile. "Watching you is more fun than sleeping."

He realized the sheet was around his ankles, and he cocked a brow at her. It was easier to breathe now, with her so obviously teasing. "Taking advantage of me?"

"Yes."

Mick stretched and yawned. With his initial alarm gone, he realized he felt better today, less frazzled, but not completely satisfied. He didn't think he'd be content until he had Delilah committed to him one hundred percent. And that meant getting a ring on her finger and hearing her say the vows.

When she was officially his wife, then maybe he could relax.

He'd made progress last night, though he hoped like hell she'd never put him through anything like that again. He hated rehashing the past. It shamed him, reminded him of how weak he'd been, how far he'd struggled. And whether Angel admitted it or not, he always knew he'd never have made it without her. If it hadn't been for Angel, he'd be on the other side of the law right now, the one being arrested for God only knew what, rather than a cop doing the arresting.

It was an emotional struggle he dealt with every day.

He heard Delilah sigh as he stretched his left arm high, and grinned. She was so blatant about enjoying his body, both by touch and sight. He was glad he hadn't spent his life chasing women and screwing around like so many males seemed driven to do. It made their relationship that much more special. She was the only woman who'd ever lived with him.

"I thought you'd be writing," he said as he stood and went to his dresser to get some shorts.

She turned to watch him. He knew his way in the dark, but still he flipped on the wall switch, wanting to see her better.

She looked…dreamy.

"I didn't even think about writing."

He frowned, stepped into his gray boxers and went to her. She wore his shirt, and that turned him on. Of course, if she'd been wearing nothing at all, or the sheet, or her own T-shirt, he'd have still been turned on. She couldn't breathe without making him hard.

He stood looking down at her, dreading the question he had to ask. "Did I interfere with your work?"

"How so?"

He smoothed her glossy dark hair behind her ears, touched her arched brows. "You were so upset, I thought…"

"Oh, no. When I'm upset, I usually work through it at the computer. Same when I'm excited. Or sad."

Mick shook his head. Not much got in the way of her writing.

"It's just that last night was so wonderful. *You* were so wonderful." She sighed again, a sigh of repletion and fulfillment, making him feel like that damn white knight she'd spoken of.

Then she added, "I've been thinking, too, about Neddie, about some of the stories he told me."

Slowly, Mick straightened. "Let's do this over coffee."

"Do this?"

"I have a gut feeling that whatever you're going to tell me will be the clue we've been missing. I need caffeine to digest it all, so I don't miss anything important."

Delilah stood and did her own stretching. His pulse leaped.

If this wasn't so important… He eyed the bed. But no, it *was* important, and he had to see to her safety first.

"This gut feeling of yours," she asked, "is it like a cop's sixth sense?"

Mick put his arm around her and led the way to the kitchen, flipping on the lights as he went. It was only five-thirty. It'd be another hour or so before the sun lit the sky. "I just know that somehow all this stuff is related."

She nodded, took a stool at the counter—evidently more than willing to have him wait on her, which he was glad to do. "I think it has to do with the story I'm working on."

"Your newest book?" He measured coffee and turned on the machine.

She nodded. "You got anything I can snack on? I'm starved."

He remembered she'd been too upset to eat much the night before, and guilt washed over him. He scrounged around until he found her a few cookies. "I can put some eggs and bacon on, too," he offered, and she accepted with a mouthful of cookie.

"You talk while I cook," he said.

She waved the second cookie at him. "Neddie was trying to go straight, you know? A condition of his parole was that he continue to be counseled, and part of his counseling was to own up to the things he knew he'd done wrong. So he sometimes talked to me."

"You were supposed to absolve him of guilt?"

"Not even close." She chewed on her cookie, thinking, then shuddered. "He told me some gruesome stories," she admitted. "Stuff I could never use in a book. It was too… real, and you know what they say about truth being stranger than fiction. But in a way, Neddie had this odd code of honor. He didn't hurt anyone that he didn't think needed to be hurt. I mean, he didn't just choose innocent victims."

"He hired himself out, honey. He did what he was paid to do."

"I know." She brushed the remainder of the crumbs from her hands and watched Mick lay bacon in a hot skillet. "But he only took jobs that his conscience would let him take. Like this one guy he snuffed—"

"Snuffed?" Mick eyed her, appalled at the casual way she said that.

She shrugged. "It's part of the lingo."

Didn't he know it. "Go on."

"Anyway, the guy he killed had some huge gambling debts, but Neddie said he took the job because the guy also abused his wife."

Mick made a face. "What a discerning fellow."

Delilah laughed. "That's what I said to him. And he knew it was still wrong, but he said he half enjoyed beating that guy up and then dumping him for dead, because he hated anyone who would hit a woman."

"We're in agreement on that."

In a voice as soft as butter, she said, "I know."

Mick poked at the bacon with a fork. He couldn't take her hero worship on an empty stomach, so he steered her back to the subject at hand. "What does any of this have to do with your story?"

"Well, Neddie told me that these guys tried to hire him to kill a man because the guy knew too much and wanted to come clean. They were afraid he'd turn evidence on them or something, so they wanted Neddie to kill him, then sink his car in the river."

Mick jerked around, staring at her. A limp piece of uncooked bacon dangled from the fork in his hand.

"Neddie refused. Not only because he was out of the business and trying to go straight, but because he said he sympathized with the other guy. He said they were alike, both of them wanting to be legit, and there was no proof the guy would rat. After all, Neddie said he'd never ratted anyone out before."

This is it, Mick thought with a surge of triumph. *This is the link.*

"I told Neddie about how I'd learned to escape a car that had gone into the river, and he said I couldn't have escaped if I'd been dead before it went in." Delilah tilted her head at Mick, her beautiful, light blue eyes filled with a heavy sadness. "Is that what happened to Neddie? You said he was murdered, and I know he drowned. Did someone kill him, then drive his car into the river? The paper didn't give all the details. I didn't know you were a cop, so I didn't think you'd know, either. After all, it was supposed to be confidential stuff for the ongoing investigation."

For the first time that he could remember since becoming an officer of the law, Mick didn't even consider what was right or wrong. He set a cup of coffee in front of Delilah and pulled out the stool next to her. Their bare knees touched, his on the outside of hers. "Neddie's wrists," he explained carefully, "had bruises on them, evidence that he'd been tied up, though there were no ropes or anything on him when his body was found."

Delilah reached for his hand, and Mick squeezed her fingers.

"He had a wound on the back of his head, too. The coroner said he'd been struck with a blunt object, knocked out just before the car went off the bridge—or possibly as the car went over. It'd be impossible to tell for sure, but as you just said, he wasn't given the chance to escape the car and swim to the surface. We're thinking whoever did it hoped the car wouldn't be found until time and the natural effects of water and cold had done enough damage to disguise a deliberate murder."

"He had a suicide note in his pocket?"

Mick nodded. "Yeah."

Her lips quivered, and she drew a ragged breath. "That's exactly what Neddie described, what he said the men wanted him to do." She blinked away a sheen of tears, and whispered raggedly, "I used that whole scenario in my book."

"The book you're working on now?"

"Yes. In the last book, the hero got away by keeping his head and doing the things I'd learned from submerging myself in a car."

Mick shuddered. He could *not* think about that now. Somehow he'd figure out a way to temper Delilah's more dangerous inclinations, without stifling her.

"But in this book," she continued, oblivious to his turmoil, "he was knocked out, a suicide note planted on him, and the heroine had to save him."

Just like Delilah to twist things around, Mick thought. But then, if any woman were capable of a rescue, it'd be Delilah Piper. He wouldn't underestimate her on anything, once she set her mind to it.

It was an enormous long shot, but Mick asked, "That whole scenario is too damn close to the truth to be comfortable. Does anyone know what's in this book?"

She nodded. "Tons of people, I'm sure. Remember I told you I was on the news, discussing my current project? We talked about that whole scene. I...I was laughing about it, bragging that it could happen, and that a woman might indeed be a hero. I never once considered that I could be putting Neddie in danger."

"Neddie didn't know about the interview?"

"I don't know." She covered her face. "He died shortly after that. He...he might have died because of *me*. Someone could have heard that radio program, someone who knew we'd become friends, that Neddie coached me on my research."

"And they might have assumed he'd told you too much, and that you could repeat it." If Mick thought he'd felt fear before, it was nothing to what he felt now. Someone wanted to shut her up, to make certain she couldn't repeat details that might be incriminating. But he didn't know who, and until he did know, until he could get the bastards, her life was at stake.

Delilah rocked slowly back and forth in her seat as the ramifications settled around her. "I'm to blame."

With a new fury, Mick tipped up her chin. "*Wrong.* Don't even go there, babe. When you live the type of life Neddie did, then you run the risks. That's just how it is."

"He was changing."

"Maybe just a little too late." Mick pulled her into his lap. "Did Neddie give you any names, anything that might connect him with the killers?"

She thought hard, staring down at her hands. Slowly her gaze rose to his. "You know, he did say something, but I'm not sure it'll help."

"At this point, it'd have to be more than we've got."

She nodded, her brows drawn. "He said the guys who wanted to hire him should have known better, because they'd been in prison with him in '86, all of them convicted for car theft."

It took several moments for it to sink in, before Mick allowed himself to believe. "Bingo."

"You think?"

"I think it'll be easy enough to check prison records. That might do it, with your testimony. Especially if the fingerprints from the apartment next to yours match up. We should have those today."

"Is that why they tried to kill me? They knew Neddie had been talking to me? They knew he'd...told me things?"

Mick hugged her. God, she was precious to him. And she was also smart, so there was no point in hoping to protect her. Besides, he didn't want her feeling guilty for Neddie's death, not if he could help it.

"The bruises on Neddie's wrists showed that he put up a hell of a fight, that he tried to work himself free. But he didn't make it." Mick kissed her temple, her ear. "Could be they promised to let him go if he named everyone he'd talked to."

She shook her head, adamant in Neddie's defense. "No, Neddie would never have done that, not if he thought they'd hurt me."

Her innocence amazed him. "How long did you know him, sweetheart?"

"A few months. But we were friends, Mick," she said staunchly.

"That's not enough time to really judge."

She leaned back and gave him a level look. "It's longer than I've known you."

Mick scowled, not appreciating that comparison at all. "He was an admitted murderer. A car thief. Those things are not synonymous with ethics, and any man could cave when his life was on the line."

"I won't believe that."

Mick decided to let it go. She'd been hurt enough, and disillusioning her now wouldn't accomplish a thing. "Let's finish up breakfast and shower, then I'll call Faradon. He should be up by then, and if not, well, he'll get up."

"You really think any of this will make a difference?"

"I know it will."

"I hope so," she said. "I want this behind us. I want us to

take walks in the park and go to the zoo, and I want to get back to my research."

Mick groaned. He didn't know if he could live through her special brand of daredevil study.

But he knew he didn't want to live without her, so he supposed he'd find a way to get used to it.

CHAPTER FOURTEEN

The phone rang while Mick was in the shower. He'd insisted that Del go ahead while he cleaned the kitchen, and when she'd protested, he claimed it had to be that way. If he showered with her, they'd never leave his house.

She accepted that he probably was right.

With her hair still wet and her feet bare, Del picked up the phone. "Dawson residence."

"Faradon here. Is this Ms. Piper?"

"Yes," she said shortly. Detective Faradon still wasn't one of her favorite people, not after the interrogation she'd been through.

"We got the fingerprints back and have some photos to go with them. We'd like you to come to the station and take a look, see if you can ID anyone. How soon can you be here?"

She bristled at his demanding tone. At the very least, she felt the man owed her a few apologies. "Actually, Mick and I were coming in, anyway." She didn't mention her new "evidence" because she wasn't convinced it would help. Mick could explain everything.

There was a pause, then he asked, "How soon?"

"Mick is about done showering now. I'd say we'll leave here in the next fifteen minutes."

"I'll be waiting," he said, and rudely hung up.

A few minutes later Mick came out looking nicely rugged and sexy as sin in faded, well-worn jeans and a soft gray T-shirt. He wore scuffed, lace-up black boots. As Del watched, he checked his gun.

She inched closer. "Can I see?"

He glanced up. "What? My gun?"

Nodding, she said, "A Smith & Wesson, right? Semiautomatic?"

Mick held the gun out of her reach. "No one touches my gun but me."

She rolled her eyes. "I'm not going to fire it. And I do know a little about guns."

"Research, I suppose?"

"Yes."

"Well, then you know enough to understand how dangerous they are." With a dexterity that proved how quickly he was healing, he tucked the gun into a holster at the small of his back, and smoothed his T-shirt over it. "And," he said again, "*no one* touches my gun but me."

"Fine. Whatever."

He caught her before she could turn away, and kissed her neck. It was shameful, but she immediately softened, just as he'd probably known she would.

"Who was on the phone?" he asked against her throat.

Sometimes it was annoying, loving Mick. She couldn't seem to stay angry with him, especially when he kissed her. "Your buddy, Faradon."

"He's not my buddy, he's just the lead investigator on the robbery and shooting." He kissed her again, this time nuzzling beneath her ear. It felt like her toes melted. "What did he want?"

Struggling to get her brain in gear, she succeeded in saying, "He has fingerprints and photos, and he wants us to come take a look for a positive ID."

Stepping back from her, Mick looked at the chunky black watch on his wrist. "Hell, it's barely eight o'clock. He's at it early."

Feeling hopeful for the first time, Del asked, "Do you think that means we're close to having this wrapped up?"

Mick took her arm and headed for the door. "Even with an ID, we'd still have to get hold of them, but it'd sure make it easier to track the bastards down. It's tougher to hide when everyone knows who you are. There's also the possibility that Rudy'll be more willing to talk once we have names."

The sun never did quite rise. Instead, as they stepped outside, they saw that fat purple clouds had rolled in, leaving the air heavy with the scent of rain. In the distance, lightning flickered.

Mick cursed. "Did you want to grab a jacket or umbrella?"

"I won't melt."

She saw his surprise, then his smile, as he opened the car door for her. "I'd forgotten your affinity for rain," he said.

When she raised a brow, he explained, "The day I finally met you, the day of the robbery. Everyone else had an umbrella, but you didn't even seem to notice how soaked you'd gotten." He slid his hand over her waist and squeezed suggestively. "I noticed."

Del smiled at that. It was nice being reminded that the awesome attraction went both ways. If Mick had indeed noticed her when she looked like a used rag mop, then his interest was as keen as hers. Maybe more so, because she hadn't paid him a bit of mind until the shooting.

Once he folded his big body behind the wheel, she told him, "I love running in the drizzling rain. It's peaceful and it stimulates my muse."

He started to make a nasty crack, no doubt about stimulating her, and Del elbowed him. They both laughed and she thought how nice it was, how right, to be with Mick this way. She wondered, once everything was settled, what would happen. When it was no longer necessary for her to stay with him for protection, would he ask her to leave? Would he ask her to stay?

Half an hour later she was still pondering that when the sky opened up. No slight drizzle this, but a raging summer storm full of power. The stuffy, humid air came alive with electricity, crackling and snapping all around them. Trees bent and dipped, leaves and debris danced across the rain-washed roadways.

Del slanted Mick a look. "Rainstorms are sexy," she whispered.

"You're sexy. Rain or no rain," he replied, keeping his gaze on the road.

She grinned, about to tell him how she'd like to spend the afternoon once they finished at the station, when they were blinded by a sudden glare. In the darkness of the morning storm, an approaching car's bright lights reflected off Mick's door. He flinched, throwing up a hand, but it didn't help. The car came from an empty side street, and rather than slowing, it accelerated to a reckless speed across the slick roadway, coming right for them.

Mick glanced out his window, gripped the wheel tightly and muttered with icy calm, "Hold on."

The car struck the back side-panel, throwing them into a spin. Del's seat belt tightened; she yelped in alarm, barely keeping her wits enough to twist around, trying to see what happened.

At the force of impact, Mick first overcompensated, and the car slewed off the road and into the mud before grasping the slick pavement again.

Del, assuming it was an accident—a result of the rainy conditions—wondered why Mick didn't just pull over. She looked over her shoulder, wide-eyed, in time to see the other car straighten and shoot toward them again.

Mick's hand flattened on the top of her head, and he shoved her down in the seat. "Stay there!"

The rear windshield exploded, glass flying everywhere. "Dear God!" Del held Mick's thigh, her face pressed into his side. This couldn't be happening! She tried to sit up, wanting only to protect Mick.

"Keep down," Mick barked, again flattening her in the seat. It suddenly hit her who was after them and why.

Del felt another impact, this time to the rear fender of the car, and there was no way to steer out of it. The car swerved off the road, slinging mud and fishtailing, and finally colliding with a scrawny tree, jarring them both hard.

Mick's head hit the wheel and he slumped.

"Mick!" She screamed his name, scrambling to get her seat belt off, to reach him. Her heart leaped into her throat, her vision clouded with fear. Before she could reach him her door was jerked open. The thunderous roar of the storm intruded, along with a spray of rain and turbulent air. Hard hands grabbed her, yanking her back. She fought them, seeing the trickle of blood on Mick's forehead, the stillness in his body.

He needed help, a hospital! But already her feet were being dragged through the mud, and no matter how she fought, she couldn't escape. The hands holding her only tightened with bruising force.

Someone grabbed her hair and wrenched her head back. "Do you want me to go back and put a bullet in him to make sure he's dead?"

That voice was rough, familiar, and Del froze, choking on her terror. "No."

"Then come along and be quiet."

A hard shove landed her facedown in the front seat of the other car, and she barely had time to right herself before two men squeezed in around her. The battered car had been left running, idling roughly. The interior smelled of smoke and stale liquor. It was dirty, cluttered.

The man on her right pressed a gun to her ribs, hard enough to make her groan, and with enough intent to scare her witless. She recognized them as the same men from the jewelry store—the men who wanted her dead.

"What do you want?" she asked around her fear, wanting, needing Mick. *Dear God, please let him be all right.*

"Shut up."

The car lurched away, tires squealing, zigzagging with a distinct lack of caution for the weather and road conditions. Wet tendrils of hair stuck to Del's face and throat. She swiped them aside and twisted to see Mick's car as they made a screeching U-turn and sped away. Right before he was out of view, she could have sworn she saw him lift his head, but it was hard to tell with the rain streaking the dirty windows and the strobing effects of the electrical storm.

Del closed her eyes on another silent prayer. Mick *had* to be okay. The gun prodded her when they made a sharp turn, keeping her own danger in acute perspective. She felt icy cold inside and out, and couldn't stop the racking shakes that made her teeth chatter and her head hurt.

Keep them talking, she thought. "How did you know where to ambush us?" she asked.

Smirking, the man lifted his hand to his head, finger and thumb extended as if it were a phone. "This is Faradon," he mimicked. "We need you to come to the station."

Her stomach roiled. "You had us bugged again?" Had these disgusting men heard Mick's heartfelt admissions about his past? She couldn't bear it.

"Nope. I didn't overhear the call, I *made* the call. Your protector was rather accommodating, sharing his home number with Faradon and asking him to leave any messages concerning the robbery on his message machine. He didn't want you to know he was a cop, you see, but he still wanted to stick his nose where it didn't belong. The son of a bitch was determined to get hold of us." He shrugged. "He called his house and took his messages that way, and you went on in blissful ignorance, thinking you screwed a PI, not a cop."

Reality sank in. One more lie Mick had told. Strangely enough, she felt more concern for his guilt, if he should find out, than she did for the lie. She understood him. She knew why he hadn't confided in her. She'd meant it when she'd said she forgave him for that. "You got Faradon's name and Mick's number from a call he made at my place."

"That's right. So, no, Faradon isn't expecting you. He won't send out the cavalry."

Del looked through the mud-spattered windshield and saw they were headed toward the river. Not the Ohio—no, that would be too obvious. This was a much smaller, much dirtier river. But it was deep. And fast. Mostly isolated excepted for the occasional fisherman. But not today. Today the river was deserted.

And she knew why they were going there.

Do not get hysterical, she told herself, even as her breath hitched and her lungs constricted. She could smell the two of them in the stuffy, steamy interior of the car. She could smell her own fear and their excitement. Bile rose in her throat.

They pulled off the main road and drove through a patch of weeds and scrub. A ramshackle outbuilding sat to their right, and a long wooden pier, probably private, stretched along the shore, then angled out into deeper water. The car bumped onto it, tires thumping along the uneven, weather-worn boards.

Though they moved slowly now, edging nearer and nearer to the end of the dock, Del felt time speeding past her. A cabin cruiser docked to their right blocked them from view of the road.

Over the river, lightning danced, temporarily illuminating the sky and emphasizing the blackness of the deep, churning water. They meant to drown her, to kill her and sink the awful, dirty car with her inside it.

The driver laughed, reaching for her upper thigh and giving her a lecherous squeeze. "It's a shame we have to end this so quickly," he sneered. "Watching you with that cop makes me want to taste you myself."

Del slugged him.

She didn't think about it, didn't weigh the wisdom with the folly. She simply snapped, then reacted on instinct. Using a technique she'd learned in self-defense classes, she brought her elbow up and back. Hard, fast. Right into his face.

"Fucking bitch." The driver grabbed for his bleeding nose and temporarily lost control of the car. The other man grabbed Del by the neck, squeezing as he shouted orders.

In that single moment of chaos, everything became clear for Del, and she knew what to do.

She ignored the fist clamped around her throat, making it impossible for her to draw air, and instead put her efforts into a hard shove on the driver. He lost his balance, and Del wedged her foot down to the floorboards. She found the gas pedal and jammed down.

With a loud roar of the engine, the car lurched forward. The driver shouted, gripping the wheel, but Del had clamped both hands on it. They wrestled, but he sputtered blood and went blind with panic.

The hand at her throat let go to grab her shoulder. It felt like her arm had been wrenched from the socket—but it was too late. The old car went airborne off the far end of the dock, suspending time and sound and reality, then dumped hard into the icy river with an enormous splash. Hissing and sputtering, the car tipped, engine first, and began sinking.

Both men forgot about Del in their panic. They pounded at the windows, screamed as the blackness engulfed them and water began rushing in.

Del concentrated on regaining her breath. Her throat felt crushed; it hurt to swallow, even to breathe, but she did it, slow, deep. The gun had dropped onto the seat beside her, forgotten. She tucked it into her pocket. The man to her right got the window open, and a great gush of frigid river water knocked him backward into Del. His elbow caught her shoulder, his foot dug into her thigh as he scrambled frantically to get to the window again, bent only on escaping the car.

On her knees so that her head stayed in the pocket of air inside the car, Del inhaled deeply, then slithered to the back seat. Water closed over her face just as her fingers found the window handle.

She thought of Mick, thought of everything she wanted to tell him, and did what she had to do.

Mick wiped blood from his face with one shaking hand and maneuvered the slippery, winding road with the other.

After smacking his head on the steering wheel, he'd come to in enough time to see the car leaving with Delilah—but not in enough time to stop them.

Going seventy miles an hour to diminish their lead, he'd called for backup. His actions had been by rote, because both his mind and his heart stalled the second he'd realized what had happened.

He reached the river just in time to see the car sail off the dock and hit the churning water with crunching force. Terror blinded him. He wasn't aware of slamming on his brakes. He wasn't aware of the other police cars pulling up at the same time, sirens blaring and lights flashing.

He threw open his car door and hit the ground running, his only thought to get to Delilah. The storm surrounded him, lashing his face, making his feet slip in the wet weeds and slimy mud. Just before he reached the end of the dock, he got tackled hard and then held down. He fought the restraining hands without thought, hitting someone, kicking another.

"No, goddamn it," Faradon shouted when Mick almost wrenched loose. "Hold him!"

Mick barely heard. Three men gripped him, twisting his arms, making his wounded shoulder burn like fire, but it was nothing compared to the agony in his heart.

They jerked him to his feet, and all around him men shouted orders, while sirens continued to squeal and blue lights competed with the white flashes of the storm.

Numb, Mick continued to strain against the arms holding him. Faradon stepped up close. "We have a team preparing," he said not two inches from Mick's face. "Dawson, do you hear me? They'll be in the water in ten minutes tops."

Mick shook his head. In ten minutes she would be dead.

With renewed strength he lurched forward, taking the men

by surprise. They lost their footing on the slippery, weathered boards and their holds loosened. Mick broke free.

He'd taken two running steps when someone shouted, "Look!"

A spotlight searching the surface of the water reflected off Delilah's inky-black hair. She sputtered, coughed. Mick went into the water in a clean dive. With several hard fast strokes, he reached her.

When he closed his hands around her, she at first fought him.

"It's all right, baby," he said, spitting dirty water, "it's me."

"Mick?" She dog-paddled, swallowed some of the water and choked, then cried, *"Mick!"*

She clung to him. Mick felt so weak it was all he could do to drag in air. Then several men surrounded them, catching them both and pulling them to the docks.

He hoisted Delilah up first. Faradon himself leaned down. "Give me your hands, miss," he said, and Delilah reached upward.

Sloshing, shivering, she landed on the dock, and someone rushed to put several blankets around her.

"M-M-Mick?"

He heard the shivering alarm, the need, and helped to drag himself out. Officers tried to cover him, too, but he wanted only Delilah. Weaving on her feet, she reached for him, and then he had her, tight in his arms where she damn well belonged and where she'd damn well stay.

He heard her crying, and his knees went weak. He tangled his hands in her wet hair, knowing he was too rough, but unable to temper his hold. "I've got you," he said gruffly, and crushed her to him.

"Mick, c'mon, man," said a gentle voice. "Let's get her out of the rain."

As if from far away, Mick heard Faradon speaking to him. He wrapped Delilah closer and allowed them both to be led to the outbuilding. It was dry inside, that was the best to be said for it.

Faradon stood there, looking slightly embarrassed. "We're, uh, fetching some dry clothes."

Mick gulped air, swallowed choking emotions and a love so rich he couldn't bear it. Delilah clung to him, and he didn't know if he'd survive the fear of thinking he'd lost her. He lifted his head. "The bastards who took her?"

"We're looking for them. If they surface, we'll fish them out. If not, we'll start diving until we find them."

Delilah struggled for a moment, and Mick loosened his hold.

"Take this," she said, digging a gun out of her baggy jeans pocket. She held it out to Faradon, and he carefully accepted it.

"You disarmed them?" he asked, his voice heavy with awe.

Mick pressed her face to his shoulder. "She can explain to you later."

Faradon didn't look like he wanted to wait until later, but then a cop wearing a slicker stepped into the doorway. He held out a bundle of clothes, wrapped in another slicker, then nodded and excused himself.

Mick said to Faradon, "Get out. And don't let anyone else in."

Half grinning, shaking his head, Faradon said, "Right."

The door shut behind the detective, and Mick forced himself to loosen his arms from around Delilah. The small building was dim, crowded with boat trailers, ski equipment, tools. Mick bent, touched his nose to hers and whispered, "Let me get you dry, okay?"

She nodded. "I'm all right now."

"I know you are." He strangled on the words and had to

stop, had to draw in a shaky breath. His hands trembled as he stripped away her sodden blankets and started to work on the fastening of her loose jeans.

"I lost my shoes in the river," she said.

Mick wondered if she was in shock. He needed to get her warm and dry, needed to get her to a hospital.

He needed… Swallowing hard this time didn't help. He hated it, hated himself, but tears clogged his throat. He felt unmanned, vulnerable.

Without the gentleness that he intended, he removed her clothes and turned to rummage through the bundle inside the slicker. He found a loose jacket, two more blankets.

"Lift your arms," he murmured, and she obliged. The jacket, apparently donated by one of the officers milling around outside, hung to her knees. Mick shook out another blanket, this one thankfully dry, and draped it over her.

Delilah clutched the edges together and said, "It's not really cold. I mean, it must be eighty-five outside. I'm just chilled…." Her teeth chattered, making her explanations difficult.

"Shh," Mick said, and stripped off his own shirt so he wouldn't get her wet. There was nothing he could do about his pants. He sure as hell wasn't going to run around bare-assed. He pulled one slicker over Delilah's head, then another over his own. "Let's get you to the hospital so you can be checked over," he said, deliberately concentrating on only one thing at a time.

Her fingers clutched at his arm, gripping the slicker with surprising force. "Mick, I don't…I don't want to go back out there yet."

His heart hit his stomach with her trembling words. He turned to her, opened his arms.

And she launched herself into him. "I was so—so scared," she said on a wail.

Mick wanted to absorb her into himself, to surround her always and keep her from ever being hurt again. Those damn tears got him again, and he squeezed her tighter, assuring himself that he had her, that she was okay.

Rain drummed on the metal roof of the shed and wind howled through every crack and crevice in the aged boards.

Then Delilah said something that made his knees give out. "I thought I'd lost you."

"What?"

She sniffed, shook her head while tears mingled with the wetness on her cheeks. Her words were broken, scattered and rushed. "I saw the blood on your forehead and I thought you might be dead or dying. You've already been hurt so much because of me." She leaned back to gently touch his face. "Are you all right? Truly?"

Mick dropped to his knees and stared up at Delilah, not caring that he cried, having totally forgotten about his own cut head. "*You* almost died," he groaned.

"Oh no. I knew what I was doing." She smoothed his sodden hair, her hand tender, loving. "I was afraid at first. Terrified really. But I kept thinking about you. I kept thinking what if I survived and you didn't? When I realized it was you in the river with me, I went weak. I was…well, I was doing fine until then."

Mick pressed his face into her belly. The chill had left her body and she felt warm, smelled musky and damp, and he knew he couldn't stand it, knew he was going to embarrass himself.

He held her tighter but it didn't help.

Faradon rapped at the door. "You two about done changing?"

"Go away!" Delilah yelled impatiently. "We'll be out in a minute."

Faradon grumbled something, but he didn't open the door.

Mick felt her cool hands cup his face, but he couldn't let her go, couldn't unclench his muscles. He hated feeling like this, powerless and weak and… He opened his hands on her behind and squeezed her closer, grinding his face into her, trying to absorb her.

He heard Delilah's smile as she said, "I love you, Mick Dawson. More than anyone or anything, now and forever."

He drew a shuddering breath and rubbed his face over her belly, on her borrowed blanket, drying his eyes and attempting to regain control. He had to get hold of himself. He had to…

"Tell me you love me, too," she whispered.

"I do," he said without hesitation. Only a trace of tears remained in his raw voice, not that he gave a damn. Delilah deserved to know everything about him.

"You do?" she asked.

"So much it hurts."

"I don't want you to hurt."

"Then don't ever leave me."

"Never." She slipped to her knees in front of him, still cupping his face. She kissed him, then kissed him again. She even smiled. "Will you stop calling me Delilah and call me Del?"

His shoulders shook. "No."

"Oh." She sounded surprised and disgruntled, and that went a long way toward helping him regain his discipline. Even at the worst of times, she amused him.

Finally she asked, "Well then, will you marry me?"

He actually laughed, but it turned into a groan. "I was going to ask you, you know."

"Sorry."

He touched her face, her sodden, tangled hair, her small breasts and narrow hips and long thighs. "God, I love you, every inch of you. I'll always love you, I swear it." When she gave him a brilliant smile, he added with more strength, "You've stolen forty years off my life with that last damn stunt!"

Her smile never wavered. She stood and held out her hand to him. As if *he* needed *her* assistance to stand!

He did.

He still felt wobbly, but as long as he didn't think about the moment that he'd seen that car go into the river…

He shuddered, took her slender hand and let her help haul him to his feet.

She put an arm around him and leaned her head into his shoulder. "I lost fifty years, leaving you behind in that car, bleeding. Nothing has ever scared me like that."

They headed for the door together. Just as Mick opened it, someone shouted, "I've got one of 'em!"

They followed the spotlight, and saw several cops converge on a man trying to crawl onto the muddy, thickly weeded shore. He was promptly handcuffed.

It wasn't until the next day that the police finally found the other man's body and confirmed his death. But they had two of them, Rudy Glasgow and the driver. They also had fingerprints, both from the apartment next to Delilah's and the gun she'd retrieved from the car.

It was over.

Del flitted from one person to the next. She loved being in a large family, even if most of that family was male and not really family at all. They felt like family, treated her as such, and they loved Mick to distraction. That in itself made her more than a little fond of them.

At the moment, Angel and Celia were perusing Mick's new bookcases, now holding her books. Del had pretty much taken over his house. His spare bedroom served as her office, and he'd already had an extra phone line put in.

The kids were all outside playing, but they could be heard through the open windows. Every minute or so one of the adults went to check on them.

Dane and Alec were seated on the couch, Josh and Zack in adjacent chairs, all of them watching a sports channel. Now that Del was used to them, Dane no longer seemed so imposing and Alec was nowhere near as frightening. But they were still fascinating characters.

Grinning, Del dropped down on the seat between them, using each hand to pat a hard masculine thigh. The two men looked at her warily. "Now that I've finally finished my current book and got it all turned in," she said, "I've been thinking of doing a book about two PIs who—"

Mick, who'd sauntered over to stand behind the couch, covered her mouth with a large hand. Del froze.

"If either one of you wants to remain in my good graces you won't tell her anything about anything...dangerous."

Alec saluted Mick with his cola. "Sorry, but Celia knows everything dangerous involved in my job, and she's been chewing Del's ear for the past hour."

True enough, Del thought, appreciating both Celia's forthright information and the way everyone had taken to calling her "Del," once she'd explained that she only used the name "Delilah" for writing.

Everyone except Mick, that is, who swore he loved her name as much as he loved her. The charmer. He even claimed "Delilah Dawson" had a very nice ring to it. Del couldn't wait for that to become her name in fact.

Dane nodded. "Yep, I'm afraid you're preaching to the choir here, Mick. You should have gagged the women, not us."

Mick groaned with heartfelt sincerity. He'd promised to

be understanding about her research, though Del knew he wanted to keep her in a cotton-lined box so she didn't so much as stub her baby toe.

Del pulled his hand away and tipped her head back to see him upside down. "How'd you sneak in here behind me?"

Mick rolled his eyes. "Sweetheart, when your brain is plotting, a herd of buffalo could tramp through and you wouldn't notice."

Since that was true, she said instead, "But I thought you were outside playing with the kids."

"They did me in. They're vicious little brutes who keep singing about how I was saved by a woman."

Del frowned, feeling a good dose of jealousy. "What woman?"

Mick leaned down to kiss her. "You."

"Me?" He nodded, and Del said, "But I didn't save you."

The awful nightmare of the car wreck, of Mick's head injury and her dousing in the river was two weeks old now, but she still shivered whenever she thought of how close she'd come to losing him.

Angel sidled up behind the couch, too, and hugged Mick. Celia joined her, resting her hands on Alec's shoulders. Zack and Josh twisted in their seats to face Del. She felt hemmed in by them all—but now the feeling was nice, sort of comforting.

She was surrounded by friends and family.

Mick smoothed his hand over her hair, something she was now more than familiar with. "Of course you saved me," he said. "You love me, right?"

"Absolutely."

"There, you see?" Alec chimed in, nudging her with his rock-hard shoulder. "You saved Mick from being a cynical fool who didn't believe in love."

Del looked at Mick again. With the way these people adored

him, she found that hard to believe. "You didn't believe in love?" she asked skeptically, but at the same time she thought it probably explained his reticence in admitting his feelings to her. Now, of course, he told her how much he cared in a thousand different ways—including the simple words *I love you*.

Mick just smiled.

Dane nudged her next, almost knocking her into Alec's lap. "You saved him from being a control freak, too."

Del righted herself and laughed; Mick was still very much a controlling man, and she doubted that would ever change.

Zack said, "You saved him from living his life like a monk."

With a very slight blush, Del said, "Okay, you got me there." Everyone laughed.

Mick was a voracious lover, and he couldn't seem to keep his hands off her. Which she appreciated because she loved when he touched her. He'd also become a voracious reader. He'd devoured her books and claimed he couldn't wait for the next one. She'd been nearly beside herself with his praise.

Josh tossed back a drink, then asked, "So when is this wedding we're all anticipating?"

Mick frowned at his friend, but said, "I just got the church reserved for the first Saturday of next month."

"You're all invited," Del announced, "as long as you know it won't be too fancy. No tuxes, and definitely no long white lace gowns." She pulled her jeans-clad legs up onto the couch and hugged her knees. "I hate dressing up."

"I'll be lucky to get shoes on her," Mick teased, and Angel promptly corrected him. She'd been with Del when the dress *and* matching shoes were bought.

Del noticed Josh heading for the kitchen, his head down, his hands shoved into his pants pockets. She smiled at Mick, rose from the couch and went to her friend. She found him standing at the sink, watching the children play through the window. "Josh?"

He turned to her, but said nothing.

"You're happy that Mick's marrying me, aren't you?"

He looked surprised, then wary. "Why?"

"Because you're one of his best friends. I don't want to come between you."

That made him laugh. "You belong between us, honey. Mick's a lucky guy, and yeah, I'm happy for you both."

"I hesitate to point this out, but you don't exactly look happy."

"No?" He studied her face, his green eyes dark, his slight smile crooked, chagrined.

She shook her head. "*Morose* might be a better word."

Mick's arms slid around her, lacing over her stomach. "*Defeated* might work, too," he said gently.

Josh snorted.

Mick tightened his hold, surprising Del, then said, "There are plenty of women out there, Josh."

"Yeah?"

Zack stepped up. "That's right, and I intend to find one."

All eyes turned to him. Del grinned. "You're bride hunting?"

"Why is that such a surprise?"

Josh said, "Because you seldom date? Because you're the quintessential bachelor? Because no woman will ever come before Dani?"

Del slugged Josh, making him jump and rub his shoulder while grumbling.

Still frowning, she said, "No *good* woman would want to come before his daughter! Children should always be first. At least until they're self-sufficient. Besides," she added, patting

Zack's chest and smiling, "Zack has enough love for a wife and several children."

"One daughter is enough! All I want now is the wife to complete the set. After all, Dani is crazy about you, Del. It made me think about what she's missing."

"Like what?" Mick asked. "You take great care of her."

"I try," Zack admitted, "but she needs a female role model. Someone quiet and intelligent and sincere."

"And sexy?" Mick asked.

Zack shrugged. "I'd rather she was domestic, if you want the truth."

"I wish you luck," Josh said with mock sincerity.

"I don't need luck, because I already have a plan. And I'm starting tomorrow."

Mick and Josh groaned, but Zack just smiled, confident in himself and his eventual success.

The rest of the family filed into the kitchen, including the children. Zack scooped up his daughter, hugged her tight.

"Time for us to go," Dane announced. "Tomorrow is a school day."

There were kisses all around, and everyone gradually left except Zack and Josh. Zack's daughter had fallen asleep on his shoulder, her blond curls disheveled, her mouth smooshed on her daddy's shoulder.

Zack pulled Del close with his free arm and gave her a smacking kiss on the mouth. "Congratulations again on the engagement," he whispered. He patted her cheek and stepped aside.

Josh set down his drink and reached for Del, catching her shoulders in his hands. He gave her the softest look she'd ever seen from him, leaned forward—and Mick's hand was suddenly between them, covering her mouth.

Mick bared his teeth at Josh and said, "Out."

Laughing, Josh pushed him aside and kissed Del on the forehead. "Your future husband is a jealous lout, did you know that?"

She waved his comment away. "Nonsense. He knows I'm crazy about him."

Josh and Mick exchanged a certain look that Del didn't understand in the least.

Shaking his head, Josh gave her a squeeze. "I'm glad you're so happy."

Holding his daughter to his shoulder, Zack grabbed Josh's collar and hauled him toward the door. "Let's go. Dani is starting to snore, and you're pressing your luck."

After they'd gone, Del asked Mick, "Okay, what was that all about?"

"What?" he asked, pretending innocence.

"That business with Josh. What's wrong with him?"

Mick looked briefly harassed. "Nothing that he won't get over," he said, and it almost sounded like a threat.

Before she could ask any more questions, he took her hand and herded her toward the bedroom.

"What do you think about Zack wanting a wife?" she asked.

Mick lightly pushed her down on the bed, then covered her with his body. He touched her cheek, her chin, the corner of her mouth. "I think he's a little jealous, too."

"Too?"

Mick kissed her. "Everyone knows I'm the luckiest man alive. When I think about the fact that you're mine, I almost can't bear it, it's so incredible. I want to tell the whole world." He smiled. "I love you, Delilah Piper."

"I'm lucky, too," she said softly. "I have you. And I did tell the whole world."

Startled, Mick leaned back. "You did?"

"Wait until you see the dedication in my next book. It's to

my very own hero, the finest man alive." She cupped his face. "And everyone knows that's you."

Mick frowned for just a moment, then his frown lifted and he shook his head. "Damn, I do feel like a hero. After all, the hero always gets the girl in the end, right?"

Del laughed. "In my books, he sure as heck does."

★ ★ ★ ★ ★